About the Authors

USA TODAY bestselling author **Jules Bennett** has penned more than fifty novels during her short career. She's married to her high school sweetheart, has two active girls, and is a former salon owner. Jules can be found on Twitter, Facebook (Fan Page), and her website julesbennett.com. She holds contests via these three outlets with each release and loves to hear from readers!

Susan Carlisle's love affair with books began when she made a bad grade in maths. Not allowed to watch TV until the grade had improved, she filled her time with books. Turning her love of reading into a love for writing romance, she pens hot medicals. She loves castles, travelling, afternoon tea, reads voraciously and hearing from her readers. Join her newsletter at www.SusanCarlisle.com

Jennifer Taylor has been writing Mills & Boon novels for some time but discovered Medical Romance books relatively recently. Having worked in scientific research, she was so captivated by these heart-warming stories that she immediately set out to write them herself. Jennifer's hobbies include reading and travelling. She lives in northwe _____ ____ blog at jennifertaylorautl

Summer of Love

Summer of Love: Forever You

JULES BENNETT

SUSAN CARLISLE

JENNIFER TAYLOR

MILLS & BOON

First Published in Great Britain 2021
By Mills & Boon, an imprint of HarperCollins*Publishers* Ltd
1 London Bridge Street, London, SE1 9GF

www.harpercollins.co.uk

HarperCollins*Publishers*
1st Floor, Watermarque Building,
Ringsend Road, Dublin 4, Ireland

SUMMER OF LOVE: FOREVER YOU © 2021 Harlequin Books S.A.

From Best Friend to Bride © 2015 Jules Bennett
His Best Friend's Baby © 2015 Harlequin Books S.A.
Best Friend to Perfect Bride © 2015 Jennifer Taylor

Special thanks and acknowledgement are given to Susan Carlisle for her
contribution to the Midwives On-Call series

ISBN: 978-0-263-30244-8

MIX
Paper from
responsible sources
FSC
www.fsc.org   FSC® C007454

This book is produced from independently certified FSC™ paper
to ensure responsible forest management.

For more information visit: www.harpercollins.co.uk/green

Printed and bound in Spain
by CPI, Barcelona

FROM BEST FRIEND
TO BRIDE

JULES BENNETT

There's nothing like spending all of your days with your best friend. This book is dedicated to not only my best friend, but my real-life hero. Love you, Michael, and I love our very own happily ever after.

Chapter One

"You know how to please a man."

Megan Richards desperately wished those words coming from her best friend's kissable lips had been said in a different context. Alas, Cameron St. John was only referring to the medium-well steak she had grilled, and not a bedroom romp.

One day she would shock them both when she declared her desire, her need for the man she'd known since kindergarten, when he'd pulled her pigtails and she'd retaliated by taking her safety scissors to his mullet. A mutual respect was instantly born, and they'd been friends since—sans pigtails and mullet.

"I figured you'd been eating enough take-out junk and needed some real food," she told him, watching in admiration as he picked up their dinner plates and started loading her dishwasher.

Oh, yeah. His mama had raised him right, and Megan didn't think there was a sexier sight than a domestic man…especially one with muscles that flexed so beautifully with each movement.

Since his back was turned, she soaked up the view. The man came by his rippled beauty honestly, with hours dedicated to rigorous workouts. She worked out, too—just last night she'd exercised with a box of cookies—which would be the main reason his body was so perfectly toned while hers was so perfectly dimpled and shapely.

Cameron closed the dishwasher door and gave the countertop a swift swipe with the cloth before turning to face her. With his hands resting on either side of his narrow hips, he might have looked all laid-back and casual, but the man positively reeked of alpha sexiness. His impressive height and broad shoulders never failed to send a sucker punch straight to her active hormones.

Too bad he was married to his job as chief of police in Stonerock, Tennessee. Besides, she was too afraid to lose him as a friend to really open up and let years of emotions come pouring out. Well, that and Cameron and his family had been the only true stability she'd known since her parents were killed in a car accident during a snowstorm when they'd been traveling up north to visit friends. Megan couldn't risk damaging the bond she had with Cam.

Oh, and he'd made it perfectly clear on more than one occasion that he wouldn't get into a committed relationship. Not as long as he was in law enforcement, thanks to an incident involving his partner when they'd been rookies.

Yup, he didn't do relationships; just like he didn't do healthy food.

"I don't eat junk," he defended himself.

Megan tipped her head, quirking a brow.

"I'll have you know that Burger-rama is real food, and they know my order without me even repeating it." Cameron crossed his arms over his wide chest and offered her that lady-killer smile.

Laughing, Megan came to her feet. "I rest my case."

With a quick glance at his watch, Cameron pushed off the counter and sighed. "I better get going. I need to rest before heading out tonight."

She had no clue what he was working on; she rarely did. He was pretty adamant about keeping his work absent from their conversations. He'd tell the occasional funny drunken-fight story, but when it came to a serious investigative case, he was pretty tight-lipped.

Whatever he was working on must be major, seeing as how he'd been heading out to work at midnight several nights a week—not something a chief normally did. The new lines between his brows and the dark circles beneath his eyes spoke volumes about his new schedule.

"You're working yourself to death. You know that, right? Between all the crazy hours and the junk food. You can't be getting enough sleep."

One corner of his mouth tipped up in a smile. That cocky, charming grin always had the same heart-

gripping impact. How many women had been mes-
merized by that beautiful, sexy smile?

"I'll be fine," he assured her, pulling her into a
friendly hug. "This case should wrap up soon, and
I'll be back to somewhat normal hours, complete with
sleep. The junk food remains, though."

Two out of three wasn't too bad. Besides, normal for
him meant ten-hour days instead of twelve or fourteen.
Reminding him of his father's bypass surgery last year
would do no good. The St. John men were a stubborn
bunch. She should know; she'd been the family side-
kick since grade school.

Megan kept her mouth shut and wrapped her arms
around his waist as she slowly inhaled his familiar
scent. Closing her eyes, she wished for so much. She
wished Cam would wake up and see how deeply she
cared for him, she wished her brother would straighten
his life out and she wished she knew what to do about
the out-of-town job offer she'd just received.

None of those things were going to happen right
now, so she held on tight and enjoyed the moment of
being enveloped by the man she'd loved for years. If
friendship was all they were destined for, then she'd
treasure what she had and not dwell on the unattain-
able.

Cameron eased back, resting his firm hands on her
shoulders. "You okay? You seem tense."

Really? Because she'd pretty much melted into his
embrace. The cop in him always managed to pick up
every little detail around him, yet the man in him was
totally oblivious to the vibes she sent out. It would be

so much easier if he just magically knew how she felt and took that giant first step so she didn't have to. The passive-aggressive thing was never her style, but in this instance she really wished he'd just read her mind.

"I'm fine," she assured him, offering a grin. "Just a lot on my mind lately."

Wasn't that an understatement?

His dark brows drew together as those signature bright blue St. John eyes studied her. "What can I do to help?"

Oh, if he only knew. One day.

"Nothing." She reached up, patted his stubbled jaw and stepped back to avoid further temptation. "Go rest so you can head out and save Stonerock from all the bad guys."

The muscle in his jaw jumped. "I'm working on it."

"I hope you're careful," she added, always worried she'd get a phone call from one of his brothers or his parents telling her the worst. Because Cameron would put his life on the line for anybody. He just wouldn't put his heart on the line.

He laughed. "Yes, Mom, I'm careful."

Swatting him on his hard pec, Megan narrowed her eyes. "I have to ask. You make me worry."

"Nothing to worry about," he assured her, with a friendly kiss on her forehead. "I'm good at my job."

"You're so humble, too."

With a shrug, he pulled his keys from his pocket. "Eli and Nora's baby is being christened tomorrow. You're still planning on coming, right?"

"Are you going to make it?"

Cameron nodded and headed toward the back door. He always came and went via her back door. He never knocked, just used a key when it was locked and made himself at home.

"I'll make it," he told her, his hand resting on the antique knob. "I may even have time to run home and nap and shower for the occasion."

"How about I pick you up?" she offered.

He lived in her neighborhood, and they tended to ride together when they went anywhere. They were pretty much like an old married couple, you know, just without the sex and shared living quarters.

"Be there at nine." His finger tapped on the doorknob. "Lock up behind me."

Rolling her eyes, she gave him a mock salute as he left. The worry was definitely a two-way street.

Now that she was alone with her thoughts, she had to face the unknowns that circled around in her mind. This job offer had come out of nowhere.

Was it a sign that she needed to move on? She'd been in Stonerock nearly her entire life; she was still single and had nothing holding her back.

Except Cameron.

After scrubbing her sink and table, Megan was still no closer to making a decision. She loved being a therapist at the local counseling center; she loved her patients and truly felt as if she was making an impact in their lives.

The new job would be in Memphis, nearly two hours away. The new facility would offer her a chance at helping more people, even taking charity cases, which would allow her to comfort and guide people she never could've reached otherwise.

How could she say no?

As she sank onto the chair at her kitchen table, she thought of her brother. He was an adult, but he'd never been able to take care of himself. The questionable decisions he made kept snowballing into more bad decisions—each one seemingly worse than the last. He always counted on her as a crutch to fall back on. What would happen to him if she left? Would he finally man up and take control of his life? See just how dependent he'd become and actually want to change?

More to the point: What would happen with Cameron? Before she made the decision, she would have to seriously consider gathering up the courage to tell him the secret she kept in the pit of her soul.

This job was a catalyst for pushing her in that direction. She needed to move on one way or another… though she'd rather move on with him. Either way, she'd know if years of wanting and dreaming had been for naught.

She'd wanted a relationship with him since they'd graduated high school, but the timing to reveal her feelings had never been right. Between her parents' deaths, his deployment and Megan always putting her life on hold to help her brother, she just had never found an opening.

Cameron was the only solid foundation in her life. What happened if she told him how much she loved him and it ruined their friendship? Could she take that risk?

He'd told her he'd never consider being in a committed relationship. He'd shared the story of the night his partner had died and how he'd had to witness the widow's complete breakdown. Cam had told her he'd never put anyone through that.

Still, she had to let him know how she felt. She couldn't go through life playing the what-if game forever, and he deserved to know. By not giving him a chance to make a decision, she could be missing out on the best thing that had ever happened to her.

Megan folded her arms across the table and rested her head on them. She really had no choice...not if she wanted to live her life without regrets.

Some risks were worth taking. She knew without a doubt if Cameron wanted to take things beyond friendship, the joy would be totally worth the bundle of nerves that had taken up residence in her stomach.

Cameron had managed about a three-hour nap before the christening. He'd also showered and shaved for the occasion. His mother would be so proud.

He'd just finished adjusting his navy tie when his front door opened and closed. Heels clicked on the hardwood floor, growing louder as Megan approached the hallway. He assumed the visitor was Megan, unless one of his brothers had opted to don stilettos today.

He knew of Megan's love for breakneck shoes when she wasn't wearing her cowgirl boots. Didn't matter to him if she was barefoot. Cameron had fought his attraction to Megan for a few years now. At first he'd thought the temptation would go away. No such luck. Being a cop's wife, even in a small town, wasn't something he'd put on anyone he cared about. He couldn't handle knowing he'd put the worry and stress of being a cop's wife on Megan, so he pulled up every bit of his self-control to block his true feelings.

Unfortunately, Cameron had never wanted to avoid his best friend as much as he did right this moment. Dread filled his stomach as he recalled the things he'd witnessed last night while monitoring the drugstore parking lot. The events that had unfolded on his watch put a whole new spin on this case…and quite possibly his relationship with Megan. No, not quite possibly. Without a doubt the new developments would shatter their perfect bond.

Her brother had gotten involved with the wrong crowd—a crowd Cameron was about to take down.

She deserved to be happy, deserved to live free from her brother's illegal activities, and Cameron would do anything and everything to keep Megan safe.

Although he was torn about whether or not she should find out, he was obligated to his job first, which meant he had to keep every bit of this operation to himself. She would be hurt and angry when she discovered what her brother was doing, and even more so when she realized Cameron had hidden the truth from her.

"You wearing pants?" she called out.

With a chuckle, Cameron shoved his wallet and phone into his back pocket. "Pants are a requirement?"

When he stepped into the hall, he stopped short. *Damn.* Megan had always been beautiful, and she always presented herself as classy and polished for work, but this morning she looked even more amazing than usual. There went that twist to his heart, the one that confirmed she was the most perfect woman for him. But he couldn't let her in, wouldn't subject her to his chaotic schedule, his stress from the job. Because if he was stressed, he knew she'd want to take some on herself to relieve him of any burden. He'd signed up for this career…Megan hadn't.

With her fitted red dress, a slim black belt accentuating her small waist and rounded hips and her dark hair down around her shoulders, she stole his breath— something that rarely happened with any woman. Always Megan. Everything was always centered around Megan. She was special.

Which was why he shouldn't be looking at her as if she were a woman he'd met at a bar and wanted to bring home for the night. Not that he remembered what that was like. He hadn't been in a bar for personal recreation in so long, never mind bringing a woman back to his bed.

Megan deserved to be treasured, to be loved and come first in any man's life. Unfortunately he could only offer two of the three.

Cameron had always figured one of his brothers would scoop Megan up, and the thought had crippled him each time the image crept through his mind. Thankfully, both Eli and Drake had found the loves of their lives. Cameron was thrilled for them, but love wasn't for all the St. John boys. Cameron barely had time to catch any sleep, let alone devote to a relationship.

"Should I go back home and change?" she asked,

raising a brow with a smirk on her face. "You're staring at me."

"No, no." He adjusted his jacket, hating the confining garment and feeling somewhat naked without his shoulder holster. "You're just looking exceptionally beautiful this morning."

"You mean my old paint-stained tank and tattered shorts I had on yesterday didn't make me look beautiful?" She fluttered her eyelids in a mocking manner he found ridiculously attractive.

He loved that no matter what life threw at her, she always found a way to be a bit snarky. Why hadn't some guy come along and swept her off her feet? Any man would be lucky to have her. She grilled an amazing steak, she was always there for him no matter what, she joked and she even drank beer with him.

If she married someone who loved her and treated her the way she deserved to be treated, Cameron might be able to get this notion that he was worthy of her out of his head. Because he sure as hell knew that was false. He wanted to see her happy with that family she'd always wanted. But she wasn't even dating anybody. Still, he couldn't tell her his feelings because there wasn't a happy ending if he chose that path. Telling Megan would only cause an awkward, uncomfortable wedge between them, and hurting her in any way would destroy him.

As she stood in his hallway, looking like a classy pinup model with all her curves, Cameron cursed himself for allowing his thoughts to travel where they had no business going. Her curves weren't new, but when the two of them got together she never dressed like this.

It was the dress. That perfectly molded dress. He was used to seeing her in professional work clothes or old tees and shorts. If he was looking at her in a way that stirred him, how would other men be looking at her today? They were attending a church service, for crying out loud, and he was standing here fighting off an ever-growing attraction to his best friend. There was so much wrong with this situation he didn't even know where to start.

"I'm ready." He moved into the foyer, careful not to touch her as he passed, and retrieved his keys from the side table.

After he'd locked up behind them, Cameron followed her down the stone path toward her black SUV parked in his drive. They'd barely gotten their seat belts fastened before her cell chimed. Casting a quick glance down to where it rested on the console, Cameron spotted Evan's name on the screen. More anxiety filled his stomach, but he kept his mouth shut. Now was not the time to expose him. He'd actually made a point to not come between Megan and her brother. Their issues went way beyond those of regular siblings. He might not be able to tell Megan what had happened last night, but Cameron would throw himself in front of her to protect her from anyone...including Evan. Family loyalty meant everything to him; unfortunately, her brother was only loyal to himself.

Megan's bright green eyes darted up to his as she sighed. "I'm sorry."

Wasn't that the story of her life? Always apologizing for her brother, always coming to his defense? Megan was never fully able to live her own life the way she wanted because she'd had to play mom, dad, sister and therapist to the ungrateful punk for years.

She snatched her cell on the second ring. "Hello."

Cameron couldn't make out what Evan was saying, only the rumble of a male voice filtered through the SUV. Not that Cameron needed to know what Evan was saying. The man only called his sister to ask for money, use her car or some other random favor.

Megan's head fell against the back of her seat as she gripped the phone with one hand and her steering wheel with the other. "I can't, Evan—I'm busy right now."

Cameron resisted the urge to pull the phone from her hand and tell Evan to grow a set and quit using his sister as plan A. The man, and he used the term loosely, had never held a job that Cameron was aware of…or at least not a legal one. Evan had been a troublemaker in school, getting kicked out of two before he even started junior high. Megan's parents had moved the family to the next town as a result of Evan's troubles, causing Cameron and Megan to lose touch for a year. Thankfully Megan had transferred back and their relationship had picked up right where they'd left off—with them goofing off and her hanging at his house with him and his brothers.

Unfortunately, switching schools had only made Evan angrier, resulting in his behavior growing more reckless. Now, as an adult, he had made no strides to clean himself up. Actually, after what Cameron had witnessed last night, he knew Evan was even worse than he'd thought. The man was straight up running drugs. And there was no way in hell Megan knew the trouble her brother was in.

No wonder Megan adored Cameron's family so much. They were all she had in the form of a loving, solid foundation.

"I'm sorry, Evan," she went on, her tone exhausted. "That's not something I can do right now. If you can wait until this afternoon, then I can help. Otherwise, I don't know what to tell you."

The more Megan argued, defending herself, the more Cameron felt his blood pressure soar. He was thankful that even though he and his brothers had been hellions in school, they'd never crossed the line into illegal activity. They'd been standard cocky teens. There just happened to be three of them with that arrogant attitude, and when one had done something, the others had jumped on board.

"No, Evan, I—"

Cameron refused to let this go on another second. He pried the phone from her hand and ended the call without a word. Megan jerked toward him, but Cameron clutched the device in his hand, holding it by his shoulder as a silent sign he wasn't giving in.

Her deep red lips parted in protest before her shoulders sank and her hands fell to her lap. Megan's head drooped. With all her hair tucked back, he could see every emotion that slid over her face, even though he could only see her profile. Her eyes closed, she bit her lip and her chin trembled. She looked positively defeated.

That right there was why Cameron loathed Evan Richards. The man constantly deflated the life out of fun-loving, bubbly Megan. Moments ago, when she'd stood in Cameron's hallway, she'd been sassy, confident and vibrant...everything he loved. What he didn't love was how quickly one person could bring her down. Evan was nothing but a bully, always seeking his own selfish desires and not giving a damn who he hurt along the way.

"Don't you dare feel bad," he scolded, maybe harsher than he should have. "That's exactly what he wants, Meg. He plays that guilt card with you because he knows you'll give him anything he wants."

"I know," she mumbled. Smoothing her hands down her fitted skirt, she let out a sigh and turned to face him. "I'm trying, really. It's way past time he stood on his own two feet. It's just so hard..."

She shook her head and reached for the keys in the ignition. After sliding his hand over her slender arm, Cameron gripped her hand.

"That's what he's counting on." Cameron gave her a gentle squeeze as he softened his tone. She wasn't a perp; she was his friend. "He continually plays the poor sibling, expecting you to ride to his rescue. He's the one who made this mess of his life."

Cameron seriously doubted she knew just how much of a mess Evan was in. There was no way he could protect her from the end result. The helpless feeling in the pit of Cameron's stomach nearly made him sick.

Tears brimming in her eyes, she held his gaze. "You think I don't know how much Evan has screwed up? That he doesn't use me on a daily basis? You don't know what I go through, Cameron. You have the picture-perfect family. I have no parents and a brother who'd just as soon wipe out my bank account as spend five minutes talking with me on how to straighten his life out, how to help him. I'm praying maybe one of these times he comes to me, he'll be there for more. I'm praying he'll let me help him, that he'll be ready to turn his life around. So if I have to get stepped on along the way, it's worth it."

The last sentence came out on a choked sob. Well, hell. Now he was the one feeling guilty. He never wanted to make her cry, make her feel as if his life was better than hers.

After placing her phone back on the console, Cameron reached across and wrapped his arms around her the best he could, considering their positions.

"I'm sorry." Her silky hair tickled his cheek, and her familiar floral scent reminded him she was nearly everything to him and he'd die before he'd hurt her. "I don't mean to be hard on you. I just hate seeing what he does to you."

Megan's hands slid up his torso between his jacket and his shirt, coming to rest against his chest. "What I deserve and what I'll have are two different things."

Easing back, Cameron studied her face. "You deserve everything you've ever wanted."

A sad smile spread across her face as she reached a

hand up and cupped his freshly shaven jaw. "All I've ever wanted may not want me back."

What?

Before he could question her further, her hand fell away and she started the vehicle. Whatever secret longing she kept locked deep inside was obviously something she'd all but given up on. Cameron refused to let Megan give up on any dream or goal she had.

He vowed that once this major case was over, he'd find a way to make her happy, living the life she desired and deserved. It would be worth everything to him. For years he'd seen her always put her needs behind everyone else's. And while he may not be the man to settle into her life intimately, he would do everything in his power to make sure her dreams were fulfilled.

Chapter Two

"I'm so glad you could make it."

Bev St. John hugged Cameron after the christening service, then looped her arm through his as they walked back up the wide aisle of Santa Monica Church.

"You don't know how much this means to me to have all my boys here for my first grandbaby's milestone," Bev said, her wide smile spreading across her face.

Straight ahead, near the tall double doors, Nora and Eli stood with Megan. Megan held his infant niece, who was just over a year old. Cameron's heart filled. The glow on Megan's face as she placed a kiss on top of Amber's curly blond head solidified the fact he couldn't be the man for her. She would be an amazing, loving, selfless mother. Just not to his kids.

Cameron's dad, Mac, approached and looked over Megan's shoulder, smiling down at his granddaughter. Cameron didn't know where Megan would be if it weren't for his family. She'd taken to them even before her parents had died suddenly, but she'd really leaned on them during that difficult time. Even as strong as Megan was, she'd been so blindsided by the shock of losing both parents, and then taking over the care of her younger brother when she'd barely gotten out of high school herself. "I'm so glad Megan could make it." His mother's soft tone pulled him back. "I just love that girl."

Over the years his mother had made it no secret she wouldn't mind Megan being part of the family—in the legal, choosing-china-patterns type of way. Of course now that Eli and Drake were taken, his mom would just have to settle for Megan being a friend and the daughter she'd never had.

Cameron steered them toward the little grouping, and Megan glanced up, caught his eye and smiled. Yeah, there was that invisible pull once again that threatened to wrap around his neck and strangle him.

He wanted her. Wanted her so much sometimes he physically hurt. But she deserved more.

The memory of the darkest time in his life took over. His partner had taken a bullet meant for Cameron. On his last breath, his partner had made Cameron promise to make sure his wife knew he loved her.

That moment changed everything. Letting a woman into his life, letting her get close enough to be devastated like his partner's wife had been, was not something he'd ever take a chance with. If he entered into a deeper relationship with Megan and something happened to him, it would kill her. Besides, worrying about her while he was trying to do his job was a sure way for him to get hurt. He needed to concentrate, needed to keep Megan out of his mind.

If he could only figure out how the hell to do that.

"Megan, you look beautiful, as always." His mom leaned forward and kissed Megan's cheek. "Thanks for being here today."

"I wouldn't miss it."

"Are you and Megan coming to eat with us after?" Eli asked Cameron. "We're heading to that new Italian place just outside of town."

Cameron started to agree, but Megan chimed in. "I have to get home, but if you want to go, go ahead."

Oh, no. If she was going home to wait on her free-loading brother to show, Cameron would be right there with her. No way would Evan try to pull her into this latest mess. Hell no.

"I need to head out, too," Cameron stated. Work was always beckoning, so he knew everyone would just assume that's why he needed to go. "And she's my ride."

Cameron and Megan said their goodbyes and stepped out of the church. The bright sun hit them as they descended the concrete steps. Cameron pulled his glasses from his jacket pocket and slid them on to block the brightness. A headache from lack of sleep and plenty of worry had settled in, and the fiery glare was making it worse.

"Skipping out?"

Cameron turned to see his other brother, Drake. Right at his side was his fiancée, Marly, and Marly's daughter, Willow.

"Megan and I need to head out," he told Drake.

"You look pretty," Willow said, standing beside Megan and looking up at her as if she were looking at a movie star. "I like your hair."

The free-spirited little six-year-old had on her beloved cowgirl boots, as usual, and was sporting a new grin, sans two teeth.

Megan bent down and slid her hand through Willow's long ponytail. "I love yours, too. I used to wear my hair just like this when I was your age. You have good taste."

"I was going to call you," Marly told Megan. "Nora and I were hoping for a girls' night sometime soon. You interested?"

Megan smiled and nodded. "Sounds good. Just let me know when."

More goodbyes were said, and finally Megan and Cameron were settled back in her SUV and headed toward their neighborhood.

"That was a beautiful service," she commented after a bit. "Thanks for inviting me."

"You're family." Cameron tried to hold back the yawn but couldn't. Damn, he was getting too old to pull all-nighters. "You belong here, too."

"You know, one day you may actually replace me with a girlfriend or a wife. I doubt she'll understand if I'm still hanging around your family."

Cameron snorted, shifted in his seat and rested his

elbow on the console. "For one thing, you could never be replaced. For another, I think you know my stance on committed relationships and marriage."

"Your reasons may be valid, but they can't be your crutch for life."

"It's not a crutch," he muttered in defense.

Megan threw him a glance and a smile as she pulled onto their road. "You never know when the right woman will come along and claim you."

The only woman he'd ever allow to "claim" him was sitting right next to him, but he'd never do that to her. He'd seen firsthand what being a cop could do to even the strongest of marriages. Even though he and Megan had a bond that rivaled the toughest relationships, he wouldn't put that kind of strain on something, or someone, so important.

She was part of his life in the deepest way he could allow and he'd just have to be satisfied with that. The fact she would likely marry one day was something he couldn't even think about right now. If he thought of Megan with another man, Cameron would likely lose that wall of control he'd built up.

Megan put on her signal to turn into his drive.

"I'm going to your house," he told her.

Totally ignoring him, she pulled up to his garage. After throwing her SUV in Park, she turned to face him, her green eyes studying his face. "You need to go in and get more sleep."

She was preaching to the choir. Unfortunately, even if he went in, he wouldn't be able to just close down and relax. Besides, he wanted to make sure Evan didn't show up and try to pour on more guilt or ask for any favors.

"I'll be fine," she assured him, patting his leg as if he were some toddler. "I know what you're doing, but don't worry. I've handled Evan long enough."

Cameron slid his hand over hers and squeezed. "And that's the problem. You shouldn't have to deal with a grown man whose behavior is that of an out-of-control teen."

Megan tilted her head, and her hair spilled over her shoulder; the strands tickled his arm on the console. "I deal with you, don't I?"

He couldn't help but smile. "You only keep me around to set your mousetraps in the winter."

"True." With a smile, she turned her hand over in his and squeezed. "Seriously. Go sleep."

Stroking his thumb along the backs of her smooth fingers, Cameron stared into those eyes that were too often full of worry—eyes that had captivated him on more occasions than he could count.

"I'm a guy and a cop. I can't help but want to take care of you."

Drawing in a shaky breath, she offered a sweet smile, one he'd witnessed for years and never grew tired of seeing. Megan's genuine, contagious smile that came from within, that lit up a room…that's what kept him going.

"I love you for that," she told him. "But really, you need to take care of yourself, and I'm going to make sure you do. Now go."

Stubborn woman. She wouldn't pull out of this

driveway until his butt was out of her car. *Fine.* He was just as stubborn, but he knew how to play the game. He knew his Megan better than anyone else did. She would always put herself out to make others comfortable, to keep those around her happy. But Cameron wasn't about to let her fall down his priority list. She was, and always had been, at the top. Just like family.

"All right," he conceded. "You will call me if you need anything."

It wasn't a question, but she nodded anyway as she leaned over to kiss his cheek. "Go on, Chief. You can't protect the town if you're dead on your feet."

"Yes, Mommy."

Cameron tugged on the handle and stepped from the SUV. Turning to rest his arm on the open door, he peered back inside. "You know, tough love is a good thing."

"Yeah." Megan sighed, and her shoulders fell slightly. "It's just easy to say and harder to do."

Cameron hated how torn she was between loyalty and forgiveness. He, too, was torn between loyalties right now. Megan had been his everything for so long. Yet he couldn't protect her, couldn't even warn her of the evils hovering so close to her life.

Tapping the top of her car, he stepped back. "I'll call you later."

As he made his way up to his porch, Cameron knew he wouldn't be sleeping. Too much was on his mind, and it all involved work and Megan. She always seemed to be the center of his thoughts. Unfortunately, this scenario had nothing to do with his desires.

Yet Megan's odd declaration earlier alluding to something or someone she wanted still weighed heavily on his mind, too. They shared everything…at least all the personal stuff. What was she keeping from him?

Granted, he'd been holding back his own feelings for so long, but he didn't think she reciprocated those emotions. Or did she? That would put a whole new spin on things and add another layer of worry to his already stressful life. Damn it, why couldn't he just have those friend feelings or that brotherly bond? When had he taken that turn into wanting more?

Cameron waited until Megan headed down the narrow road toward her own house before he turned in the opposite direction and took off for a much-needed walk around their neighborhood. He needed to clear his head and figure out how best to approach this delicate situation with Evan.

Cameron also needed to figure out how to get the image of Megan in that classy yet sexy-as-hell red dress out of his mind. No other woman could shoot for polished and timeless and come off as a siren. Megan's beauty had always been special, but today she'd taken it to a whole new level. The more time passed, the deeper his feelings went. There was nothing he could do; he'd tried denying it, tried ignoring it. Unfortunately, Megan had embedded herself so deeply into his life that he had no clue how to function with all of these lies.

Yeah, a walk was definitely what he needed to get his head on straight because losing himself in his thoughts where Megan was concerned was only throwing fuel on the proverbial fire. Too often when they were close together in a car, on her sofa watching a movie, he'd fought not to kiss her, not to touch her. The struggle he battled with himself was a daily occurrence, but he'd sacrifice anything, even his desires and his sanity, to keep her happy and safe.

Lust, love or anything other than a simple friendship had no room in the well-secured bond they'd honed and perfected since childhood.

So focusing on this case from hell that had just taken a turn for the worse was the only thing he had time to dwell on. Because in the end, no matter his feelings for Megan, she would hate him for standing by and watching her brother make mistake after mistake, for waiting to take down him and his criminal friends. But Cameron didn't have a choice. His job had to come before his feelings for Megan.

Clothes were strewn around her room, hanging over the treadmill, draped across her bed, adorning the floor mirror in the corner. Pretty much every stationary object had taken a hit from the purging of her closet.

Megan tugged on the black tank-style dress that used to be her favorite. When she gave a pull to cover her rear end, it pulled the scoop neck down. When she tried to pull the material up over her breasts, her butt nearly popped out.

Damn that new Ben & Jerry's flavor. Ice cream was her weakness, and now she'd discovered something else to feed her addiction…and her thighs.

So here she was, going through her closet because she needed to de-clutter. Nobody needed this many clothes, and she'd gained a few pounds, so why keep all this stuff? If she ended up losing the extra weight, she deserved a shopping spree, anyway. And if she opted to take that new job in Memphis, she would want to start fresh. That meant getting rid of this too-tight, hoochie-mama-looking dress.

Besides, reorganizing her overflowing closet was a great stress reliever and a good way to keep her mind off Cameron.

With a laugh, she fingered through the pile of too-small clothes on her bed. Like Cameron was ever off her mind. She'd nearly slipped up and bared her soul to him earlier when he'd declared he wanted her to have all she'd ever desired. Could the man be so blind that he couldn't see she desired him? Did he pay no attention to the fact she rarely dated and when she did it was only one date because nobody could ever compare with Cam?

She knew why he didn't go out with women. He was married to his job. But he'd never questioned her on why her social life was nonexistent.

Or perhaps she was the blind one. Maybe she wasn't ready to face the fact that he truly didn't want anyone in his life, and even if he did, she would only be a friend to him.

Though he had given her a visual sampling when he'd first seen her before the christening. That was a good sign…right? Or maybe he'd just had indigestion from all the garbage he ate the night before. Who knew?

Groaning, she started to attempt to get out of the

body-hugging dress when she heard her back door open and close. Jerking around, she tried to listen to the footsteps.

Evan? Cameron? Either way she was clearly not dressed for company.

"You wearing pants?"

A slight sigh of relief swept through her as she laughed at Cameron echoing her earlier question to him. Her body was half hanging out, but extra pounds or not, men usually just saw skin and got excited. Could this work to her advantage? Maybe being a bit more out there, literally, would get Cameron to wake up.

"Actually, no," she called back, then stepped into the hall to tell him she'd be right out.

As soon as she left her room, she ran into Cameron's solid chest. Firm, strong hands immediately came up and gripped her shoulders. Her breasts, already spilling out of her dress, pressed against his hard pecs. Megan sucked in a breath, unable to think of anything but how nicely they molded together in all the perfectly delicious ways.

The way his eyes widened, his nostrils flared and his fingertips bit into her bare skin told her he wasn't so unaffected by her femininity.

Game on.

Chapter Three

Holy—

Cameron couldn't breathe, couldn't think, couldn't form a damn thought with Megan's curvy body pressed against his. This was his best friend, yet with the way her breasts were all but spilling out of her barely-there black dress, his thoughts weren't very friend-like at the moment.

Hadn't he just pep-talked himself into trying to keep his thoughts out of the gutter?

"Wh-what are you doing here?" she asked.

Why was her voice all breathy and sultry?

Cameron dropped his hands and took a step back, but that didn't help his hormones settle down. Now he was able to see just how hot she looked wearing that second-skin dress that hit her upper thigh at a very indecent level and scooped low enough to show off her breasts.

Jealousy ripped through him. "Where the hell are you going like that?"

She flinched. Maybe he'd sounded a tad gruff, but seriously? Every visual that came to mind involved a bedroom.

Megan lifted her chin defiantly as she crossed her arms, doing nothing to help her cause of breast spill-age. "For your information, I'm cleaning my closet and trying things on. Now, why are you here and not home asleep?"

He was starting to question that himself. "I couldn't sleep."

Not that he'd tried, but she didn't need to know that. He glanced into her room and laughed. Megan always had everything in its place, but something tragic had transpired with her clothes. He wasn't dumb enough to make a comment because he was pretty sure that some rage had been unleashed in that room.

"Not a word," she growled, as if daring him to com-ment on the chaos. "Let me change real quick."

Before she turned away, the back door opened and closed. Cameron nearly groaned. Nobody else would just walk in other than him or Evan.

Megan let out a sigh. "Be nice," she whispered. "I'll go change."

Cameron turned away just as Evan rounded the hall corner. His disheveled hair and black eye were so pre-dictable. He looked like a deadbeat who'd obviously been on the wrong end of one of his "friends'" fists.

Cameron wouldn't allow him to come in here and make Megan feel like crap.

"Am I interrupting something?" Evan asked, his narrowed eyes darting between Cameron and Megan.

Cameron wanted to tell the guy yes, but he didn't figure Evan would leave and the lie would only make Megan upset. No matter what, he was treading a fine line because if this weren't Megan's only living relative, Cameron wouldn't think twice about hauling his butt in if for nothing else than to shake him up a bit.

Megan stepped into her room and came out seconds later tying a robe around her waist. At least she was covered now. Cameron didn't like that judgmental glance that Evan had thrown at them. Even if Cameron and Megan had been doing something intimate, that wouldn't have been Evan's business...or anyone else's for that matter.

"What happened?" Megan asked, stepping toward her brother.

Evan waved a hand, his eyes still moving between Cameron and Megan. "Nothing for you to worry about."

Cameron knew those blow-off comments hurt Megan. The woman obviously cared for her brother, and Evan didn't even acknowledge the fact.

"I do worry," she told him with a softer tone.

Cameron maintained his place between the two siblings. No way was he budging. When it became clear that Evan wasn't going to offer any more feedback over his recent fight, Megan sighed.

"What do you need, Evan?" Megan asked as she took a step back, landing her next to Cameron.

Good. Cameron wanted her to feel safer with him there. The silent gesture clearly showed who she trusted, who she felt more comfortable with. The primal part of Cameron liked to think her easing closer to him showed whose side she was on, as well.

"I need to talk to you," Evan told her, then shifted his eyes to Cameron.

"Go ahead," Cameron replied, resting his hands on his hips and in absolutely no hurry to budge.

"Alone."

Megan moved down the hall, squaring her shoulders. "I'm not giving you money," she informed him as she got closer. "If you want to visit with me, that's fine."

Evan raked a hand through his hair, then threw another glance at Cameron and back to Megan. Cameron didn't move, didn't even consider giving them privacy because he wanted Megan to know he was here for support. He wouldn't chime in, wouldn't say a word unless he saw she couldn't be strong. But he had faith in her. He knew she was getting tired of her brother only coming around for money.

Evan leaned down, whispered something to Megan and gripped her arm. Cameron went on full alert.

"No, Evan," Megan said softly, shaking her head. "I don't have it to give. I'm sorry."

"You're not sorry," he spat as he released her with a forced shove. "I don't need that much."

Megan stumbled back a step, but caught herself as she crossed her arms and tipped her chin. "I have obligations, too, Evan. I can't always give you money because you get into trouble."

Evan's focus darted over Megan's shoulder, and Cameron merely narrowed his eyes, silently daring Evan to cross the line. The arm incident was more than enough to have Cameron ready to smash his face, but Megan wouldn't like Cameron interfering. Plus as an officer of the law, Cameron couldn't just go around punching all the people who pissed him off. Such a shame.

Cameron would like nothing more than to show Evan some tough love, but Megan was right. That was easier said than done. And as much as Cameron loathed the man, he *was* Megan's brother and she loved him.

"I'll come back when we can talk in private," Evan said, looking back to Megan.

"My answer won't change," she informed him. "But you're always welcome in my house."

Evan merely grunted and started to turn.

"I love you," Megan said, her voice shaky.

Evan froze, didn't look back, didn't comment, just paused before he disappeared around the corner. Moments later, the back door opened and closed again.

Megan turned, a fake smile pasted across her face, and started down the hall toward her room, skirting around him. "Well, let me change and then maybe we can do dinner. You want to go out? I'm not sure I have a lot here—"

Cameron followed her into the bedroom and watched as she jerked off her robe and tossed it onto the mound of clothes on her bed. As she glanced into the mirror and sighed, Cameron came up behind her, resting his hands on her shoulders and meeting her gaze in the reflection.

"You don't have to pretend with me."

Her bright green eyes held his. "I'm not pretending," she assured him. "I'm ignoring the fact that for years I've been an enabler to someone who really doesn't care about me, and I'm done. I'm also starving, so while I change, figure out what you want to eat."

Cameron knew there was so much more in her, but he wasn't pressing the matter...not when she was staring back at him with such vulnerability and was half-naked. They were back to that damn body-hugging dress again, and Cameron didn't know if he wanted to keep looking or if he wanted her to cover up.

Megan's entire body relaxed against his. Her bottom nestled against his groin, and Cameron tried to ignore the innocent gesture as he wrapped his arms around her shoulders and held her securely. She needed comfort, needed to lean on someone even though it was against everything she stood for. She'd never admit she needed to draw from his strength, but Cameron was freely giving it.

Unfortunately, his fingertips barely brushed across the tops of her breasts before he could complete his hold. A shiver racked her body and vibrated through his.

"I'm glad you're here," she whispered, her eyes still locked on his in the mirror.

Looking at her reflection was quite different from being face-to-face. He didn't know why, but in the mirror he saw so much, too much. Her vulnerability stared back at him at the same time that her killer body mocked him. He was her friend, damn it. He shouldn't be having these thoughts of how perfect she felt against him, how sexy she was.

"I wouldn't be anywhere else." Even though his libido was taking a hard hit, it was the truth.

With a deep breath, Megan straightened and turned, all but brushing those breasts against his chest. Okay, really. He was a guy already on the brink of snapping the stretched line of control, and there was only so much more of this he could take.

"Are you working tonight?" she asked, oblivious to his inner turmoil.

"No." He dropped his arms to his side and took a slight step back, away from that chest, the killer body that was slowly unraveling him. "Why don't I run to the store and grab something while you change?"

"A night in?" She beamed. "Only if I get to pick the movie."

Cameron groaned. "If I have to watch *The Godfather* again..."

With an evil laugh and a shrug, Megan stepped around him and started digging through clothes. "You choose the meal—I choose the movie. You know that's how we work."

Yeah, that's how they worked. They'd been working like this for years, before his deployment and since. But in all the years they'd had this routine of spontaneous date nights with each other, never once had the urge to peel her out of her clothes been this strong.

Of course now that he'd seen her, held her and visually enjoyed her in this dress, he could think of little else. So in a moot attempt at holding on to his sanity, and their friendship, Cameron conceded.

"You win," he told her. "I'll be back."

Even if he removed himself from the situation, Cameron knew he was screwed. Now that he'd seen her lush, curvy body, and felt it so intimately against his, he couldn't *not* see it. The image, the feel of her, was permanently ingrained into him.

Penance for his sins of lying to her.

Every single time they settled in for a movie, Megan fell asleep within the first hour without fail. Tonight was no exception.

She'd curled her feet beneath her, rested her head on his shoulder and before the mobsters could leave the gun and take the cannoli, Megan was out.

Cameron propped his feet up on her coffee table and slid farther down on the sofa. Carefully, he adjusted Megan so she lay down, her head on his lap. Resting his own head against the back cushion, Cameron shut his eyes and attempted to relax. Her delicate hand settled right over his thigh as she let out a soft sigh.

With his hand curled over her shoulder, feeling the steady rise and fall, Cameron realized he actually preferred resting just like this to his bed at home. At least here he had company. At home he had thoughts that kept him awake and staring at the ceiling fan. Work never fully left him—occupational hazard.

But here, with Megan, he could let work shuffle to

the back of his mind. He didn't want to burden her with his stress, so he purposely tried to be a friend first and a cop second whenever he was with her. Added to that, he reveled in the fact she was comfortable and sleeping soundly. He wanted to be her protector, her stable force. Somehow knowing he was all of that allowed him to let down his guard just a bit.

Crossing his ankles, Cameron rested an elbow on the arm of the couch. He'd muted the movie once Megan had fallen asleep, but the flicker of the screen lit up the room. As always, when they had movie night, all lights were off.

A shrill ring pierced the silence, and Cameron jerked awake. The TV had gone black, indicating he'd dozed off for a good bit, but he didn't really recall how long ago that had been. The ring sounded again. He grabbed his side, but Megan's phone on the table was the one lit up. Normally his phone was the one that rang at all hours.

She was still out with her head on his lap. He didn't recognize the number on the screen. Shocked the caller wasn't her brother, Cameron nudged Megan's shoulder.

"Meg."

She groaned and rolled to her back, blinking as she looked up at him. The sight of her utterly exhausted and rumpled from sleeping on his lap shouldn't have his body stirring. Damn that red dress from the christening and the skimpy number she'd had on earlier.

The third ring ripped through the silence, and Megan was on instant alert. She jerked up, grabbed the phone and answered.

Cameron shifted his legs to the floor, immediately getting some blood flow back. They'd obviously been asleep for a while, which was what they had both needed.

Megan came to her feet and spoke in hushed tones as she walked into the other room. He assumed it was a client. Megan often counseled long after regular office hours were over. She was so good at her job because of how caring she was, how much she sacrificed to make sure her clients' needs came first.

Cameron got to his feet, then twisted at the waist until his back popped in all the right places. He was getting too old to sleep on a couch, a car, his office. Unfortunately, he didn't see an end to his bad habits anytime soon.

He turned off the TV, sending the living room into utter darkness. Megan rounded the corner from the kitchen just as he started to reach over and click on the lamp, but his hand bumped the stand and sent the light to the hardwood floor. He cringed at the racket.

"Don't move." Megan turned on the kitchen light, sending an instant glow shining into the living room. "Let me grab my broom."

"You're barefoot," he told her. "Let me clean it up."

"You don't have shoes on, either." She disappeared down the hall and came back with broom and dustpan in hand. "Sit on the couch, and I'll get this."

Like hell. Ignoring her, he reached down to pick up the cockeyed lampshade and the remains of the lamp. The bulb and base had completely shattered.

"I'll bring you a new one later." He set the awkward

shade and lamp guts on the coffee table and reached to take the broom.

Stepping around him, she handed him the dustpan and started sweeping. *Stubborn woman.* No wonder they were best friends. Nobody else would put up with how hardheaded they both were.

He squatted down and held the pan while she scooped in the shards. "At least this wasn't a family heirloom," he joked.

Shoving her hair from her eyes, she threw him a glance. "Funny."

Cameron headed into the kitchen to toss the debris. As he was tying the bag, the vacuum kicked on in the living room, the occasional cracking noise indicating she was removing the rest of the slivers from the floor.

He tugged the liner from the trash can and tied it, wanting to get it out so she didn't cut herself later. As Cameron jerked the knot in place, a hunk of glass he hadn't seen poking from the small hole sliced through the edge of his hand.

Damn. That hurt.

He opened her back door, tossed the bag into the larger can on her patio and closed and locked the door. The vacuum shut off in the other room as Cameron headed to the sink. Running his hand beneath the cool water eased the burning sensation and washed away the mess, allowing him to see just how deep the cut was. Megan didn't need to know he'd hurt himself. She'd make a bigger deal of it than need be.

After rinsing his hand, he examined the area further. Instantly he started bleeding again. Apparently it was deeper than he thought.

"Hiding something?"

Cringing, Cameron ripped off a paper towel, pressed it against the side of his hand and turned toward his accuser. Megan rested one shoulder against the door frame, arms crossed over her chest, and merely lifted a brow.

"Just a scratch." That hurt like hell. Apparently he was old and wimpy. Great combo for the police chief.

Cameron's eyes locked on to her shapely legs as she crossed the room. *Damn it.*

Carefully, she took his hand and pulled the paper towel away. "Oh, Cam. This needs stitches."

She examined his hand, then brought her gaze up to meet his. In the middle of the night, with everything so quiet and intimate, Cameron knew for a fact he was starting to delve into a territory he had no business being in.

Her eyes held his, dropped to his mouth, then traveled back up. That gesture said more than any words could. But this was Megan, his best friend, the girl who'd been his senior prom date and the girl who'd sneaked out with him and his brothers that same night and got absolutely plastered near the lake.

She was pretty much family. So why was she looking at him beneath those heavy lids? Why was he enjoying this rush of new sensations, wondering if she had deeper feelings? He shouldn't want her to have stronger emotions for him. That added complication was the last thing either of them needed.

"Come with me."

Cameron blinked. "Excuse me?"

Megan smiled. "To the bathroom. You're too stubborn to go get stitches, so I'll fix you up with my first-aid kit."

When she turned and headed back down the hall, Cameron released a breath he hadn't been aware he'd bottled up. Had he been the only one thinking about what would happen if they kissed? The way she'd looked at him, his mouth, as though she wanted more, wasn't something he'd made up. But the desire flashing in her eyes was gone in a second.

What was going on in that head of hers? More to the point, what the hell was he going to do if her feelings did match his?

"Cam?"

Pushing off the edge of the counter, Cameron moved through the kitchen. They were both sleep deprived; that was all. He'd been without a woman for so long, was so wrapped up in work, and Megan had quite a bit on her plate, as well.

Once daylight came, once reality settled back in and the ambience was gone, this intense moment would be forgotten. Wouldn't it?

Chapter Four

Megan squeezed her eyes shut and willed her hands to stop shaking. That was a close call. She'd nearly ignored every single red flag waving around in her mind and kissed Cameron.

She'd been examining his hand one second and the next she'd found herself lost in those St. John signature blue eyes. After just coming off a phone call with one of her teen clients, Megan had wanted to lose herself in Cameron, even if only for a moment. Bad idea, bad timing.

Heavy footsteps sounded down the hall. Megan stepped aside to give Cameron room. Her guest bath was the smallest in her house, but it was where she kept her first-aid kit.

Without a word he came in and sat down on the

edge of the garden tub. If she thought the bathroom was tiny before, having a man of Cameron's size there only solidified the fact.

"I can take care of this at home," he informed her. "It's the middle of the night."

Ignoring him, Megan cleaned the area, concentrating on her task and not the enclosed space or the warmth radiating from Cameron's body…or the fact she stood directly between his spread legs and only had on a tank and a pair of old boxers.

You'd think she'd at least take a bit more pride in her appearance when he came over, but this was Cameron. He knew her better than anybody so if she donned something halfway dressy, he'd wonder what was wrong.

Megan feared she'd doomed herself into the friend category for life where Cameron was concerned. She'd had feelings for him for years, yet the man was utterly oblivious.

Once the area was clean and dry, Megan quickly placed butterfly bandages over the cut. The strips weren't nearly as effective as stitches, but she wasn't fighting with the stubborn man. Men were like children—you had to pick your battles.

Megan turned to throw away the used supplies and wrappers, only her body and her mind weren't in sync and she swayed slightly. Strong arms circled her waist, holding her steady in an instant.

"You okay?"

Nodding, Megan closed her eyes as his caring words

and warm breath washed over her. "Yeah. The room started spinning for a second. I'm just tired, I guess."

With a gentle power she'd come to appreciate, he eased her down onto his leg. Megan twisted to face him, wondering if this would turn awkward. She didn't want awkward anywhere near their perfectly built relationship. They'd been friends too long to allow anything negative or evil to slip in.

When Cameron's uninjured hand covered her bare thigh, Megan's first thought was how she was glad she'd shaved that day...or the day before, considering it was after midnight.

Her second thought was that she hoped he didn't feel her body trembling beneath his touch. Unfortunately, keeping her body controlled around Cameron was impossible.

"Was that call earlier from a client?" he asked, his thumb tracing an invisible pattern over her thigh.

Staring into those eyes, Megan could only nod.

"You're working yourself too hard, Meg." His bandaged hand slid up, pushing her hair off her shoulder and down her back. "I know you want to be there for your patients, be there for your brother, but when will you do something for yourself?"

Actually, being on his lap right now fell nicely into the "doing something for yourself" category.

"Are you the pot or the kettle?" she asked with a smile.

A corner of his mouth tipped up into a tired grin, causing the corners of his eyes to crease. "Whichever one you aren't."

Megan yawned. "Sorry. You want to crash in the guest room tonight?"

"I'll just walk home."

As Megan came to her feet, Cameron stood with her and kept a hand on her waist.

"Dizzy?" he asked.

Shaking her head, Megan started putting the first-aid kit back. "I'm fine. I've just not been sleeping lately and with the call and then your injury, I think my body was trying to crash before I was ready."

Without even looking at the man, she knew his eyes were on her. She could feel them, feel him.

"Is your client all right?"

Megan thought back to the call. No matter how many years she'd been counseling, certain topics never got easier to deal with, and there were those special cases that truly touched her heart. Megan wished more than anything she could wave a magic wand and heal all the hurt she dealt with on a daily basis.

"Honestly, no." Megan put the kit back under the vanity. She leaned back against the counter and crossed her arms over her chest. "She's unstable, scared and can't live a normal teenage life. It's not fair and I want to go get her and bring her here. She needs love and guidance and to be able to sleep without worrying about her family."

After taking one step, Cameron stood in front of her. His good hand came down and rested on the edge of the sink beside her hip.

"You can't make up for the past, Megan."

How easily this man could see through her. He

knew how she equated every teen to her brother when he'd been an out-of-control hellion after their parents' deaths. Still, the day Megan quit caring about her clients would be the day she quit her job.

"I can't," she agreed, trying not to think about how close he was, how his breath tickled her face or how his body was nearly covering hers. "But I can help one person. I can help steer them toward a better future."

Cameron wrapped his other arm around her shoulders and pulled her against his hard chest. Tilting her head to rest her cheek against him, Megan inhaled the familiar masculine scent. What she wouldn't give to be able to wrap her arms around him and have the embrace mean so much more than friendship. An embrace that led to something intimate, something that would take them to the next level.

"Why don't you concentrate on getting sleep for what's left of the night?"

Megan eased back and smiled. "You sure you don't want the spare room?"

Cameron shook his head and took a step back. "I need to be back at the station early. I'll just head home."

A sliver of disappointment slid through her, but Megan kept smiling. Seriously, if he stayed it wasn't like she'd make a move, even though she'd thought she was ready to admit her feelings. Why couldn't she be more forward about what she wanted? She admired women who targeted a man and went after him.

Megan walked him to the door, rubbing her tired, burning eyes. "If that hand still looks bad by afternoon I want you to think about getting stitches. I'm not a nurse, you know."

Cameron glanced down to the bandage and shrugged. "It's not my shooting hand. I'll be fine."

Rolling her eyes, Megan reached around him and opened the front door. The living room and foyer were still only illuminated by the light spilling in from the kitchen.

"I have a crazy schedule the next couple of days, but I swear I'll get that lamp replaced."

"Don't worry about it." Megan covered her mouth as another yawn slipped out. "I'll just take one from the spare room until I get to a store. No big deal."

The screen door creaked open as Cameron stepped onto her porch. A cool breeze drifted through as he turned and studied her once more. He opened his mouth as if to say something, but he ended up tightening his lips. Megan wanted to know what he was thinking after they'd shared those intense moments.

Finally he swallowed and nodded. "Lock up behind me."

Megan reached for the screen door to prevent it from slamming. "Always."

"You've got to be kidding me."

Cameron crossed his arms over his chest and stood back, admiring the gaudy gold dragon lamp he'd found on his lunch break at one of the antiques stores in town.

"What?" he asked, pretending to be offended. "It puts out more light than the one you had—plus it was only eight bucks."

Megan laughed. "You got screwed if you paid more than a dime for that hideous thing."

"So you'd rather pay more for something that does the exact same thing?"

Megan stepped closer, bending down to inspect the new piece. She wrinkled her nose, squinted her eyes and her mouth contorted into an expression that looked as if she'd just inhaled the sickening aroma of a sewer plant.

This was the exact reaction he'd expected...which was why he'd bought the ugly thing.

"You did this on purpose," she accused, turning her scrunched face to him. "You know how I am about gifts, and you know I'll keep it just because you got it for me."

Cameron shrugged. "Maybe. Do you still have that unicorn salt-and-pepper-shaker set?"

Her eyes narrowed as she crossed her arms and mirrored his stance. "You know I do. I just don't get it out of the cabinet."

For years he'd randomly bought her tacky things from time to time just for a laugh. He knew how she treasured every present because she hadn't had much growing up and gifts were few and far between. Megan had a loving heart, and she'd never give away something someone bought her.

And now this tacky dragon lamp, with the light shooting out of the open mouth directed toward the ceiling, adorned her neutral-toned living room. A dragon that projectile vomited light? This was a new level of tacky. Cameron had to really bite the inside of his cheek to keep from bursting out laughing.

"I thought you were too busy to see me today."

The list of things Cameron needed to do flooded his mind. Tonight he'd be staking out another parking lot, waiting for the familiar crew of drug runners to pass through. Cameron only hoped Evan wasn't with them this time. He truly hoped Megan's brother would get away from that crowd. This case would not have a positive ending, and Cameron didn't want to arrest Evan and help convict him of a felony. That crushing blow would kill Megan.

"I'm on my way back in," he told her. "But when I saw this, I just knew you had to have it. I couldn't wait to see your face."

"There will be retaliation," she promised with a gleam in her eyes.

"I can't wait," he retorted, laughing.

Rain started splattering the windows as the gray clouds moved over the sun, blocking out the natural light.

"Got this lamp in just in time," he said, not even trying to hold back his grin. "It's supposed to storm all night. It'll be good for you to sit in here and read."

"I'd hate for the power to go out and my lamp to have some malfunction due to the storm."

Cameron patted the top of the beastly thing. "This is an antique. I'd say she's been around through many storms. Don't worry."

"She? You're giving that thing a gender?"

Cameron may have initially been drawn to the lamp

because of the shock factor and the entertainment value of presenting it to Megan, but there was more. After he'd gotten over the amusement, he realized in some weird way, this dragon reminded him of Megan. Sturdy and fierce. Of course, if he mentioned any of that to her she'd probably launch the heavy atrocity right at his head.

"You can give her a name," he added, just wanting to get under her skin. The unladylike growl was perfect. "Think about it. No need to call her anything right now. You'll want to acquaint yourself."

"I'm thinking of a few names," Megan said through gritted teeth. "None of them are for her, though."

Cameron swatted her arm. "See? You're already thinking of the lamp as her. You'll have her named by the end of the day."

Another unladylike growl escaped Megan as her eyes narrowed to slits. "Don't you have a city to protect?"

More so now than ever, yet he found himself not wanting to leave. This was the first time in a while he actually smiled for good reason. Added to that, he felt they needed this ridiculous moment after way too many close calls. His control was about to snap.

Even if he had wanted to risk their friendship and delve into a more intimate relationship, he couldn't ignore the flashes of his old partner that ripped through him. The man had been married to his job and he'd had a beautiful young wife at home. Now she was a widow. Cameron tried to check in on her from time to time, and he would never forget her face when she'd learned her husband had been killed in the line of duty. Killed by a bullet meant for Cameron. The guilt used to eat at him, but now he realized he would've done the same thing. Jumping into the line of fire wasn't something you thought about, you just did it.

"Cam?"

Megan's hand on his arm and her soft tone pulled him from his thoughts. "Yeah. Sorry."

"You left me for a minute." Her arched brows drew in. "You can talk to me. I know you can't discuss open cases, but you can at least get out some frustration."

No, he couldn't because the second those words left her lips, he found himself studying her mouth. The very thought of kissing her should have made awkwardness rise to the surface, but he found himself curious how she would taste, how she would respond. There was only one way to get her out of his system.

"I'm fine," he assured her. Well, as fine as he could be considering he was now fantasizing about kissing his best friend and keeping the fact that her brother was in way over his head with drug runners a secret. "I need to get going."

Megan reached out, wrapping her arms around him. She held on tighter than usual and damn if that didn't send a shot of arousal straight through him. Cameron slid his arms around her waist, loving how she just knew when he needed a connection most.

"Be careful," she whispered just before she stepped back. "I know you're working on a big case, but promise me you're cautious."

Cameron swallowed, hating the worry that settled

in her bright eyes. This was the reason he wouldn't subject her or any other woman to his line of work.

"I promise," he told her. "Text me and tell me what you name her."

Megan's eyes darted to the dragon lamp and back to him. "Distracting me from worry won't work."

Cameron gave her shoulder a squeeze and headed to the door. "No need to worry. Call me if you need anything."

"You know I won't call you." She smiled and tipped that adorable defiant chin up a notch. "I'm perfectly capable of taking care of myself."

Yes, but she didn't know what she was up against if her loser brother opted to somehow use her in his latest dealings. Cameron had to be on full alert because the likelihood of Evan trying to get something from Megan or bringing the rest of the cronies into her life was viable. Cameron might be watching the entire city, but his focus was zeroed in on keeping Megan safe and oblivious to the activity hitting way too close to home.

Granted, this was a small town, but that didn't mean evils wouldn't try to reach their arms in and infiltrate anyone who proved to be an easy target. Cameron wouldn't allow his town to be overrun by corrupt, illegal activities as long as he was chief.

Cameron headed back to the station, where he would be meeting up with an FBI agent to discuss the case. Too often cops developed inflated egos and didn't want outside assistance. Cameron wasn't that stupid. When the FBI had come in, he had welcomed the extra help. He'd do anything to keep his town safe, to keep drugs from filtering into the schools and homes of innocent, unsuspecting kids.

He wasn't naive enough to believe he could stop all drug trafficking, but he was damn sure going to stop this group from bringing shipments into Stonerock. Every bust, every seller taken off the streets, could possibly be saving someone's life.

Cameron couldn't wait for this case to wrap up. They had a good amount of evidence so far, but they needed a bit more. An undercover FBI agent had been placed deep in the runners' inner circle months ago. Another reason Cameron was elated to have them all on board.

All they had to do was wait on his signal, and then the group would be taken down.

Glancing back at Megan's one-story cottage, complete with cheery colorful flowers and a yellow front door, Cameron only hoped he could save her from the pain of seeing her own brother in prison. Unfortunately, Cameron didn't think that was possible.

Chapter Five

The storm had ripped through the night, putting off the surveillance. Cameron and a few other officers and FBI agents had waited around the station, hoping the storm would pass. Unfortunately, with lightning bolting across the sky and claps of thunder raging at the same time, even the dealers weren't stupid enough to be outdoors.

At around three in the morning, Cameron headed home, ready to get a few hours of sleep before coming back. Their informant had told them another meet was scheduled to happen in three days. Cameron honestly thought of taking a day off to do absolutely nothing. He was running on fumes. All he wanted to do was fall face-first into his bed and sleep for a good solid eight hours. Was that too much to ask?

He and the other agents and officers were convinced

it would only take one or two more meets before they could bring the group down. The day wouldn't come soon enough.

His headlights cut through the darkness as he pulled into his drive. He needed a shower and a bed. He actually needed food, but that would have to wait. He was too exhausted to even pry open a package of toaster pastries at this point.

After letting himself in the back door, he removed his shoulder holster and gun. After carrying it through the darkened hall, he stepped into his bedroom and placed the gun on the dresser just inside the door. Turning around, he went into the bathroom directly across the hall from his room.

The shower was quick, hot and enough to loosen his sore muscles and have him one step closer to falling into oblivion as soon as he slid between his sheets.

Wrapping the towel around his waist and tucking the edge in to secure it in place, Cameron padded back across the hall. He kept his blackout shades pulled at all times, seeing as how he never knew when he'd get shut-eye and he wanted to keep the room nice and dark. Of course tonight, with the storm, the moon wasn't even out to offer a glow.

Cameron jerked off the towel and hung it on the closet doorknob. Shuffling toward the king-size bed, Cameron nearly wept at the thought of falling asleep. Now, if he could stay asleep that would be a miracle.

Jerking back the covers quickly revealed two things: there was a woman in his bed, and there would be no sleep tonight.

* * *

His hands glided over her bare skin, sending ripples of satisfaction coursing through her. Finally, after all these years, she would finally know what making love to her best friend was like.

A soft groan escaped her lips; her body arched in eager anticipation.

"Megan."

Even his voice aroused her. That low, throaty tone. She'd imagined him growling her name while looking into her eyes as his body leaned over hers.

"Meg."

The firm grip on her shoulder had her lifting her lids, blinking. Darkness surrounded her, but the shape before her was so familiar, so close. She reached up, slid her hands over his stubbled jaw and pulled him down. Her mouth covered his and for a second she wondered why he wasn't responding.

The thought was fleeting as Cameron's hesitant state snapped; his hold on her shoulders tightened. His mouth opened, his tongue plunging in to tangle with hers. Yes, this is what she needed, what she craved.

The weight of his body pressing hers back into the bed, the sheer strength of this man, consumed her in every single way and made all her fantasies seem so minor in comparison.

The euphoria of coming from a dream into reality—

Megan froze. Dream into reality? *Oh, no.* She had been dreaming earlier…now she wasn't.

As if sensing her detachment, Cameron stilled and lifted his head. She lay on the bed, the top half of his body covering hers, the tingling sensations still rippling through her as she focused back on the cold, harsh reality.

"Cam?"

"Yeah." His husky voice did nothing to rid her body's ache. "Um...sorry. That was...I don't...why did you kiss me?"

With her palms plastered to his bare chest—his bare, damp chest—Megan closed her eyes and battled with telling the truth or saving her pride.

"I was dreaming."

Pride won out. How could she tell her best friend she'd been dreaming of seducing him and fully succeeding? How could she tell him that for years she'd dreamed of taking control and making him see just how amazing they'd be together?

"That was one hell of a dream." He eased himself off her, and as her eyes fully adjusted to the darkened room, she realized he wore... *Oh, mercy.* He wore absolutely nothing.

Embarrassed, yet incredibly still aroused, Megan shoved her hair away from her face. "I didn't want to bother you at work and I thought I'd be gone by morning since I figured you'd be out all night." She realized she was rambling, but nerves had taken over and she'd lost all control. As she rambled, though, it gave him time to retrieve a towel from the closet knob and secure it around his waist. "I couldn't sleep at my house and had you been home I would've taken the couch, but since you were out..."

Cameron smiled as she trailed off, and she figured

she sounded as nervous as she felt. Silence settled between them, and he crossed his arms over his chest, as if wearing only a towel was the most comfortable thing in the world.

Was he not affected at all by that kiss? She knew for a fact he'd been somewhat aroused when he'd been on top of her, but now he merely looked at her with that lopsided grin she'd come to love.

"I don't mind a bit that you came here," he informed her. "But what was wrong with your house?"

Restless on so many levels, Megan came to her feet and started smoothing out the covers. "My back door had been tampered with and the lock was broken. I wasn't comfortable sleeping there. I didn't figure you'd mind."

"What the hell, Meg?" Reaching around her, he clicked on the bedside lamp. "Someone broke in and you were afraid to call my cell?"

"I wasn't afraid," she defended herself, testing every bit of her self-control as she kept her eyes on his and not on the stark white towel riding low on his hips or the sprinkling of dark hair across his bare torso. "I knew you were busy and…can you put some pants on? I can't talk like this."

A corner of his mouth kicked up into a grin. "You've seen me in swim trunks, Meg."

Yes, but in those instances he hadn't just been lying on top of her, kissing her back as if she were his next breath of air. Would her lips ever stop tingling from all that heat? His body's imprint was permanently ingrained onto hers.

Her eyes darted to the bed, re-creating an image of how close she'd been to attaining her greatest fantasy. When she glanced back up, Cameron's jaw was clenched, his eyes holding hers as if he knew exactly where her thoughts had traveled and he was having a hard time keeping his own from going there.

"It's not the same," she whispered.

With a nod, he turned, pulled a pair of shorts from his drawer and slid them on beneath the towel. With a flick of his wrist, the towel came off and he hung it back on the doorknob before he crossed the intimate room to stand within a breath of her.

"Now, tell me what the hell is going on. What happened at your house?"

Megan pulled in a deep breath, giving herself an extra minute to figure out how to control her emotions and get back on track to where their conversation needed to be.

"My back door had been kicked in or something. It was open and the lock was busted."

Cameron raked a hand over his still-damp hair and muttered a curse. "You'll call me next time anything happens. Me, not the department, not another officer. You'll call my cell."

A little surprised at his demanding tone, Megan propped her hands on her hips. "What would you have done? Left whatever you've been working undercover on for months?"

His narrowed eyes held hers as he eased forward just enough for his bare chest to brush against her. "Yes."

He'd put work second? That was a first. Work never

came after anything for Cameron. He took pride in keeping his town's reputation favorable and the crime rate low. To know he would've dropped everything for her caused a new warmth to spread through her, overlaying the previous heat from their intimate encounter moments ago.

"I didn't need to call you for a busted door," she said. "I knew you'd look at it sometime in the morning. I just wanted to sleep. Like I said, had I known you'd be home, I'd have taken the couch."

While his small cottage had two bedrooms, the second bedroom was full of workout equipment that aided in bulking up his already magnificent physic.

"I'll take the couch," he told her. "Go on back to sleep."

Oh, sure. As if she could crawl back into that bed after what had just happened. She'd had a hard enough time getting to sleep in the first place because she'd nearly suffocated herself by burying her face into his pillow and inhaling that familiar masculine scent. She really needed to get a grip before she made a complete fool of herself.

"I'll take the couch." She smiled up at him, hoping the friendly gesture would ease the tension. Granted, the tension was most likely all one-sided. "You've been up long enough and there's no way you'll fit."

"What kind of gentleman and friend would I be if I booted my best friend to the couch?"

Best friend. Had he thrown those two words at her to remind her of their status? Had she completely freaked him out when she'd attacked him, rubbed herself all over him and claimed his mouth? Part of her was mortified; the other part of her was a bit relieved she'd finally kissed him. She'd not only kissed him, she'd full-out devoured him. But now she knew how he tasted, how he felt. That knowledge was both a blessing and a curse.

"I either take the couch or I head home where it may not be safe."

True, she wasn't fighting fair because no way would he let her go if he thought for a second she wasn't well protected. He studied her for a moment, and Megan tried not to look away or fidget beneath that hypnotic gaze. Would she ever stop tingling? Would she ever forget how perfectly his body felt pressed against hers? She hoped not. Those were memories she'd want to relive over and over for as long as possible.

"You're stubborn."

Megan shrugged. "One of my many talents," she told him, patting his bare shoulder because she was having a hard time resisting all that glorious skin mere inches away. "Sleep tight."

Inching around him, inhaling that fresh-from-the-shower scent, Megan made her way out of his room and headed to the couch. She may as well just head on home because there was no way she could sleep now, not after that kiss. But she would stay. If Cameron knew she was home, he wouldn't rest, either, and he desperately needed to before he worked himself to death.

Megan pulled a blanket from the back of the couch, fluffed the throw pillow and lay on her side, facing the hallway. The darkened space offered nothing of comfort or peace. The silence was equally as empty.

Was Cameron already lying in bed? Had he already slid between the sheets she'd just come from? Had that kiss even made an impact on him, or was he completely repulsed at the fact his best friend had tried to consume him?

More than likely the man's head had barely hit the pillow before he was out. At least one of them would get some sleep tonight.

Chapter Six

How the hell could a man rest after finding a woman in his bed, being kissed in such an arousing way by said woman and now smelling her fruity scent on his sheets?

Cameron laced his fingers over his abdomen and stared up at the ceiling fan. Whoever Megan had been dreaming about was one lucky man. The way she'd all but plastered her curvy body against his had him instantly responding. Hence the problem with sleeping. How the hell did he react to this? For a few brief moments, he'd found something with Megan he'd never experienced with any other woman. Ever.

What was the protocol for discovering your best friend kissed like every man's fantasy? He knew he'd wanted her on a primal level, but to actually have evidence of the fact only added to his confusion.

This was Megan, the woman who knew all his secrets, all his annoying quirks. They'd been through everything together from riding their first rollercoaster to her brother's ups and downs.

She was like family, only he was feeling close to her in a way that had nothing to do with family. He'd secretly hoped if he ever got his hands or lips on her, he'd get her out of his system because he'd feel nothing. Unfortunately, that was completely the opposite of what had just happened. He felt too much, too fast.

Cameron's body still hadn't settled back down, and it wouldn't anytime soon. Who the hell had Megan been dreaming about? She wasn't dating anyone, unless she was keeping it a secret.

Damn it. Jealousy was an ugly, unwelcome trait.

Swiping a hand down his face, Cameron cursed himself. Here he was, dead on his feet, unable to sleep for fantasizing about his best friend dreaming about a mysterious man. How messed up had his life become in the past hour?

Licking his lips, he still tasted her. He couldn't want more. Wanting anything more from Megan was out of the question. Their friendship was solid—why mess that up just because she kissed like every dream he'd ever had?

Movement in the house made him focus on the darkness instead of his wayward thoughts. Bare feet slid over the hardwood. The refrigerator door opened, closed, followed by the sound of a cabinet being shut softly. She was trying to be so quiet, but he wasn't sleeping and he was trained to hear even the slightest disturbances.

This new tension that had settled between them wasn't going anywhere. She may have tried to act calm after what they'd shared, but he knew her well enough to know she was anything but. Her nerves and emotions were just as jumbled, just as buzzing, as his were.

With a sigh, he sat up and swung his legs over the side of the bed. Might as well face this head-on. He didn't want uneasiness to become an uninvited third party in their relationship. Maybe she really was just dreaming, but the way his body responded, the way she'd been jittery afterward, told him there was more.

He padded his way down the hall, his eyes adjusting to the darkness in his familiar surroundings. The living room was empty, so he turned toward the kitchen, where he saw her. Leaning against the counter, looking out onto the backyard, Megan held a glass in her hand. Cameron studied her in a new light. He couldn't deny her beauty, with her perfectly shaped curves and hair that tumbled down her back. Those green eyes could pierce you in an instant, and now he knew that mouth could render a man speechless.

Still clutching the glass and staring, Megan hadn't moved one bit since he'd stood here. Something, or someone, consumed her mind.

"Who is he?"

Megan jumped, turned and the glass she'd been clutching dropped to the floor with a crackling shatter.

"Damn it." He started to move forward but stopped. He reached around the doorjamb and flicked on the light, blinking against the bright glare. "Don't move. Neither of us have shoes on."

First the lamp at her house and now this. They hadn't even delved into relationship territory, and already things were breaking all around them. A metaphor for things to come?

He ran back to his room and shoved his feet into a pair of tennis shoes at the foot of the bed. When he got back to the kitchen, Megan was bending over, picking up pieces of glass.

"I told you not to move," he growled, not knowing which situation he was angrier at.

"I didn't take a step. I'm just picking up the large pieces."

He jerked open the small built-in utility closet and grabbed the broom and dustpan. After sweeping up the majority of the glass, Megan set the shards she'd held into the dustpan, too.

After dumping the mess into the trash, he went back and scooped her up into his arms without a word.

With a squeak of surprise, Megan landed against his chest and he had no idea how to react to the fact his body warmed and responded with her against him once again.

"This is overkill—don't you think?" she asked, sliding one arm around his neck.

"I need you out of the way so I can get the rest and you're not wearing shoes. So no, I don't think it's overkill."

He deposited her on the couch in the living room and made his way back to clean up the water and make sure all the fragments were swept up. Several minutes later, he headed back into the living room to find Megan gone.

Heading down the hall, he heard water running from the bathroom. She'd left the door open, allowing the light to spill into the hallway. When he peeked into the room, Megan was at the sink, holding one hand under the water. Blood seeped to the surface of her palm as soon as water could wash it away.

"Why didn't you tell me you'd cut yourself?" he asked.

"Like you told me the other day?" Throwing him a glance over her shoulder, Megan shrugged. "You were cleaning up the mess. Seriously, it's very minor. I could use a bandage, though."

Stepping forward, Cameron reached around, shut the water off and held on to her wrist to examine her hand. Her hair tickled the side of his face, and the pulse beneath his fingertips sped up. Gritting his teeth to shove aside any emotions outside the friend zone, Cameron inspected the injury.

"It is small," he agreed, still inspecting the area.

She glanced up, catching his eyes in the mirror. "It just needs to be cleaned up and a bandage. I wasn't lying."

When he continued to stare at her, she merely quirked a brow. Damn woman would make a nun curse like a sailor.

"Sit," he said, pointing to the toilet lid. "It's my turn to take care of you."

Grabbing the first-aid kit from beneath the sink, he

shuffled the supplies around and found what he needed to fix her up.

He took a seat on the edge of the tub and balanced the supplies on his thigh. With careful movements, he uncurled her fingers and examined the cut again. It was bleeding pretty good, but it wasn't deep at all.

"I'm thinking you and I need only plastic, child-safe things in our homes," she joked.

"At the very least, we should stop handling glass in the middle of the night."

Cameron appreciated her attempt to lighten the mood, but he'd come out of his room for a reason and he needed to get this off his chest.

"Why couldn't you sleep?" he asked, keeping his eyes locked on his task as he swiped her palm with gauze.

"Insomnia has become a close friend of mine lately."

That was something he definitely understood. Still, she'd been sleeping just fine earlier in his bed.

"I'll make sure your door is fixed so you can sleep in your bed." Confident the bleeding had slowed enough not to come through the bandage, Cameron held a fresh gauze pad over the cut and applied pressure. "I'm sorry I startled you earlier."

Her hand tensed beneath his touch. "What were you asking me when you came into the kitchen, anyway?"

Keeping his thumb over the pad, he lifted his gaze to hers. Those bright green eyes outlined by dark lashes held him captivated and speechless for a second. "Nothing. Forget it."

"You asked who he was," she went on. "What *he* are you referring to?"

Knowing she wouldn't back down, Cameron opted to face this head-on as he'd originally intended. He was chief of police, for crying out loud, yet the thought of discussing another man with Megan had him trembling and nearly breaking out into a sweat…not to mention ready to punch someone in the face.

"I wanted to know who you were dreaming about."

Megan lowered her lids, took a deep breath and let it out. "I'm not sure you're ready for that answer."

Not ready for the answer? What was she about to tell him? Was she fantasizing about someone he didn't care for? Cameron got along with nearly everybody on the right side of the law.

"It's none of my business," he repeated, not sure he was ready for the answer, either. "The way you kissed me…"

Megan stared at him as his words died in the crackling air between them. "I was dreaming of you."

Nerves and fear settled deep in her stomach as if weighted by an anchor. She kept her gaze on his, refusing to back down or show weakness. He wanted the truth—he got it. Now they would both have to deal with the consequences because she'd just opened a door and shoved him right on through into the black abyss. Neither of them had a clue what waited for them.

Cameron's warm hand continued to hold hers, protecting her injury. He clenched the muscle in his jaw as if he was holding back his response. Not knowing what was going on in his head was only adding to her worry.

"Say something." She tried for a smile but swallowed instead, blinking as her eyes began to burn with the threat of tears. *Oh, no.* She wouldn't break down. Not here, not now. "It was a kiss, Cam. No big deal."

Okay, so she'd tried to be strong and not back down, but right now, in the wake of his silence, she figured backpedaling was the only approach.

"Don't lie to me," he commanded. "I was on the receiving end of that kiss, and it was definitely a big deal."

Megan pulled her hand away and got to her feet, causing him to scoot back and try to catch all the supplies from his lap before they scattered to the floor.

"I was still asleep, Cameron. I was in your bed, surrounded by your scent. I can't help what I was dreaming."

Lifting the pad from her hand, she studied her palm. The cut only stung a little, not enough to keep her focus off the fact she was in this minuscule bathroom with Cameron and she'd just told him she'd been fantasizing about him. There wasn't enough air or space because he came up right behind her, practically caging her in between his hard, broad body and the vanity.

"So you're saying if I kissed you now that you're fully awake, you wouldn't respond like earlier?"

His bold, challenging question had her jerking her gaze up to meet his in the mirror. Slowly turning to face him, brushing against every plane of his torso in the process, Megan clutched her injured hand against her chest. Though the cut was insignificant in the grand scheme of things, holding on to it gave her a prop she needed to calm her shaky hands.

"It's late...or early," she told him. "Let's forget any of this happened and try to salvage what's left of the night. We both need sleep."

He braced his hands on the sink, officially trapping her in between his arms. "You're not a coward."

"No, I'm not. But this little exercise is ridiculous."

Lowering his lids, he stared at her mouth. "Then this won't be a problem."

His mouth slid over hers, and Megan pulled up every ounce of self-control to keep from moaning. Earlier she'd been half dreaming when she'd kissed him, but now she was fully awake and able to truly enjoy how amazing her best friend was in the kissing department.

Even though he was demanding and controlling, Cameron somehow managed to also be gentle with his touch. One strong hand splayed across her back, urging her closer. Her injured hand remained trapped between their bodies, and she fisted the other at her side because she didn't want to show emotion, not now. As much as she yearned to wrap herself around him and give in to anything he was willing to offer, she wasn't ready.

Cameron nipped at her lips, easing his way out of the kiss. But he didn't stop. No, the man merely angled his head the other way and dived back in for more.

The way he had her partially bent back over the vanity, Megan had to bring up her good hand to clutch his bare shoulder. She couldn't recall the last time she'd been so thoroughly kissed. No matter the time, she'd certainly never been kissed as passionately, as intensely, as now. Even those kisses that led straight to the bedroom had never gotten her this hot, this turned on.

Cameron fisted her T-shirt in his hand, pulling it tighter against her back as he lifted his head slightly. His forehead rested against hers.

"You're awake now," he muttered. "Feeling anything?"

Because she needed to think, and she knew *he* needed to think, Megan patted his shoulder and smiled. "You're a good kisser, Cam. No denying that. But I'm not dreaming anymore."

Cameron stepped back, hands on his narrowed hips where his shorts were riding low. "Tell me that didn't make your body respond."

She knew for a fact his body had responded, but she wouldn't be so tacky as to drop her gaze to the front of his shorts. They both knew she was fully aware.

Cameron had never even hinted he wanted to kiss her before. And even though she knew she should take this chance to tell him how she felt, she found herself lying to his face to save hers.

"Like I said, you're a great kisser," she told him. "But I've had better."

With that bold-faced lie, she marched from the bathroom and straight to the sofa, where she lay down facing the back cushions and covered up with the throw.

Megan wasn't quite sure if she'd put this experiment to rest or if she'd awakened the beast inside Cameron.

She had a feeling she'd find out soon enough. Thrills of anticipation coursed through her at the prospect.

Chapter Seven

Cameron needed this break. Between work and keeping track of Evan at various late-night meetings and that semierotic evening spent with Megan, he was about to lose it.

Drinking a beer on Eli's new patio with his brothers while their wives sat in the house discussing babies or shoes or some other frightening topic was exactly what he needed to relax.

Of course the incident with Megan had happened only two days ago and he still hadn't been able to get a grasp on how much that kiss, both kisses, had affected him.

"We've lost him again," Eli mocked, pulling Cameron from his daze.

"He's still working in his head." Drake took a pull of

his beer, then let the bottle dangle between his knees. "You're off the clock right now. Enjoy it."

Cameron rested his forearms on the edge of the deck railing and glanced out into the wooded backyard. Eli had built an addition on his home and then added the deck. He and his wife of nearly a year, and their baby, lived in their own little corner on the edge of town.

Drake, with his new bride and adorable stepdaughter, was embracing family life, as well. Drake had even mentioned how he and Marly wanted to try for a baby of their own.

Cameron couldn't be happier for his brothers, but they could keep their minivans, grocery lists and scheduled bedtimes. That wasn't a lifestyle he saw himself settling into anytime soon…if ever.

"I'm not working in my head," he defended himself. "I'm just enjoying listening to you two go on about recipes and paint swatches like a bunch of old ladies at a hair salon."

"Someone's grouchy," Eli muttered.

"Maybe he doesn't have a recipe worth sharing and he's embarrassed," Drake added with a low chuckle.

Cameron turned, flipping his brothers the one-finger salute. He missed getting together with them. They used to try to have a cookout or something once a week, especially since Eli's deployments were over and he was officially a civilian now, but Cameron's schedule was anything but regular. He hated putting work ahead of his family, but sometimes he couldn't help the matter. The criminals didn't seem to keep nine-to-five hours.

"Oh, hell," Drake whispered as he sat straight up in his deck chair. "You've finally got woman issues."

Eli's head whipped around, his gaze narrowing on Cameron. "Seriously? Because if you have woman issues, that means you have a woman, which is a damn miracle."

Finishing off his beer, knowing full well he needed something stronger to get into this discussion, Cameron tossed his empty bottle into the bin.

"I don't have a woman," he ground out, dropping onto the settee. "I have a headache over one."

Why did he have to go and issue Megan that challenge? Why did he have to push her into proving she was lying? Because all he'd gotten out of the deal was a hell of a great kiss, sleepless nights full of fantasies fueled by his best friend and a whole lot of anger with himself for crossing the line.

His own issues aside, how could he actually move to another level with Megan knowing her brother was well on his way to prison? Hell, Cameron was having a hard time keeping that bottled up now, and they were just friends. How could he keep secrets if he allowed intimacy to slip into the picture?

"Who is she?" Eli asked. "Oh, is it the new lady in town that lives out behind the grocery store? I hear she's single and if those tight-fitting clothes and spike heels aren't an invitation—"

"An invitation to what?" Nora asked from the patio door with her arms crossed over her chest, a quirked brow and a knowing grin on her face.

Eli cleared his throat. "Hey, babe," he said, crossing the wide area to wrap an arm around her waist. "I was just thinking about you."

She swatted him in the stomach. "If you think I'll ever dress like I work a pole every night, you're insane."

Eli groaned. "Please, don't mention a pole."

Cameron and Drake exchanged a conspiratorial look before they busted out laughing. "Still scarred from the image of Maddie Mays?"

Squeezing his eyes shut, Eli shook his head. "I'm trying to forget, but she was in again yesterday. Why does she always bring up her workout regime with me?"

"Because you're her doctor," Cameron smirked, enjoying the idea of his brother in such an awkward position. "Aren't you sworn to secrecy? I don't think you should share such things with us."

Eli blinked, narrowing his gaze. "If I have to suffer at the image, then so do you two."

"Mad" Maddie Mays had seemed to be a hundred years old when they were kids. At this point she may have been the same age as Noah and survived by hiding out on the ark. She'd never been a fan of the St. John boys and found their shenanigans less than amusing. More often than not, she'd chased them out of her yard wielding a rolling pin, baseball bat or sometimes both to really get her point across.

Now with Eli taking over their father's clinic, Maddie had no choice but to associate with at least one of the St. John boys, unless she wanted to find a doctor in a neighboring town. Apparently she'd warmed up to Eli. Perhaps sharing her unorthodox exercise routine was just her way of getting back at him for being a menace as a kid.

"If you guys are done discussing that poor woman, I wanted to know if you all had mentioned date night to Cameron." Nora took the bottle from Eli's hands and took a drink.

"What date night?" Cameron eyed his brothers. "You two aren't my type."

Nora smiled. "Actually we were wondering if you'd like to play the cool uncle while we went out. I was hesitant to ask you, but Eli and Drake assured me you wouldn't mind if you weren't busy."

Stunned, Cameron considered the idea, then shrugged. "Sure, I can do it." He'd just schedule the diaper changing and mac-and-cheese dinner around watching for drug smugglers. "How hard can watching a baby and a six-year-old be?"

His brothers exchanged a look and nearly turned red trying to hold back a comment or laughter. *Oh, they think I'm not capable? Challenge accepted.*

"Seriously?" Cameron went on. "You're already thinking I'm going to blow this? I run a town, for pity's sake. Surely I can handle two kids."

Nora stepped forward, patted his arm and offered a smile that was a bit on the patronizing side. Did nobody have faith in him?

"Just tell us when you're free," she told him.

Running his crazy schedule through his mind, Cameron knew there wouldn't be a great night, but he could surely spare a few hours. "I could do it Sunday eve-ning."

"I work until four, but we could go after that," Drake chimed in.

"Great." Nora beamed. She leaned down, kissed Cameron on the cheek and patted his shoulder. "I'll go tell Marly."

She raced back into the house and Cameron leaned his head back against the cushion on the settee. Both brothers stared down at him.

"What?"

"You're not getting off the hook about this woman that has you tied in knots just because you're babysit-ting," Eli insisted. "We'll get the truth out of you one way or another."

Cameron didn't even know what there was to tell. Megan had kissed him, he'd kissed her and since then they hadn't spoken. What a mess, and most of it was his fault. If he hadn't insisted on challenging her, if he'd let her lie her way out of the first kiss, they would've moved on and ignored that pivotal turn they'd taken.

No way would he reveal Megan's name to his brothers. She was like a sister to them, and he wasn't sure they'd be on board with how Cameron had treated her.

But damn it, she'd tied him up in knots the second she'd slid her body against his.

"Come on—you can't sit there brooding and not fill us in." Drake leaned an elbow against the railing. "It has to be someone you know since you work every waking second. You don't have time to meet women unless it's someone you're arresting. Please, tell me you don't have some prisoner-guard romance going because if you do we're staging an intervention."

"Do you ever shut up?" Cameron asked, without heat. "Can't a guy keep some things to himself?"

"No," Eli and Drake replied in unison.

Raking a hand down his face, Cameron came to his feet. He couldn't stay any longer. If he did, they'd figure out who had him in knots and he couldn't afford to let that out right now, not when he was so confused. And he had no clue what was going through Megan's head, either.

"Now he's leaving." Eli laughed. "This must be bad if you're running from your own brothers."

"It's a small town," Drake added with a smile that stated he'd get to the bottom of it. "Secrets don't stay hidden long. The truth will come out eventually."

Cameron glared at his brothers before heading into the house to say goodbye to his sisters-in-law and his nieces.

The truth coming out was precisely what he couldn't have happen. But he knew he wasn't telling anybody about the incident and he doubted Megan would tell anyone, so that left the secret bottled up good and tight.

The question now was: When would it explode?

Megan hadn't even made it home from work when her cell rang. She'd just pulled onto her road when she answered without looking.

"Hello."

"I'm sorry to bother you."

Instantly Megan recognized the voice of one of her clients…a girl who'd just been in earlier that afternoon and the same one who'd called in the middle of the night days ago. Farrah wasn't the most stable person, and Megan made a point to really work with her. Megan cared for all her clients' well-being, but Farrah was extremely unstable and truly had no one else to turn to.

"Don't apologize," Megan insisted as she neared her driveway. "I'm here for you anytime."

"Earlier you told me that moving forward was the only way to start over."

Megan eased her car into the detached garage. "That's right."

Farrah sniffed. "I'm going to look for a job tomorrow. It's time I move out and try to make my life my own."

Megan had been waiting for Farrah to see that she needed to stand on her own two feet, to get away from the controlling man who held so much power over her. Megan had tried to stress how control can often quickly turn to abuse.

"I just wanted to thank you for today, and maybe… Could I put you down as a reference?"

Megan smiled as she killed the engine. "That would be fine. I'm really proud of you, Farrah."

Farrah thanked her, then ended the call. By the time Megan gathered her things and headed across the stone walkway to her back door, her phone was ringing again. She glanced at the screen and saw Evan's number. She hated how her first instinct was to groan.

How was it she could counsel total strangers, yet her own flesh and blood refused to take her advice or even consider for a moment that she wasn't trying to control him?

With a sigh, she answered as she shoved her key in her new doorknob. "Hi, Evan."

"Can I stay with you for a few nights?"

Stunned, Megan froze with her hand on the knob. She wasn't shocked at his abrupt question without so much as a greeting, but at the request. It was unusual for him not to ask for money first.

"Are you all right?"

"Yeah, yeah. I just…I need a place to crash. You going to help me or not?"

Closing her eyes, Megan leaned her head against the glass on the door. Even though his tone was put out and angry, he was at least coming to her for support.

"I'll always help you, Evan. But are you asking because you're ready to make changes in your life or because you're hiding?"

"Forget it," he grunted. "You're always judging me."

"No, Evan. I'm not judging—I'm worried."

Silence filled the line. Megan straightened and strained to hear.

"Evan?"

"If I wanted to change, could you help me?"

Now his voice came out in a near whisper, reminding her of the young boy he'd once been. At one time he'd looked up to her. When did all of that change?

"I'd do anything for you," she assured him. "Do you need help? I can come get you right now."

Again silence filled the line. She waited, not wanting to push further. This was the first time he actually sounded as if he may want to let her in. Megan prayed he would take the olive branch she'd been holding out for so long.

Commotion from the other end of the line, muffled voices and Evan's swearing told her the conversation was dead.

"I'll, uh, I'll call you later," he whispered as if he didn't want to be heard.

Gripping her phone, Megan pushed her way into the house. She didn't know why she'd let herself get her hopes up for those few seconds. She didn't know why she was constantly beating herself up over a man who might just continue to use her for the rest of their lives. But he was her brother and she would never give up. She may be frustrated and oftentimes deflated, but she wasn't a quitter and she would make damn sure he wasn't, either.

He'd called; that was a major step.

After hanging her purse on the peg by the back door, Megan slid her keys and phone inside. Her stomach growled, reminding her that she'd skipped lunch again in order to squeeze in one more client. Her supervisor kept telling her she needed to take breaks, but how could Megan justify them when someone's life could very well be in her hands? What if it was the patient who was contemplating suicide or leaving a spouse and they needed to talk right then? Megan couldn't turn them away.

Her eyes landed on the letter she'd tacked to the side

of her refrigerator. The letter outlining every detail for the new position she'd been offered in Memphis. The job was almost too good to be true, but it meant leaving Cameron, leaving the chance for something she'd wanted her whole life.

The directors had certainly pulled out all the stops to get her to take the position. The opportunity to help launch a free clinic in an area of town where people had been forgotten, left to their own devices. Megan wasn't married, didn't have kids and had been recommended for this job by her boss. How could she say no?

Two very valid reasons kept her from jumping at this chance of a lifetime: Evan and Cameron. Both men were fixtures in her life, and both men needed her whether either of them admitted it or not.

She hadn't spoken to Cameron in a few days, and emptiness had long since settled into that pit in her stomach, joining the fear and worry there. This was precisely why she hadn't made a move before, why she'd kept her feelings to herself. If a few kisses had already wedged an awkward wall between them, what would've happened had she told him she wanted to try a real relationship with him?

Megan glanced at the letter again and sighed. Maybe she should go. Maybe she needed to get away from the man who was a constant in her life but would never fill the slot she needed him to. And perhaps her new start would be the perfect opportunity for Evan to make a clean break, as well.

Chapter Eight

"**I** need you." Cameron surveyed the chaos around him and cringed. "How soon can you be at my house?"

Shrill cries pierced his eardrums for at least the fifteenth time in as many minutes. Every single parent in the world officially had his respect and deserved some type of recognized award for their patience.

"Where are you?" Megan asked. "What's all that noise?"

Cameron raked a hand over his hair and realized he needed to get a cut. He'd add that to the many things he'd slacked on lately. Right now, though, he was groveling to his best friend to come save him even though he'd been a jerk and hadn't spoken to her since.

His house was a complete war zone thanks to a spunky six-year-old and an infant.

Willow was dancing her stuffed horse in front of Amber's reddened, angry, tear-soaked face in an attempt to calm the baby, but Cameron figured that was only making it worse. Not to mention the fact that Willow had a slight goose egg on her head after tripping over the baby and falling into the corner of the coffee table.

Why had he insisted on watching the kids at his house? A house that was as far from baby proof as possible. He was a bachelor. Unfortunately, his bachelor pad had now tragically converted into a failing day-care center.

"Please," he begged. He never begged. "I'm home, and you can't get here fast enough. I'm…babysitting."

Okay, so he muttered that last word because he knew Megan well enough to know she'd burst out laughing and he wasn't in the mood.

"I'm sorry. Did you say *babysitting*?"

Cameron bent over and pulled Amber into his arms. "Front door's unlocked," he said right before disconnecting the call and sliding his cell back into his pocket. He had no time for mockery; this was crisis mode. Code red.

Megan would most likely dash down here within minutes, if nothing else to see firsthand how out of his comfort zone he was. The humiliation he was about to suffer would be long lasting, but at this point he didn't care. He needed reinforcements in the worst possible way.

This was not how he'd intended to apologize to Megan or how he'd planned on contacting her for the first time since he'd all but consumed her in his bathroom. Cameron hadn't mapped out a plan, exactly, but he knew he needed to be the one to take the next step. But the step he wanted to take and the step he needed to take were on opposite ends of the spectrum.

Cameron patted Amber on her back and tried to console her. How could someone so tiny be so filled with rage? Fatherhood was not his area of expertise. He wished there was some how-to manual he could read. Did Eli have this much trouble with his little girl? Cameron had never seen this side of his infant niece.

"Maybe you should sing her a song," Willow said, smiling up at him with a grin that lacked the front two teeth. "Do you know any songs?"

AC/DC's "Back in Black" sprang to mind, but he didn't figure an infant would find that particular tune as appealing as a nearly forty-year-old man did.

"I bet you know some," he countered. "What songs have you learned in school so far?"

Brows drawn, Willow looked lost in thought. Apparently, something brilliant came to her because she jumped up and down, her lopsided ponytails bouncing off her shoulders.

"'Wheels on the Bus'! That's my favorite."

After taking a seat on the sofa, Cameron adjusted Amber on his lap so the infant could see Willow and hopefully hear the song.

What else could he do? He'd fed her. Then she'd played on the floor with her toys, and now she was angrier than any woman he'd ever encountered on either side of the law.

Willow started singing, extremely off-key and loud, but hey, the extra noise caught Amber's attention and for a blessed moment she stopped screaming.

Then she started again, burying her face against his chest. Unfazed, Willow continued to sing.

The front door flew open, and Megan stepped in, instantly surveying the room. A smirk threatened to take over, but Cameron narrowed his gaze across the room, silently daring her to laugh.

He'd never been so happy to see another person in his entire life.

Willow stopped singing the second the door closed. "Hey, Megan. I didn't know you were coming over."

Megan smiled and crossed the room. "I didn't, either, but here I am."

Cameron tried to focus on the reason he'd called her here, but his eyes drank in the sight of Megan wearing a pair of body-hugging jeans and a plain white T-shirt with her signature off-duty cowgirl boots. With her hair pulled back in a ponytail, she looked about twenty years old.

Megan reached for Amber and held the infant against her body. Without giving Cameron another glance, she turned and started walking around the room, patting Amber's back and singing softly.

Well, what did he expect? He'd called her to help with the situation he obviously had lost control over, not to take up where they'd left off the other night.

Still, the fact she didn't say a word to him made him wonder if he'd hurt her more than he realized. He was botching up their relationship in every way, and he didn't blame her for being upset or angry.

Almost instantly the crying ceased. "Seriously? You hold her and she stops?"

Megan laughed, easing back to look Amber in the face. "I don't think it was me at all," she corrected him. "I think her stomach was upset. I just felt rumbling on my hand."

Cameron glanced to Megan's hand resting on Amber's bottom. Realization hit him hard. "Oh, no."

Willow giggled. "She feels better now."

Megan lifted Amber around to face Cameron. "She doesn't smell better," Megan said, scrunching up her nose.

Oh, please, please, please. There were few things that truly left him crippled, but the top of that list was changing a diaper...a dirty, smelly diaper.

Slowly rising to his feet, Cameron locked eyes with Megan. "I'll give you a hundred bucks to change that diaper."

Megan quirked a brow, her eyes glazed over with something much more devious than humor. "Keep your hundred bucks. I'll decide payment later."

Oh, mercy. Was she flirting with him? No, she was upset...wasn't she? Chalk this up to reason number 947 as to why he didn't do relationships. He'd never understand women. Ever.

"Where's the diapers and wipes?" she asked.

"Oh, I know," Willow raised her hand as if she were in school. "Follow me."

Megan trailed after Drake's stepdaughter and went down the hall to his bedroom. His bedroom.

"Don't change that diaper on my bed," he yelled. Laughter answered him, and he knew he was in for it. This was all part of his punishment.

The reeking smell in his bedroom was the least of his worries, because in just over an hour his brothers would be back to retrieve their kids—leaving him and Megan alone once again.

She should've left when everyone else did, but she'd put her pride and her emotions aside because she and Cameron needed to talk. He also needed help picking up his living room. Between the fort with couch cushions and blankets and the towels Willow had used as capes, making sure Cameron and Megan were superheroes, too, the place was anything but organized. The furniture had been pushed aside to allow room for "flying," and Megan hadn't even walked into the kitchen yet. She'd started making marshmallow treats with Willow just before she left and the mess was epic. She had to get in there before Cameron, with all his straight, orderly ways, had a heart attack.

Another thing she and Cameron saw eye to eye on. They both had a knack for cleanliness and keeping everything in its place...except for these emotions. They were all over, and nothing was orderly about them.

Best to start in the kitchen. Not only could she get that back in order, she could think of how best to approach being back in his house and all alone together...

Especially after that giant gauntlet she'd thrown down when he'd offered her a hundred bucks.

What had she been thinking? The flirty comment had literally slid out of her mouth. Clearly she needed a filter.

She'd been so amused by him babysitting, at the chaos his normally perfectly polished house was in. Then she'd seen him holding Amber and something very female, very biological-clock-ticking, snapped in her. She'd always known Cameron was a strong man who could handle anything. Yet the sight of those big tanned hands cradling an infant, of Cameron trying to console her with fear and vulnerability in his eyes, had sent her attraction to a whole new level. As if she needed yet another reason to be drawn to every facet of her best friend.

Surveying the cereal on the floor, Megan tiptoed carefully through to the other side of the kitchen to get the broom from the utility closet. In the midst of sweeping, a tingle slid up her spine and she knew she wasn't alone.

"Sorry." She went back to her chore, keeping her back to him. "Willow wanted to do everything on her own, so I let her. She's too cute to deny. I'll get this cleaned up and be gone."

When a warm, firm hand gripped her arm, Megan froze. Her heart kicked up, and she hated how she'd become this weak woman around her best friend. A part of her regretted sneaking into his bed. She'd cursed herself over and over for dreaming of him. The timing of the all-too-real dream at the same time he'd tried to wake her had thrown her control completely out the window.

But she couldn't wish away those kisses. No matter how she wanted things to be different between them right now, she would cherish those moments when his mouth had been on hers, his body flush against her own.

"Stop avoiding me." His low tone washed over her, and Megan closed her eyes, comforted in that familiar richness of his voice. "We haven't talked in days, and when the kids were here you barely said a word to me."

So she'd been using two innocent children as a buffer. What was a girl to do when she was so far out of her comfort zone she couldn't even see the zone anymore?

"You called me to help, so I helped." She started sweeping the dry cereal again, her swift movements causing Cameron's hand to fall away. "Let me get this cleaned up before you step on it and make it worse."

"Damn it, would you turn around and look at me? Stop being a coward."

That commanding tone had her gripping the broom, straightening her shoulders and pivoting, cereal crunching beneath her boots.

"Coward?" she repeated, ready to use her broom to knock some sense into him. "You could've contacted me, too, you know. How dare you call me a coward after that stunt you pulled? Did you think I'd wither at your feet or declare my undying love? What did you want me to say or do when you all but challenged me?"

She hated how anger was her instant reaction, but damn it, the man was dead-on. She had been a coward. She'd purposely not contacted him. Still, in her defense, he could've texted her or something.

"I'm not trying to start a fight." That calm, controlled cop tone remained in place, grating on her nerves even more because now she was fired up and he wasn't proving to be a worthy opponent. "I just wanted to talk."

"Fine," she spat. "You talk while I clean."

Angrier at herself for letting her emotions take control, Megan went back to focusing on the floor. With jerky movements, she had a rather large pile in no time. When she glanced out the corner of her eye and saw Cameron with his arms crossed over his chest, she had to grit her teeth to keep from saying something even more childish. The last thing she wanted was to be the reason this relationship plummeted, and if she didn't rein in her irritability about the fact he'd called her out, that's exactly what would happen.

Once she'd scooped up the mess and dumped everything into the trash, she put the broom and dustpan back in the closet. The counters weren't as bad, but the big brute was blocking them.

Propping her hands on her hips, Megan stared across the room. "You're going to have to move."

He moved—leaning back against the counter, crossing one ankle over the other. "You can't seriously be mad at me. Let's put the kissing aside, which I know for a fact you enjoyed. An hour ago you flirted with me and now you're ready to fight. What has gotten into you?"

The way he studied her, as if she were a stranger,

made her want that proverbial hole to open and swallow her. To be honest, she didn't know what had gotten into her, either. One minute she was ready to tell him her true feelings; the next minute she was angry at him for not reading her mind and at herself for being afraid to risk dignity.

Yeah, she was all woman when it came to moods and indecisiveness.

"We've already established the kisses were good," she agreed. "I didn't want your hundred bucks, and now I have leverage over you when I actually need something."

"I think you know I'd do anything for you," he told her. "You don't need to hold anything over me."

With a shrug, Megan went to the sink to wet the rag. "Fine, then get out of my way so I can clean and get home. I've had a long day, and I'm pretty tired."

She wrung out the water and turned, colliding with a hard, wide chest. Megan tipped her head slightly to look into Cameron's blue eyes. Those signature St. John baby blues could mesmerize any woman... She was no exception.

"Thank you for coming." He slid his hand up her arm, pushing a wayward strand of hair behind her ear and resting his hand on her shoulder. "I'm sorry for how I treated you the other night. Sorry I made you uncomfortable. But I'm not sorry I kissed you."

Megan heard the words, even processed what he was saying; she just couldn't believe Cameron was confessing this to her.

"Cam—"

The way his eyes locked on to hers cut off whatever she was about to say. The always-controlled cop she'd known most of her life looked as if he was barely hanging on. The level of hunger staring back at her was new. Had she misread him? Had he responded to that kiss in a way that mirrored her own need? Physically he'd responded, but what about emotionally?

"I won't lie and say I haven't thought of you as more than a friend before," he started. "I can't deny you're stunning, and you know more about me than anyone outside of my family."

Why did this sound like a stepping-stone to a gentle letdown?

"You don't have to defend your feelings," she told him, offering a smile. "I'm not asking for anything. I feel the same way."

Those strong hands came up to frame her face. "I liked kissing you, loved it, if I'm being honest."

Between that firm hold he had on her and his raw words, Megan wanted to let that hope blossom, but she wasn't ready to start celebrating just yet. The worry lines between Cameron's brows, the thin lips and the way he gritted his teeth between sentences were all red flags that he was in a battle with himself. Nothing spoke volumes like that raw passion staring back at her.

"Then why do you look so angry?" she asked.

His hands dropped to her shoulders, his fingertips curling into her skin. "Because this is such a bad idea on so many levels, Meg."

Heart beating fast, nerves swirling around in her

stomach, Megan forced all the courage she could muster to rise and take center stage.

"Why is that?" she countered with a defiant tip of her chin. "You're afraid of what it would do to our relationship? You think this is just some random emotion and it will pass?"

"Yes to both of those." His clutch on her shoulders lessened as he leaned in so close, his warm breath tickled her face. "And because if I start kissing you again, I won't stop."

Every nerve ending in her entire body instantly went on alert at his declaration. How could he drop a bomb like that and not expect her to react? Did he think he was helping matters? Did he truly believe with this knowledge she now possessed that she would give up?

"What if I don't want you to stop?"

By his swift intake of breath, she knew she'd shocked him with her bold question.

"You don't mean that," Cameron muttered.

Megan flattened her palms against his chest, slid them up to his shoulders and on up to frame his face. Touching him intimately like this was just the first step of many she hoped they'd take together. She wanted him to see she wasn't blowing this off anymore, wasn't pretending whatever was happening between them wasn't real.

"I mean every word. If you want something, why not take it?"

The way he continued to stare at her, as if listening to both the devil and the angel on his shoulders, made her take action into her own hands.

Rising to her toes, she pulled his head down and captured his lips with her own. She knew she'd made a good judgment call when Cameron instantly melted against her.

Chapter Nine

Every single valid reason for keeping his distance from Megan flew out the window with her lips on his. He'd always admired her take-charge attitude, but she'd never fully executed that power with him before.

He didn't know if he should be terrified or turned on.

Wrapping his arms around her, pulling her flush against his body, just seemed to happen without him even thinking. One second he was talking himself out of kissing her ever again. Then he'd touched her, and the next thing he knew she was on him…which wasn't a bad thing.

Cameron held one arm against her lower back, forcing her hips against his, and slid one hand up to the nape of her neck to hold her right where he wanted her.

Soft moans escaped Megan, and he couldn't stop the dam of need from bursting.

Bending her back, Cameron eased his fingertips beneath the hem of her shirt. Smooth, silky skin slid beneath his touch. The ache he had burning inside completely blindsided him. He'd known he'd wanted her, but the all-consuming passion that completely took hold of him was new.

Megan's hands traveled down to the edge of his shirt and the second her petite hands roamed up his abdomen, Cameron nearly lost it. It wasn't as if he hadn't been touched by a woman before, but never by the one woman he'd craved for years. Her touch was so much more hypnotizing than he'd ever imagined...and he'd imagined plenty.

Megan tore her mouth from his, tipping her head back and arching against him. "Cam," she panted.

Hearing his name on her lips in such an intimate way was the equivalent of throwing cold water on him. This was Megan. Evan's sister. A guy he was within days of arresting.

Cameron jerked back, his hands falling from beneath her shirt. Megan got tangled in his until he lifted the hem and took another step back.

Her moist, swollen lips seemed to mock him, showcasing what he'd just had and what he was turning down. He clenched his fists at his side, trying to grasp on to some form of control. Lately, where Megan was concerned, he was losing every bit of it.

"This can't happen."

Why did it sound as if his vocal chords were rubbing

against sandpaper? He couldn't put up a strong front if he didn't have control over his own voice.

Her eyes searched his, and Cameron hated the confusion laced with arousal staring back at him. Of course she was confused. He'd all but taken over the second she'd touched him and nearly devoured her; then he told her no and backed away as if she had some contagious disease.

Megan pushed off the counter. "What is the problem?"

Swallowing the truth, Cameron gave her another reason that was just as valid. "Sex would take us into a whole new territory. Who's to say that once we give in to this lust, that we won't resent each other or regret what happened?"

She crossed her arms over her breasts and shrugged. "Judging from that kiss, I can't imagine either of us would have regrets. So maybe we would actually enjoy ourselves and find that we may want to keep moving and building on our relationship."

That right there was the biggest worry of all. No way would he go through with this knowing he would have to tear her and her brother apart. Megan would hate Cameron when that time came, and if he slept with her now, she would hate him even more. He couldn't handle it. He only hoped their friendship would carry them over this hurdle once Evan went to jail and Megan understood that Cameron had no choice but to do his job.

Besides, if they went beyond the lust, beyond the sex, Cameron refused to let Megan lead a life married to a cop.

Married? Yes, he loved Megan more than any other woman, but marriage was not in his future.

"There's a reason I don't have relationships, Megan. You know that."

After staring at him for another minute, she laughed and threw her arms out. "So, what, you're just giving up before anything can get started? You're denying yourself, denying me what we both want because you already know the outcome?"

Pretty much.

"We can't come back to this after we have sex," he retorted.

"Come back to what?" she asked, taking a step closer, fire blazing in her eyes. "Friendship? We already crossed that threshold when your mouth was on mine and your hand was up my shirt."

Her angry, frustrated tone matched the turmoil raging inside him. What could he counter with when she was absolutely right? The second they'd crossed that line, an invisible wall had been erected, preventing them from turning back.

Why had he allowed this to happen? Why hadn't he let it go after she'd kissed him when she'd been dreaming? Even though she'd been dreaming of him, he could've moved on to save their friendship. But Megan's kiss had turned something inside him; something had clicked into place...something he couldn't identify because he was too scared to even try.

Megan threw her arms in the air and let out a low groan. "Forget it. Clearly you don't even know what you want. Or, if you do, you're afraid to face it. I don't have time for games."

"Games?" Cameron all but yelled, and he never yelled at anyone, let alone his best friend. "You think I'm playing a game here?"

When she started to walk by him, he reached out and snagged her arm until their shoulders were touching, her face tipping up toward his. The fury in her eyes wasn't something he'd seen too often and never before directed at him. Her chest rose and fell as her heavy breathing filled the silence. He didn't release his grip on her arm, apparently because he wanted to torture himself further by feeling that silky skin beneath his fingertips once more.

"Let me go," she whispered, her chin quivering.

Even with her eyes starting to fill, the anger penetrated through the hurt. As he watched her struggle with holding her emotions together, Cameron's heart jumped as he reluctantly slid his hand down her arm, stopping at her wrist and finally releasing her.

"I'm not trying to hurt you." That pitiful statement sounded flat and cold even to his own ears. "You're the last person I want to make cry."

A watery laugh escaped her. "You think I'm crying over you? These tears are over my own foolishness."

One lone tear slid down her cheek. Just as she reached up to swat it away, he caught her hand in his and used the pad of his thumb to swipe at the moisture.

He turned toward her and tugged her until she fell against him. Wrapping his arms around her, ignoring her protest, Cameron waited until she stopped struggling before he spoke.

"I don't want this between us, Meg. I can't lose you."

Her head dropped to his chest as she sniffed, her palms flattened against his shoulders. "This is just a really bad time, and my emotions are getting the best of me. Don't worry."

Cameron stroked her back, trying to ease all the tension, knowing he'd never fully get her relaxed and calm. But that wouldn't stop him from trying.

"You don't have to defend yourself," he muttered against her ear. "We've both had pressure on us lately. Finding you in my bed the other night and then kissing you, it was all unexpected and it takes a lot to catch me off guard."

Megan eased back, lifted her eyes to his and blinked. Wet lashes framed her green eyes as a wide smile spread across her face. "The fact that I manage to keep you on your toes after all these years makes me happier than it should."

The way she worded that, *after all these years*, sounded so personal. More personal than friendship. Married couples said such things to each other.

"I'm not blaming those kisses on pressure or the chaos in my life," she told him. "I realized soon after your lips touched mine that I wasn't dreaming anymore. I could've stopped, but it just felt so good and you were responding."

Hell yeah, he'd responded. He hadn't been with a woman for so long, but even he couldn't make that his excuse. Cameron had to at least be honest with himself. The second her lips had touched his, her arms encircled his neck, he'd been pulled under. All control had slid from him to her in the span of a second, and he hadn't minded one bit.

Then reality had come crashing back and he'd known what a mistake he'd made. Unfortunately, he'd gotten her in his system and now he was paying the price.

Damn it.

"I need to get going." She pulled completely away, eased around him and headed toward the living room. "The kitchen is done. Can you handle the living room?"

Why did his eyes have to zero in on the sway of her hips? Why was his body still humming from the way she'd been leaning against him?

Years ago he'd wondered, but he'd never made a move because either she or he had been dating someone. Then they got to a point where they were just perfectly happy being friends and not expecting anything more. He'd been deployed and hoped when he'd returned the feelings would've lessened. They hadn't. And then he'd become a cop, lost a partner and hardened his heart toward anything permanent.

So here they were, still best friends who each knew just how well the other one kissed. Cameron was also extremely aware of exactly how Megan liked to be touched and how hard and demanding she wanted those kisses. Her sighs, her moans, the way she arched her body against his were all images he'd live with forever.

He had to endure his own personal hell because he couldn't have her, wouldn't put her through coming in second to his job. And he damn well wouldn't expect her to want more once she learned he'd spent months bringing down a drug ring that now involved her brother.

Megan grabbed her keys off the small table just inside the entryway. "I'll be out of town Thursday and Friday," she told him without turning to look at him as she pulled open the door. "I should be home late Friday night."

"Where are you going?"

With her hand on the knob, she tossed her hair over her shoulder and stared back at him. "Just something for work."

Cameron curled his fingers around the edge of the wood door. "Is it a conference?"

"You might say that."

She was lying. Whatever she was doing, she didn't want to tell him.

"I don't expect you to share every aspect of your life," he told her. "But don't lie to my face."

Megan reached up, patted his cheek. "Kind of like you lying about not wanting more with me? That goes both ways, Cam."

Before he could respond, the cell in his pocket vibrated. *Damn it.* Now was not the time to deal with work unless it was to bring this ring down once and for all.

He pulled the phone out, saw his brother's number and didn't know if he was disappointed or relieved that work wasn't calling him in.

"Hang on," he told Megan. "It's just Eli. I'm not done with you."

Her eyes flared, and he realized how that sounded considering all that had transpired between them within the past week.

"What?" he growled into the phone.

"Mom fell." Eli didn't bother with any pleasantries. "I'm pretty sure her ankle is broken."

"Oh, hell." Cameron ran a hand down his face and sighed, meeting the concerned look in Megan's eyes. "Want me to meet you at the hospital?"

"I've already got her here," Eli answered. "You don't have to come, but I wanted to let you know what was up. Dad is home, and he's watching Amber for me. Nora came with me to sit with mom. Drake got called into work when one of his guys reported in sick."

"I'll be right there."

Cameron shoved the phone back in his pocket and yanked his keys from the peg by the door.

"Mom fell," he said, answering Megan's worried look. "Eli thinks her ankle is broken. I'm heading to the ER now. Dad is babysitting for Eli."

Megan stepped out onto the porch, holding the screen door open for him. "I'll go by your parents' house and sit with Mac and Amber. I'm sure he's worried. Keep me posted."

Before she walked away, Cameron reached out, wrapped his hand around the nape of her neck and looked her straight in the eyes. "I meant what I said. We're not done talking."

Megan's eyes locked on to his, her shoulders

straightened and that defiant chin lifted. "I'm pretty sure we're done discussing just how much you're denying both of us something that could be amazing. Until you're ready to face the fact you enjoyed kissing me, rubbing your hands on me, and admit you're just running scared, don't bring it up again."

She pulled away and bounded down the porch steps. "Just text with an update on your mom. No need to call."

And with that she headed toward her house, leaving Cameron to stare at those mocking hips.

Yes, he'd liked kissing her, thoroughly appreciated the feel of her curves beneath his hands. He was a man and she was a sensual woman whom he'd wanted for years. So what if he was running scared? Better to stop the disaster before it completely ruined their friendship.

As Cameron headed to his truck, he had a sinking feeling their friendship had already rounded a curve and was speeding out of control, and there wasn't a damn thing he could do about it.

Chapter Ten

"This fuss isn't necessary." Bev tried to maneuver her new crutches as Eli and Cameron flanked her sides, assisting her into the house. "I'll be fine. There's no need for everyone to hover."

"You will be fine," Eli agreed. "But for now we're going to hover. Just be glad Drake had to go in or you'd have all of us."

Megan held the door open with one hand and propped Amber on her hip with the other. "You know it's useless to argue with these guys, Bev," Megan said, catching the woman's grin. "Just let them think what they want to boost their egos."

Cameron's gaze swung to hers, and Megan merely lifted a brow. If he wanted to apply those words to the turmoil they had going on, so be it. Wasn't her fault if he had a guilty conscience.

Megan closed the door and pulled Amber around to settle against her chest as the baby continued chewing on her cloth rattle.

"I've already brought your pillows and pajamas down to the guest room," Mac stated, moving forward to take the place of his sons. "We'll be sleeping down here until you're healed and can do the stairs."

"And I'll be stopping by in the mornings," Nora stated, coming in through the door, holding Bev's purse. "I can do your grocery shopping after work so Mac doesn't have to worry about anything."

"One of my patients has volunteered to babysit Amber until you're feeling better," Eli added.

"Oh, for pity's sake." Bev stopped in the foyer and sighed, shooting glares at all those around her. "I can get through these next six weeks without rearranging everyone's lives."

Mac placed a hand over her shoulder. "Complain all you want, but when I had bypass surgery, you all steamrolled me and took care of me. Now it's our turn to cater to you."

A lump formed in Megan's throat at the sincere, loving way Mac looked to Bev. They'd always been such a dynamic couple, always strong even when dealing with hellion teen boys and all their shenanigans.

Megan knew that Mac's bypass surgery last year had rocked them all because the pillar of the family wasn't as indestructible as they'd all thought him to be.

Megan's eyes traveled to Cameron. Her breath caught in her throat when she found herself under the scrutiny of his bright blue eyes. Amber started fussing, pulling Megan's focus back to the infant in her arms.

"It's okay, sweetheart." Megan patted her back. "You're just getting sleepy, aren't you?"

Nora smiled, set the purse down on the accent table and reached out. "I can take her. She's not used to being awake this late."

"I'll run Eli home," Cameron chimed in. "Go on ahead and take her."

Nora said her goodbyes in a frantic attempt to get her unhappy child out the door. Once she was gone, Mac assisted Bev down the hall and into the spare room.

"I'll get her meds from the car," Eli volunteered. "She won't need any more tonight, but I'll put them in the kitchen where Dad can see them."

Eli headed out the front door, leaving Cameron and Megan alone. Why did they always somehow gravitate toward these situations? Before last week she wouldn't think twice about being alone with Cameron, but with all this tension crackling between them, she truly didn't know what step to take next. And she'd made it clear that the ball was in his court.

"I'm heading out," she told him. "Let your mom know I'm here if she needs anything. I'm free all weekend once I get back."

Cameron nodded. "Thanks for your help."

She waited for him to say something else, but he continued to stare in silence. Eli came back inside, carrying a small white pharmacy bag. He glanced between Megan and Cameron.

"Everything okay?" he asked, his brows drawn together.

"Fine," Megan and Cameron replied in unison, still eyeing each other.

"O-kay," Eli whispered as he moved on through to the kitchen.

Shoving her hair away from her face, Megan gritted her teeth as she reached into her pocket and pulled out her keys. Without another word, she headed out the front door and into the cool evening. She'd just hit the bottom step when she heard the screen door slam.

"Is this how it's going to be?" Cameron yelled. "This awkward, sometimes-polite chitchat like we're virtual strangers?"

Megan took in a deep breath before turning to face the man on the porch illuminated by the soft glow of outdoor lights. With his hands on his narrow hips, black T-shirt stretched tightly over toned shoulders and that perfectly cropped hair, Cameron gave off the impression of someone in control and pulled together.

Megan knew better. She'd experienced just how much he relinquished that power when she'd touched him, kissed him, pressed her body to his. And that interesting tidbit of information was something worth hanging on to.

The chill in the air slid through her. A shiver racked her body as she wrapped her arms around her midsection.

"If you feel awkward around me, then it sounds like you have some issues to work out," she threw back. She wasn't going to make this easy on him, not when he was being so infuriating. "I've always heard intimacy helps people relax."

Maybe she shouldn't poke the bear, but they'd already gone past the point of no return. She may as well toss it all out there.

Cameron took a step forward, his eyes still locked on hers. "Why are you acting like this?"

Megan shrugged. "Maybe that kiss was a wake-up for both of us, and I'm willing to face it instead of run from it."

Cameron bounded down the steps, coming to stand right in front of her. So close, she could feel his warm breath, but he didn't touch her.

"You keep coming to me," she added, looking up into those eyes filled with torment. "You keep provoking me, too, but then you back off. You can't have it both ways, Cam."

He gripped her arms in an almost bruising manner as he leaned over her, giving her no choice but to lean back to keep her gaze locked on to his.

Without a word, his mouth crushed hers. The instant demand had her clutching his shoulders and cursing herself for giving in to his impulses so easily. But damn it, she was human. She'd wanted this man for as long as she could remember, and she was going to take what she could get…for now. She wasn't settling for seconds; she was biding her time until Cameron realized this was right. Everything about them coming together was perfectly, wonderfully right.

Reluctant, Megan tore her mouth away. "If you're

only kissing me because you're angry with yourself or you're trying to prove a point, then stop."

His forehead rested against her temple, those lips barely touching her jawline. "I don't know, Meg. You make me crazy. I can't do relationships, and I won't do a fling—not with you. But part of me can't seem to stop now that we've started."

Not quite the victory she'd hoped for, but one she would definitely take. She had him torn, had him thinking. Still, she wanted, *deserved*, more.

"I won't be someone you figure things out with along the way," she told him, sliding her hands away from his taut shoulders. "If you want more, you say so."

She stepped back, waited until he looked at her before she continued. "Be damn sure if you come to me that you want what I've offered because there's no going back."

Megan waited, giving him an opportunity to respond. When silence greeted her and the muscle in Cameron's jaw moved, Megan swallowed, turned on her heel and headed to her car.

Maybe her going out of town would give them the space they both needed to regroup. Maybe the time away would give her the insight she needed on whether to stay or go.

That reminded her—she still needed to inform Evan that she'd be gone. Hopefully he wouldn't tell his questionable friends that her house sat empty. She wanted to be honest with him, wanted him to know that she trusted him, but in all honesty, she didn't. She knew the group he was with was only making his attitude worse, hence his phone call. She had no clue what he truly did with his free time, but she had a feeling it wasn't legal.

Evan had obviously felt himself sinking deeper into a place he didn't want to be when he'd reached out to her. Megan could only pray while she was gone for these two days that the most important men in her life came to some decisions...and she hoped the outcomes would be what she wanted.

"Care to explain what I just saw?"

Cameron winced as he stepped back into his parents' house. Eli stood in the foyer near the sidelight like some Peeping Tom.

"Yeah, I care," Cameron mumbled. The last thing he wanted was to discuss what had just happened because each time he lost his damn mind and kissed Megan, he always felt worse afterward. He was using her to feed his desires, knowing he couldn't go any further.

"Then would you like to tell me why you and Megan look like you're ready to fight one minute and the next thing I know I look out and see you all but devouring her?"

Cameron clenched his fists at his side. Eli's arms crossed over his chest as his eyes narrowed. Eli had married his high school sweetheart, but Megan had been around for so long. And they'd all been friends. *Damn it.* Cameron hadn't even thought of how his brothers would react if they knew...

Hell. Cameron couldn't even put a label on the debacle he'd made of his life in the past month.

"Leave it," Cameron warned as he started down the hall to check on his mom.

"She's resting and Dad's in there." Eli moved quickly, coming to block the entrance to the hall. "I told them we'd lock up and turn off all the lights."

"Fine. You get the lights. I'll check the back door."

Eli made no attempt to move. Raising his gaze to the ceiling, Cameron sighed. He should've known this wasn't going to be easy.

"I have no idea what's going on," he conceded, looking back to his brother. "We've kissed. I know on every level it's a bad idea, but I can't stop myself."

A little of the anger in Eli's eyes dimmed as his shoulders relaxed. "How does she feel?"

Cameron couldn't help but laugh. "Oh, she's made it clear she's ready to step from the friend zone to something more."

Eli tipped his head and shrugged. "And you're angry about this?"

"You know I've made it clear for years I don't want a commitment. Megan's heard me say it over and over." Damn her for making him so confused. "I won't use her, Eli. She's the type of woman who deserves stability and a family. I can't give her either."

"Can't or won't?"

No, he wasn't getting into this. Cameron maneuvered around Eli and went to make sure the back door was locked. When he came back to the front, Eli had turned off the lights except the small lamp on the accent table.

Eli opened the door and gestured for Cameron to

go on ahead. Once they were on the porch, Cameron started to head down the steps, but Eli had to open his mouth again. Ridiculous to think he'd be able to make a break for it.

"You can't be married to your job forever," Eli called out. "At some point you're going to be lonely. Megan's a great girl. You two would be good together."

Cameron spun around. "I'm not looking for advice on my love life. There are complications that you don't know about and I can't get into. So just drop it, and don't mention what you saw to anybody."

Eli stared back, not saying a word.

"Promise me," Cameron demanded. "Not Drake, not Mom or Dad."

After a minute, Eli nodded. "Fine. But you better not mess around and hurt Megan. She's the only woman in your life other than your mother who puts up with your moodiness and your unruly schedule."

Cameron turned back, heading toward his truck parked last in the driveway. He wasn't even entertaining thoughts of how much Megan had put up with. Because then he'd have to admit how much she truly did care for him.

Cameron knew he wasn't going to get any sleep at all tonight, so he headed to the station. Might as well check in with his guys and see if there were any new developments. Of course, if there had been anything, he would've been called. Still, he couldn't go home because Megan's presence was in every single room… especially his bedroom.

His office was practically Megan-free, and he always had work he could do. But Eli was right. Cameron was afraid to go deeper with Megan. How could he be anything else? Too much rested on his shoulders, and no matter what weight he relieved himself of, he'd have more taking its place.

Everything in his life, both personal and professional, all pointed back to Megan somehow. There wasn't a damn thing he could do to save her from his choices, regardless of the path he took.

Chapter Eleven

Megan thought for sure that after visiting the new facility and meeting the staff she'd potentially be working with, she'd have a clearer insight on a decision.

As she maneuvered her car onto the exit ramp that would take her back into Stonerock, she was more confused than ever.

Yes, the facility was beautiful. But the nicest computer equipment or fancy waiting areas, complete with a waterfall wall for a calming atmosphere, weren't going to sway her into making a life-altering decision.

What Megan cared about was the people she'd be able to reach, to help, the difference she could make in their lives. Megan's potential supervisor had gone into great detail about the areas the clinic planned to target. Topping the list were poverty-stricken neighborhoods where alcoholism and drug abuse had spiked in the past few years.

Just the mention of that area had pulled Megan's mind back home with Evan. She knew he had a problem, and she'd give anything to fix him. That's what she did; she had a degree to fix people. But if he didn't want to change completely, she could use all the fancy words and textbook cures in the world and he'd still remain in the pit he'd dug for himself. Though she didn't think he was using drugs—she hadn't seen the telltale signs—she did believe he was mixed up with a group who wasn't immune to the industry. Why else did he always need money? Why else would he always be worried about his safety?

So did she truly want to leave, risking Evan choosing to stay behind? Or did she want to stay in Stonerock where she'd already developed relationships with clients? Those clients trusted her, counted on her. Would they feel as if they were being abandoned if she accepted the new position?

Megan's cell rang, cutting off the radio. Pressing the button on her steering wheel, Megan answered.

"Hello?"

"Hey, Megan." Marly's chipper voice came through the car speakers. "Are you busy?"

"Just driving. What's up?"

"Nora and I were wondering if you were free tonight. I know it's last minute, but Eli said he didn't mind keeping the girls for us."

As exhausted as she was from her whirlwind trip, a girls' night out sounded like the reward she needed.

Megan couldn't remember the last time she'd been out with a group of friends. Going out with Cameron didn't count, not that they went out. They tended to grill at his house or watch movies, and then she'd go back to her house.

"Count me in," Megan said, turning onto her road. "I'm almost home. I need to change, but I can meet you all somewhere."

"We're heading to Dolly's Bar and Grill."

They arranged the time and Megan suddenly found herself getting another burst of energy. She wouldn't think about Evan, Cameron or her work situation. She'd have a beer, chat with the girls and have a good time. A simple, relaxing evening.

With the days losing light earlier and earlier, she too often found herself in pajamas by six o'clock. When had she gotten to that stage in life that the best part of her day was spent in pj's? Mercy, she was getting old.

As soon as Megan examined her closet, she knew she wanted to dress a little sassier than usual tonight. Even if she was just going out with Nora and Marly, Megan had that female urge to step up her game a notch.

When had she let herself get so dowdy and boring? Lately she'd only donned the barest of makeup for work, and she couldn't remember the last time she'd pulled out her curling iron or straightener. If she looked under her bathroom sink, she'd probably find them overtaken by dust.

Glancing at the clock, Megan decided she had time to put some effort into her appearance tonight. After a quick shower, she opted for the big iron and put large, bouncy waves into her hair. A little more shadow than usual made her green eyes pop. Why didn't she do this more often? Just what she'd done so far had boosted both her energy level and confidence.

After pulling on a simple yellow tank-style dress, Megan wrapped a thick belt around her waist, threw on a fitted navy cardigan and pulled on her favorite cowgirl boots. Surely she had earrings that went with this outfit. Digging through her meager stash of jewelry, she managed to find some dangly hoops and a chunky silver bracelet.

Megan grabbed her purse and headed out the door. She hadn't heard from Evan in a couple of days, and, surprisingly, her house hadn't been bothered while she'd been gone.

The guilt of expecting him or his friends to steal something weighed heavily in her gut.

Megan shook off all negative thoughts as she pulled into Dolly's. It being a Friday night, the place was bustling with cars filling the parking lot and people piling in through the front doors.

Music blasted out of the bar as a group of guys held the door open and gestured for her to enter. Smiling her thanks, Megan stepped inside, quickly scanned the room and found Nora and Marly in a booth along the wall.

With a wave, Megan wove her way through the crowd as a slow country song filled the room. Hand in hand, couples made their way to the scarred wooden dance floor. Megan refused to allow the image of her and Cameron dancing to occupy her mind. She was here for fun and for a girls' night. Nothing more.

Nora slid over, giving Megan room to ease onto the leather seat.

"You look beautiful," Nora said with a huge smile. "I was just happy to shower and actually attempt to fix my hair."

Marly laughed. "You're always gorgeous, Nora. But, seriously, Megan, you look great."

"Thanks." Megan sat her purse between her and Nora and thanked God she'd taken some extra time to get ready. "I was going for the fun Megan instead of therapist Megan."

"Well, honey, you nailed it." Nora waved her hand at a waitress. "First round's on me."

"I need a drink," Marly stated. "I've been sewing on Willow's Halloween costume for a week and it still looks like a hot mess. Why the hell did I think I could be supermom instead of just buying one?"

Nora patted Marly's arm. "Because you're an awesome mom and Willow doesn't care what it looks like. She's just excited her mom is making the Darth Vader-cowgirl-princess getup."

Marly moaned. "I suppose. I think letting her pick her favorite themes was a bad idea. I meant one character, not three combined."

Once they ordered their drinks plus a basket of chips and salsa, Megan turned to Nora.

"How's Bev? She getting used to those crutches?" Megan asked.

"Eli said she's still complaining about using them,

but he told her she'd get used to it." Nora rested an elbow on the dull wooden tabletop and smiled. "As long as Mac is there, though, she doesn't have to get up for anything except to use the bathroom. He's right at her side making sure she doesn't even have to ask."

Marly laughed, pushing back a wayward curl from her forehead. "The St. John males have a tendency to go overboard with protecting and assisting their ladies."

Megan thought about how Cameron had wanted her to show Evan some tough love. Cameron was ready to step in and be her human shield, but she had held him back. She remembered a time in high school when a guy was insistent she leave a party with him and all but dragged her toward his car. Cameron had stepped in then, as well, and punched the guy in the face.

The waitress came back with the drinks and each woman took a long, sigh-worthy sip. Megan licked the frothy, fruity foam off her top lip and glanced up to see the other two staring at her.

"What?"

"You were daydreaming." Nora quirked a brow while sliding her fingertip over the condensation on her tall, slender glass. "I know this is absolutely none of my business, but we've known each other a really long time."

Megan braced herself for whatever Nora was about to ask.

"Any chance you and Cameron…" Nora let the silent question settle between them as she pulled the toothpick full of pineapple out of her drink and plucked a piece off.

Marly eased her forearms onto the table and leaned forward, obviously eager to hear the answer, as well.

Megan shrugged. "We're best friends." That was the truth. "I'm not sure we would know how to be anything else."

"Have you tried?" Marly asked.

The waitress returned, setting a giant basket of tortilla chips and three small bowls of salsa on the table.

Megan pretended to look for the perfect chip while she contemplated the answer she should give over the answer she wanted to give.

"I believe the silence speaks for itself," Nora proudly stated as she dipped her chip. "There's no way a man like Cameron can ignore you for years."

Yeah, well, he had. At least in any form beyond friendship. But when his mouth had been on hers, his hands up her shirt, he'd certainly given off the vibe he was staking a claim.

"How long have you guys been a secret?" Nora asked, leaning in just a bit more, a wide, knowing smile spread across her face.

Megan sighed. "There's no secret. To be honest, we only kissed for the first time last week and that was because I was sleeping, he startled me from a dream and I..."

"Please, please don't stop there." Marly reached across and squeezed her arm. "I may not have known you that long, but I'm wrapped up in this and I know it's not my business. So, tell Nora and just let me listen in."

Megan laughed and took a drink, welcoming the chill of the strawberry-flavored, alcohol-enriched slush. "I yanked him down and kissed him," she muttered.

Both women's eyes widened as their grins spread even wider. Megan couldn't help but smile back because she so had to get this off her chest. And there wasn't a doubt in her mind these two ladies would offer her some much-needed advice.

"Then he cornered me in his kitchen the other night after we watched your kids during your date." Megan found herself moving forward with the story without being prompted. She wanted to blame the alcohol, but after only two sips, that defense fell flat. "He was angry at the kiss we'd shared."

"If he cornered you and was angry, sounds to me like he's turned on and is mad at himself," Nora supplied. "Probably for just now taking notice, if you ask me."

"Yeah, well, we argued. That led to another kiss and his hand up my shirt."

Nora and Marly high-fived each other across the table, and Megan felt her face flush. "This is silly." She laughed. "I feel like I'm in high school."

"Better than high school," Marly chimed in. "Way better. So what happened next? This is the best girls' night ever."

Megan reached for another chip. "Sorry to disappoint, but he pulled back and we argued again. I just don't know what to do."

Nora shifted in her seat and all smiling vanished as she looked Megan straight in the eyes. "Take my advice. Don't wait to tell him how you feel, what you truly want. I did that with Eli the first time. We let a lot of years and hurt build between us, and then we had to overcome so much to be together. You're not guaranteed a tomorrow."

Megan felt the quick sting in her nose as her eyes started to fill. Nora had been in love with Eli in school, and then he had gone into the military. After a few years, Nora married Eli's friend, who had ultimately died while deployed. Nora had taken the long, hard road to find love, and Megan could only nod as the lump formed in her throat.

"Damn it." Marly yanked her napkin from under her drink and dabbed beneath her eyes. "I had my makeup so nice, too, thanks to that pin I saw on Pinterest."

"I didn't mean to cause tears," Nora defended herself, passing another napkin over to Marly. "I'm just trying to help."

Megan blinked back her own unshed tears and gripped her icy-cold glass. "You did help. I know I need to tell him how I feel, but I guess I just needed encouragement. I'm a bit of a coward. What if we mess up? He's the most stable person in my life, and I can't lose him as a best friend."

Nora nodded. "I understand the fear, but if he loves you beyond friends, isn't that worth the risk? Is he worth it?"

Without a doubt. Cameron was worth risking everything for.

Her phone chimed from her purse. She thought it was rude to be on the phone when out with a group of people, but it could be a patient in need.

"Sorry," she said, digging out the phone. "Give me one second."

The caller ID flashed her brother's name. Megan swiped the screen and answered.

"Evan?"

"I'm ready."

Those two words held so much meaning. "You want me to come and get you?"

"Yeah, um, I was dropped off at the parking lot beside the old gas station that closed. You know where that's at?"

Megan nodded, even though he couldn't see her. "Yes. I'll be there in five minutes."

She hung up, quickly pulled money from her purse and tossed it on the table before explaining to the girls that she had to get her brother. There was no time to go into further details because Evan changed his mind so often, she wanted to jump through this window of opportunity.

Besides, he might be in danger if he was in a parking lot at night all alone.

Megan raced for her SUV. As she pulled into the lot, at first she didn't see anybody. As soon as she got out, she felt the presence of someone behind her. Spinning around, her heart leaped into her throat. The hulking figure wasn't Evan.

Pulling all her experience and courage to the surface, Megan lifted her chin and squared her shoulders. "Where's my brother?" she asked.

The sneer on the stranger's face sent a cold chill down her spine. He stepped closer, all the while raking his eyes over her. Curse this dress she'd felt beautiful in earlier. Why was she now feeling as if she was being punished for wanting to look nice?

"I'm right here."

Megan jerked around to see Evan, hands in his pockets, staring across the open space. She could barely see him for the glow from the streetlight that was at the other end of the block. But the tone of his voice worried her. He sounded sad, nervous, almost desperate.

"What's going on?" she asked Evan as she started to take a step forward.

The man behind her gripped her arm. Megan had taken a self-defense course, a requirement for her job. Instantly the lessons came flooding to her mind. She whirled around and shoved the palm of her free hand straight up into the man's nose.

With a howl, he dropped her arm and covered his face. She shook out her wrist and glanced over her shoulder to Evan.

"Get in my car," she ordered, her gaze volleying back and forth between her brother and the man who would no doubt be angry. She didn't want to be there when he decided to retaliate. "Now, Evan."

"I can't."

Another man seemed to materialize behind Evan. This man held a gun...pointed at her. The hulk behind her gripped her arm once again, this time tighter as he yanked her back against his chest.

"They'll kill us if we don't do what they want," Evan told her. "I had no clue they were setting me up, Meg. I'm sorry."

Apologies could wait. Right now she needed to figure out how to get them out of here without getting shot. "What do you want?" she asked, still trying to keep her voice calm though she was anything but.

"Your brother here owes us twenty thousand dollars," the man behind her stated, his hot breath against her cheek making her gag. "And after that stunt you just pulled on me, I'm adding another five K."

Why hadn't she paid more attention to her brother? Whatever mess he'd gotten wrapped up in had apparently been going on awhile if he owed that kind of money. Still, all that could be dealt with later. Right now she needed to figure out a way to survive the night. She wanted Cameron. He wouldn't be afraid; he would arrest these guys and save her and Evan. But Cameron wasn't here, and she'd have to fend for herself.

"I'm sure you know I don't have that much money on me," she told them, her eyes darting to the gun still aimed at her.

Sirens filled the night, and Megan nearly wept with relief. She forced herself to keep in mind her surroundings and the men who were threatening her. She may not be a cop like Cameron, but she'd counseled enough addicts to know that if they were high, they didn't care who they hurt. They had nothing to lose. Which meant she was expendable.

Before she knew it, the man behind her let go, causing her to stumble back from the force of his departure. The man with the gun patted Evan on the shoulder as if they were the best of friends.

"Come on, man." The guy shoved his gun in his waistband. "You ain't waiting to talk to no cops. You're with us till you pay up."

Evan threw her one last pained look and mouthed "sorry" before turning and running off into the night with the men who'd just threatened their lives. With shaky knees and tremors overtaking her body, Megan sank to the cool concrete. Moments later, a cruiser pulled in, too late to save her brother.

Chapter Twelve

Never in his life had fear crippled him to the point of losing control and being ready to throw it all away.

But the sight of Megan in the clutches of notorious gang leader "The Shark" was an image that would haunt him forever.

Then the gun had appeared, and Cameron had to get a patrol car sounding that second. He knew those guys. He knew they wouldn't shoot Megan unless provoked. The siren did its job and the criminals fled—including her lowlife brother. Cameron wanted to get ahold of that man and punch him in the face for not protecting his sister.

What the hell had Megan been doing there, anyway? His heart had nearly exploded in his chest when he saw her black SUV pull into the lot. He'd gotten a good look at her sexy little dress and cowgirl boots, showcasing those shapely legs. But even that punch of lust had vanished the second those dangerous thugs had surrounded her.

Now, an hour later, Cameron stood on her porch. He knew she was inside because his officer had told him he'd driven Megan's car home while another officer drove her in his cruiser. She was too shaken up, too scared to drive.

Cameron slid his key into her lock and let himself in. The second he stepped over the threshold, he called her name, not wanting to alarm her because he'd come in the front door and not the back as he normally did.

He heard the sound of her boots clicking over the wooden floor from the rear of the house. Megan came down the hallway, her arms wrapped around her midsection, her face pale.

For her fear alone he vowed to get enough evidence on these guys to put them away for a long, long time. Right now, though, he wished he wasn't on the right side of the law. He wished more than anything he could track them down and beat them within an inch of their lives, forgetting about the justice system altogether and saving the taxpayers' dollars.

"I knew they'd call you." She pasted on a smile that fell short of convincing. "Did they find Evan? I've texted and called him, but…"

Fury threatened to take over. She was worried about Evan? After a man had held her at gunpoint while another practically held her captive?

"My officers were more concerned with you." Only

because the FBI was still out there right now keeping an eye on the traffickers…and because Cameron had told his two officers to make sure Megan was watched until he arrived. "Evan is a big boy."

Anything else he said would be out of anger, and the last thing he wanted to do was fight. Between the way her vulnerability had settled between them like a third party and the way that dress hugged her body, Cameron was having a really difficult time prioritizing his emotions.

"Are you okay?" he asked, taking a step forward, then another, until he was within reaching distance. But he fisted his hands at his side. "My officers told me you weren't hurt, but I needed to hear it from you. I needed to see you."

Those bright green eyes seemed even more vibrant than usual. Cameron didn't know if he was just now noticing or if she'd done something tricky with her makeup. Regardless, the way she watched him, the way she seemed to be holding herself back, had him nearing the breaking point. He'd been holding on by the proverbial thread for so long now; it was only a matter of time before he fell.

Megan reached up, shoved her hair back from her face. "I'm fine."

Her action drew his gaze to her arm, to the fingerprint-size bruises dotting her perfect skin. Cameron clenched his teeth, reining in his anger because none of this was her fault and he wouldn't make her the target simply because she was the only one here once the rage fully surfaced. The only thing he could fault Megan with was having a kind heart and wanting to help people who would continue to stomp on her and use her.

Cameron gripped her wrist in one hand and slid a fingertip from his other over around the marred skin. "You're not fine. This never should've happened."

He'd cursed himself for standing by and watching as events unfolded, but had he gone charging for her as he'd wanted to, as his heart told him to, his cover would've been blown and she would have known the cops were watching Evan. *Cameron* was watching Evan.

That heavy ball of guilt was something he'd have to live with. If there had ever been any doubt before, tonight just proved that he would choose his job first every single time. He hated himself for it, but that's how he was made up.

"They're just bruises," she whispered, her eyes still on his.

Goose bumps raised beneath his fingertips as he continued to stroke her skin. "I don't like them."

Megan placed a hand over his, halting his movement. Her lids closed as she whispered, "Please, Cam. I just…"

Bowing her head, Megan sighed.

"You what, baby?"

"I wanted you to come," she muttered beneath the curtain of her hair that had cascaded around her face. "I wanted you here because I knew I'd feel safe. But now that you're here, I can't let you touch me." Slowly lifting her head, she brought her eyes up to lock on to his. "It makes me want things. Want you."

Damn it. There went that last thread he'd been holding on to.

Cameron stepped into her, trapping their hands between their bodies. The tip of his nose brushed against hers, leaving their mouths barely a whisper apart.

"You are always safe with me," he told her, slowly moving his lips across hers with the lightest of touches. "And tonight you're mine."

"Just tonight," she agreed. "We don't need to put a label on it, and I don't want to think beyond now."

Cameron captured her mouth, completely ignoring all the warnings pounding through his head. Totally shoving aside all the reasons this was a terrible idea: the investigation, the risk of losing his best friend and the fact he'd just admitted to himself that his job would always come first. All that mattered was Megan and this ache he'd had for her for years. It wasn't going away no matter how noble he tried to be. His hormones didn't give a damn about his morals or standards.

Megan's mouth opened beneath his as she tried to pull her hands free. Cameron was quicker, holding them firm as he broke from the kiss.

"You're mine," he repeated, nipping her lips, her chin, trailing a line down to her collarbone. "I don't know why you have on this dress with these boots, but it's driving me crazy. Tell me you weren't on a date earlier."

Tipping her head back, arching into him, Megan let out one of those sweet moans he was starting to love. "No, no date," she panted. "I was out with Nora and Marly."

The fact she was out with his sisters-in-law thrilled him because if she'd been out with a guy, Cameron would've had to admit jealousy.

Cameron released her hands and slid his palms over her curvy hips. He gripped her and pulled her pelvis flush with his as he continued to rain kisses along her exposed skin just above the dip in her dress. Just above the perfect swell of her breasts.

Megan wrapped her delicate fingers around his biceps and squeezed as he yanked down the top of her dress. Material tore, but he didn't care. He'd buy her a new one.

"Cam."

He froze at her plea. "Meg, I'm sorry. After what you went through tonight, I wasn't thinking."

Her lips curved into a smile. "I wasn't complaining. I know you'd never hurt me."

Seeing her lips swollen from his kisses, her neck and the tops of her breasts pink from arousal, an instant flood of possessiveness filled him. The only mark he ever wanted on her was from him, from passion.

"If you keep this up, I don't know how much longer I can stand." Her arms slid around his neck as she rubbed her body against his. "You make my knees weak and we're still fully clothed."

"I'm about to fix that problem."

He unbuckled her belt and let it drop with a clatter to the wood floor. He gripped the hem of her dress, yanked it up and over her head, then tossed the unwanted garment aside.

The sight of her standing before him wearing a pale pink bra and matching panties along with those cowgirl boots was enough to make his own knees weak.

Megan reached for his shirt, but he pulled it off before she could touch him. In record time their clothes were mere puddles on the floor. From the way her eyes kept sampling him, Cameron knew if he didn't try to keep some sort of control, this night would be over before he could truly enjoy it.

"I've waited to see you look at me like that," Megan told him, rising up on her toes to kiss his jawline. "Like you really want me."

She was killing him. With the way the lace from her bra pressed against his bare skin, her raw, honest words and the delicate way her mouth cruised over him, Megan was gradually overpowering him.

Gliding his hands around her curves, Cameron lifted her until her legs went around his waist. The leather from her cowgirl boots rubbed his back, but the fact he finally had this woman wrapped all over him overrode his discomfort.

"I'm too heavy for you," she argued, nipping at his ear.

Palming her backside, his thumb teased the edge of her lacy panty line. "Baby, you're the perfect weight for me," he growled as he headed toward the living room and the L-shaped sofa. "Absolutely perfect."

Without easing his hold, Cameron settled her onto

the corner of the couch as his lips took hold of hers once again. He could kiss her forever.

Too bad he couldn't do forever. Selfishly, he was doing now, tonight, and he'd hate himself later for taking advantage even if she had given him the green light.

Megan's legs fell away from his waist, her boots landing on either side of his feet. Cameron eased back, picked up one leg at a time and pried off her cowgirl boots. She watched him beneath heavy lids, her chest rising and falling as she licked her lips in anticipation.

Coming to his full height, Cameron stared down at this magnificent woman practically laid out for him. His throat grew tight with emotions…emotions he could certainly identify but he couldn't allow to take over.

"You're stunning," he told her, completely taking in the display.

Without a word, Megan sat up, reached behind and unfastened her bra. After sliding it down her arms and tossing it to the side, she hooked her thumbs beneath her panties and slid them down, never once taking her eyes off his. The minor striptease was the most erotic moment of his life, and it had lasted all of ten seconds. Megan had a power over him that no other woman could match.

"Tell me you have protection," she whispered as she reached for him. Flat palms slid up over his chest and around his neck.

Cameron allowed her to pull him down, and he loved the feel of her beneath him. He had to remind himself not to get used to this, not to want this ever again.

"I don't have anything." One fingertip slid up and over her breast. "But I'm clean. I have regular physicals for work and I've always used protection. It's your call."

"I'm clean, too, and I've always been protected." Megan smiled, wrapping her legs around Cameron's narrow waist once again. "So what are we waiting for?"

The darkness that had settled into Cameron's blue eyes revealed so much. Who knew her best friend had a possessive streak when it came to intimacy? The way he held her, spoke to her, dominated her, thrilled Megan in a way she'd never before experienced and she knew without a doubt that this was it for her... *He* was it for her. No other man would compare with Cameron St. John.

She wanted to lose herself in him, wanted to forget all the ugliness and worries in her life. She wanted him to show her how beautiful they could be together because her fantasy had already paled in comparison.

"Tell me what you want," he murmured against her lips.

She trembled beneath his touch. No, that wasn't her. Cameron's hands were shaking as he slid them over her breasts.

Framing his face with her hands, she held his gaze. "You're nervous." She didn't ask and she wasn't making fun of him.

Cameron closed his eyes, resting his forehead against hers. "Nobody else has ever mattered this much."

Megan didn't know what to say to that revealing piece of information, so she tucked it in the back of her mind. Stroking his bottom lip with her thumb, she kept her eyes on his.

"I want anything you're willing to give," she said, answering his earlier question. "Anything you want to do."

A low groan escaped him. Then, as if some invisible barrier broke, Cameron consumed her. His hands took journeys all over her body, leaving goose bumps in their wake. That talented mouth demanded kisses, demanded passion.

Cameron settled himself between her legs, gliding one hand down her quivering abdomen to cup her most aching area. Megan tilted her hips, ready to burst for just one simple touch. She was officially at his mercy.

Easing his hand away, he held on to her waist. "Look at me," he demanded. "Only me."

"Only you."

As he slid into her, Megan gasped. Every dream, every waking fantasy she'd ever had about her best friend, didn't prepare her for the onslaught of emotions, waves of pleasure and such an awakening. They moved together as if they'd been made for each other, as if their bodies automatically knew how to respond to each other.

Cameron's arms wrapped around her as he lifted her off the couch. Still connected, he turned and sat, leaving her to straddle him…surrendering all power and control to Megan.

In that moment, she knew he loved her. He may not say it, he may not want to face the fact, but there was no way this man could look at her, make love to her, as if she were the only woman in the world and not love her.

Ripples of pleasure began to build, each one stronger than the last. Megan wanted to be fully fused with him when her body flew apart. Gripping his shoulders, she leaned down and claimed his mouth. Seconds later spasms took hold. With one hand firmly against the small of her back and the other cupping the nape of her neck, Cameron held her tight against his body as he stilled and trembled right along with her.

Moments after they fell over the edge together, Cameron still held on to her, still commanded her lips. The man wasn't done just because his body had hit the finish line.

His tongue slid along her bottom lip, his kisses softer, shorter...as if he didn't want this moment to end. At least, that's how she hoped he felt.

"Stay with me," she muttered around his kisses. "In my bed. Just for tonight."

His darkened, heavy-lidded gaze met hers. She thought for sure he'd deny her—they'd only agreed on this one time—but she had to ask. She wasn't ready to let him go.

Circling his arms tighter around her waist, Cameron came to his feet. Megan's legs instinctively wrapped around him.

"You seem to like my legs here," she joked, hoping to break the tension because he still hadn't answered her.

He headed out into the hall and toward her bedroom. "I intend to keep them here."

Chapter Thirteen

He'd guaranteed nothing beyond that night. Hadn't promised pretty words or a happily-ever-after. Megan had known exactly what she was getting into with him. He'd made his intentions perfectly clear before he'd peeled her out of her clothes.

So why did he feel like a jerk for leaving her before she woke?

Because he was.

Cameron sat on his deck, looking out over the pond as the morning sun reflected off the water. He didn't take time out here anymore, didn't just relax and enjoy life.

Last night he'd enjoyed life to the absolute fullest, which only made him want more. But his career didn't mesh well with a personal life. He couldn't compartmentalize and keep things separated, neat and orderly anymore. But he wanted Megan in one area, the friend area. He wanted her far away from anything that could harm her, like her useless brother who hadn't been able to protect her last night.

Cameron cursed, propping his bare feet up on the rail. He hadn't been able to protect her, either. Apparently he was no better than Evan at this point.

Opting to beat himself up over how everything went down last night was better than rehashing all that could have gone wrong in those few seconds. It also kept his mind off what had happened afterward.

Okay, so that was a lie. Even Cameron couldn't pretend to be unfazed by what had happened at Megan's house. How could he forget how perfectly they'd come together? How she'd clung to him? He could practically still feel her breath on his cheek, feel her curvy body beneath his hands. Those sighs of pleasure tickling his ear and the way she called his name on a groan were locked so deep in to his soul, he knew forgetting the intimacy they'd shared was impossible.

Closing his eyes, Cameron clenched his fists on the arms of his Adirondack chair. He hadn't given a thought to what would happen after he'd made love to Megan. Hadn't cared about feelings or excuses after the fact. All Cameron had wanted was to feel her, consume her. The fantasy come to life had been his only focus, and now here he sat with a sated body and a guilty conscience.

Between his ever-evolving feelings and the worry he'd seen in her eyes when he'd arrived at her house,

Cameron had told himself he was there to console her. That was a flat-out lie. He'd needed to comfort himself because he'd been a trembling mess.

Now his priority was to check in with the station, where some of the FBI agents had set up temporary headquarters until this case was over. He knew if something major had happened, he would have been notified. Still, as the chief, he needed to check in and get an update.

His cell vibrated in his pocket. Dropping his feet to the deck floor, he slid the phone out and read the screen.

I didn't take you for a coward

The harsh words hit right where Megan intended… his heart. Her text couldn't have been more accurate. He was a coward, and she'd called him out. One of the things he loved about her was her ability to never back down.

He honestly had no clue how to reply, and this wasn't a conversation to be had via text. He wouldn't be that guy and he sure as hell would treat Megan with more respect. The thought was laughable, considering he'd done the walk of shame out her back door, but he would make it up to her. Somehow.

Ignoring the text wasn't an option, either. Cameron quickly replied.

Be at my place at noon

That would give him time to check in with the station, figure out where the hell Evan was and grab a quick shower. Cameron planned to have a little talk with Evan. Cameron had to play every scenario out in his head because he couldn't tip off the guy. But he had every intention of making it clear that dragging Megan into his illegal mess was unacceptable and intolerable.

The phone vibrated in his hand.

If I have time

Smiling, Cameron came to his feet. She'd be there. He was sure of it. If she wasn't, then he'd find her. They weren't done. Not by a long shot.

Now he just had to figure out what the hell to do with his feelings and how to eliminate the possibility of hurting hers. Because, damn it, he still wanted her. Wanted Megan with a passion that went beyond all they'd shared last night. How could he tell her that and still try to keep her at a distance? How could he even try to take a chance with her but keep her safe and away from his job?

Granted, he worked in a small town and the crime rate, for the most part, was low. But there were instances that crept up, and he was the man to take control. He couldn't have his life both ways, and the decision ate at him because he knew he'd have to give up something—or someone—he loved.

Cameron headed inside to make a few calls. First things first. Right now he needed to find Evan and have a man-to-man talk. Then he'd deal with Megan.

If Cameron St. John thought he could turn her world inside out with a few orgasms, leave without a word and then have the nerve to summon her to his house, he truly didn't know her.

Megan took a deep breath, counted backward from ten and mounted the steps to Mac and Bev's house. She hadn't seen Cameron's truck in the drive or along the street, so she figured now would be a good time to stop and check on Bev. No doubt the woman was fed up with St. John testosterone ordering her to stay put while they did everything for her.

Megan didn't want to go in all angry and frustrated because then she'd have to explain. There was absolutely no way she'd be revealing to Cameron's parents why she was a bit irritable this morning.

After ringing the doorbell, Megan stepped back and waited. Mac pulled the door open, sending the fall floral wreath swaying against the glass.

"Megan." Mac extended his hand, taking hers and pulling her into the foyer. "I'm so glad to see you."

Laughing, Megan allowed herself to be ushered in. "Wow, I've never had such a lovely greeting before."

"I think Bev hates me," he whispered. "She just threatened to bash me with her crutch if I asked her one more time if she needed anything."

Megan patted Mac's arm and smiled. "I'm sure the threat was out of love."

Glancing toward the living room, Mac shook his head. "I doubt it," he said, turning back to her. "If you're going to be a few minutes, would you mind if I ran out to the hardware store? I hate to leave her even though she's told me to go."

Megan nodded. "You go on. We'll be just fine."

Mac seemed to breathe a sigh of relief as his shoulders relaxed. "Thanks, Megan. I'll only be twenty minutes, at the most."

"Take your time."

Mac eased around her, grabbed his keys from the table and headed out the door. Still amused at the fear in Mac's eyes, Megan headed to the living room, where Bev had her feet propped up on the footrest of the recliner. Some cooking channel was muted on the TV.

"Thank God he's gone," Bev said as soon as Megan stepped into the room. "That man needs to stop hovering."

Megan sank onto the edge of the old sofa, angling her body to face Bev. "He just loves you."

Bev dropped the remote into her lap. "I know. I keep telling myself that, but it's a broken ankle. I'm not dying."

Megan glanced around the walls at all the years of memories, family vacations and military medals adorning the space. This family was full of love, full of life and always so supportive.

She couldn't help but wonder what her life would've been like had her parents survived. What would her brother's life have been like? Would he still have felt that urge to rebel at every single thing? "You okay, honey?"

Glancing back to Bev, Megan nodded, swallowing the lump of emotions threatening to clog her throat. "I've been better," Megan answered honestly. "But I came to check on you, not discuss me."

Bev waved a hand. "Oh, please. Everyone has checked on me. I'm fine. What's got you so worried?"

There was no way Megan would get into all the issues that swirled around in her mind. Whatever she and Cameron had going on—or not going on—would remain between them. She had no label for it, had no way of knowing where the next step would take them.

Bev knew enough about Evan, though, that Megan found herself opening up about him. She explained what happened the night before, stopping at the point where Cameron ended up staying the night. Megan had been around this family for so long, Bev had seen Evan's downfall, witnessed Megan's frustration.

"As a woman who raised three hellions, let me tell you that you can only do so much." Bev shifted in her chair until she could reach out and take Megan's hand in hers. "You guide them the best way you can, but in the end they have to make their own decisions."

These were all facts Megan knew, but she still ached for a peace she may never find with her only living relative.

"Those were your kids. It's a bit different with Evan because he's always quick to throw in my face how I'm not his mother." Megan smiled and shrugged. "Besides, your boys all turned out perfect."

Bev's laughter filled the cozy living room. "Oh, honey. They're far from perfect. I had a full head of gray hair by the time I was thirty-five. I swore I wouldn't make it through their teen years without getting a call from the cops about one or all three. They seemed to travel in a pack."

Megan couldn't help but laugh herself. "Yeah, they got me drunk during my senior prom."

"Oh, mercy," Bev whispered, shaking her head. "I think I'm better off not knowing some of the things they did. I cringe just thinking of the stuff I know about."

Megan took comfort in Bev's gentle hand. So many times she'd wanted motherly advice and she'd always known she could turn to Bev at any time. Unfortunately, with the Cameron situation, Megan wasn't about to seek support. She'd have to figure out that one all on her own.

"Evan wouldn't keep in contact with you if he didn't love you," Bev went on. "He may take some time, but you're the only stable person in his life. He'll come back to you."

Megan squeezed Bev's hand. "I hope so."

Because even though she didn't have concrete evidence of his extracurricular activities, she wasn't stupid. If he didn't change his ways, the end result would be either jail or death. Megan didn't know if she had the strength to get through either of those.

Cameron kept his voice low, his back to the brick building, so he could keep an eye on the open end of the alley. He'd found out Evan was in the shady part of a neighboring town, just outside Cameron's jurisdiction.

After throwing on a ball cap and sunglasses, Cameron had gone into the pool hall and firmly told Evan to meet him out back.

Now the coward had the nerve to look worried.

"Maybe you should've been a little more concerned last night for your sister." It took every ounce of Cameron's self-control to keep him from pummeling Megan's brother. "Do you have any idea how scared she was? You may run with these guys, but she doesn't, and she has a heart of gold. You realize that afterward she was more worried about you than what could've happened to her?"

Evan glanced away, but Cameron wasn't having it. Cameron smacked his cheek. "Look at me. Megan said one of your so-called friends had a gun on her. Do you want to see your sister wrapped up in this mess you're in? Do you want to see her hurt or worse?"

Something flared in Evan's eyes. Anger, hatred, who knew what, but at least there was some sign that he actually cared about Megan.

"You have no idea what's going on in my life," Evan spat.

Cameron didn't react, didn't say a word. No sense in giving away that he in fact knew nearly everything that was going on. Knew so much that warrants were about to be processed for the arrest of two major players in the drug-running ring and for Evan, though Evan's charges weren't as harsh. Still, Cameron wanted the charges to stick. He wanted Evan to hit rock bottom so he'd get the help he needed and maybe eventually be the brother Megan deserved.

Disgusted that he was getting nowhere, Cameron started to turn away. "Keep her safe." Evan's low, pleading words froze Cameron in his tracks.

Glancing over his shoulder, Cameron met Evan's

eyes and for the first time he actually saw a man who showed genuine concern and fear for someone other than himself. "She doesn't have anybody else," Evan stated, still holding Cameron's gaze.

Cameron nodded. "Whose fault is that?"

When Evan continued to stare, as if waiting for affirmation, Cameron replied, "I won't let anything happen to her."

As he walked away and headed back toward his truck, he wondered if he'd just lied. Could he honestly keep Megan from getting hurt? Oh, he could prevent her from physical harm, but what about her heart?

The mental scars from this entire scenario would live with her forever. She'd blame herself; she'd question every decision she ever made where her brother was concerned. And she'd hate Cameron.

He slid behind the wheel and brought the engine to life. The clock on his dash showed only thirty minutes until she was due at his house. Knowing Megan, she'd keep him waiting out of spite—which was fine. He needed the extra time to calm down from seeing Evan, from realizing that so much was about to come to a head. All Cameron could do was sit back and proceed with his job...just like always.

Chapter Fourteen

So what if it was nearly two o'clock? Megan wished she could chalk up her tardiness to stubbornness or even the fact she'd been visiting with Bev and Mac. In reality, she'd stuck around with Bev out of nerves.

What would she and Cameron discuss? How did they jump from best friends to the most intimate experience of her life to her waking up alone? Did he really think they would just pal up, watch a movie, grill a steak and hang like they always did on their days off?

Only one way to find out.

Megan mounted the steps and raised her hand to knock. She'd never knocked before. Letting out a sigh, she opened the screen door and twisted the knob on the old oak door. She wouldn't put it past Cameron to lock it since she was late, but the knob turned beneath her palm.

She stepped over the threshold, nerves swirling in her stomach as the familiar scent of Cameron's masculine aroma surrounded her. She'd inhaled that woodsy scent when her face had been pressed into his neck as he'd lowered her into her bed. Never again could she breathe in Cameron's signature scent and not instantly be taken to the time when he'd fulfilled her every desire, her every wish.

Closing the door at her back, Megan sat her purse and keys on the built-in bookshelf to the left of the doorway. The same place she always sat her things when she came in, as if this were her home, too.

Silly thought, really. They'd slept together, not exchanged rings or vows.

A part of Megan wouldn't mind doing just that, but she wouldn't beg any man to love her. Either Cameron would want the same things she did or he wouldn't. No matter how this next phase played out, Megan was a big girl and she'd survive.

But even knowing they'd taken another step deeper into their relationship, Megan still didn't know what to do about the job in Memphis. Being with Cameron was more important than any position she could ever have. She'd give up her dream job in order to have a life with him, but was that something she could convince him of?

She didn't want to have to convince him, though. Megan wanted Cam to come to the realization they belonged together.

And if he didn't, Megan knew she'd have to make

the move because she couldn't live here, see him every day and act as if her heart wasn't shattered.

Heavy footsteps sounded from overhead. Megan glanced toward the stairs just as Cameron came down the first set, then stopped on the landing. His piercing blue eyes held hers as she remained by the door.

"Contemplating whether to stay or go?" he asked.

Shoving her hands in the pockets of her favorite pair of faded jeans, Megan tipped her head. "I don't run away."

Cameron rested his hand on the newel post as he continued to stare down at her. What was he thinking? And why did he look even sexier today now that they'd been intimate?

Keeping his eyes on hers, Cameron slid his hand down the banister as he descended the steps. Megan didn't move, didn't glance away even though her heart was pounding so hard. Cameron came to stand directly in front of her. The way he towered over her had Megan tipping her head back to hold his gaze. Nowhere did he touch her, yet his demanding presence commanded her body to react.

Cameron leaned forward, his lips by her ear. "Don't call me a coward again," he growled.

Pleased he was just as affected by their predicament as she was, Megan forced herself to remain still, to not reach for him and cling as she desperately wanted to. And that was the problem wrapped in the proverbial nutshell. She was desperate for this man's touch, his passion.

When Cameron eased back, just enough for a sliver

of sunlight from the windows to pass through, Megan smiled.

"Hit a nerve, did I?"

"You knew you would."

"Maybe."

Was he just going to stand within a breath of her and not touch her? Maybe he wasn't as affected by their connection as she'd thought. Or perhaps he was into torturing her.

"What's the protocol here, Cam?" she asked, unable to stand the tension for another second. Someone had to step up and start this conversation. "What happens now?"

"What do you want to happen?" he countered.

Megan pulled in a deep breath, knowing full well she walked on a tightrope. "I think I've made things pretty clear. It's you who seems to be torn about what you want."

The muscle in his jaw jumped. He gripped her wrists with one hand, tugging them over her head, causing her to lean back against the door. He trailed his other hand down her arm until she trembled, all the while keeping his eyes locked on hers. She held her breath, unable to fully comprehend the power he had over her and the helpless state she was currently in.

"I'm not torn," he corrected as he brought his palm up to cup her cheek, his thumb stroking her lips. "I know exactly what I want."

That low, sultry tone of his made her body hum with anticipation. Or maybe she was still shaking from the simple touch of his fingertips. Perhaps every single thing about the man made her tingle now that she had let her guard down.

His eyes held hers. "What I want and what is possible are two different things."

It took a moment for the words to register. Megan made to pull his hands away, shaking her head. "That makes no sense," she all but shouted. "You're an adult. You pretty much decide what you want. Do you not want me? I can handle it if that's the case."

Okay, she might not handle it very well, but she would move on. She wasn't playing around anymore.

"I'd say after last night it's obvious I want you."

"Nothing is obvious," she hissed, hating how she still was held captive by him. "I have no clue what's going on with you, Cam. What are you fighting against?"

Cameron opened his mouth as if to say something, but then he shut it. Glancing toward the ground, he muttered a curse as he rubbed the back of his neck and released his hold on her.

He was battling some inner turmoil. Whatever it was, he wasn't opening up about it. The fact he was keeping something that obviously involved her locked inside had Megan hurting in a way she hadn't known possible.

"You know what, forget it." She sighed, throwing her hands in the air. "We'll go back to being friends. We'll chalk last night up to a—"

His eyes narrowed in on her. "Don't say mistake."

"An amazing experience," she finished slowly. "I

won't call it a mistake. What we shared can't be labeled as a mistake. But it won't happen again."

When he merely nodded, a portion of the hope she'd been clinging to died. He offered nothing but that simple gesture of agreement, as if his entire life hadn't changed after the intimacy they'd shared.

Seeing as how he was not much into conversation today, Megan turned toward the built-in and grabbed her keys and purse. In an instant, Cameron's hands covered hers, his body was plastered to her back, his arms stretched out with hers.

"Don't go," he whispered in her ear.

Closing her eyes, Megan dropped her head between her shoulders. "Why did you tell me to come?"

"I wanted to see you." He nuzzled his way through her hair, his lips barely brushing against the side of her neck. "I had no clue what I'd do once you got here. I told myself to keep the friendship above my desire for you. But I can't."

His fingers laced through hers as he placed open-mouthed kisses over the side of her neck and down onto her shoulder. Megan didn't want to respond, wanted to make him work for it, but her head tipped to the side before she could even think.

"I don't know what the hell to do here, Meg."

So much tension radiated from him. She wanted to turn, to hold him and comfort him. Whatever war he waged with himself was something he felt he needed to face alone.

"I've fought this for so long," he went on as his lips continued to travel over her heated skin. "I never wanted to cross this line with you because I knew once I had you, it wouldn't be nearly enough."

Well, that certainly sounded promising.

"Then why do you sound so upset?" she asked, trying to focus on his unspoken problem and not the way he was setting her body on fire with each simple touch of those talented lips.

"I've always said I won't get involved." His fingers tightened around hers, balling their joined hands into fists. "I'm married to this job. The stress, the worry, I wouldn't put that on anybody, least of all you."

Everything always came down his job. She loved how noble he was, but, damn it, he was a man, too. A man with needs, desires. And he was ready to shove it all aside for the sake of his badge?

"I don't mind," she answered honestly. "Maybe you wouldn't feel so stressed if you had someone to share the burden with."

"I can't," he muttered, resting his forehead on her shoulder. "You don't understand."

She started to turn, but he held her away. "Damn it, let me look at you," she cried.

Finally he eased back, releasing her hands. When Megan fully turned to face him, angst and torment stared back at her. She'd never thought she'd see a day when Cameron St. John seemed anything but strong and resilient.

They needed to get off this emotional roller coaster. They needed to return to familiar territory where they weren't so wrapped up in what the next step should be. If that step happened to be in opposite directions, then so be it. But they couldn't lose sight of what was important.

Megan slid a fingertip along the worry lines between Cameron's indrawn brows. "We need a break. *You* need a break." Smiling, she dropped her hand. "I have the perfect idea. Don't go anywhere. I'll be back in thirty minutes to pick you up."

His eyes narrowed. "What do you have in mind?"

"Oh, please." She laughed. "After the shenanigans you and your brothers got into, you're afraid of me?"

His gaze darted to her lips, then back up. "More than you know," he whispered.

How could her body continually respond to his words, his tone and those heated looks? How much did she have to endure before she was put out of her misery and he either moved forward or stepped away? In all honesty, she was done playing. So she was going after all she wanted...and she wanted him.

"I'll be back," she told him. "Just be ready."

"I'm not sure that's possible," he said.

So Cameron didn't miss the meaning in her final warning. *Good.*

Chapter Fifteen

How the hell did he go from telling himself he'd keep the intimacy and sexual tension out of his mind to sitting in Megan's SUV heading toward an unknown destination, fantasizing about peeling that dress up and over her head?

Cameron gritted his teeth and watched out the side window as his familiar town flew by. Megan may be teetering on the edge of speeding, but he wasn't about to say anything. In all honesty, he could use the distraction. He needed to focus on something other than the way she'd shown back up at his door with a wide smile, a little white dress that shifted against her thighs when she turned and those beat-up brown cowgirl boots. She'd done this on purpose. He wasn't a fool, and he knew Megan better than he knew any other woman. When she set her mind to something, she got it. Which meant he was not only fighting himself; now he'd be battling her.

He didn't stand a chance.

"Where are we going?" he asked, still not turning to look back at those tanned thighs peeking beneath the lacy edge of her dress.

"You're like a little kid." Megan turned onto a dirt road just outside the city limits. "This property is for sale and there's a cute little pond. We're having a picnic. Nobody is around, and I doubt there's even cell service here because it's nestled in the woods. It's too nice of a day to waste inside. The temperature is perfect."

Private. Woods. No cell service. Yeah, she'd definitely be the end of him. They were officially going to be alone, and Cameron knew without a doubt he wouldn't be able to keep his hands off her no matter how good his intentions may be. He was human, and every part of him wanted Megan for himself.

She pulled her SUV under a canopy of trees and killed the engine. Before he could pull on his door handle, Megan reached over the console and gripped his hand.

"No pressure, Cam." Her eyes held his; her unpainted lips called to him. "I just wanted to get away and relax. You've been tense the whole way here."

"I wouldn't say tense," he defended himself.

Megan laughed, smacked a brief kiss on his lips and patted his arm. "You're right. Not tense. Terrified. Now help me get the stuff out of the back."

Cameron had no choice but to follow her around to

the back and pull out the basket she'd hidden beneath a large red blanket. Allowing her to lead the way, Cameron had a hard time keeping his eyes off the sway of the hem of her skirt as the lace edge shifted against her skin. He knew firsthand how silky she felt, how perfectly his fingertips slid over her.

Those damn cowgirl boots were only adding to his arousal. She was so modest, so small-town girl, yet everything about her called to him on a level so primal and carnal she'd probably be terrified if she discovered just how much he craved her.

Beyond the physical pull he had toward her, Megan was the only woman who made him want more for his personal life. She was the only woman who inspired him to want to make the impossible actually work.

"I can practically hear you thinking," she called without looking back. "You're not relaxing."

Megan stopped near the edge of the pond. After giving the folded blanket a jerk, she sent it floating down over the grass. Cameron set the basket down and took a seat. She was right. The weather was rather warm for this time of year and he doubted they'd have many days like this left. Taking advantage of the time was a great idea. Now he just had to figure out how to remain in control here.

"For your information, I'm more relaxed now than I have been in weeks," he told her as he flipped the lid on the basket.

Easing down onto the blanket, Megan shifted her legs to her side and smoothed her skirt around her knees. "Liar. You've barely said a word. That tells me you're analyzing something." She pulled out two bottles of water. "Most likely you're overthinking us."

Us. They were an *us* at this point whether he wanted to admit it or not.

Megan continued to pull out items from the basket, as if discussing their confusing relationship with the surmounting tension was an everyday occurrence. Grapes, slices of bread, peanut butter, chips and cookies were all scattered around the blanket before he felt confident enough to speak.

Damn it. He was police chief, for pity's sake. He'd put up with quite a bit in his years on the force, dealt with even more before that when he'd been in the army. Yet here he was, trying to find the right words, the courage to talk to Megan as if nothing had changed.

Everything mattered where she was concerned. That's why he was so nervous about hurting her.

"Can I be honest?" he asked.

Her hand froze in the middle of smearing a generous amount of peanut butter onto a slice of bread. Her eyes lifted to his as a slow smile spread across her face.

"You must really be torn up about something. You've never asked permission to do anything and I've never known you to lie to me." She quirked an arched brow. "Have you lied to me?"

That smile held in place, and he knew she was joking. Little did she know how close she was to the truth. He had lied to her—by omission. He'd kept a secret that would most definitely crush her. And that was just the one about her brother, never mind the truth behind his feelings toward her.

"Okay," she muttered as she went back to making a sandwich. "Apparently your lack of smile or response tells me all I need to know. I never thought you'd actually lie to my face."

Cameron reached out, wrapping his hand around her slender wrist until she looked at him again. "There are things I can't tell you, Megan. You know that. Right now I wanted to talk about what's going on with us. I know you wanted me to relax, but I can't when there's so much between us that we're both trying to ignore."

"Oh, I'm not ignoring anything," she countered. "I'm giving you space to come to grips with the fact we slept together."

A soft breeze filtered through, picking up the curled ends of her hair and sending them dancing. Those silky strands had slid all over his body, he'd threaded his fingers through them, and right now he itched to touch her intimately once again.

"I handled that entire situation wrong," he told her, releasing her wrist.

She reached for another slice of bread and put it on top of the peanut butter. When she offered him the sandwich, he shook his head and started making his own.

"You were so vulnerable," he started, still recalling exactly how she'd trembled. "I was, too, for that matter. I'd hit a breaking point, though. I couldn't hold back anymore."

Megan swallowed a bite of her sandwich, reached for a bottle of water and took a drink before responding. "I don't understand why you denied either of us for so long when we wanted the same thing."

"Because in the end we *don't* want the same thing," he corrected her. "You know my stance on serious relationships, and I know you want a family. We're better off as friends, and I never meant to cross the line because now we're having a damn hard time finding our way back."

Megan plucked off a grape and popped it into her mouth. "There's no reason to turn back. Unless you think sleeping with me was a mistake."

The way her green eyes held his, the way so many questions stared back at him, Cameron found himself shaking his head. "No. That wasn't a mistake. I didn't plan on it, but no way could I call what happened a mistake."

"But you don't want it to happen again."

She couldn't be more wrong. "It can't happen again. Big difference."

With a cocky smile, she went back to her sandwich. He had no clue what that smile meant; more than likely he'd find out because he had no doubt she was plotting something. Cameron finished his sandwich and dived right into the BBQ chips, his favorite. She always kept them on hand for him at her house.

And it was all those little things that added up to make a giant impact on his life.

"So how did you know this property is for sale?" Cameron stretched his legs out in front of him, resting his hands behind his back.

Megan started putting the leftover food back into the

basket. "I have a coworker whose sister is the Realtor. She told me I could come anytime and fish or swim until the property sold. I guess the land was their parents' and now the sisters don't want it, so they're selling it and splitting the profit."

Cameron looked around at all the old oak trees, the perfectly shaped pond, complete with a small dock for fishing or jumping off. He could practically picture a large, two-story cabin-like home off in the distance on the flat stretch of land.

"Beautiful, isn't it?" she asked.

Cameron glanced back to her. "It is."

He watched as her eyes surveyed the land, saw a soft smile settle on her face. Such a look of happiness and contentment.

"You want this land, don't you?"

Blinking, she met his gaze and shrugged. "Who wouldn't? It's just another daydream, though."

He wanted her to have this, wanted her to achieve all those dreams because her entire life she'd put everyone ahead of her own needs. He knew she'd already fantasized about having a family here, kids running through the field and jumping off a dock into the pond. "Buy it," he told her. "Nothing is holding you back. Buy this land and it will be here when you're ready to build."

Megan lay on her back, her head on his thigh and her booted ankles crossed. She laced her fingers over her abdomen and stared up at the sky.

"There's so much holding me back." Her reply came on a soft sigh as she smiled. "I just want to lie here and pretend for a bit longer. I love the sound of absolute nothing. There's something so peaceful, so perfect about it. Like the world is one big happy place."

Her eyes drifted closed, and Cameron's heart broke for her. All she'd ever wanted was for everyone around her to be happy and have a peaceful life. She wasn't naive by any means, but Cameron wondered if she truly believed she could make that happen. The woman was relentless; she'd try to help everyone she knew or she'd go down swinging.

Unable to keep his hands from her another moment, he smoothed her hair away from her face, trailing his fingertip down along her shoulder. "What's holding you back from buying?" he asked.

He knew she was extremely frugal with her finances and she rarely bought anything for herself. Her house and SUV were both paid off. She wasn't a shopper like some women he knew.

Those bright green eyes focused on his. Sometimes looking at her physically hurt him, because he knew one day she'd find the one. She'd settle down and marry, probably have children. And all that happiness was exactly what he wanted for her. He just couldn't be the one to supply her needs.

"I may be moving."

Cameron's hand stilled, and the fine strands of her hair slid right out of his fingers. "You're moving?"

"I haven't decided yet."

All Cameron could do was stare. The air seemed a bit thicker as the severity of her words hit him like a punch to the stomach. He hadn't seen this coming, and it took a lot to send his shock factor gauge soaring.

"Where would you be moving?" he asked.

"Memphis."

Almost two hours away. Not terribly far, but not down the street, either, as he'd grown used to. He'd already told himself he couldn't have his job and her. Something had to give. He just hadn't been prepared to let her go so far. Damn it, he didn't want this, but she had to make her own choices.

"I was offered a position at a new facility," she told him, her tone soft as if she was afraid to go into details. "That's where I was when I went out of town."

Nodding, Cameron rested his hand at his side. "Did you like the place?"

Why did the selfish part of him want her to say she hated it? Why did he hope she would turn this opportunity down? Hadn't he just told himself he wanted to see her happy, to see all her wishes and dreams come true for once?

Yet here he was, craving her, knowing he wouldn't give in to his own desires all because he wanted her to live the life she deserved and not be tied to the stress and obligations of being with a cop.

"I did." Megan focused back on the sky as the sun took cover behind a large white cloud. "There's just so many pros and cons no matter what decision I make."

"You need to do what's best for you, not what's best for everyone else."

There, that was the right thing to say. Still, the thought of her leaving was like a vise on his heart. He didn't want her to go, but he wouldn't sway her decision unless she asked his opinion. Even then, he wouldn't tell her to stay because he selfishly couldn't stand the thought of going days or even weeks without seeing her.

She was obviously just as torn or she would've told him her decision sooner. "Have you talked to Evan about the move?"

Megan sighed. "No. On one hand, I think leaving and having him come with me would be the fresh start he needs. On the other hand, I don't know that he would come."

Cameron really wished he could tell her that most likely Evan would be in jail before long.

"Don't let Evan factor into this," he commanded, a little harsher than he'd meant to.

Megan's eyes snapped to his. "How can I not?" she asked, jerking up into a sitting position. The way she twisted to confront him had their faces within inches of each other. "He's my only family, and he needs me."

"He needs to help himself for once."

Anger flashed through her eyes. "I won't fight with you about this again. You love Eli and Drake no matter what they do, and I love Evan no matter how much he screws up. He's still my brother."

Cameron wasn't about to state the obvious, that Evan wasn't near the men Eli and Drake were. Megan knew exactly how those three men lived their lives.

Tamping down his worry and frustration, Cameron lifted his hand to her cheek. Stroking his thumb along her soft skin, he held her gaze.

"I want you to make a decision that is strictly selfish," he told her. "I want you to do whatever you want without thinking of the consequences, without thinking of who will be hurt or angry. What does Megan want?"

Without a word, she shifted away and came to her feet. Toeing off her cowgirl boots, she kept her eyes locked on to his. In a move he hadn't seen coming, she lifted the hem of her skirt and pulled the dress over her head, tossing the garment to the side. Seeing her standing before him in a simple white cotton bra and panties shouldn't have turned him on as much as it did, but every single thing about Megan had his body responding.

"What are you doing?" he asked, cursing his raspy voice.

Reaching around to unfasten her bra, Megan let the straps slide down her arms. "I'm making a selfish decision. Right now, I want to go lay at the edge of the pond and get lost in a fantasy." She met his gaze as she hooked her thumbs in her panties and pulled them down. "With you."

He'd never been one to turn away from a challenge. No matter how many warnings blared through his head, there wasn't a man alive who would turn Megan Richards away.

Even with the high, full trees, sunlight filtered through and seemed to land right on the perfect body she'd placed on display for him.

"What if someone sees us?" he asked.

Megan laughed. "Well, we're pretty secluded and nobody is around. We'll hear a car if it comes up the road. Plus I'm the only one naked, so I guess I'm the only one who should worry about being seen. Am I right?"

She quirked a brow and turned away, heading toward the deck. Cameron came to his feet and began to strip, all the while watching that soft sway of those rounded hips.

There would be no good outcome to this story. Not one. He figured he might as well enjoy every moment with her that he could, because once those warrants came through, Megan would not be throwing those sassy, sultry smiles his way any longer. She'd look at him with disdain, and the thought crushed him.

Right now, he wanted to feel her in his arms, wanted to show her he truly did love her...even if he could never say the words aloud and mean them the way she needed him to.

Chapter Sixteen

Out of all the spontaneous things she'd done in her life, not that there had been many, making love with Cameron out in the open without a care in the world had to top the list.

Come to think of it, making love with Cameron had topped any and all lists she'd ever made or ever would make.

As Megan pulled into her drive after dropping Cameron off, she realized they'd been out much later than she'd meant and she hadn't left a porch light on. The street lamp was enough for her to see, but she still hated coming home to a dark, empty house.

She didn't regret one moment of today, though. Spending the day with Cameron, not worrying about Evan or how this change in her and Cam's dynamic would affect their friendship was quite refreshing.

Speaking of refreshing, her body still tingled as she recalled how Cameron had lifted her naked body against his and walked into the water. The water had been surprisingly warm. When Cameron had knelt down, with her wrapped all around him, and made love to her as the water lapped at their waistlines, she'd fallen completely in love with him. The moment had been perfect, the man even more perfect. And she knew she'd loved him all along, but that moment, that beautiful, special moment, had opened her eyes to what was truly happening between them.

Megan pulled into the garage, grabbed the basket from the trunk and headed to the back door. Holding up her keys toward the glow from streetlights, Megan squealed when a shadow of a man stood on her back steps.

"It's just me."

Heart pounding nearly through her chest, Megan gripped her keys and the basket. "Evan, you scared me to death. Why are you out here in the dark?"

"Can I stay here? At least for tonight?"

Megan stepped forward, still unable to see him very well. "Of course you can. You're my brother."

He shrugged. "I just…I didn't know after the other night."

"Let's get inside and then we'll talk."

She opened the back door and ushered him in ahead of her. After flicking on the kitchen light and setting the basket on the dinette table, she turned to Evan.

"What happened?" she asked, examining his swollen eye and cut lip. This looked far worse than the injury from the other day. And this was the other eye because the other one still sported a fading purple bruise.

Evan sank into a wooden chair at the table. "Wrong place, wrong time. Story of my life."

She wanted to tell him he'd written his own story and it was never too late to start a new chapter, but she figured all that psychoanalyzing would only irritate him even more. It would be the equivalent of teaching a drowning person to swim. Not the time.

So, for now, she'd tend to his wounds and listen. He was here because he felt safe, and she wasn't about to run him off with all the questions swirling around in her mind or by scolding him like a warden.

"Let me get my first-aid kit."

By the time she came back, Evan had flipped the lid off the basket and was making a sandwich.

"I can make you real food if you're hungry." She sat in the chair at the head of the table and checked the supplies in the kit. "I know I have some spaghetti and a quesadilla I could heat up."

Evan shook his head. "This will be fine."

After pulling out the things she needed to fix Evan up, she turned toward him. "I only have one question."

His eyes came up to meet hers. Eyes so like hers, but they'd dimmed somewhere along the way. Perhaps the process had been slow, and that's why she hadn't noticed. Most likely the light started fading when he'd been kicked out of two schools in two years, before junior high. They'd had to move, but eventually Megan came back to her school in Stonerock because she'd missed Cameron and his brothers.

Evan's eyes definitely lost some shine on the night their parents died. Since then he'd been at a rapid decline and spiraling into a territory she feared she'd never rescue him from.

"Are you ready to get out?" she asked.

Evan reached across the space between them and gripped her hand. "Yes."

Relief flooded through her. "Are you on something now?"

She didn't need to go into details; he knew exactly what she was asking.

"No. I don't use. I only supply."

As if that made his position any better? Megan sandwiched his hand in her grip so he'd understand how much she wanted him here, how much she loved him and would support him on all levels.

"We'll get through this, Evan," she promised. "But first we need to go to the police."

"No." He jerked back, shaking his head. "I can't do that. You don't know what those guys are capable of."

Megan repressed a shudder as the memory of being held at gunpoint flashed through her mind. "I've got a pretty good idea," she told him. Easing forward, she pleaded, "Cameron can help, but you have to tell him everything."

Evan closed his eyes and sighed. "I can't right now."

Megan started to say something, but Evan opened his eyes and offered a weak smile. "Just let me get some rest tonight. Okay? Can we discuss this tomorrow?"

He was exhausted and broken. Megan's heart ached for him. But he was making progress, and she wasn't about to upset him further and risk driving him away.

The job opportunity in Memphis was weighing heavily on her mind, especially after being with Cameron again. He'd seemed stunned and speechless about her offer, but she desperately needed to know how he felt about her moving, how that would impact anything they had. At some point he was going to have to be honest with her about what he wanted.

Megan dabbed at the cut on Evan's swollen eye with a cotton ball. After applying some antibiotic ointment, she placed a small butterfly bandage on the wound and turned her attention toward his mouth.

"If we could move away, would you go?" she asked.

"Where would we go?"

Shrugging, Megan didn't want to give too much away about the job offer. "I've thought about Memphis, but I wouldn't do anything without discussing it with you."

"I like it here."

Megan nodded. "If you want to escape the mess you're in, you need to get away, and not just in theory."

A frustrated sigh escaped him. "I don't want to fight. I just want to rest."

"Fine." She wasn't going to get anywhere right now. She had to be patient. "You're more than welcome to stay. Will they come here looking for you?"

"I don't think so."

Megan finished up and started putting supplies

away. "If they come, I am calling Cameron. No arguments. Got it?"

Evan straightened in his seat. "Meg—"

She held up her hand. "No. Arguments." This was her turf, and no way in hell was it going to be penetrated by guys who were only out to cause harm.

"Fine."

He scooted away from the table, rising to his feet as he grabbed his side.

"What's wrong?" She started to reach for him, but he stepped back. "Are you hurt there, too?"

"It's nothing but some bruised ribs. I'm gonna go crash."

With that, Evan turned and headed toward the spare bedroom. Megan stared at the empty doorway, wondering how the conversation would go in the morning. Would Evan still be ready to talk about a new life or would his current fear disappear?

For now, he was safe and she wouldn't go to Cameron unless someone from Evan's circle showed up. She would do anything to keep her brother safe, and now that he was in her home, nobody would get through. She kept a gun for security in her closet. She'd never had to use it before, but she wouldn't hesitate to defend her family. No matter what.

Megan was thankful today was Sunday and she could relax. She tended to work a few hours on Saturday, so Sunday was her only full day off.

Halloween was tomorrow night. She enjoyed seeing the kids in her neighborhood all dressed up in adorable costumes. She couldn't wait until the day she got to parade her own little gremlin or witch around.

Megan had finished making breakfast an hour ago, and when Evan continued to sleep, she covered his plate and set it in the microwave. She wanted him to have a nice home-cooked meal because she doubted anyone else truly cared for him.

Her phone vibrated on the kitchen table. Glancing at the screen, she read Cameron's message.

Still coming to the cookout at my parents'?

Megan hesitated. She'd forgotten all about the cookout and bonfire, complete with s'mores, at Mac and Bev's. But she couldn't leave her brother behind to go to the St. Johns' house, and she couldn't very well take him.

Until she knew how the day unfolded, she wasn't going to respond.

By the time Evan woke, Megan had already cleaned the entire kitchen and dusted her living room. Wearing only his jeans, Evan shuffled in and sank onto the couch. His dark hair stood on end, the bruises over his face and along his right side more prominent this morning. He hadn't let her look last night and she wasn't going to coddle him today. He was a grown man, and he was here for security, not lecturing.

"Morning," he mumbled, raking a hand over his face, the stubble along his jaw and chin bristling beneath his palm. "Thought you'd be at work."

Megan leaned a hip against the back of her oversize chair and crossed her arms. "I don't work on Sunday."

"It's Sunday? I've lost track of the days." He eyed her, drawing his dark brows in. "You have plans?"

"Not really," she replied with a shrug. "You have anything you want to do?"

Evan scratched his bare chest. "I need to get my stuff sometime."

"Where is it?"

"All over. My clothes are at Spider's place. He's cool, though, so I can go there alone. I have a few things at this girl Mary's house, but she's probably sold it all by now."

As Megan listened to her brother go through his list of minute belongings scattered all around, another layer of how different their lives were slid into place. He had no stability, while she thrived on a solid foundation. He had no real friends, and she'd had Cameron and his family since grade school. Evan worried about day-to-day life, whereas Megan worried about advancing in her already successful career.

Where had she gone wrong? At some point along the way she'd missed something.

"If you have plans, go on and do them," Evan told her. "I'm going to go get my clothes and just chill here. I don't expect you to put your life on hold for me."

"I'm not putting my life on hold," she corrected him, easing around the chair. Taking a seat on the edge, she angled her body to face him fully. "Do you have a plan beyond today?"

"Not really." Wincing and grabbing his side, he

started to sit up. "I know you like details and sched-
ules, but that's not me, Meg. I'm not sure about moving, but I wouldn't mind staying here for a while if
you don't mind."

Reaching out to pat his leg, she offered a smile.
"You're always welcome here, Evan. I just can't have
the group you hang around with. I've worked hard to
get where I am and I'll do anything to help you. Consider this your home, but if anyone jeopardizes my little world, I won't back down. I'm not afraid of them."

Covering her hand with his, Evan's eyes held hers.
"You should be afraid. They're ruthless, Megan. They
don't care who they hurt, so long as they have money
and drugs. Maybe I should stay somewhere else."

"No," she answered without thinking. "I worry
when I don't see you or hear from you. You're staying
here, where I can help you."

The muscle moved in his jaw, and his eyes darted
down, then back up. "I don't even know if getting out
is possible."

"We'll make it possible," she promised.

The back door opened at the same time Cameron's
voice called out for her. "Megan?"

"Living room."

Evan's face went from worry for her to instant stone.
"You didn't respond earlier so—"

Cameron's words died as he stepped around the corner and froze in the entryway. "Evan."

The tension between these two was so thick it was
like a concrete block had been dropped into the room.

Still, she loved them both, and if they loved her, they'd just have to grow up.

"Evan needed a place to crash," she explained.

Cameron didn't take his eyes off Evan. "Looks like he was already in a crash."

"Something like that," Evan muttered.

They'd never made it a secret they weren't buddies, but still, couldn't they at least try to be civil while she was around?

Megan twisted in her seat, letting go of Evan's hand. "What's up?"

Cameron stared at Evan another few seconds before turning his attention to Megan. "I didn't hear from you earlier, so I thought I'd see if you were coming tonight."

"Actually, I probably won't."

"Megan, go," Evan told her. "Don't stay here because of me."

She glanced back to her brother, knowing he expected her to just leave him in pain. He'd just have to get used to the fact that not everyone abandoned him. Damn it, she wanted him to see that she was here no matter what and his needs came before her own.

"I really don't want to leave you alone."

"Because you don't trust me?" he asked, masking his hurt with a rough tone.

"No," she told him, purposely softening her voice. "Because I worry about you, especially after last night."

"You can come, too."

Both Evan and Megan turned to Cameron as his invitation settled in the air between them.

"You're inviting me to your family dinner?" Evan asked.

With a shrug, Cameron leaned a shoulder against the door frame. "Sure. It's no big deal, and you have to eat, too."

Megan held her breath, her eyes darting between the two men. She was beyond shocked that Cameron had invited Evan. That was the type of noble man he was. Cameron was reaching out all because he cared for her and—dare she hope—loved her.

"I don't think your family would want me there," Evan said as he came to his feet.

"They won't mind. Come with Megan if you want or don't come. No big deal. Just extending the offer."

Megan caught Cameron's gaze and mouthed "thank you" when Evan wasn't looking. Cameron's eyes held hers, a small smirk formed on his lips and Megan knew he was only doing this for her.

If she hadn't already loved him, this would've sealed the deal. He was trying. Did that mean he wanted to try more with her, as well?

"I was just heading out for a run and thought I'd swing in," Cameron stated, pushing off the frame. "Megan, I'll see you tonight."

So, he wanted to see her whether Evan came or not. When the front door closed again, Evan glanced down to where she remained seated.

"He's in love with you."

Jerking her eyes up to him, Megan laughed. "Don't be ridiculous, Evan. We've been best friends since grade school."

"The guy has always been territorial with you, but he was looking at you like… Oh, great." Evan shook his head and laughed. "Tell me you didn't fall in love with him. Come on, Meg. He's a cop."

Yeah, he was a cop. He was also perfect for her little world, amazing in bed and irreplaceable.

"Who I love or don't love is really none of your concern," she told him. "I'm not being rude, but you have your own issues to work out. Now, if you want to come with me later, that's fine. If you don't, that's fine, too. I'll be leaving at six."

Megan turned and left Evan alone. She didn't want to hear anything else about why she should or shouldn't fall in love with Cameron. The reasons were moot at this point because she'd already fallen so deep, she'd never find her way back out.

Chapter Seventeen

Keep your friends close and your enemies closer.

Cameron had always hated that saying. Having enemies so close made him twitchy and irritable.

As he glanced across the field toward Evan, who sat in a folding chair all by himself, Cameron figured if Evan was here, he wasn't getting into anything illegal. Megan could rest easy tonight.

Speaking of Megan, she'd gotten cold earlier when the sun had gone down and he'd grabbed a hoodie sweatshirt from the back of his truck. The fact she was wrapped in his shirt made him feel even more territorial. The way she all but disappeared inside the fleecy material made her seem even more adorable. How could a woman be so many things at once? Sexy, cute, intriguing, strong... Megan was all of that and much more.

She laughed at something Eli said before turning her gaze and meeting his. Instantly the air crackled. Nothing else mattered but Megan. The case should be wrapped up by tomorrow evening when the next "trade" took place. He knew all key players were supposed to be in attendance, according to their inside source.

Maybe once all of this was tied up, maybe once Evan was out of the picture and not weighing so heavily on Megan's mind and conscience, she would figure out how to seek that happiness she deserved.

Drake came to stand beside Megan, and she turned, breaking the moment. Only Eli knew of the tension between them, and Cameron doubted anyone else was picking up on the vibes he and Megan were sending out.

Cameron's gaze darted back to Evan...who was shooting death glares across the distance. Okay, maybe one more person knew something was happening between him and Megan, but Cameron didn't care what Evan's opinion was.

"You seem quiet tonight."

Cameron merely nodded as his father came up beside him. "Been a stressful time at work," Cameron replied.

"Looks to me like you have something else on your mind."

Cameron glanced to his father, who was looking straight at Megan. She excused herself, picked up a roasting stick and took it over to her brother. Cameron watched as they talked, and finally Evan came to his feet, took the stick, and he and Megan went over to the fire to roast marshmallows.

"I figured you two would figure this out eventually," his father went on.

Cameron groaned inwardly. "There's nothing to figure out, Dad. We're friends."

"Friends is a good start," Mac agreed. "Building on that only makes a stronger relationship."

Frustration slid through him. He really didn't want to get into this right now with his dad...or anybody else for that matter.

"Look, Dad—"

"Hear me out." Mac turned to face Cameron. The wrinkles around his father's eyes were more prominent as he drew his brows together. "You are overthinking things, son. Megan isn't going to wait around for you to come to your senses."

Clenching his fists at his side, Cameron nodded. "I don't expect her to. Things would be easier if she met someone and moved on."

"Easier for you?" he asked. "Because from where I'm standing, Megan only has eyes for one person. I figured you'd be smart enough to make your friendship more permanent."

"You don't get it," Cameron began, absently noting that Evan had taken a phone call.

"Get what?" Licking marshmallow off his thumb, Drake came up beside their dad.

"Nothing," Cameron stated.

"Your brother is having women problems."

Still focused on his gooey thumb, Drake laughed. "Megan giving you fits?"

What the hell? Is nothing sacred around here?

"I'm going to kill Eli," Cameron muttered.

Drake's smile widened. "He didn't tell me. Marly

did. Women just seem to be in tune with each other, but I think something happened when they all went out to Dolly's the other night."

Had Megan mentioned him to Marly and Nora? Surely she hadn't.

When he sought her out again, she was helping Willow roast a marshmallow. She fit in perfectly with his family. What would happen if he decided to take a chance? What would happen if he gave in to both of their needs and took this friendship beyond the bedroom?

"For what it's worth," Drake went on, "I think Megan is great. I always figured you guys would end up together."

Apparently every single person in his family had some creepy psychic ability because Cameron had fought the urge for years to ever make Megan more than a buddy or a pal. Unfortunately he knew firsthand just how sexy and feisty his "pal" was.

Evan rushed to Megan's side as he slid his phone back into his pocket. Just as Evan said something to her and hurried toward the front of the house, Cameron's cell vibrated in his pocket.

"Excuse me," he told his father and Drake.

Stepping away from the crowd, he pulled out the phone and read the text.

Moving day changed. 30 min.

Damn it. That's why Evan rushed out?

Cameron caught Drake's eye. "Something came up. Tell everyone—"

Drake waved him away. "Go—we know."

This family was more than used to Cameron getting called away. All three St. John brothers were in high demand in Stonerock, so it wasn't unusual for at least one of them to get called away from a family gathering.

Cameron rushed to his house to grab his work gun and Kevlar vest. Thankfully, the designated parking lot was less than ten minutes away. By the time he pulled in, he still had ten minutes to spare.

The outcome tonight was not going to be good, but right now all Cameron could focus on was doing his job. Just when he'd been about to open himself up to the possibility of a relationship with Megan, this call had come through. Was it a sign that keeping his distance was the right thing to do?

Cameron settled in with his fellow officers and FBI agents. Now all they had to do was watch and wait, and hopefully this entire ordeal would be wrapped up tonight.

He had no idea if he should be elated or terrified.

Megan had no clue where Evan had run off to and then Cameron had gotten called into work. She'd stayed behind and chatted with Nora and Marly, roasted more marshmallows than her stomach appreciated and now lay curled up in the corner of her sofa trying to read a book by the vomited light of the evil dragon.

Megan couldn't help but look at that tacky piece and laugh. Because if she didn't laugh, she'd surely cry. Some people had a beautiful art sculpture or painting as the focal point in their living rooms. Nope, Megan had this monstrosity.

Flipping through the pages of her book, Megan wanted to see when the good scenes were coming up because the current chapter was nearly putting her to sleep.

Before she could decide whether or not to give up, her cell rang. Dropping the book on the end table, she picked up her phone, not recognizing the number. Most likely a client.

"Hello?"

"Meg. I've been arrested."

Jumping to her feet, Megan started toward her bedroom to put clothes on. "What happened, Evan?"

Dread flooded her. Whatever he'd hightailed it out of the St. Johns' party for had obviously not been a good idea.

"Your boyfriend brought me in." Evan's tone was filled with disgust. "I wasn't doing anything, Meg. I need you to come get me."

Cameron arrested Evan? How the hell had the night gone from roasting marshmallows to her brother being thrown in jail?

"How much is bail?" she asked, shoving her feet into her cowgirl boots.

"I don't think they're allowing it to be set."

Megan froze. "What did you do?"

"Listen, I need you to fix this, Meg," he pleaded, near hysterics. "I don't want to be here. Call your attorney and get me out of this place."

Megan sank onto the edge of her bed. "If bail isn't an option, there's nothing I can do right now. I'll call my lawyer, but I doubt he can do anything tonight, either."

"Maybe you should tell Cameron I'm innocent," he spat, seconds before hanging up.

Defeated, angry and cold, Megan stared at the cell in her hand. In her heart she'd known this day was coming. Evan had reached out to her for help only twenty-four hours ago…obviously too late to make a difference.

Before she could allow her mind to travel into what Cameron knew about this situation, she had to call her attorney. Evan's fear had been apparent through the line. She knew from a few of her clients just how terrifying being arrested for the first time could be. No matter what the attorney's fee would be, she'd pay it and do every single thing in her power to get him away from this city where he was only staying in trouble. If he wanted to truly get away, he needed a fresh start away from the thugs he'd been with.

Hours later, Megan was still wound tight. She'd discovered there was nothing to do for Evan right now. There would be a hearing on Monday morning to decide the next step.

Megan had hung up with her attorney thirty minutes ago and couldn't go in to bed if she tried. She glanced at the book on the end table and knew that wouldn't hold her interest, either.

Heading to the hall closet, she was just about to sink to a whole new level of desperate and pull out her vacuum when her back door opened and closed.

The late hour didn't stop Cameron from letting himself in. *Great*. She wasn't sure she was ready to deal with this, with him. She was still shaking from the fact that her brother was behind bars with criminals and her best friend had arrested him.

Moving down the hall, she met Cameron just as he stepped out of the kitchen. The dark bruise beneath his eye, the cut across his other brow and his disheveled clothes stopped her in her tracks.

"What the hell happened tonight?" she cried. "Evan's arrested and you've been in a fight."

Cameron's tired eyes closed as he shook his head. "I wanted to be the one to tell you about Evan, but I knew there was no way I could finish everything up and get here before he called you."

Anger coursed through her. "You knew my brother was in trouble. Enough trouble to get arrested, didn't you?"

Slowly, his lids opened, those signature baby blues locked on her. "Yes. I've been watching him for some time now. Him and several others."

Megan felt as if someone had taken a pointy-toed shoe and kicked her straight in the stomach.

"Evan wasn't a key player," Cameron went on. "He just fell in with the wrong crowd and ended up deeper than I think he intended."

Bursts of cold shot through her system. Megan wrapped her arms around her waist and pushed past Cameron.

"So you just arrest him anyway?" she asked, moving to the living room to sink onto the sofa. "You know he's trying to break away and you still arrest him like some hardened criminal?"

Cameron rested his hands on his hips, remaining across the room. "He is a criminal, Meg. He was with the group we've been tracking for months. Evan has been running drugs."

No. This was her brother, her baby brother. She didn't want this to be his life even though he'd admitted as much to her just yesterday. He'd said he wanted to get out. She'd give anything if he would have come to her sooner; maybe they wouldn't be in this position now.

Bending forward, her arms still tight around her midsection, she wanted to just curl up and cry or scream. "You should go," she whispered, already feeling the burn of tears in her throat.

"I'm not leaving until we talk."

Of course he wasn't.

"I know you aren't happy with me right now," he started. "But you have to know I was doing my job. I can't let our relationship prevent me from keeping Stonerock safe."

A laugh erupted from her before she could prevent it. Megan sat back up and rested her elbows on her knees.

"I don't expect you to not do your job, Chief. But I never thought you'd be spying on my brother one minute and sleeping with me the next."

Okay, he deserved that. Megan needed to get all her anger out because he'd had months to deal with the fact that Evan was into illegal activities. While Megan had suspected her brother's involvement, tonight she'd been dealt some cold, hard facts—and then learned her best friend was the arresting officer.

"How could you do this to me?" she asked, her voice husky from emotion. "How could you use me like that? We've been friends so long, Cam. I trusted you with everything in my life and you just…"

Her words died in the air as she covered her face with her hands. Sobs tore through her, filling the room and slicing his heart. Cameron knew full well that right at this moment she felt she hated him, but that didn't stop him from stepping forward and squatting down in front of her.

"I didn't use you," he said, realizing how pathetic he sounded. "I couldn't tell you, Meg. I wanted to. I wanted you to know what you were in the midst of. I wanted to somehow soften the blow, but my hands were tied."

Her hands dropped to her lap as she focused her watery stare on him. Tear tracks marred her creamy skin, and Cameron knew if he attempted to reach out to wipe away the physical evidence of her pain, she would push him away.

"You mean you chose your job again over everything else. Over me."

Cameron eased up enough to sit on the edge of the coffee table, his elbows on his knees, as he fought the urge to take her hands in his. She had to get all this anger out, and he had to absorb it. There was no other way to move beyond this mess…if they even could move on.

"Wait." Megan sat up straighter, her gaze darting to the floor, then back up to his. "You were there, weren't you? The night I was with Evan and those guys showed up?"

Regret filled him, cutting off any pathetic defense he could've come up with. As if the entire lying-by-omission thing weren't enough, now he had to face the ugly truth that he'd not done a damn thing to help her.

She continued to stare at him, continued to study him as if she didn't even recognize him anymore. "Tell me you weren't there," she whispered.

Swallowing a lump of rage and remorse all rolled into one, he replied, "I can't."

He expected her to slap him, to stand up and charge from the room or start yelling and throwing things. He expected pure anger. Anger he could've dealt with.

But when she closed her eyes, unleashing a fresh set of tears as she fell back against the couch, defeated, Cameron knew he'd broken something between them. He'd broken something in her, and he had no idea how to fix it or even if their relationship was repairable.

"I want to hate you right now."

Those harsh words from such a tiny voice was the equivalent of salt to the wound…a self-inflicted wound. He had absolutely nobody to blame but himself.

Megan eased up, just enough to look him in the eye. "I want to hate you so you'll be out of my life, so I never have to see you again," she told him through tears. "But I can't because no matter how deeply you hurt me, I still love you. Damn it, Cameron, I love you more than I've ever loved anybody. I was prepared to turn down this job in Memphis for you. I was ready to fight for you, for us."

Her voice shook as she went on, swiping at the tears streaking down her cheeks. "I was ready to live with your dedication to your job. I foolishly thought you could love me just as much, but now I know I'll never be equal, never be enough."

Cameron had no clue he'd shed his own tears until he felt the trickle down his cheek. He'd never cried over a woman. Hell, he couldn't recall the last time he'd cried at all. But Megan was worth the emotion; she was worth absolutely everything.

"Stay," he pleaded. "Don't take the job. We can get through this."

"Can we?" she tossed back. "And how would we do that? You spied on my brother for who knows how long. You watched me from a distance during one of my scariest moments. I think that is enough to prove you'd never put me first, so don't preach to me about staying to make this work. I've been here for years, Cam. Years. I can't help it if you're just now ready."

Megan came to her feet, anger fueling her now if the way she swatted at the tears on her face was any indication. Cameron eased back on the table but didn't rise. He knew she needed the control, the upper hand here.

"You always said you wouldn't ever make a woman compete with your job," she went on. "But what do you think I've been doing all this time? I was with you during deployments, during the police academy and your entire law-enforcement career. You think I worried less because we were friends and not married? You think I didn't play the 'what-if' game while you were overseas or if a day or two went by that I didn't hear from you?"

Reality hit him square in the gut.

"You're right." Slowly, he got to his feet. Considering she didn't back away, he reached for her hands. "You were there for me every step of the way. I didn't see your angle until now, or maybe I was afraid to."

Megan fisted her hands beneath his. "You need to go. I'm exhausted. I've got to figure out what I can do for Evan, and I need to make arrangements for Memphis."

The last bit of hope he'd had died as he released her fists. "You're leaving."

Megan's gaze slid to the floor as she nodded, not saying a word. Conversation over.

There had never been such an emptiness, such a hollow feeling in his soul. The bond they'd honed and strengthened for years had just been severed in the span of minutes. He'd known how this would hurt her, but he hadn't expected her to erect this steel wall between them, completely shutting him out.

Cameron turned, headed toward the back door.

"Did you ever love me?" Megan's question tore through the thick tension.

Stopping, Cameron leaned a hand on the door frame to steady himself. Not only was he starting to tear up again but his knees were shaking.

"I've always loved you," he told her. "More than you could ever know."

When she said nothing in reply, Cameron headed straight out the back door. He had to keep going or he'd drop to his knees and beg her forgiveness. But Megan wasn't in the frame of mind to forgive.

He had a feeling after all he'd done to destroy their friendship and the intimacy they'd discovered, she never would be.

Chapter Eighteen

Two weeks later, Evan was still in jail. She'd been able to see him several times and each time she went her heart broke even more. He'd hinted that maybe he'd be getting out soon, but she couldn't get details from him.

After taking another picture from the wall, Megan wrapped it in bubble wrap and placed it in the box with the other fragile items. Her new job was to start in two weeks and she was moving in to her new rental within days.

The thought of leaving this house that she'd loved for so long had her reminiscing with each room she walked through, each item she boxed up. She'd yet to pack the dragon lamp because each time she passed by the hideous thing, she started tearing up once again.

In the two weeks since she'd last seen Cameron, her

emotions had been all over the place. She'd gone from angry to depressed, from crying to yelling at the empty space. Other than during his deployments, she'd never gone this long without seeing or talking to him. How could her best friend since childhood be out of her life so fast? How did she move on without the stability and support he'd always offered?

By sticking to her plans. She would move towns, make new friends and start a new life. And if Evan somehow miraculously got out, he could join her.

Of course, all of that would be in a perfect world, and she knew she lived in anything but.

Tomorrow she'd have the difficult task of telling her clients that she was leaving. She'd really formed some wonderful friendships during her time at the counseling center. Her supervisor was sorry to see her go, but understood, considering she'd been the one to recommend Megan for the position.

Before she could pull another piece of artwork from the wall, the doorbell rang. Glancing around the boxes, bubble wrap and her own state of haphazardness, Megan shrugged. She wasn't expecting company, though she'd been surprised Cameron hadn't attempted to contact her again. A piece of her was disappointed and a little more than hurt at the fact, but she'd told him to go and he was honoring her wishes. Noble until the end, that man was.

Adjusting her ratty old T-shirt and smoothing back the wayward strands that had escaped her ponytail, Megan flicked the lock and tugged on the door.

Speak of the devil.

Only he didn't look like the devil at all. He didn't even look worn and haggard as she did. Damn the man for standing on her porch looking all polished and tempting. The fall breeze kicked up, bringing his familiar scent straight to her and teasing her further.

His eyes darted behind her, no doubt taking in the chaos.

"When do you leave?" he asked, returning those baby blues to her.

Gripping the door frame, she prayed for strength, prayed to be able to hold it together while she figured out the reason for his visit.

"Next week."

He glanced down, then back up and sighed. "Can I come in? Just for a minute?"

Said the lion to its prey.

Megan stepped back, opening the old oak door even more to accommodate his broad frame. As soon as he entered, she closed the door, leaned back against it and waited while he continued to survey the room.

"I came to fill you in on Evan."

He turned to face her, and now that he was closer, she could see the worry lines etched between his brows, more prominent than ever. The dark circles beneath his eyes were evidence he'd been sleeping about as much as she had.

"What about him?" she asked, crossing her arms over her chest, resisting the urge to touch Cameron just one more time.

"I'm not supposed to tell you this, so please don't say anything. This could cost me my badge."

Megan stood up straighter. He was here as her friend, putting her above his job for once. A piece of the hard shell around her heart crumbled.

"Is he in more trouble?" she asked, fearful for the unknown.

"No." Cameron toyed with the open flap of a box on the coffee table. "He's actually going to take a plea bargain. He was offered immunity in exchange for every bit of information he knows."

Elation filled her. Megan clutched the scoop neck of her T-shirt and sucked in a deep breath. "Thank you," she whispered, unable to say anything else.

"There's more."

She tensed up at Cameron's hard stare. Whatever the "more" was apparently wasn't good news.

"He's going to go into Witness Protection first thing in the morning."

Witness Protection. The words registered but not fully at first. Then she realized what Cameron was truly telling her.

"I won't see him again?"

Shaking his head, Cameron held her gaze for a moment, then looked away as if he couldn't bear to see her. "I tried to get you in, but that power is above me. I had to fight to get the immunity. He had some stiff charges against him, but since he was a latecomer to the group, we needed the big names he could provide."

Megan nodded, hating what he was saying but knowing this was for the best. This was the only option for her brother to make a fresh start and stay safe.

"Could I write him a letter or something?" she asked. "Maybe you could get it to him?"

The muscle in Cameron's jaw jumped. "I can't."

Megan pulled in a shaky breath and pushed away from the door. Heading back to her task, something she had control over and something she could concentrate on, she pulled a picture off the wall and tore off more bubble wrap.

Methodically, she wrapped the frame, all the while coming to grips with the new level of pain that had settled deep into her chest.

"If you happen to have something that needs to be said, I could perhaps stop by and tell him before they take him away."

Cameron's generous offer hovered between them. After placing the package in the box, she closed the flaps and held her hand over the opening as she focused on Cameron.

"Tell him...just tell him I'm proud of him and I love him." Megan couldn't believe she'd never be able to tell him in person again, but if this was all she had, she was going to take it. Cameron nodded and turned to go. Megan stared at his back. Had he only come to deliver the message? Weren't they going to talk about anything or even pretend to be...what? What could they discuss at this point? She'd thrown him out weeks ago, and she hadn't extended a branch to him since.

"Cam," she called just as his hand fell to her doorknob. "Wait."

Glancing over his shoulder, he raised a brow as his eyes locked on to hers.

Gathering her strength and courage, she stepped around the coffee table and crossed the room to stand in front of him. He turned to face her, but the minuscule space between them may as well have been an ocean for all the tension that settled in the slot.

"Thank you."

Megan looked up at him, at the man she'd fallen so deeply in love with, and seriously had no clue how she would go on without Evan or Cameron in her life.

"I know Evan and I had our issues," Cameron started. "But we have one thing in common. We both love you."

Megan swallowed the tears that threatened. The last time Cameron had been here she'd cried enough to last a lifetime.

"We both want to see you happy," he went on. "Unfortunately we both had a terrible way of showing it."

Cameron started to reach out, then stopped. She glanced at his hand, hovering so close, and slid her fingers through his.

"They always say the ones you love the most can hurt you the most." The feel of his hand in hers sent a warmth spreading through her—a warmth she'd missed for two weeks. "I didn't know that to be true until recently."

Cameron's free hand slid along the side of her face. Megan tilted her head just enough to take the comfort he was offering.

"To know that you did this for Evan means everything to me," she added. "The thought of not seeing him again hurts, but it's far better than seeing him through glass. He'll have freedom and he'll be able to start over. That's all I've ever wanted for him."

"What about you?" Cameron's thumb stroked her cheek, the simple touch sending chills all over her body. "Are you going to start over?"

"That's my plan," she muttered. "It's my only option at this point."

Cameron's mouth covered hers without warning. The hungry kiss started so demandingly, Megan had no choice but to clutch at his wide shoulders. Just as she was getting used to being overtaken, Cam lightened his touch, turning the kiss into something less forceful but every bit as potent and primal.

By the time he eased away and rested his head against hers, they were both panting.

"I'm begging you, Meg. Don't leave." Both his hands framed her face; the strength of his body covered hers, and the raw words hit her straight in her heart. "I don't care if I look weak or pathetic. I'll beg you to stay. I need you so much more than you need me. You're so strong, and I know you would be just fine in Memphis. But I would not be okay here without you."

Wrapping her arms around his waist, Megan couldn't hold back any longer. The dam completely burst and tears she'd sworn never to shed in front of him again came flooding out. Cameron enveloped her, pulling her tighter against his chest as she let out all her fear, worry and uncertainty.

"I know I broke something in you with the choices I made." His hand smoothed up and down her back, comforting her. "I'll spend the rest of my life making all of that up to you. Please, please give me a chance."

"I'm scared, Cam," she murmured into his chest. "What happens when another big case comes along? What happens the next time you shut me out? What will I do when you decide the job is more important than I am or we are?"

Pulling back, Cameron looked her in the eye. "Nothing is more important than you are. Nothing. I came here expecting nothing from you, Megan. I came here to tell you about Evan, knowing full well that I could lose my job if anyone found out. I don't care. You are worth every risk, every chance I'll ever take."

Megan hiccupped as the next onslaught of tears took over. "I'm a mess," she told him, wiping the backs of her hands over her cheeks. "Look what you do to me."

His eyes focused on her. "I'm looking, and I've never seen a more beautiful woman in my life. You're it for me, Megan. I want to marry you and start a family with you. I know that's a lot to absorb right now, but just stay so we can work this out."

Megan couldn't believe what he was saying. He wanted to marry her?

"If you can't stay, if you're already committed and cannot get out of the Memphis job, or if that's really where your heart is, we can buy a place between here and there and we'll commute." Cameron kissed her lightly once more. "Just say you'll give us a chance."

"How could I refuse you?" she told him, raining kisses over his face. "How could I ever let you go?"

Cameron picked her up and started toward the hallway. "You'll never have to find out."

By the time they hit the bedroom, Megan knew she wasn't going anywhere for a long, long time.

Epilogue

"How much farther?"

Cameron squeezed Megan's hand and laughed. "Just don't move that blindfold. We're almost there."

"I think you're just driving in circles," she mumbled. "If you keep going too much farther, I'm going to get carsick. We're supposed to be on our way to our honeymoon."

They'd been married for three hours. He'd promised her a memorable wedding night, and he intended to deliver, but they weren't going far. He'd requested she keep her wedding dress on, told her it was important to him.

He glanced over, still a little choked up at the vision in white lace beside him. Her strapless gown fitted her body beautifully from her breasts to her waist with such a delicate fabric, he was afraid to touch her. In just a few short minutes she'd see why he wanted to keep her in her wedding gown. The airport could wait until tomorrow.

Tonight, he had a special surprise.

Cameron turned onto the dirt road and brought his truck to a stop just in front of the clearing. "Don't move. I'll come around to get you."

By the time he'd gotten Megan out of the truck and stood her beside him, she was looking a bit pale.

"You feeling okay?" he asked. "I thought you were joking about the carsick thing."

Megan whipped off her blindfold. "I'm not carsick— I'm pregnant," she cried.

Shock slid over him at the same time she gasped as she took in her surroundings. "What are we doing back here?" she asked.

Cameron couldn't think, couldn't speak. His gaze darted to her flat stomach beneath her vintage gown and all he could think was he was going to be a father. He and Megan were going to be parents.

With a shout, he wrapped his arms around her, picked her up and spun her in a circle, the train of her dress wrapping around his feet.

"Sickness, remember?" she yelled.

Easing her down, Cameron kissed her thoroughly. "How long have you known?" he asked when he pulled back.

"I just took a test at home this morning. I wanted to wait until after the reception to tell you, when we were alone, but then you said you had a surprise for me so I waited."

The flash of her coming down the aisle, smiling with tears in her eyes took on a whole new meaning now. She'd been radiant, beaming, a bright light coming toward him to make his life complete. She'd been there all along, and he was so thankful she hadn't given up on them.

Their ceremony had been perfect, planned by his sisters-in-law, his mother and Megan. The church had been covered in a variety of flowers, vibrant colors splashed all around. No doubt all of it was gorgeous, but he'd only had eyes for Megan. There was nothing more beautiful than seeing your best friend walk toward you, knowing you were going to start down a path that would forever bind you in love. And when she'd kissed him, he'd felt every bit of her love. And he wanted to spend the rest of his life showing her how precious she was to him.

Cameron choked back his own tears because this was the happiest day of his life. He didn't deserve all of this, but he was going to embrace every bit of it and build a family with the only woman he'd ever wanted.

"You've picked the perfect time to tell me." Laughing, Cameron held out his arms and eased the train aside with his foot. "This is it. I bought this for us to build our house on."

A wide smile spread across her face. "You're serious? You mean it?"

Seeing how happy she was made draining his entire savings completely worth it. A baby on the way, a new house and a wedding just around the holidays was a whole lot to be thankful for.

"I wanted to see you here, on our land in that dress." He reached out and stroked her cheek. "I wanted to capture this moment, this memory with you because I know it's only going to get better."

"I'm so glad I decided not to take that job in Memphis," she told him, still smiling. "How did you keep this a secret from me?"

Cameron shrugged. "It wasn't easy and I know I promised not to lie to you ever again, but I really wanted this to be a surprise."

"Oh, Cameron." Megan plastered herself against his side, wrapping her arms around his waist. "This is going to be perfect for our family. And maybe by this time next year we'll have our house done, and we can have all of your family over for the holidays. We'll have our little baby for everyone to fuss over."

Kissing the top of her head, Cameron smiled as he surveyed the land. "I think that sounds like a plan. First thing we'll move into the house will be—"

"Don't say it," she warned.

"Come on," he joked. "The lamp has to come with us."

Megan tipped her face up to his. "The only place that lamp needs to go is the Dumpster."

Squeezing her tight, Cameron rubbed her back. "Well, we can negotiate that later, but I think it would be a great piece for the nursery."

Smacking his abdomen, Megan groaned. "I will not give our child nightmares."

"You're right. It should stay in the living room. It has made quite a conversation starter."

Megan laughed, easing up on her toes to kiss his cheek. "You know I love you, but it's either me or the dragon lamp."

Turning to fully engulf her in his arms, Cameron smiled and slid his lips across hers. "You. It's always been you."

* * * * *

HIS BEST FRIEND'S
BABY

SUSAN CARLISLE

Joseph.

Thanks for being a great tool.

CHAPTER ONE

WHAT AM I doing here? Phoebe Taylor asked herself for the hundredth time, pulling her light coat closer. She could no longer get it to meet in the middle. Bowing her head against a gust of Melbourne, Australia, wind, she walked on. It would rain soon.

She looked at the name on the street sign. Morris Lane. This was the correct place. Phoebe didn't even have to check the paper in her hand that was shoved into her pocket. She had it memorized. She'd read it often during the past few weeks.

When had she turned into such a pathetic and needy person?

It had happened slowly, over the last eight months as her middle had expanded. She'd always heard that a baby changed you. She'd had no idea how true those words were until it had happened to her. She was even more fearful of the changes she faced in the weeks ahead. The fact she'd be handling them all on her own, had no one to rely on, frightened her.

She started down the cobblestone street lined with town houses. Joshua had written that if she needed anything she could contact Ryan Matthews. But who was she to him? An old army buddy's wife. People said those types of things all the time but few meant them. But she had no one else to turn to. There were teachers she worked with, but they all had their own lives, husbands and children. They didn't have time to hold her hand. There were plenty of acquaintances but none that she would call on. She'd take this chance because Joshua had said to. And this was Joshua's baby.

But would this guy Ryan help her? Be there for her during the delivery afterwards? Take Joshua's place at the birthing suite? *Yeah, right.* She didn't see any man agreeing to that job. Who took on someone else's widow and unborn child? She could never ask that of him. Would she want to? She didn't know this man outside of Joshua saying he was an upstanding mate.

When the walls of reality had started closing in on her and panic had arrived, she'd been unable to think of where to turn. Joshua's letter had called to her. Seemed to offer her salvation. Phoebe inhaled and released a breath. She'd come this far. She wouldn't turn back now. What was the worst Ryan Matthews could do? Send her away? Act like he'd never heard of her?

What she was sure of was she didn't want to feel alone anymore. She wanted someone to lean on. Be near a person who had a connection to Joshua. Hear a story or two that she could tell her son or daughter about their father. Joshua and Ryan had been brothers in arms. Been there for each other. Joshua had assured her in his last letter seven months ago that if she needed anything, *anything*, Ryan was the person to find. Desperate, she was going to his house to see if that was true.

Phoebe located the house number. It was painted above the door in black against the white frame of the Victorian house. The car traveling down the street drew her attention for a second. She pulled the paper out and looked at the address again, then at the entrance once more. Studying the steps to the door, she hesitated. Now she was stalling.

What was she going to say to this guy?

She'd been rehearsing her speech for days and still didn't know if she could get it out. On the tram coming across town she'd practiced again but couldn't seem to get it right. Everything she'd planned made her sound crazy. Maybe she was. But she had to say something, give some explanation as to why she'd turned up on his doorstep.

Hi, I'm Phoebe Taylor. You were a friend of my husband's. He said if I ever needed anything to come see you. So here I am.

That should get his attention. She placed a hand on her protruding middle and chuckled dryly. *His first thought will probably be I'm here to accuse him of being the father.*

The wind gusted again as she mounted the steps. There were no potted plants lining them, like most of the other houses. Holding the handrail, she all but pulled her way up to the stoop. Could she get any bigger? Her midwife Sophia had assured her she could, and would.

After catching her breath, Phoebe knocked on the door. She waited. Thankfully, the small alcove afforded her some shelter from the wind.

When there was no answer, she rapped again. Seconds went by and still no one came. She refused to go back home without speaking to Ryan. It had taken her months to muster the courage to come in the first place. It was getting late, surely he'd be home soon.

To the right side of the door was a small wooden bench. She'd just wait for a while to see if he showed up. Bracing a hand against the wall, she eased herself down. She chuckled humorously at the picture she must make. Like a beach ball sitting on top of a flowerpot.

She needed to rest anyway. Everything fatigued her

these days. Trying to keep up with twenty grade fivers
wore her out but she loved her job. At least her students
kept her mind off the fact that she was having a baby
soon. Alone.

Phoebe never made a habit of feeling sorry for herself,
had prided herself on being strong, facing life head-on.
She'd always managed to sound encouraging and supportive when Joshua had prepared to leave on tour again and
again. When they'd married, she'd been aware of what she
was getting into. So why was the idea of having this baby
alone making her come emotionally undone?

Pulling her coat tighter and leaning her head into the
corner of the veranda, she closed her eyes. She'd just rest
a few minutes.

It was just after dark when Ryan Matthews pulled his
sporty compact car into his usual parking spot along the
street. It had been drizzling during his entire drive from
the hospital. Street lamps lit the area. The trees cast shad-
ows along the sidewalk and even across the steps leading
to homes.

He'd had a long day that had involved more than one
baby delivery and one of those a tough one. Nothing had
seemed to go as planned. Not one but two of the babies
had been breech. Regardless, the babies had joined the
world kicking and screaming. He was grateful. All the
other difficulties seemed to disappear the second he heard
a healthy cry. He'd take welcoming a life over dealing with
death any day.

Stepping out of the car, he reached behind the driver's
seat and grabbed his duffel bag stuffed with his street
clothes. Too exhausted to change, he still wore his hospital uniform. As much as he loved his job, thirty-six
hours straight was plenty. He was looking forward to a

hot shower, bed and the next day off. It would be his first chance in over two weeks to spend time in his workshop. A half-finished chair, along with a table he'd promised to repair for a friend, waited. He wanted to think of nothing and just enjoy the process of creating something with his hands.

Duffel in hand, a wad of dirty uniforms under his arm, he climbed the steps. The light remained on over his door as he'd left it. Halfway up the steps he halted. There was an obviously pregnant woman asleep on his porch. He saw pregnant women regularly in his job as a midwife at Melbourne Victoria Hospital's maternity unit. Today more than he'd wanted to. As if he didn't have a full load at the hospital, they were now showing up on his doorstep.

By the blue tint of the woman's lips and the way she was huddled into a ball, she'd been there for some time. Why was she out in the cold? She should be taking better care of herself, especially at this stage in her pregnancy. Her arms rested on her protruding middle. She wore a fashionable knit cap that covered the top of her head. Strawberry-blond hair twisted around her face and across her shoulders. With the rain and the temperature dropping, she must be uncomfortable.

Taking a resigned breath, Ryan moved farther up the steps. As he reached the top the mysterious woman roused and her eyes popped open. They were large and a dark sable brown with flecks of gold. He'd never seen more mesmerizing or sad ones in his life.

His first instinct was to protect her. He faltered. That wasn't a feeling he experienced often. He made it his practice not to become involved with anyone. Not to care too deeply. He tamped the feeling down. Being tired was all there was to it. "Can I help you?"

The woman slowly straightened. She tugged the not-

heavy-enough-for-the-weather coat closer as she stared
at him.

When she didn't answer right away he asked in a weary
voice, "Do you need help?"

"Are you Ryan Matthews?" Her soft Aussie accent carried in the evening air.

His eyes widened and he stepped back half a pace, stopping before tumbling. Did he know her? She was such a
tiny thing she couldn't be more than a girl. Something
about her looked familiar. Could he have seen her in the
waiting room sometime?

Ryan glanced at her middle again. He'd always made it
a practice to use birth control. Plus, this female was far too
young for him. She must be seeking medical help.

"Yes."

"I'm Phoebe Taylor."

Was that supposed to mean something to him? He
squinted, studying her face in the dim light. "Have we
met before?"

"I should go." She reached out to touch the wall as if
she planned to use it as support in order to stand. When
she did, a slip of paper fluttered to the stoop.

Ryan picked it up. In blue pen was written his name,
address and phone number. Had she been given it at the
clinic?

He glared at her. "Where did you get this?"

"I think I had better go." She made a movement toward
the steps. "I'm sorry. I shouldn't have come. I'll go."

"I'm afraid I don't understand."

"I don't know for sure what I wanted. I need to go." Her
words came out high-pitched and shaky.

He put out a hand as if she were a skittish animal he
was trying to reassure. "Think of the baby." That must be
what this was all about.

Her eyes widened, taking on a hysterical look. She jerked away from him. "I've done nothing but think of this baby. I have to go. I'm sorry I shouldn't have come." She sniffled. "I don't know..." another louder sniffle "...what I was thinking. You don't know me." Her head went into her hands and she started to cry in earnest. "I'll go. This is..." she sucked in air "...too embarrassing. You must think I'm mad."

He began to think she was. Who acted this way?

She struggled to stand. Ryan took her elbow and helped her.

"I've never done anything...like this before. I need to go."

Ryan could only make out a few of her garbled words through her weeping. He glanced around. If she continued to carry on like this his neighbors would be calling the law.

She shivered. What had she said her name was? Phoebe?

"You need to calm down. Being so upset isn't good for the baby. It's getting cold out and dark. Come in. Let your jacket dry." He needed to get her off the street so he could figure out what this was all about. This wasn't what he had planned for his evening.

"No, I've already embarrassed myself enough. I think I'd better go."

Thankfully the crying had stopped but it had left her eyes large and luminous.

She looked up at him with those eyes laced with something close to pain, and said in a low voice, "You knew my husband."

"Your husband?"

"Joshua Taylor."

Ryan cringed. Air quit moving to his lungs. JT was part of his past. The piece of his life he had put behind him. Ryan hadn't heard JT's name in seven months. Not since he'd had word that he had been killed when his convoy had been bombed.

Why was his wife here? Ryan didn't want to think of the war, or JT. He'd moved on.

They had been buddies while they'd been in Iraq. Ryan had been devastated when he'd heard JT had been killed. He'd been one more in a long list of men Ryan had cared about, shared his life with, had considered family. Now that was gone, all gone. He wasn't going to let himself feel that pain ever again. When he'd left the service he'd promised himself never to let anyone matter that much. He wasn't dragging those ugly memories up for anyone's wife, not even JT's.

Ryan had known there was a wife, had even seen her picture fixed to Joshua's CHU or containerized housing unit room. That had been over five years ago, before he'd left the service. This was his friend's widow?

He studied her. Yes, she did bear a resemblance to the young, bright-faced girl in the pictures. Except that spark of life that had fascinated him back then had left her eyes.

"You need to come in and get warm, then I'll see you get home." He used his midwife-telling-the-mother-to-push voice.

She made a couple of soft sniffling sounds but said no more.

Ryan unlocked the door. Pushing it back, he offered her space to enter before him. She accepted the invitation. She stopped in the middle of the room as if unsure what to do next. He turned on the light and dropped his bag and dirty clothes in the usual spot on top of all the other dirty clothes lying next to the door.

For the first time, he noted what sparse living conditions he maintained. He had a sofa, a chair, a TV that sat on a wooden crate and was rarely turned on. Not a single picture hung on the walls. He didn't care about any of that. It wasn't important. All he was interested in was bringing babies safely into the world and the saws in his workshop.

"Have a seat. I'll get you some tea," he said in a gruff voice.

Bracing on the arm of the sofa, she lowered herself to the cushion. She pulled the knit cap from her head and her hair fell around her shoulders.

Ryan watched, stunned by the sight. The urge to touch those glowing tresses caught him by surprise. His fingers tingled to test the texture, to see if it was as soft and silky as it looked.

Her gaze lifted, meeting his. Her cheekbones were high and a touch of pink from the cold made the fairness of her skin more noticeable. Her chin trembled. The sudden fear that she might start crying again went through him. He cleared his throat. "I'll get you that tea."

Phoebe watched as the rather stoic American man walked out of the room. Why had he looked at her that way? Where was all that compassion and caring that Joshua had written about in his letter? Ryan obviously wanted her gone as soon as possible. He wasn't at all what she'd expected. Nothing like Joshua had described him. She shivered, the cold and damp seeping through her jacket. What had she been thinking? This wasn't the warm and welcoming guy that Joshua had said he would be. He hadn't even reacted to her mentioning Joshua.

He was tall, extremely tall. He ducked slightly to go through the doorway. Joshua had been five feet eleven. Ryan Matthews was far taller, with shoulders that went with that height.

Though he was an attractive man with high cheekbones and a straight nose, his eyes held a melancholy gaze. As if he'd seen things and had had to do things he never wanted to remember, much less talk about.

A few minutes later Ryan handed her a mug with a tea-bag string hanging over the side. He hadn't even bothered to ask her what she wanted to drink. Did he treat everybody he met with such disinterest?

"I'm a coffee drinker myself. An associate left the tea here or I wouldn't have had it."

She bet it was a female friend. He struck her as the type of man who had women around him all the time. "You are an American."

"Yes."

"Joshua never said that you weren't Australian."

He took a seat in the lone chair in the room. "I guess he didn't notice after a while."

She looked around. Whatever women he brought here didn't stay around long. His place showed nothing of the feminine touch. In fact, it was only just a step above un-livable. If she had to guess, there was nothing but a bed and a carton for a table in the bedroom.

Phoebe watched him drink the coffee, the smell of which wafted her way as she took a sip of her tea.

Quiet minutes later he asked, "How long were you on my doorstep?"

"I don't know. I left home around four."

"It's after seven now." His tone was incredulous. "You've been waiting that long?"

"I fell asleep."

The tension left his face. "That's pretty easy to do in your condition."

"I can't seem to make it without a nap after teaching all day."

"Teaching?"

"I teach at Fillmore Primary School. Grade Five."

He seemed as if he was trying to remember something. "That's right. JT said you were going to school to be a teacher."

At the mention of Joshua they both looked away.

He spoke more to his coffee cup than to her. "I was sorry to hear about Joshua."

"Me, too." He and Joshua supposed to have been best buddies and that was all he had to say. This guy was so distant he acted as if he'd barely known Joshua. She wouldn't be getting any help or friendship from him.

He looked at her then as if he was unsure about what he might have heard. "Is there something you need from me?"

Phoebe flinched at his directness. Not anymore. She needed to look elsewhere. She wasn't sure what she'd expected from him but this wasn't it. Joshua's letter had assured her that Ryan Matthews would do anything to help her but this man's attitude indicated he wasn't interested in getting involved.

"To tell you the truth, I'm not sure. You were a friend of Joshua's and I just thought..."

"And what did you think? Do you need money?"

"Mr. Matthews, I don't need your money. I have a good job and Joshua's widow and orphans' pension."

"Then I can't imagine what I can do for you, unless you need someone to deliver your baby?"

"Why would I come to you for that?"

"Because I'm a midwife."

"I thought he said you were a medic."

"I was in the army but now I work as a midwife. I still don't understand why you're here. If you need someone to deliver your baby you need to come to the Prenatal Clinic during office hours."

"I already have one. Sophia Toulson."

His brows drew together. "She's leaving soon. Did she send you here?"

She lowered her head.

Had he heard her say, "I just needed a friend, I guess." *A friend?*

He couldn't believe that statement. What kind of person showed up at a stranger's house, asking them to be their friend? Surely she had family and friends in town. Why would she come looking for him now? After all this time. She said she didn't need money so what did she want from him?

"Where's the father of the baby?"

Phoebe sat straighter and looked him directly in the eyes. "Joshua is the father of the baby."

"When…?"

"When he was last home on leave. I wrote to him about the baby but he was…" she swallowed hard "…gone by then." She placed the cup in the crack between the cushions, unable to bend down far enough to put it on the floor. Pushing herself to a standing position, she said, "I think I'd better go."

He glanced out the window. The rain had picked up and the wind was blowing stronger. He huffed as he unfolded from the chair. "I'll drive you home."

"That's not necessary. I can catch the tram."

"Yeah, but you'll get wet getting there and from it to your house. I'll drive you. Where's home?"

Despite his tough exterior, she liked his voice. It was slow, deep and rich. Maybe a Texan or Georgian drawl. "I live in Box Hill."

"That's out toward Ferntree Gully, isn't it?"

"Yes."

"Okay. Let's go."

He sounded resigned to driving her instead of being

helpful. This Ryan Matthews didn't seem to care one way or another. Had Joshua gotten him wrong or had Ryan changed?

"If you insist."

"I do." He was already heading toward the door.

"Then thank you."

This trip to see Ryan had been a mistake on a number of levels. But she had learned one thing. She was definitely alone in the world.

Forty-five minutes later, Ryan pulled onto a tree-lined street with California bungalow-style houses. The lights glowing in the homes screamed warmth, caring and permanency, all the things that he didn't have in his life, didn't want or deserve.

Since they'd left his place Phoebe hadn't tried to make conversation. She'd only spoken when giving him directions. He was no closer than he'd been earlier to knowing what she wanted.

"Next left," she said in a monotone.

He turned there she indicated.

"Last house on the right. The one with the veranda light on."

Ryan pulled his car to the curb. He looked at her house. It appeared well cared-for. A rosebush grew abundantly in the front yard. An archway indicated the main door. The only light shining was the one over it.

"Is anyone expecting you?"

"No."

"You live by yourself?"

"Yes. Did you think I lived with my parents?"

"I just thought since Joshua was gone and you were having a baby, someone would be nearby. Especially as close as you're obviously getting to the due date."

"No, there's no one. My parents were killed in an auto accident the year before I married. My only brother had moved to England two years before that. We were never really close. There is a pretty large age difference between us." The words were matter-of-fact but she sounded lost.

"Surely someone from Joshua's family is planning to help out?"

"No."

"Really? Why not?"

"If you must know, they didn't want him to marry me. They had someone else picked out. Now that he's gone, they want nothing more to do with me."

"That must have been hard to hear."

"Yeah. It hurt." Her tone said she still was having a hard time dealing with that knowledge. He couldn't imagine someone not wanting to have anything to do with their grandchild.

"Not even the baby?"

She placed her hand on her belly. "Not even the baby. They told me it would be too hard to look at him or her and know Joshua wasn't here."

"You've got to be kidding!" Ryan's hands tightened on the steering wheel.

"No. That isn't something that I would kid about."

"I'm sorry."

"So am I. But I just think of it as their loss. If that's the way they feel, then it wouldn't ever be healthy for the baby to be around them. We'll be better off without them."

Ryan looked at the house one more time. By its appearance, the baby would be well cared for and loved. "I'll see you to the door."

"That's not necessary." She opened the car door.

He climbed out and hurried around the automobile. She'd started to her feet. He held out a hand. After a second she accepted it. His larger one swallowed her smaller one. Hers was soft and smooth, very feminine. So very different from his. A few seconds later she seemed to gather strength. She removed her hand from his and stood taller.

"Come on, I'll see you to the door." Even to his own ears it sounded as if he was ready to get rid of her.

"I'll be fine. You've already helped enough by driving me home." She started up the walk lined with flowers and stopped, then looked back at him. "I'm sorry to have bothered you."

Ryan waited to see if she would turn around again, but she didn't. When the light went out on the porch he pulled away from the curb.

Phoebe closed the door behind her with a soft click. Through the small window she saw the lights of Ryan's car as he drove off.

What had she expected? That he would immediately say, "I'll take care of you, I'll be there for you"? She moved through the house without turning any lights on. She knew where every piece of furniture and every lamp was located. With the exception of the few times that Joshua had been home during their marriage, no one had lived with her. Nothing was ever moved unless she did it.

Their marriage had consisted mostly of them living apart. They had met when she was eighteen and fresh out of school. The tall, dark man dressed in a uniform had taken her breath away. Joshua had made it clear what it would be like, being married to a serviceman, and she had been willing to take on that life. She was strong and could deal with it.

It hurt terribly that his parents had said they wouldn't be around to help her with the baby. He or she needed grandparents in their life. With her parents gone they were the only ones. She'd been devastated when she'd received the letter stating they would not be coming around. They had sent some money. Phoebe had thought about returning it but had decided to start a fund at the bank for the baby instead. Not knowing their grandchild would be their loss.

For her the baby was about having a small part of Joshua still in her life. Her hope was that Joshua's parents might change their minds. Either way, right now she was on her own. Not a feeling she enjoyed. In a moment of weakness she'd gone to Ryan's house, but she didn't plan to let him know how bone deep the hurt was that Joshua's parents wanted nothing to do with her. How lonely she was for someone who'd known and loved Joshua.

She turned on the lamp beside her bed and glanced at the picture of her and Joshua smiling. They'd been married eight years but had spent maybe a year together in total. That had been a week or two here, or a month there. They had always laughed that their marriage was like being on vacation instead of the day in, day out experience of living together. Even their jobs had been vastly different. Joshua had found his place in the service more than with her. She'd found contentment in teaching. It had given her the normalcy and stability that being married to a husband who popped in and out hadn't.

Each time Joshua had come home it had been like the first heart-pounding, whirlwind and all-consuming first love that had soon died out and become the regular thud of everyday life. They'd had to relearn each other and getting in the groove had seemed harder to achieve. As they'd grown older they'd both seemed to pull away. She'd had her set life and routine and Joshua had invaded it when he'd returned.

Removing her clothes, she laid them over a chair and pulled her pj's out of the chest of drawers. She groaned.

The large T-shirt reminded her of a tent that she and Joshua had camped in just after they'd married. The shirt was huge and still she almost filled it.

Pulling it over her head, she rubbed her belly. The baby had been a complete surprise. She'd given up on ever having children. She and Joshua had decided not to have them since he hadn't been home often enough. She wasn't sure whether or not she'd cared when they'd married or if she'd believed he would leave the army and come home to stay. The idea of having a family had been pushed far into the future. It had become easier just not to consider it. So when she'd come up pregnant it had been a shock.

Her fingers went to her middle, then to her eye, pushing the moisture away. She'd grown up with the dream of having a family one day. Now she was starting a family but with half of it missing.

She pulled the covers back on the bed and climbed in between the cool sheets. Bringing the blanket up around her, she turned on her side, stuffing an extra pillow between the mattress and her tummy. The baby kicked. She laid her hand over the area, feeling the tiny heel that pushed against her side.

The last time Joshua had been home they'd even talked of separating. They'd spent so little time together she'd felt like she hadn't even known her husband anymore. She not only carried Joshua's baby but the guilt that he'd died believing she no longer cared. Friendship had been there but not the intense love that she should have had for a husband.

CHAPTER TWO

THE NEXT MORNING Ryan flipped on the light switch that lit the stairs that led down to his workshop. He'd picked out this town house because of this particular space. Because it was underground it helped block the noise of the saws from the neighbors. The area was also close to the hospital, which made it nice when he had to be there quickly.

Going down the stairs, he scanned the area. A band saw filled one corner, while stationed in the center of the room was a table saw. The area Ryan was most interested in right now was the workbench against the far wall. There lay the half-made chair that he had every intention of finishing today. He would still have to spend another few days staining it.

Picking up a square piece of sandpaper, he began running it up and down one of the curved rockers. He'd made a couple of rockers when the nursery of the hospital had needed new ones. A number of the nurses had been so impressed they'd wanted one of their own. Since then he'd been busy filling orders in his spare time.

Outside the moments when a baby was born and offered its first spirited view of the new world with a shout, being in his shop was the place he was the most happy. Far better than his life in the military.

When he could stand it no longer, he'd resigned his commission. He'd had enough of torn bodies. He ran his hand along the expanse of the wood. It was level but not quite smooth enough. Now he was doing something he loved. But thoughts of Phoebe kept intruding.

He couldn't believe that had been Joshua's wife at his home the night before. Ryan had been living in Melbourne for five years. Joshua had always let him know when he was home, but in all that time he'd never met his wife. It had seemed like his friend's visits had come at the busiest times, and even though the two of them had managed to have a drink together, Ryan had never seen her. Now all of a sudden she had turned up on his doorstep.

Even after he'd gotten her calmed down he hadn't been sure what she'd wanted. It didn't matter. Still, he owed Joshua. He should check on her. But first he'd see what Sophia could tell him.

The next morning, at the clinic, Ryan flipped through his schedule for the day. He had a number of patients to see but none had babies due any time soon. Maybe he would get a few days' reprieve before things got wild again.

"You look deep in thought."

He recognized Sophia's voice and looked up. "Not that deep. You're just the person I wanted to talk to."

The slim woman took one of the functional office chairs in front of his desk. "What can I do for you?"

"I was just wondering what you know about Phoebe Taylor."

"Trying to steal my patients now?" Her eyes twinkled as she asked.

Ryan gave her a dubious look.

She grinned. "She's due in about five weeks. What's happened?"

"She was waiting for me when I got home yesterday. At first I thought she'd gotten my name and address from you. That you were sending her to me because you would be on your honeymoon when it was time to deliver."

Sophia shook her dark-haired head. "Oh, no, it wasn't me. But I remember she mentioned you at one of her appointments and said she had your address."

"I thought maybe she was looking for a midwife. She later told me she was the wife of an army buddy of mine."

"Yes, she told me that you were good friends with her husband. Did she seem okay?"

"Not really. It was all rather confusing and she was quite emotional. I let her get warm, gave her something to drink and took her home."

"She's usually steady as a rock. I'll find out what's going on at her next appointment."

"Thanks, Sophia. I owe her husband."

"I understand. You are coming to my wedding, aren't you?"

Sophia was marrying Aiden Harrison in a few weeks and she wanted everyone there for the event. Ryan wasn't into weddings. He'd never been so close to someone he'd felt like marrying them. After his years in the military he was well aware of how short life could be. Too young to really understand that kind of love when he'd entered the army, he'd soon realized he didn't want to put someone through what Phoebe Taylor had been experiencing.

He didn't understand that type of love. Knew how fleeting it could be. His parents sure hadn't known how to show love. His foster-parents had been poor examples of that also. They had taken care of his physical needs but he'd always been aware that they hadn't really cared about him. The army had given him purpose that had filled that void, for a while. That had lasted for years until the hundreds of faces of death had become heavier with every day. He well understood that losses lasted a lifetime. Even delivering babies and seeing the happiness on families' faces didn't change that. Those men he'd served with were gone. Yet, like JT, they were always with him.

He smiled at Sophia. "I plan to be there. I'll even dust off my suit for the occasion."

"That's great. See you later."

Ryan had seen his last patient for the day and was headed out the glass doors of the Prenatal Clinic in the hospital. A woman was coming in. He stopped to hold the door for her, then glanced up. It was Phoebe Taylor.

"Ah, hey."

"Hello." Her gaze flicked up at him and then away.

Phoebe must have been coming here for months. How many times had he passed her without having any idea who she was? She looked far less disheveled than she had two days ago. Her hair lay along her shoulders. Dressed in a brown, tan and blue dotted top over brown slacks and low-heeled shoes, she looked professional, classy and fragile.

"Are you looking for me?" Ryan asked.

"I'm here for my appointment with Sophia."

Another mother-to-be came up behind Phoebe. She moved back and out of the way, allowing the woman to go past her. Ryan held the door wide, moving out into the hall. He said to Phoebe, "May I speak to you for a minute?"

A terrified look flicked in her eyes before she gave him a resigned nod. He had the impression that if she could forget they had already met, she'd gladly do so.

Before he could say anything she started, "About the other evening. I'm sorry. I shouldn't have put you on the spot. I had no right to do that."

Here she was the one apologizing and he was the one who should be. "Not a problem. I should have visited you after Joshua died."

Her look was earnest. "That's all right. I understand. Well, I have to get to my appointment."

Apparently whatever she'd needed had been resolved. "It was nice to meet you, Phoebe."

"You, too." She walked by him, opened the door and went through it. With a soft swish it closed behind her.

Why did he feel as if he needed to say or do more?

Ryan made it as far as his car before curiosity and a nagging guilt caused him to return to the clinic. He waited until Phoebe was finished with her appointment. Phoebe might not agree to him taking her to dinner, but he was going to try. He needed to know why she'd come to see him and even more if there was some way he could help her.

Now that she had contacted him he felt like he owed Joshua that.

On the way to his office he passed a nurse and asked that she let him know when Mrs. Taylor was finished.

Thirty minutes later the nurse popped her head in the door and said Phoebe was on her way out.

Ryan hurried to the waiting room and spotted her as she reached the door. When he called her name she stopped and turned. Her eyes widened in astonishment, then filled with wariness.

"I thought you had left." Phoebe sounded as if she had hoped not to see him again. After his behavior the other night he shouldn't be surprised.

"I came back. I wanted to ask you something."

She raised her brows.

Phoebe wasn't opening the door wide for him. She wouldn't be making this easy.

Thankfully this late in the day the waiting room was empty. "I wondered if I could buy you dinner?"

Phoebe turned her head slightly, as if both studying and judging him. He must have really put her off the other evening. He prided himself on his rapport with people, especially pregnant women and their families. He had let this one down. The guilt he'd felt doubled in size.

"Please. I'd like to make up for how I acted the other night."

"You don't owe me any apologies. I'm the one who showed up on your doorstep unannounced."

"Why don't we both stop taking blame and agree to start again?"

Her eyes became less unsure. "I guess we could do that."

"Then why don't we start by having a burger together?"

"Okay." She agreed with less enthusiasm than he would have liked.

"I know a place just down the street that serves good food. Andrew's Burgers."

"I've heard of it but never been there."

"Great. Do you mind walking?"

"No, I haven't had my exercise today."

Ryan looked at her. If it hadn't been for the baby, she would have been a slim woman. With her coloring she was an eye-catcher, pregnant or not. Her soft, lilting voice was what really caught his attention.

"If you'll wait I'd like to lock up my office."

She nodded. When he returned she was sitting in one of the reclining chairs in the waiting room with her hands resting on the baby.

"I'm ready."

Phoebe looked at him. She pushed against the chair arm to support herself as she stood. "I think this baby is going to be a giant."

"Every mother-to-be that I see thinks that about this time."

As they made their way down the hall to the elevators, Ryan asked, "So how're you and the baby doing?"

A soft smile came to her lips. "Sophia says we're both doing great. I'll have to start coming to clinic every week soon. I just hate that I'm losing her as my midwife. I've become very attached."

"You are getting close."

"I am."

There was depression in her tone that he didn't understand. He knew little about her, but she struck him as someone who would be ecstatic about holding a new life in her hands and caring for someone. Yet he sensed a need in her that he couldn't put a finger on.

They went down the six floors to the lobby of the art deco building and out into the sunlight. The restaurant was a few blocks from the hospital.

"Let's cross the street. I know a shortcut through the park."

She followed him without question. A few minutes later they exited the park and were once again walking along the sidewalk. A couple of times they had to work themselves around other people walking briskly in the opposite direction. Ryan matched his stride to her shorter one and ran interference when someone looked as if they might bump into her.

"I can walk without help, you know."

He glanced at her. She was small but she gave off an air of confidence. It was in complete contrast to her actions that night at his house. Something was going on with her. "I know, but I wouldn't want you to accidentally fall and Sophia would have my head for it."

"I think they gave up chopping off heads in Australia a long time ago," she said in a dry tone.

"Still, I'm kind of scared of Sophia. I don't know if I could face her if I let you get hurt."

That got a smile out of her. "Here we are," Ryan said as he pulled the glass door of the restaurant open and allowed Phoebe to enter ahead of him.

She wasn't sure sharing a meal with Ryan was such a good idea. He'd asked nicely enough and she hadn't eaten out in so long she hadn't had the heart to say no. She suspected either his curiosity or some kind of obligation he felt toward Joshua had made him ask. No way had he changed overnight into being the emotional support she'd naively hoped he might be. A nice meal shared with someone was all she expected to get out of the next hour.

When Ryan was asked if they wanted a booth or table he glanced at her middle and grinned. He had a wide smile and nice even teeth. "I guess we'd better go for a table."

They were directed to one. The restaurant was decorated in a 1950s diner style, all chrome, red-covered chairs and white tile on the floor. Lighting hung over each booth and table. It was still early for the dinner crowd so it wasn't noisy. Phoebe wasn't sure if she considered that good or bad.

She took a seat. Ryan sat in the chair across the table from her.

"So I need to order a hamburger, I'm thinking." Phoebe took the menu out of the metal rack on the table.

"They have good ones. But there are also other things just as good."

The waitress arrived and took their drink order. Phoebe opened a menu but Ryan didn't. When the waitress returned with their glasses, she asked what they would like to order. Phoebe decided on the burger without onions and Ryan ordered his with everything.

The waitress left and Ryan asked, "No onions?"

"They don't agree with me."

"That's typical. I know a mother who said she couldn't cook bacon the entire first three months of her pregnancy."

"Smells used to bother me but that has become better."

Ryan crossed his arms and leaned on the table. "So do you know if it's a boy or a girl?"

"I don't know."

"Really?"

Phoebe almost laughed at his look of shock. "Don't want to know. I like surprises."

"That's pretty amazing in this day and age where everyone is wanting to know the sex and you don't. I wouldn't want to know, either. One of my favorite moments during a delivery is the look on the parents' faces when they discover the sex."

Phoebe got the impression that she'd gone up a notch in his estimation.

"You know, I don't know any other male midwife."

"There are only a few of us around. More in Australia than in the US."

"So why did you become one?"

"I wanted to do something that made me smile." He picked up his drink. "I was tired of watching people's lives being destroyed or lost when I was in the service. I wanted to do something that involved medicine but had a happy ending. What's better than bringing a life into the world?"

He was right. What was better than that?

The waitress brought their meals. They didn't speak for a while.

It fascinated Phoebe that they were virtual strangers but seem to be content sharing a meal together. This evening stood in sharp contrast to when they had met. Being around this Ryan put her at ease for some reason. After their first meeting she would have sworn that couldn't be possible.

She ate half her burger and chips before pushing them aside.

"You're eating for two, you know," Ryan said with a raised brow.

"The problem is that when this baby comes I don't want to look like I ate for three." She wiped her mouth with her napkin and placed it on the table.

"How's your weight gain?"

Phoebe leaned back in her chair. "That's certainly a personal question."

"I'm a midwife. I ask that question all the time."

"Yes, but you aren't my midwife."

He pushed his empty plate away. "I'll concede that. But I'm only asking out of concern."

"If it'll make you feel better my weight is just fine. I'm within the guidelines."

"Good. You look like you're taking care of yourself."

"I try to eat right and get some exercise every day." She looked pointedly at her plate. "Not that this burger was on the healthy chart."

He shrugged. "No, it probably isn't, but every once in a while it's okay."

They lapsed into silence again as the waitress refilled their glasses and took away their plates.

A few minutes later Phoebe said, "I know this might be tough but I was wondering if you might be willing to tell me some stories about Joshua. Something I could tell the baby. Something about him outside of just what I remember."

Ryan's lips tightened and he didn't meet her gaze.

"You don't have to if you don't want to."

After a moment he met her look. "What would you like to know?"

"I guess anything. I feel like you knew him better than me. You spent far more time together than we did. I was wondering how you met?"

Ryan's gray eyes took on a faraway look. "The Aussie and the US troops didn't always hit it off, but JT and I did. We didn't usually work together, but I was asked to go out on patrol with his platoon. Their medic was on leave and the replacement hadn't made it in yet. My commander agreed. It was supposed to be an easy in and out of a village under our control. All went well until we were headed out, then all hell broke loose. The Iraqis had us pinned down and we couldn't expect help until the next morning.

"A couple of JT's men were seriously injured. While we spent long hours hunkered down together we got to know each other pretty well. He told me about you, and I told him about growing up in Texas.

"When I told him that I was tired of having to patch up people that another human had destroyed, he encouraged me to do something different. Even suggested I move to Australia for a new start. He joked that if he ever left the army he'd use his skills to become a police officer."

Phoebe had never heard Joshua say anything about wanting to do that. He had told Ryan things he either hadn't wanted to share with her or couldn't. It made her sad and angry at the same time. She and Joshua had just not been as close as a married couple should have been.

"After that kind of night you know each other pretty well. We started getting together for drinks whenever we had leave at the same time." His eyes didn't meet hers. "JT found out that I didn't get much mail so he shared his letters with me."

For seconds Phoebe panicked, trying to remember what

she had said in her letters. Misery overtook the panic. During the last few years of their marriage her letters had been less about them personally and more about what was happening with her students, how Melbourne was changing, what she was doing at the house. It had been as if she'd been writing to a friend instead of her husband.

"I always looked forward to your letters. They were full of news and I liked to hear about your class. The letters your students wrote were the best. There was something about them that helped make all the ugliness disappear for a while."

"I'm glad they helped. My students liked writing them. Thank you for telling me about Joshua. I guess I just wanted to talk about him. This is his baby and he isn't around. Just hearing about him makes him seem a little closer. But it's time for me to go." She needed to think about what Ryan had told her. The fact that someone had known her husband better than she had made her feel heartsick.

Ryan stood and Phoebe did also. She led the way to the door. Outside Ryan turned in the direction of the hospital.

"I need to go this way to catch the tram. Thanks for dinner." She turned toward the left.

"I'll give you a ride home," Ryan said.

"I don't want you to drive all the way out to my house."

"I don't mind and you don't need to be so late getting home. Don't you own a car?"

"No, I can take the tram to almost anything I need."

"But you're making two-hour round trips to see Sophia. In America we can't live without a car. There isn't public transportation everywhere."

"Yes, but that's only once a month and it's worth it to have Sophia as my midwife. I wish she was going to be there for the delivery."

"I realize that I live in Australia, but I can't get used to prenatal care being called antenatal. It took me forever to tell the mothers I saw that they needed to come to the antenatal clinic. I just think prenatal."

"The ideas and ways we grow up with are hard to change."

"Yes, once an idea gets fixed in my head it's hard to make me budge. And with that thought, not to make you feel bad, but you look like you could use some rest. I'm driving you home."

"I am tired and I know now that you won't change your mind. I'm going to accept the ride."

"Good."

Ryan escorted Phoebe back to the hospital and to his car. The sidewalk wasn't near as busy as it had been earlier. It had been a long time since he'd done something as simple as stroll through a park with a woman. He couldn't remember ever doing so with one who was expecting. People smiled and greeted Phoebe. She returned them. A number of times they turned to him and offered their congratulations. The first time he began to explain but soon realized it was a waste of time. Instead, he nodded noncommittally.

"I'm sorry," Phoebe said after the first incident.

"Not your fault. You can't help what they think."

He had hardly pulled out of the parking area before Phoebe had closed her eyes. She was tired.

Ryan got a number of reactions when he told someone he was a midwife. He'd gotten used to it. But the one thing he couldn't get used to was not being able to understand all the nuances of the female body when a baby was growing inside it. The sudden ability to go to sleep anywhere and in any position was one of those. It must be like being in the army. He had learned to sleep anywhere at any time.

* * *

Phoebe blinked with the small jolt of the car stopping. She'd fallen asleep again. It was getting embarrassing.

"I'm sorry. I didn't mean to go to sleep."

"Not a problem. You're not the first woman I've put to sleep."

Phoebe gave him a questioning look. She bet she wasn't. What had her thinking of Ryan in that suggestive way?

"I'm the one sorry this time. I didn't mean it like that."

"Like what?" She gave him her best innocent look.

"You know, like…"

Phoebe enjoyed his flustered expression and the pink-ness that began to work its way up his neck.

She rested her hands on each side of her belly. "I'm well aware of the facts of life and how a man can satisfy a woman."

He grinned. "You're laughing at me now."

Phoebe chuckled. "I guess I am." She opened her car door. "Thanks for the burger and the ride. Also thanks for telling me about Joshua. You have no idea how much it means to me."

"Hey, wait a minute."

Before she could get completely out of the car Ryan had come round and was standing on the path, reaching to help her. His hand went to her elbow and he supported her as she stood. He pushed the door closed behind her and it made a thud.

"Listen, if there's anything that I can do for you…"

He sounded sincere. "I appreciate it… Uh, there is one thing I could use some help with."

"What's that?"

His voice held an eager tone as if he was looking for a chance to atone for his earlier behavior. She hated to ask him but couldn't think of another way to get it done before the baby came. "I had a bed for the baby delivered but it needs to be put together. I would pay you."

Ryan looked as if she had slapped him. "You will not. How about I come by Saturday afternoon? If I have to work I'll call and let you know, otherwise I'll be here on Saturday."

"Thank you, that would be wonderful." And she meant it. She'd spent more than one night worrying over how she was going to get that baby bed assembled.

"Not a problem. Do you have tools or do I need to bring mine?"

"You might want to bring yours. I have a few but only necessities like a hammer and screwdriver."

"Then it's a plan. Why don't you give me your number?" Ryan took out his cellphone and punched in the numbers she told him.

"I'll be here after lunch on Saturday, unless you hear differently from me."

"Thank you."

"No worries. Furniture I can do."

Something about Ryan made her believe that he had many talents if he was just willing to show them.

"Come on. I'll walk you to your door."

Phoebe didn't argue this time.

"See you Saturday." With that he turned and left her to enter her home.

She was putting her key in the lock when she noticed the curtain of her neighbor's house flutter. Mrs. Rosenheim had been watching. She would no doubt be over the next afternoon to get all the particulars about who Ryan was and how Phoebe knew him.

Ryan was as good as his word. He was there on Saturday just after lunchtime with a tool bag in his hand. Mrs.

Rosenheim was sitting at Phoebe's kitchen table when the knock came at the door.

"I won't stay but I am going to check this boy out before I go."

Phoebe would have argued but it wouldn't have done her any good. Despite the fact that Mrs. Rosenheim was probably older than Phoebe's grandmother would be, she was a commanding presence and was only concerned for Phoebe's welfare. They had started taking care of each other two years ago when Phoebe had moved in.

Joshua had only been home once since she'd been living there. He'd not been impressed with Mrs. Rosenheim, calling her the "old busybody bird." Phoebe had learned to appreciate her concern. If nothing else, she knew someone would miss her if she didn't come home.

She opened the door for Ryan. "Come in."

"How're you doing?"

The question sounded like he was making pleasant conversation, but he was also looking at her with a trained eye. He smelled of sawdust with a hint of citrus. It made her want to step closer. Take a deeper breath.

"I'm feeling fine." She smiled and he nodded.

"Good. I told Sophia that I would check."

Mrs. Rosenheim shuffled into the room.

Ryan looked from her to Phoebe. "Ryan, this is my neighbor, Mrs. Rosenheim."

He sat his tool bag on the floor at his feet and extended a hand. "Nice to meet you."

"You're American."

"Yes, ma'am. Texan."

Mrs. Rosenheim made a noncommittal sound low in her throat. Ryan gave Phoebe a questioning look. She shrugged her shoulders.

"So you knew Mr. Taylor."

A guarded look came over Ryan's face. "Yes, JT and I served in Iraq together."

"Bad thing, leaving Phoebe here all by herself all the time. A man should want to be at home with his wife. She needs someone to watch over her. Help her."

Phoebe didn't miss the color wash out of Ryan's face.

"It was his job. The army," Phoebe said quietly.

"I know, sweetie. But a woman not only wants a man to help put a roof over her head but to be around when the times are hard." She directed the last few words at Ryan.

"Uh, Mrs. Rosenheim, I think we need to let Ryan get started on the bed. I'm sure he has other places he needs to go today." Phoebe shook her head at him when she started to say something.

"I'm next door if you need me." Mrs. Rosenheim made her way out with a last glance at Ryan.

"Formidable lady," Ryan said with a grin.

"Yes. She and Joshua didn't like each other on sight, but she's been good to me. She was with the men who came from the military department to tell me about Joshua. I don't know what I would have done without her shoulder to cry on. She's also the one who realized I was pregnant when I started being sick."

Phoebe suddenly needed to focus on something else. She shook away the memories. Ryan was the first male to have come into her home in over a year. He seemed to take up the entire space. "Anyway, let me show you where the bed is."

Ryan followed Phoebe down a hallway that had four doors leading off of it. She stopped at the next to last one and nudged the door open.

Against one wall was a large brown box that Ryan

guessed was the baby bed. That didn't surprise him. What did were the piles of books stacked around the room and the desk painted in a folk art style with a chair of the same kind sitting in one corner. The walls were painted a dark gray. Two cans of paint sat in another corner. He fully expected to see a room decorated in all the frills and with toys waiting for a baby. He'd listened to enough mothers talk about what they had done in the baby's room or were going to do to know that Phoebe was far behind in her preparations.

She placed her hand on the box. "This is the bed."

"Great. I'll get it put together."

Walking to the door, she looked back at him. "You didn't have to agree to this, but I really appreciate you doing it."

"Not a problem."

He'd been working for an hour when Phoebe returned to stand in the doorway. His back was to her but he felt her presence.

"I brought you something to drink." She moved to the desk and placed the drink on it.

Ryan stood from where he'd been tightening a screw on the back of the bed. He picked up the glass, took a long swallow of water and put it back on the desk again.

Phoebe had an odd look on her face that quickly disappeared.

Ryan said, "I guess I'm doing pretty well. I don't think I'm going to have but two screws and one thingamajig left over."

She laughed.

Had he ever heard anything more beautiful? It was almost musical. He vowed then to give her a reason to laugh often.

"My father always said that if you didn't have parts left over then you didn't put it together correctly."

"Where did you grow up?"

"In a small town about fifty miles from here."

"Is that where you met JT?"

"Yeah. We had a military base nearby. I worked at a local restaurant and Joshua and some of his mates came in for dinner one night and sat at my table."

"And, as they say, the rest was history."

"Yes, it was. I was wondering if…uh, you might like to stay for dinner? I do most of my cooking on the weekends so that I don't have to stand up any more than necessary during the week. How do grilled lamb chops with three vegetables sound?"

When had been the last time he'd eaten a home-cooked meal? Ryan couldn't remember. He grabbed what he did eat from the hospital cafeteria or from a fast-food place. The thought of sitting down to a real meal was more than he could resist. "That sounds great."

"Good. Then I'll go finish up."

She'd already moved to leave when he said, "Phoebe, I couldn't help but notice that you don't have this room set up for a baby."

Making a slow turn, she faced him. "I don't need you to make me feel ashamed. I bet you think I sank so far into feeling sorry for myself that I didn't pay attention to getting ready for the baby. I was still in shock over Joshua when I found out I was pregnant. I just couldn't bring myself to do anything for a while. Anyway, it has been pushed back. Maybe I'll have time to do something after the baby comes."

That wasn't going to happen. Ryan had also heard the new mothers talking about how they never got anything done any more. "I didn't mean to make you feel ashamed or defensive. I was thinking I could help. I see you have paint. How about letting me do the walls for you? I could also move this desk and chair to where you want it and the books."

"I hate to have you do all that."

"I don't mind. All you'd have to do is tell me where to put everything."

She rested her hand on her middle. A wistful look came to her eyes. "It would be nice to have the room ready for the baby. I had planned to buy some stuff for the walls."

"We could do that together." It was the least he could do for Joshua. This was practical stuff that needed doing. He had a strong back and could take care of them. He couldn't fix the fact she was having this baby all by herself but he could help with the everyday aspects of adding a new person to her household.

"That sounds like I'm asking too much."

"You're not asking. I volunteered. I'd like to do it. If JT were here, he'd be doing it. This will be my way of helping him out, like he did me."

Her eyes darkened for a second and then she nodded. "Then thanks. I'll gladly accept your help, but I'm going to warn you that you may wish you hadn't."

"How's that?"

"I have so many ideas for this room you'll get tired of me telling you what to do."

"We'll see. I'll be through here in about ten minutes, then I'd like to get started on the painting. Do you have any paint supplies?"

"They're in the shed in the backyard. When you get done, come to the kitchen and I'll take you out and show you where they are."

"Will do."

He watched her leave. Even with the bulk she carried

she had a graceful stride. What had possessed him to get this caught up in doing a baby's room? He made a practice of not getting involved.

Guilt, pure and simple.

CHAPTER THREE

PHOEBE HAD SPENT so much time without a man or his help it made her nervous to have Ryan in her house. While he'd been putting together the bed, she'd been in the kitchen, cooking. Still, she'd been aware of every clatter or thump that had come from the direction of the bedroom. On occasion she'd heard a swear word. She smiled. More than once her father had bloodied his knuckles, putting a toy together for her or her brother.

It was nice to have someone in the house. She'd considered getting a dog or cat a couple of times just so there would be a living, breathing thing around. She'd decided to wait because she didn't want the poor animal alone in the house all day.

Ryan came around the corner. "All done. Come see what you think."

She put the plate on the table and headed down the hall, well aware of him following her. He'd pushed the bed up against the wall across from the window. It looked like the perfect place for it. She ran her hand along the railing. "It looks wonderful."

"Do you have a mattress for it?"

"Yes, it's in the other bedroom."

"I'll get it."

He soon returned with a mattress covered in protective

plastic. Together they worked to remove it. Ryan lifted the bedding and dropped it into place.

"It almost makes it real," she said with a note of wonder.

"What?"

"A baby coming."

He chuckled. "I would think that large mound you're sporting out front would make it seem pretty real."

"It does but the bed is something tangible."

"What about a rocker or any other furniture?"

She shrugged. "I'll have to go buy something. I was hoping I could find some pieces at a garage sale that I could redo. I wanted to paint it bright and add animals and plants, that sort of thing."

"You mean like the other folk art you have in the living room?"

She looked at him with a brightness that said they were talking about a passion of hers. "You know about folk art?"

"Only what it is. I'm more a straight paint and stain kind of guy. Fancy painting isn't my thing. So, if you'll show me where you want these books, I'll start moving them."

"They go in my bedroom."

She went out the doorway and turned toward the end of the hall, then went through an open doorway. Ryan followed more slowly. Why did it bother him that he had just been invited into his buddy's wife's bedroom? She hadn't even thought about what she was saying. When she looked back he was standing in the doorway.

"They go on this bookshelf. If you'll bring them to me, I can shelve them."

Ryan returned with an armload of books. She'd taken a seat on the floor in front of the shelving while he'd been gone.

He stacked the books on the floor and she went to work, putting them in place.

* * *

Ryan looked down at Phoebe. He saw pregnant women day in and day out, but there was something almost angelic about the way her golden hair covered a portion of her face and her small hands put the books so neatly into their spots.

He shook his head and strode toward the door. Had he been spending too much time in his shop alone? The sawdust was filling his brain.

Fifteen minutes later he had all the books moved. Phoebe hadn't worked as fast as he so she was still shelving books. Not wanting to sit on her bed, he stood near the door until she was finished.

"Thanks for doing this. I've been dreading it for weeks. That's why it hasn't been done." She continued to work.

Ryan's cell phone rang and he pulled it out of his pocket. "I have to get this."

She nodded.

"Ryan Matthews."

"It's Julie Habershire. My waters just broke."

"Okay. No need to panic. We talked about what to do if this happens. I'll meet you at the hospital. Drive safe."

"Ryan, the baby will be all right, won't it? It's early."

"The baby should be fine. Not so early it shouldn't be perfect. See you soon."

He touched the phone to disconnect the call. Phoebe looked at him with a slight smile on her face. "Are you always that calm and reassuring with your patients?"

"I try to be."

"That's a special gift."

"I just know that people are scared when they have never experienced something before, especially if it has to do with their bodies. I learned a long time ago if I don't sound upset, then they're more likely not to get upset."

"You must be good at your job."

He slipped the phone back into his pocket. "I hope my patients think so. Anyway, I've got to go. I hate to miss out on that meal, but babies don't wait."

"I understand."

"Would it be all right if I come back tomorrow and get started on that painting? Maybe get in on leftovers?"

"That sounds fine to me. After lunch?"

"Then it's a plan. See you then." He turned to head out the door and stopped. Coming back, he offered her his hand. "If I don't help you up, I'm afraid you might still be on the floor when I return tomorrow."

"Are you implying that I'm so big that I can't get up off the floor by myself?" She accepted his hand. He helped her rise. She did it with grace.

With her on her feet, he put up his hands as if defending himself. "Hey, I work with pregnant women every day and I know better than to do that. Have to go. See you later."

Her soft laugh followed him down the hall. He went out the front door with a grin on his face, something he'd done more in the last few days than he had in years.

The next afternoon Phoebe wasn't sure what was happening but she was going to take Ryan's help while it was being offered. She'd sat around for too long with no direction. Well aware that she needed to be getting the baby's room together, she hadn't had the heart to do so. It was just too sad to work on it by herself. Having the bed assembled made her want to do more. It needed sheets, blankets. There should be other pieces of furniture, pictures on the walls.

Next weekend she'd go to some garage sales and see if she could find a few items. She smiled. For once she was feeling some excitement over the prospect of being a mother. For now she'd be satisfied with just having the room painted.

She'd hardly finished her lunch sandwich when there was a knock at the door. Ryan stood there. Dressed in cargo pants and a white T-shirt that hugged his well-defined physique, he was a fine-looking man. Mrs. Rosenheim had made a point to tell Phoebe the same thing that morning. Ryan proved that just because she was pregnant it didn't mean that she couldn't be affected by a man. It took her time to draw enough breath to say hello.

"Hey," he said in that drawl that left her feeling like she was sitting beside a cool stream on a hot summer day. "How about showing me the paint supplies? If I need anything I'll still have time to go to the store before it closes."

"Okay. It's this way." This was the first time he hadn't taken time to ask her how she was doing. He seemed focused on the project. She kind of liked the fact that he didn't see her as only a pregnant woman.

At the shed, she started to raise the roll-top door. Ryan stopped her by placing his hand over hers. His hand wasn't smooth, like she had expected for a midwife. Instead, it had a coarseness to it that spoke of a man who did more than wear gloves all the time.

"Hey, you don't need to be doing that. Let me get it."

What would have taken her great effort seemed as easy for him as lifting a blind.

"The paint stuff is stacked up over there." She pointed to the right and toward the back of the shed.

"I see it." He leaned over some gardening pots to gather the items, while at the same time presenting her with a nice view of his behind.

"Would you mind carrying a couple of things?"

It took her a second to answer. "No."

Ryan looked over his shoulder and gave her a speculative look. "Here." He handed her a few brushes and a package of rollers, then came out holding an armload of drop cloths and a paint tray. "I think this is everything I need."

They walked back to the house. Phoebe held the door open for him to enter. He was laying supplies on the floor of the baby's room by the time she entered. He took what she carried from her and added them to the pile.

Scanning the room, he said, "Is the desk staying in here?"

She looked at it. Ryan's drive to get things done was surpassing what she had thought through. "I had planned to put it in the living room. But I'll need to move a few things around so it'll have a place. Give me a minute and I'll see what I can do."

"You're not moving anything by yourself."

Phoebe faced him with her hands on her hips. "I appreciate your help. Really I do, but up until a few days ago I had no help. No one telling me what I should and shouldn't do. I am fully capable of moving a few things. If it's too large for me to do so, I'll call you."

Ryan's look met hers. He pursed his lips. She'd got his attention.

"I'm sorry. I stepped over the line, didn't I?"

She nodded. "Yes. Just a little bit."

"Then please let me know if and when you need help." He bowed slightly.

"Thank you. I will." She left the room with her head held high. She was grateful for Ryan's help but she wasn't needy, despite what her behavior at his house had implied.

In the living room, she began moving small items off an end table. Ryan's soft whistle drifted up the hall. It was nice to have someone around. Her smile grew. It would be nice to have a baby in the house.

She had reached to move the end table when behind her came, "I knew I couldn't trust you."

Jerking to a standing position, she looked around to find Ryan standing with his shoulder leaning against the wall.

"Are you checking up on me?"

"Do you need to be checked up on?"

"No." The word didn't come out as confidently as she would have liked.

He came toward her. "I think you might." He placed his hands on the table and looked at her. "Where do you want this?"

She pointed to the other end of the sofa, where she'd cleared a space by moving a floor lamp.

Ryan moved the table into the spot. He ran a finger over a painted swirl on it. "This type of artwork is interesting."

"Thank you."

He looked at her. "You did this?"

"Don't act so surprised."

"I didn't mean it like that." He looked around the room. "You did all of this?"

She stood straighter. "I did, even down to making the cushions and curtains."

"I'm impressed. I like it."

She chuckled dryly. "Now I'm surprised. Joshua hated this type of decorating. He said it made us look like we couldn't afford better. I put most of it away when he came home. Pulled it out again when he had gone again."

Ryan looked at her for a long moment. "Well, I like it. It's you."

She didn't think anyone had said anything nicer to her in a long time. "Thank you. I appreciate that."

"You're welcome. Now, if I go paint another wall, can I trust you to behave?"

Phoebe glared at him. "Yes, I'll put our supper on to warm. Will that make you happy?"

"Yes." With that, he went off whistling down the hall.

Half an hour later Phoebe went to check on Ryan's progress. He was getting ready to start on the last wall. The others were already a pale yellow. A cheerful and happy color.

The room was small but he seemed very efficient. She watched as he bent to apply paint to the roller in the tray. The muscles on his back rippled. He reached up and brought the roller down along the wall. His biceps flexed and released.

Phoebe shook her head. She had been without a man for far too long and yet was far too pregnant to consider having a relationship with one now. Still, she was alive...

Ryan turned. By the look in his eyes and the way he watched her like a cat after a bird, he knew what she'd been doing. She'd never been much of a blusher but she felt the heat rising to her face.

"So what do you think?"

Thankfully he hadn't made a comment about her staring. "It looks beautiful."

"The paint goes on great."

She stepped farther into the room. "This isn't your first time to do this."

"No. My foster-father was a painter. I started working with him when I was fourteen." He moved back to filling the roller again.

Phoebe wasn't sure she should ask but she was too curious not to. "You were a foster-child?"

"Yeah. I never knew my father and my mother was a drug addict. I was five when I was taken away from her."

Her heart hurt for that little boy. "Oh, Ryan."

He shrugged. "It was tough but it was a long time ago."

Something about his attitude told her it still affected him. His focus turned to refilling the roller again.

"So your foster-father let you go to work with him?"

"It was more like made me go. I was a difficult teen and he thought it would help keep me in line. Something about idle hands leaving room for trouble."

"And did it keep you in line?"

"Not really. I ended up going into the army the day after I graduated from high school. It made my foster-parents happy, and me, too."

"Even your foster-mother?"

He glanced back at her. "She didn't mind, either. She was so exhausted from dealing with the smaller kids and my behavior she was glad to see me go. I should be finished here in about thirty minutes. Any chance I could get something to eat?"

He was apparently through discussing his childhood. She would see to it that her child felt loved and wanted. "It'll be ready."

Ryan washed up in the hall bathroom. Splashing water on his face, he looked into the mirror. What was he doing? He could feel himself getting in too deep. He'd enjoyed the afternoon more than he would have ever imagined. He spent most of his off hours in his shop and he found he rather liked being out in the daylight, spending time with someone.

He entered the kitchen. There he found more of the same decor as the rest of the house. The table had four chairs, each painted a different color yet they seem to complement each other. The eclectic look seemed to suit Phoebe.

The table was set. When was the last time he'd eaten dinner off something other than a takeout plate?

"You may sit there." Phoebe pointed to the chair closest to him and turned back to the oven. She pulled out a casserole pan and placed it in the center of the table.

Ryan leaned in close and inhaled. "Smells wonderful."

He didn't miss her pleased smile. Phoebe would make a great mother. She found pleasure in doing for others.

She handed him a serving spoon. "Help yourself."

Ryan didn't need to be told twice. He scooped two large helpings onto his plate. Phoebe took one. When she picked up her fork, he did also.

"I see you were taught manners. Not eating until everyone else does."

"My foster-mother was a real stickler about them." He put a forkful into his mouth. It was the best thing he'd eaten in years. "This is good. Real good."

"Thank you. It's my grandmother's chicken casserole recipe."

He ate a plateful and one more before he sat back and looked at Phoebe. She had only eaten about half of what she'd put on her plate.

"You need to eat more."

She looked down at her middle. "I don't think I need to get any bigger."

"You look wonderful."

"You are feeding me compliments now."

Ryan chuckled. "That wasn't my intent. But I guess I am."

"I'll take them any way I can get them." It was nice to be noticed by a male on any level.

Ryan pushed his chair back. "I guess I'd better get the paint supplies cleaned up."

He left and she cleared the table. When done, she went to see if she could help Ryan. He was in the process of moving the desk.

"That's heavy. Let me help you."

Ryan jerked around. "You will not."

"There's no way you can move that desk by yourself."

"It's all in the technique." He gripped it by each side and began walking it from one corner to the other until he'd moved it to the doorway.

"Do you have an old towel I can use?" Ryan asked.

"Just a second." Phoebe went into the bathroom and brought back the largest one she could find. She handed it to Ryan.

"You stay out here." He moved the desk out into the hall. Taking the towel, he laid it on the floor in front of the desk. Lifting one end he asked, "Can you put the towel under the desk as far as possible?"

Glad she could be of some help she did as he requested.

He then lowered the desk. "Perfect." Gathering the corners of the towel into his hands he slowly pulled the desk over the wooden flooring and down the hall.

Phoebe stepped into the doorway, letting him pass. When he was by, she stepped out and began to push.

Coming to a stop, Ryan growled, "What're you doing?"

"Helping."

"You shouldn't—"

"Stop telling me what to do. I'm not really doing much."

A grunt of disbelief came from his direction but the desk started moving again. She continued to help maneuver it, seeing that it didn't nick the walls or hit any other furniture. When the desk quit moving, she looked over it. Her gaze met Ryan's. For a second his intense gray gaze held hers. Warmth washed over her. Could he see things she'd rather keep hidden?

"Why did you stop?"

His mouth quirked. "I don't know where you want this."

Phoebe tried to squeeze through the space between the desk and the wall.

"Hold on a sec and let me move it." Ryan grabbed the desk and shifted it so she could join him.

"I want it put over there." She pointed to the space she had cleared under a window.

"Okay." He began walking and shifting the desk until it was in place. "I'll go get the chair." He left.

The desk really needed to be centered under the window. Phoebe placed one hip against the side and pushed. It only moved a few centimeters.

"I can't leave you alone for a minute." Ryan's deep voice came from behind her.

"It needs to be centered under the window."

"Then why didn't you say something?"

He put his hands on her waist or what had once been her waist. Her breath caught. Ryan gently directed her out of the way, then quickly put space between them. "I'm sorry. I shouldn't have done that."

Ryan acted as if he'd been too personal with her. "It's okay," she said.

"Stand over there, out of the way, and tell me when I have it where you want it."

"You do know I'm just pregnant, not an invalid."

He gave her a pointed look. "I'm well aware of that but some things you shouldn't be doing, whether you're pregnant or not. This is one of them. Now, tell me where you want it."

Shifting the desk an inch, he looked at her for confirmation. It still wasn't where she wanted it. "Move it to the right just a little."

Had he muttered "Women" under his breath?

"That's it. Perfect. Thank you."

He stood and rubbed his lower back.

She stepped closer. "Did you hurt yourself?"

He grinned. "No. I was just afraid that you might ask me to move something else."

"Hey, you're the one who volunteered."

"That I did. I might ought to think about it before I do that again." He continued stretching.

"Might ought to?" She liked his accent.

"Ought to. Texas. Southern. Ought to go. Ought to get."

Phoebe laughed. "I'll have to remember that. Use it sometime."

"I think you ought not make fun of me."

"And I think you ought not be so sensitive."

They both laughed.

It was the first real laugh she'd shared with someone in a long time. It felt good.

"Well, I guess I had better go. It's getting late."

"I really appreciate all your work today. The baby's room looks wonderful. I can hardly wait to go to some garage sales and look for a chest of drawers."

"And how do you plan to get something like that home?"

"I'll worry about that if I find one. Some people are willing to deliver if I ask."

"I don't have any mothers due for a couple of weeks so why don't I go with you on Saturday?"

She like the idea but didn't want to take advantage of him. "I hate to take up another one of your weekends."

"I'd like to go. I've got a buddy who has a truck and lets me borrow it sometimes."

The truck was a plus and it would be nice to have company. "I won't turn that down."

"Great. I'll be here early Saturday to pick you up."

Ryan headed out the front door. "See you then."

"Bye." Phoebe watched from the veranda as Ryan drove away. She could get used to having him around. Seeing him on Saturday gave her something to look forward to. Of course she appreciated his help but more than that she liked him. There was an easy way about him that made life seem like fun. She was far too attracted to him already. Joshua had been right about him. Maybe she had found someone she could depend on.

Warmth lingered where Ryan had touched her. A ripple of awareness had gone up her spine. What was she thinking? Joshua had been dead for less than a year and she had a baby on the way, and here she was mooning over Ryan.

Still, Saturday couldn't come soon enough.

CHAPTER FOUR

RYAN PULLED THE truck to the curb in front of Phoebe's house just as the sun became warm.

What was he doing? The question kept rotating through his mind like a revolving door. He was too interested in Phoebe. But it was hard not to be. Those large, vulnerable eyes drew him in. Still, he admired the way she had stood up to him when he'd stepped over the line to bossing her around. The brief moments he'd touched her waist had told him that he could want more than just to help her. That wasn't going to happen. Still, he'd looked forward to spending the day with her.

Phoebe met him halfway up the walk. She wore jeans and a simple white shirt. Her eyes sparkled and for a woman of her size she walked with a peppy step. A smile covered her face. She reminded him of springtime. A fresh start.

If he'd seen any woman look more alluring, he couldn't remember when. "Mornin'."

"Hi. You ready to go? We need to get going. You know the early bird gets the worm." She carried a newspaper and passed him on the way to the truck, leaving the smell of flowers swirling in the air. He was tempted to breathe deeply. Let his mind commit it to memory.

"Uh...yeah. I'm ready." Ryan wasn't able to keep the

astonishment out of his voice. He hurried to join her. Phoebe was a woman on a mission.

She had climbed into the passenger seat and closed the door before he reached the truck. He took his place behind the wheel. "So where's the fire?"

"What?" She looked up from the open paper.

"What's the hurry?"

"I think they have just what I need at a sale and I don't want it to get bought up before we get there."

"Why didn't you call me? I could have come earlier."

"I didn't know for sure until I phoned a few minutes ago. They wouldn't promise to hold it for me so we've got to go."

Ryan grinned as he pulled away from the curb. There was nothing like a woman looking for a deal. "So where are we headed?"

"South. It's about forty minutes away." Phoebe gave him directions.

"South it is."

They traveled in silence until they were out of the city and he was driving along a two-lane highway.

"Do you have an address for the place we're going?"

Phoebe read it to him out of the paper.

"I have no idea where that is." Ryan kept his eyes on the road as a delivery truck whizzed by them.

"It's another half hour down this road, then we have to turn off."

"Have you always redone furniture?" It was ironic that she enjoyed something that was so similar to his passion.

"I've been doing it for a few years. I found I needed to fill the time when Joshua was away."

"You were lonely, weren't you?"

Phoebe didn't immediately answer. "It wasn't so hard at first. But it got more so as time went on."

Her melancholy tone implied that something more than loneliness had pushed her toward finding a hobby.

"Joshua didn't care for my painting taking up my time when he was home so I always put things away then."

He remembered what she'd said before about putting away her painted furniture because Joshua hadn't like it. That had surprised him. It didn't sound like the Joshua he'd known. Maybe he had changed since they'd known each other in the service. Ryan needed to find a safer subject. "Looks like it's going to be a pretty day."

"Yes, it does. I'm glad. I don't want anything I buy to get wet."

"I brought a covering in case we need it."

She gave him a smile of admiration.

The feeling of being a conquering hero went through him. What was happening to him? He smiled back. "Glad I could be of help."

"You're going to need to take a left turn in a couple of miles."

"You know this area well."

"This isn't the first time I've been down this way to garage sales."

They lapsed into silence until Phoebe began giving him directions regularly. They turned off the main road onto a dirt road that led up to a farmhouse with a steep metal roof and a porch circling it on three sides. A large barn with its doors opened wide stood off to the side. Two other cars were parked nearby.

"They keep the stuff they're selling in the barn," Phoebe said, with the door already open.

She hurried to the barn and Ryan joined her halfway there. They entered the dim interior. In an unused stall tables had been set up that contained all types of bottles, kitchen utensils, purses and other small items. On the other side were the larger items. Phoebe headed to them. She studied a cabinet that came up to his chest. It was much too high for her to make good use of it.

Phoebe pulled the drawers out and pushed them back in. "Would you mind tipping it forward so I can look at the back's construction?"

He had to give her credit for being knowledgeable and thorough. Ryan did as she requested.

She knocked against the wood and made a sound in her throat. Her hair curtained her face so he couldn't see what she was thinking. Running a hand over the edge and back again, she made another sound. Whether it was positive or negative he couldn't tell. It didn't matter. He was enthralled just watching her.

"You can let it down now."

Ryan lowered it to the ground.

She stepped back and studied it. "I think it'll do."

"May I make a suggestion?"

She looked at him as if she'd almost forgotten he was there. He didn't like that idea. That he could that easily disappear from her thoughts. Raising her chin and cocking her head, she gave him a questioning look. "Yes?"

"I think this chest is too tall for you. You can't even see over it."

Her eyes widened. She turned to face the chest. "You know, I can't. I hadn't thought about that."

"You need one where you can use all the space. You couldn't even find the baby powder if it got pushed to the back on this one."

"You're right. I guess now that I'm in the baby mood I'm getting in a panic to buy, afraid that time is running out. That I won't get it all done."

"We have all day. You have more places on your list, don't you?"

"Yes."

"Then let's go see what they have. Maybe we can find just the right one."

He offered his hand.

She looked at it for a moment and then placed hers in his. Her fingers were soft and cool. He closed his around them. It was as if they had chosen to face a problem together and see it overcome. Somehow this relationship had gone from less about getting a piece of furniture to having an emotional attachment. He didn't release her hand when she gave his a nudge.

Together, side by side this time, they walked back to the truck.

They visited two more places and didn't find what Phoebe was looking for.

"I don't know about you but I need something to eat," Ryan said, when he saw a sign for a café and ice-cream parlor.

"I am, too, but we might miss out on my chest."

"Then there'll be another one."

"Okay," Phoebe said, but her heart didn't sound like it was in it.

He pulled into a drive much like the one at the first house they had visited. As he came to the end of it he found a house with a restaurant attached to the back. "Come on. We'll have a sandwich, maybe some ice cream and plan our attack. Bring the paper and the map."

She didn't argue and had them in her hand when he came around the truck to meet her.

Ryan held the door for her to enter the café, then directed her to one of the small square tables in the room. Phoebe took a seat in one of the wooden chairs. He sat beside her.

She looked around the space. "I like this. It's my style."

"It does look like your type of decor."

The tables were covered in floral-print cloths. The chairs were mismatched, like hers.

A young man brought them a menu. He and Phoebe studied it for a moment.

"What're you going to have?" Ryan laid the menu on the table.

"A ham sandwich and lemonade."

"I think I'll have the same."

The waiter returned and Ryan gave him their order. When they were alone again, Ryan said, "Hand me that map, then read out the places you want to visit."

Phoebe did as he asked and he circled the places on the map. "Okay, is that it?"

"Yes."

"All right. Show me on the map your first and second, then third choice."

Phoebe pointed them out. He drew a line from one to the other to the other. "This is our game plan. We'll visit these. If we don't find what you want today, then we'll try again next weekend or whenever we can. Agreed?"

"Agreed."

The waiter brought their meals.

"Now let's eat. I'm starved."

She smiled. "You're always hungry."

Her soft chuckle made his heart catch. He was becoming hungry for more time with her.

Phoebe had always enjoyed junking but never as much as she had today. It turned out that Ryan was not only efficient but also a fun person to have around. She hadn't smiled or laughed as much as she had in the last few weeks. She'd almost forgotten what it was like to have a companion or to just appreciate male company.

Even so, there seemed to be a part of Ryan that he kept to himself. Something locked up that he wouldn't or couldn't share with the world or her.

After they had finished their lunch they climbed back into the truck and headed down the road. This time Ryan was not only driving but navigating as well. It didn't take them long to reach their first stop.

"It looks like they have a lot of furniture," Ryan said as they walked toward a shed.

"Maybe they'll have just the right thing."

A man met them at the shed door but let them wander around and look in peace.

Phoebe had been studying a chest. She turned to speak to Ryan but found he was in another area, looking at a rocker. "What have you found?"

She joined him and watched as he lovingly ran a hand down the arm of the chair. Now that she was closer she could tell it sat lopsided. There was a rocker missing.

"There was a woman who lived next to my foster-family who had a rocker like this. She and only she sat in it. She said it was the best seat in the house."

"She was nice to you."

"Yeah. Her house was where I would go if things got too hard for me at the Henrys'." She could only imagine the little boy who had needed someone on his side. "It's beautiful. I like that high-back style. Gives you someplace to lean your head."

Ryan moved another chair and a small table so that he could pull the rocker out. When he had plenty of space he tipped it over.

Phoebe admired the careful way he took in handling it. Despite his size, he was a gentle man.

"I think I can fix this. The structure is sound. All that's

missing is the one rocker. Would you like to have it for the baby's room? I can fix it. You can paint it or I'll stain it."

"You don't need to buy me anything."

He looked at her. "I wasn't buying you anything. I was getting something for the baby."

Before she could argue that it was the same thing, he walked away and had soon agreed a price with the owner.

She didn't find a chest of drawers there but they left with the rocker tied down in the back of the truck. At the next place she found nothing she liked.

As Ryan drove away she looked out the window. "I don't think we're going to find what I need today."

"Don't give up yet. We still have one more place on our list."

She studied his strong profile for a minute. He had a long jaw that spoke of determination but there were small laugh lines around his eyes. His forehead was high and a lock of hair had fallen across it as if to rebel against control. Much like the man himself.

"Do you always approach everything you do with such determination?"

"I guess old habits die hard. Being in the service will do that to you."

"Tell me what it was like being in the service. Joshua would never talk about it. He always said he didn't want me to worry."

This was the last subject Ryan wished to discuss. He wanted those days long gone and forgotten. Without his heart in it, he asked, "What do you want to know?"

"Was it as bad as the news makes it out to be?"

"Worse."

"I'm sorry."

"It's war. Few people understand. War is never pretty.

It's all death and destruction. Until you have looked into someone's eyes and watched life leave them, no one can ever grasp that."

"That happened to you?"

His glance held disbelief. "Yeah, more than once."

At her gasp he couldn't decide if he was pleased he'd shocked her or disgusted with himself for doing so. "I'm sorry. I shouldn't have said it like that."

"Yes, you should have. You have experienced horrible, unspeakable things while I've been here safe in my home." A second later she asked, "How did you deal with it?"

Ryan gripped the steering wheel and kept his eyes on the road. He wasn't sure he had or was. "I did what I had to and tried not to think about how lives were being shattered."

She laid a hand on his shoulder. Even that small gesture eased the flames of painful memories. Suddenly he wanted her to understand. "There was this one guy in my unit who had lost half his face. He cried and he kept repeating 'I'm going to scare my kids, I'm going to scare my kids.' How do you reassure someone in that kind of shape that he won't?"

As if a dam had broken he couldn't stop talking. "There was another guy who had tried to kill himself because he'd received a Dear John letter. We were in a war zone and we had our own guys trying to kill themselves."

"That had to be hard to deal with."

"Yeah, more than anyone should have to deal with. We lived in metal shipping containers that had been divided into two small rooms by thin wooden walls. We showered in bath houses, ate in the same mess hall. It's hard not to get involved in each other's lives."

"I imagine you do."

"Even though we had R and R time, you never truly

got away from it. We could go to the rec building, call our families or use the internet, but the minute we stepped out of the building the fence and sentries told us we weren't at home."

He'd confessed more than he'd ever told anyone about his time in the service. Had he terrified her? He glanced her direction. A single tear rested on her cheek.

His hand found hers. "I'm sorry. I shouldn't have told you all that."

"I'm glad you did. This baby deserves to know about his daddy and what he did. What life was like for him before he died. Thank you for telling me."

Ryan went back to looking at the road. "Joshua was a strong leader. I saw more than one man panic in the kind of situation we were in in that village. He held it together. Because of him I'm alive and so are a lot of other men. You can tell the baby that his father was a good soldier and a hero."

It was a relief to see the turnoff to their next stop. The conversation had gone in a direction he'd not expected or really wanted to continue. He made the turn into the road leading to the farmhouse. He released Phoebe's hand. The feeling of loss was immediate. "I have a good feeling about this place."

"I hope you're right."

Phoebe's voice held a sad note that he'd like to have disappear. He hadn't intended to bring what had been a nice day to a standstill. Even so, he had to admit it was a relief to get some of what he felt about the war off his chest. He'd carried that heaviness too long. It was strange that Phoebe, the wife of an army buddy, was the one person he had felt comfortable enough with to do so. He had never even told his coworkers as much as he'd just told Phoebe.

The house they were looking for came into view. He pulled to a stop in the drive.

"Doesn't look like we're at the right place. Let me double-check the address." Phoebe opened the newspaper.

A woman came around the corner of the house.

Ryan stepped out of the truck. "Excuse me, ma'am, but is this the place where the yard sale is?" he asked.

"Yes, but it has been over for an hour. We've put everything away."

Phoebe joined them. "Do you still have any furniture? I'm looking for a chest of drawers for my baby's room."

"I'm sorry but we had very little furniture and what we did have is all gone."

Ryan looked at Phoebe. He hated seeing that defeated look on her face. "We'll just have to try again on another weekend."

They were on their way back to the truck when the woman called, "Hey, I do have a chest of drawers out in the old smoke house that my husband says has to go. It was my mother's. It's missing a leg and a drawer, though."

Ryan looked at Phoebe. "I could fix those things. It wouldn't hurt to look."

Phoebe shrugged. "I guess so."

She didn't sound too confident. He gave her an encouraging smile. "Come on. You might be in for a surprise."

He certainly knew about them. Phoebe had been one of those in his life.

"It's back this way." The woman headed around the house. She led them to a wooden building that looked ready to fall down and opened a door.

Ryan looked into the dark space. All types of farming equipment, big and small, was crammed into it.

"You're gonna have to move some of that stuff around if you want to get to it," the woman said from behind him.

Glancing back over the woman's shoulder to where Phoebe stood, he saw her look of anticipation. Not wanting to disappoint her, he didn't have any choice but to start moving rakes, hoes, carts and even larger gardening implements. He definitely didn't want her to do that.

Picking up things and shifting them aside to make a narrow path, he could see a chest leaning against a wall. In the dim light provided by the slits in the boards it looked the right height. His heart beat faster. It might be just what Phoebe was looking for.

He made his way to it by squeezing between a stack of boxes and a tall piece of farming equipment that he couldn't put a name to. Pulling the chest away from the wall, he leaned it forward to look at the back.

"Doesn't it look perfect? It's just right."

His head jerked toward the voice. "Phoebe! What're you doing back here?" He shouldn't have been surprised. She managed to dumbfound him regularly.

"I wanted to see."

"You should have waited until I brought it out."

"What if you had done all that work and I wasn't interested? I didn't have any problem getting back here, except for between the boxes and that piece of equipment. I'm certainly no larger than you."

He eased the cabinet back against the wall. "What's that supposed to mean?"

"You're no little guy, with your broad shoulders and height."

He wasn't and he liked that she had noticed.

She circled around him, as if wanting to get a closer look at the chest. She pulled each drawer out and examined the slot where the missing drawer went. "What do you think?"

"What?" Ryan was so absorbed with watching her he'd missed her question.

"What do you think?" she asked in an impatient tone. "Can it be fixed?"

"Yes. It has sturdy construction. With a new drawer and a leg you would be in business."

She looked at him and grinned. Had he just been punched in the stomach?

"In business?"

"What kind of business would that be?"

"The baby business," he quipped back.

"I think I'll like that kind of business." Her smile was of pure happiness.

He returned it. "And I think you'll be good at it. So do you want the chest?"

"Yes, I do."

For a second there he wanted her to say that about him. He shook the thought away. Those were not ones he should be having. He and Phoebe were just friends. That was all they could be or should be.

"If you'll slide your way back out, then I'll bring this."

"I could help—"

Ryan leaned down until his nose almost touched hers. "No. You. Will. Not."

She giggled. "I thought that's what you might say." She gave him a quick kiss on the cheek and started for the path. "Thanks. You've been wonderful."

All he could do was stand there with a silly grin on his face. What was he, ten again?

With a groan, he began manipulating the chest through the maze. With less muscle than patience, he managed to get it outside. Before he could hardly stand the cabinet against the side of the building, Phoebe began studying it with a critical eye. She pulled each of the drawers out and pushed them in again.

"What do you want for it?" Phoebe glanced at the lady.

Heck, now that he'd worked to bring it into the light of day it didn't matter what the woman wanted. He'd pay her price just to not have to put it back.

"One hundred dollars," the woman stated.

"It has a leg and a drawer missing. How about thirty?" Phoebe came back with.

"Make it eighty, then."

Ryan watched, his look going from one woman to the other like at a tennis match.

"I don't think so. There's too much work to be done. Thanks anyway." Phoebe started toward the truck.

Ryan stood there in disbelief. She was going to leave after all the looking they had done today and the trouble he'd gone to get the chest out of the cluttered building? After she'd found what she wanted?

He gave her a pointed look. She winked. He was so stunned he couldn't say anything.

"How about we make it fifty?" the woman called after her.

Phoebe made almost a ballerina turn and had a smile on her face when she faced the woman. "Deal." Phoebe opened up her purse and handed the woman some bills.

He had to give Phoebe credit, she was an excellent bargainer.

She looked at him and grinned in pure satisfaction. What would it be like to have her look at him that way because of something he'd done? Heaven.

Clearing his head, he asked, "Ma'am, do you mind if I pull the truck closer to load this up?"

"Sure, that's fine."

Twenty minutes later, Phoebe was waving bye to the woman like they were long-lost friends.

"That was some dickering you did back there."

"Dickering?"

"Bargaining."

"Thanks."

"The next time I have to buy a car I'm taking you with me."

Phoebe smiled.

"Where did you learn to do that?"

"I don't know. I just know that it usually works. And it's always worth a try."

"There for a few minutes I was afraid that I was going to have to wrestle that chest back into that building."

"I wouldn't have let that happen. I wanted it too badly. I would have paid the hundred."

"Well, I'm glad to know that."

A few minutes later he pulled out onto the main highway that would take them to the larger road leading to Melbourne.

"Oh, the little penguins. I haven't seen them since I was young," Phoebe remarked as they passed a billboard.

"Penguins?"

"You don't know about the penguins? At Phillip Island?"

"No."

"They come in every night. It's amazing to watch. They go out every morning and hunt for food and bring it back for their babies. They're about a foot tall."

"How far away is this?"

"On the coast. About thirty minutes from here."

"Do you want to go?"

"They don't come in until the sun is going down. It would be late when we got home."

She sounded so wistful that he didn't have the heart to say no.

"Tell me which way to go."

"Surely you have something to do tonight. A date?"

"Why, Phoebe, are you fishing to find out about my love life?"

She rewarded him with a blush. "No."

"I have no plans. I'd like to see these tuxedo-wearing birds."

"Then you need to turn around and head the other direction."

"Yes, ma'am."

CHAPTER FIVE

PHOEBE HADN'T BEEN to Phillip Island in years. She still had the picture her father had taken of her standing next to the penguin mascot. The area had changed. The building had been expanded and more parking added.

Ryan found a space and pulled into it. "I'm glad we ate when we did. I haven't seen any place to do so in miles."

"I was hungry, too."

Inside the welcome center they were directed outside. In another hour it would be dark. They followed the paved path that zigged and zagged down toward the beach. Other people mingled along the way.

"What's that noise?" Ryan asked.

"That's the baby chicks."

He looked around. "Where are they?"

Phoebe placed a hand on his arm. She pointed with the other at a hole in the grass embankment. "They're in there. Watch for a second and you'll catch a glimpse of them."

A grin came to Ryan's lips. "I see one."

"The penguin's mother and father leave the nest in the morning and spend all day hunting food. They return each night to feed the young and do it all over again the next day. Fifty kilometers or farther."

"Every day?" Ryan asked in an incredulous tone.

"Yes. The ocean is overfished so they have to go farther and farther. It's pretty amazing what parents will do for their children."

Ryan looked at her. "Are you scared?"

"Some. At first I was shocked, frightened, mad, then protective. It has been better here lately." She left off *because of you*.

"So it takes both parents to find enough food?"

"They are partners for life."

Ryan looked off toward the ocean and didn't say anything.

Had she made him nervous? Made it sound like she expected something from him? "I think I'm most scared that I won't be enough for the baby. That I can't be both mother and father."

"I think you'll do just fine. Your baby will grow up happy and loved. Let's head on down."

Phoebe didn't immediately move. Did he think she expected him to offer to help? That she thought he'd be around when the baby came? Would take Joshua's place? She wouldn't force commitment on any man. She was looking for someone who wanted to spend time with her. Who would put her first, over everything. Someone that would willingly be there for her and her baby.

She started walking but at a slower pace.

They walked in silence around a couple of turns before Ryan said, "Whew, the smell is something."

"There are thousands of small chicks living in this bank."

"Really?" Ryan leaned over the rail and peered down. "I don't see them."

"Most are asleep right now. When they wake up you can see their heads stick out. There is one small nest after another."

"Everywhere."

Phoebe chuckled. It was fun to be around when Ryan experienced something new. He seemed to get such enjoyment and wonderment from it. It made her see it the same way. "Yes, they are everywhere."

"If you had told me about this I wouldn't have believed it."

"You haven't seen the best yet. Come on, let's get a good seat."

"Seat for what?"

"To watch mum and dad come home." She took his hand and pulled him along the walk.

When she tried to let his hand go he hung on tighter. She relaxed and reveled in the feeling of having someone close. Ryan seemed to like having contact with her.

"What do you mean?"

"We have to go down to the beach. There are grandstands."

"Like bleachers?"

"Come on, I'll show you."

As they continued on Ryan pulled her to a halt every once in a while to peer into the bank. "I can't believe all these little birds here."

She just smiled. They finally made it down to the sand. She was glad to have Ryan's help as she crossed it and they found a seat on an aluminum bench.

Ryan looked around. "This many people will be here?"

"Yes, the three sets of bleachers will be full and there will be people standing along the rails."

"I wonder why I've never heard about this."

"I don't know but I do think it's the best-kept secret about Australia."

The bleachers filled as the sun began to set. Minutes later the crowd around them quieted.

"Look," Phoebe whispered and pointed out toward the water. "Here they come."

Emerging from the surf was a small penguin, and behind it another until there was a group of ten to twelve. They hurried up the beach and into the grassy areas.

A loud chirping rose as their chicks realized dinner had arrived. Soon after the first group, another one came out of the water. Then another. Occasionally the group would be as many as twenty.

Ryan leaned close. There was a smell to him that was all Ryan with a hint of the sea. Phoebe liked the combination.

"Why do they come out in groups?"

"For protection from predators. If they all come at once, then they all could be killed. They come out in groups and in waves. That way there will be someone left to take care of the chicks if something happens to them."

Who would take care of her child if something happened to her? She wasn't going to think about that. Glancing at Ryan, she saw that he was looking out at the water. Was he thinking about what she'd said?

As they watched the penguins, the sun went down and floodlights came on. Phoebe shivered as a breeze came off the water. Ryan put an arm around her and pulled her in close. She didn't resist his warmth. Instead, she snuggled into his side.

As they watched, a cluster came out of the water and quickly returned.

"See, that group was frightened by something. Watch for a minute and they will try it again."

Out of the water they came. Ryan gave her a little squeeze.

"You know, I expected the penguins to have black coats but they are really a dark navy."

"That was my biggest surprise the first time I saw them. Aren't they cute?"

"I have to admit they are."

They watched for the next hour. As they did so the penguins continued to come out in waves and the noise from the nests rose to almost a point to where Ryan and Phoebe couldn't hear each other.

Finally they sat there for another ten minutes and no more birds arrived. The crowd started moving toward the walkway.

"Is that it?" Ryan sounded disappointed.

"That's it for tonight."

"Amazing."

When they passed a park ranger, Ryan asked, "How many penguins are there?"

"Two thousand two hundred and fifty-one tonight."

"How do you know that?"

"We count them. There are rangers stationed in sections along the beach."

Ryan's arm supported her as they climbed the hill on the way back to the welcome center. He didn't remove it as they walked to the truck.

As they left the car park he said, "Thanks for bringing me. I'll be doing this again."

"I'm glad you had a good time."

"I did. I bet you are beat." He grinned. "You didn't even fall asleep on me today."

"I'm sorry. I can't help it."

"I'm just teasing you."

They talked about their day for a few minutes. It was the best one she'd had in a long time. Even before Joshua had died. Ryan had proved he could be fun and willing to try new things. She had more than enjoyed his company. Unfortunately, she feared she might crave it. Her eyelids became heavy and a strong arm pulled her against a firm cushion.

* * *

Ryan hated to wake Phoebe but they were in front of her house. He had given thought to just sitting in the truck and holding her all night.

Visiting the penguins had been wonderful. He'd especially enjoyed the look on Phoebe's face when the first bird had waddled out of the water. It was pure pleasure. He'd like the chance to put a look on her face like that.

That was a place he shouldn't go. He'd been more than uncomfortable when the discussion had turned to how parents protected their young. He couldn't be that person in Phoebe's life and the baby's. That devotion those tiny birds had to their young wasn't in him. He couldn't let Phoebe start believing that it was. He wouldn't be around for the long haul. That required a level of emotion that he wasn't willing to give.

Still, she felt right in his arms. Too right.

He pushed those thoughts away and settled for practicality and what was best for Phoebe. She would be sore from sleeping in the truck and he would ache for other reasons. He smirked. Plus he was liable to end up in jail when her neighbor called the police.

"Phoebe." He shook her gently. "Phoebe. We're home."

Her eyes fluttered open. "Mmm…?"

"We're at your house."

"Oh." She tried to sit up but it wasn't happening quickly. "I'm sorry, I didn't mean to fall asleep on you, literally and figuratively."

"Not a problem." And it hadn't been.

Ryan opened his door and got out before helping her out. He walked her to the door.

"What about my chest of drawers?"

"I need to fix the leg and build a drawer before you can do much with it anyway. I'll just take it home with me. You could come to my house and work on it. I'll do the paint stripping anyway. You don't need to be around those fumes."

"You've already done so much."

Ryan put a hand under her chin and lifted it. "Hey, today was no hardship for me."

She smiled. "I enjoyed it, too."

With reluctance he stepped back. "You need to get to bed."

"And you still have a drive ahead."

"I do. I'll see you in clinic Wednesday afternoon. Plan to come to my place afterward. I should have the leg on and the drawer done by then."

"Okay."

He liked the fact that she readily agreed.

"See you then."

Phoebe made her way into the hospital and up to the clinic waiting room. She hadn't been this nervous since her first visit. Her name was called and she was directed to an examination room. She was told to remove her trousers, sit on the exam table and place the sheet over her. Soon Sophia entered. "Well, have you made a decision on who you want to replace me?"

"Not yet. I hate to lose you. Are you sure you can't put off the wedding until after this baby is born?"

"I don't think Aiden will agree to that. You're going to have to make a decision soon."

"I know."

"I'm sorry that I can't be there to deliver." Sophia's smile grew. "But love doesn't wait."

"I understand. I wish you the best."

"So how's it going between you and Ryan? I know your first meeting was a little rocky."

Phoebe smiled. "That would be an understatement. It turns out he's a great guy. He's been helping me get the baby's room together. I asked him to put the baby bed together and he volunteered to paint the room."

"I'm not surprised. He's the kind of person who keeps to himself and quietly goes about helping people."

A few minutes later Sophia had left and Phoebe had just finished dressing when there was a knock on the door. "Come in."

Ryan entered. "Hey."

"Hi." She sounded shy even to herself. She'd never been timid in her life.

"So how're you feeling?"

"Fine."

"Great. No aches or pains after our adventure on Saturday?"

She appreciated his friendly manner. "I was tired but no more than I'm sure you were."

"I have to admit it was a long day. You mind waiting on me in the waiting room? I have one more patient to see."

"Sure."

She hadn't been waiting long when he came out of the office area.

"You ready?"

She stood. "Ryan, I have to work tomorrow. I can't be out late. Maybe I should just come by this weekend."

"Don't you want to see what I've done with the chest?"

Ryan sounded like a kid wanting to show off his new toy. He opened the door leading to the main hall. She went out and he followed.

"Sure I do, but I also have to get to bed at a decent hour."

"I'll drive you home."

"I don't want you to have to do that."

He looked at her. Worry darkened his eyes to a granite color. "Is something wrong? Did I do something wrong?"

"No, of course not."

"Then stop arguing and come on. I'll get you home for your regular bedtime. We'll go to my place and then walk down to a café for dinner. Then I'll take you home."

"Okay. If you insist."

"I do."

Twenty minutes later Ryan unlocked the front door to his home. She followed him in. The place looked no different than it had the last time she had been there yet everything had changed. She felt welcomed where she hadn't before.

Ryan dropped his clothes in a pile next to the door just as he had done before. "Are you thirsty?" he called from the kitchen area.

"No, but I would like to use the bathroom."

"That's right. Pregnant women and their bladders. You'll find it off my bedroom. Sorry it isn't cleaner."

"I'll try not to look."

Phoebe walked to the only doorway she'd never been through. She stopped in shock. The most perfect bedroom suite she'd ever seen filled the room. The furnishing here was nothing like what was in the rest of the house. There was such a contrast it was like being in two different worlds. She went to the sleigh-style bed and ran her hand along the footboard, then turned to study the large dresser. The workmanship was old world with a twist of the modern. She'd never seen any like it. She'd give anything to have furniture like this.

"Hey, Phoebe—" Ryan walked into the room.

"These are beautiful pieces. Where did you get them?" She walked around the end of the bed to the bedside table. She couldn't stop herself from touching it.

"I made it."

She pivoted. "You did? It's amazing. If you ever give up being a midwife, you could become a millionaire, making furniture. It's just beautiful."

A hint of redness crept up his throat.

"Thank you. I don't think it's that good. But I'm glad you like it. You ready to go downstairs?"

"Downstairs?"

"That's where my workshop is."

"I haven't made it to the bathroom yet."

"You go. The door to the basement is in the kitchen. I'll leave it open."

A few minutes later Phoebe gingerly descended the stairs. She was half way down when Ryan rushed over.

"Give me your hand and I'll help you. I forget how steep the steps are."

"I think I've got it." She took the last three steps, then looked around. The area was immaculate. There was equipment spaced around the room that she couldn't put a name to but there wasn't a speck of sawdust on the floor. It was in marked contrast to his living area upstairs. He obviously loved and spent a lot of time down here.

Her cabinet stood near a wooden workbench. Ryan walked over to it. There was a look of anticipation on his face. As if it really mattered to him what she thought. He moved from one foot to the other. The man was worried about her reaction.

"So what do you think?"

"About what?"

"The chest."

"I know what you're talking about, silly. I'm just teasing you. It looks wonderful."

As if he'd been awarded a prize, his chest puffed out.

She would have never thought that this self-assured man would be that concerned about her opinion.

"I couldn't find a leg that matched the others so I bought four new ones that were as close to the original as I could find."

"They look great. The drawer looks like it was made with it. I'm not surprised after I saw your bedroom furniture. Thank you, Ryan. It's perfect."

"I managed to strip some of the paint but it still needs more work. I was going to do some of it tonight but I promised to get you home."

"You know I'd rather have that finished so I can work on it than go out for a meal. Why don't I go down to the café and get takeout—?"

"While I work?" Ryan finished with a grin. "I think you could be a slave driver for a little bit."

"You're the one that said I shouldn't be stripping it. I would have put it out in the backyard where there was plenty of ventilation."

He propped his hands on his hips. "And just how were you planning to move it out of the weather?"

"I would have found a way. Ms. Rosenheim could help me."

"That would have been a sight worth watching."

She glared at him. "You don't think we could do it?"

He threw up his hands. "I don't think I would put anything past you two."

"Good. You need to remember that. Now, I'm going to get us something to eat and you'd better get busy."

"Yes, ma'am."

His chuckle followed her up the stairs.

Ryan was aware of Phoebe returning. Her soft footfalls crossed overhead. As she moved around in the kitchen, something about the sound made him feel good inside. When her eyes lit up at the sight of the chest of drawers he felt like he could carry the world on his shoulders. For so long he'd only seen the look in eyes of those in pain or life slipping away. He could do nothing to change it but this time he'd been able to help someone and see pure joy. It was the same feeling he had when he delivered a baby.

Taking the can of paint stripper off the bench, he poured it into an empty food can. Using a brush, he applied it to the wood of the chest.

He liked too many things about Phoebe. The way her hair hid her face like a curtain and then when it was drawn away discovering she'd hidden a smile from him. The way she insisted on helping. Phoebe was no shrinking violet. She was a survivor. JT's baby was lucky. JT's baby!

What was happening to him? Phoebe was JT's wife. *Was*. It didn't matter how attracted to her he was, she would always belong to JT. There was the bro code. You don't take your best friend's girl.

Ryan picked up the putty knife and began to scrape the paint off in thin sheets.

No matter how much you might want to.

A board creaked above him.

It didn't matter. Phoebe didn't feel that way about him. She'd been alone during a hard time in her life and she was searching for a connection to JT. All *he* meant to her was someone who had known the father of her baby. He would be her friend and nothing more.

Still, it was as if he saw the world as a better place when he was around her. Like his wounds were finally closing. That life could be good. Not black-and-white. Living or dying. But happy, healthy and hopeful.

"Hey, down there, your dinner is served." There was a

cheerful tone to her voice, like someone calling another they cared about.

Ryan's heart thumped hard against his chest. Wouldn't it be nice to be called to every meal that way? Even those little things improved life.

Phoebe was filling their glasses when Ryan's footsteps drew her attention to the door of the basement. It had been over a year since she had called someone to dinner and here she was doing it twice in less than two weeks. She liked it. There was something about it that made her feel like all was as it should be in her world.

"Smells good."

"You do know that all I did was pick it up, don't you?" she said, putting the pitcher back on the corner.

"Yes, but you did a good job with that."

He looked at the table. She had set their places with what little she could find in Ryan's woefully low-stocked kitchen. Passing a shop, she'd impulsively bought a handful of flowers. She hoped he didn't think she was suggesting that this was more than a friendly meal.

He nodded toward them. "Nice touch."

She smiled. "I like fresh flowers. I couldn't resist them."

"I'll have to remember that. Let me wash my hands."

Ryan went to the sink. With his back to her she had a chance for a good look. What would it be like to run her hands across these wide shoulders? To cup what must be a firm butt?

She didn't need to be thinking like that. But she was pregnant, not dead.

"What's wrong? You feeling okay? You have an odd look on your face."

She'd been caught ogling him. "No, no, I feel fine."

A slow smile stole over his face and his eyes twinkled, pushing the worry away. "Okay, let's eat. I'm hungry."

Had he figured out what she'd been thinking?

They each took one of the two chairs at the table.

"I didn't know what you liked so I got two kinds of soups and two sandwiches, hoping you liked at least one of each."

"It all looks good."

"I didn't move your mail off the table. I thought you might not be able to find it if I did." She pushed it toward him. Ryan's hand brushed hers when he reached for it.

The flutter in her middle had nothing to do with the baby moving. She jerked her hand back.

"Is that a valid comment on my housekeeping skills?"

"Not really, but now that you mention it I've not really seen any of those skills outside your shop."

He laughed. "I deserve that. I'm not here much and when I am I go downstairs. As for my mail, I usually let it stack up and then open anything that isn't bills when I get around to it." He glanced through the pile and pulled an envelope out, tearing it open. Slipping a card out, he studied it a moment, then laid it on the table. "It's an invitation to Sophia's wedding next weekend."

"You weren't kidding. That had to have come weeks ago."

He gave her a sheepish look. "I'm sure it did."

"I'm happy for her but I hate it she isn't going to be there to deliver this baby. I've become attached to her. It's hard to give her up. I don't want just anyone to deliver. But I've got to make a choice soon."

There was a long pause before Ryan leaned forward and said, "I'd like to do it."

Phoebe sucked in a breath. "You want to do what?"

"Be your midwife. Would you let me take over from Sophia?"

She wasn't sure it was a good idea but she didn't want to hurt his feelings by saying no immediately. She'd been looking for emotional support, not medical help. Ryan being her midwife sounded far too personal. "Ooh, I don't know if I'm comfortable with that."

"You need a midwife and I'm one."

"Yes, but isn't there something about not delivering people you know?"

His gaze held hers. "I don't see it as being a problem. And I'd rather be the one there if there's a complication than wishing I had been."

She nodded.

"Phoebe, I'd like to be a part of bringing Joshua's baby into the world."

Wasn't this what she'd been looking for? Someone to support her? Be there for her? She loved Sophia but she wasn't available. Why shouldn't Ryan be the one? Because she had feelings for him that had nothing to do with the baby.

He shifted forward in his chair. "I didn't mean to put you on the spot."

"No, no. It's okay. I'm just not sure what to say. Let me think about it."

"Take all the time you need."

She didn't have much time. He had proved more than once he was the guy Joshua had said he was. What she knew was that she didn't feel as alone as she had only a few weeks ago. Ryan had been tender and caring with her so why wouldn't he be a good midwife? Right now what she needed to do was change the subject. "Where's Sophia getting married?"

"I forget women are always interested in a wedding." He slid the card toward her.

Phoebe picked it up. It was a classic embossed invitation. "They're getting married at Overnewton. It'll be a beautiful wedding. That's an amazing place."

Ryan gazed at her over his soup spoon.

"What wedding doesn't a woman think is beautiful?"

"Mine wasn't. We got married at the registry office."

"Oh?"

"It was time for Joshua to ship out and we decided to just do it. I wore my best dress and he his dress uniform. And we did it."

"Do you wish you'd had a fancier wedding?"

"Sometimes. But that was us back then. Fast in love, fast to the altar. It seemed exciting. My parents were gone. My brother showed up and one of Joshua's friends from school was there. We all went out to eat lunch afterward. The next day Joshua was gone."

"No honeymoon?"

"We took a trip into the mountains, camping, when he came home nine months later. Those were good times."

It was nice to talk about Joshua. People were hesitant to ask about him. They were always afraid it would make her cry. What they didn't understand was that she wanted to talk about the husband she'd lost. Wanted to remember. She and Joshua had had some fun times. It was a shame they had grown apart there at the end. She'd wanted better for him. For him to think of her positively.

She picked up her sandwich. "How about you? Ever been married?"

"No."

"Not even close?"

"Nope. Never found the right one."

"I bet there have been women who thought you were the right one."

He shrugged.

"So you've been a 'love them and leave them' guy?"

Ryan looked at her. "I wouldn't say that. It's more like it's better not to get involved unless your heart is fully in it. Mine never has been."

His eyes held a dark look, despite the effortlessness of the words. There was more to it than that but she didn't know him well enough to probe further. "I guess that's fair."

"You know, Joshua used to talk about you all the time. It was Phoebe this and Phoebe that."

"Really?" She'd always thought she'd been more like a toy that he'd come home to play with and then left behind to pick up again during the next holiday. Would things have been different between them if Joshua had not been gone so much?

"He talked about how you liked to camp and hike. What a good sport you were. I liked to hear stories about places you went, things you did."

Guilt washed through her. And the last time Joshua had been home they'd done nothing special. Instead, they'd talked about getting a divorce. How had their relationship deteriorated so much? Would anyone ever love her like she needed to be loved? Want to come home to her every night? Have a family? She put down her half-eaten sandwich and pushed back her chair. "I need to get this cleaned up and get home. It's getting late."

"Do you mind if I finish my sandwich before we go?"

"I'm sorry. I didn't mean to be rude." She settled in her chair again.

"It's okay."

Phoebe watched as Ryan finished his meal. As soon as he had she started removing their plates and glasses.

"I need to put a cover over a few things before we leave." Ryan went down the stairs.

Ten minutes later she called through the door to the basement, "I'm ready to go when you are."

"I'll be right up."

Coming from Ryan, she could depend on it happening.

CHAPTER SIX

JUST UNDER AN hour later Ryan joined Phoebe on the sidewalk in front of her house.

"Thanks for the ride home."

"When are you planning to come to my house and work on the cabinet? This weekend? I'll have it ready for you by then."

"I hadn't thought about that. I guess I need to get busy. I'll bring my paints and be there early on Saturday morning."

"I can come get you—"

"No, I'll take the tram." She started up the walk.

"I don't mind."

She looked at him. "Ryan, please."

"Okay, okay. Have it your way. Come on, you're tired." He took her elbow and they started toward the door.

Phoebe stopped walking.

Ryan jerked to a stop. "What—?"

She kicked off her shoes and picked them up by two fingers. "My feet are killing me."

They continued to the door. Phoebe unlocked it, pushing it open.

"If you soak and massage your feet it would help," Ryan said behind her.

"I don't do feet." She dropped her shoes inside the door.

Ryan followed her in and closed the door behind him. "That's all right, because I do. You get a bath and come back here. Bring a bottle of your favorite lotion with you. I'll be waiting."

"It's late. We've both had a long day."

"It won't take long and I promise you'll like it. So stop complaining and go on."

Phoebe gave him a dubious look but went off toward her bedroom.

While she was gone Ryan found a cook pot and put water on to heat. Looking under the sink, he pulled out a wash pan. He added a little dish soap to it. He searched the cabinets for a container of salt and, finding it, he added a generous amount to the soap. When the water started to steam he poured it into the pan.

Going to the bathroom in the hallway, he pulled a towel off the rack. Returning to the living room, he placed the towel on the floor in front of the most comfortable-looking chair. He then went for the pan of water.

"What's all this?" Phoebe asked. She wore a gown and a housecoat that covered her breasts but not her belly. Her hair flowed around her shoulders and her cheeks were rosy. Ryan had never seen a more captivating sight.

Gathering his wits and settling his male libido, he took her hand and led her toward the chair. "I'm going to help make those feet feel better. You sit here."

She lowered herself into the chair.

"Now, slowly put your feet into the water. It may be too hot."

"This feels wonderful." She sighed, lowering her feet into the water.

He left her to get a chair from the kitchen, returned and placed it in front of her.

"What're you planning now?"

Taking a seat, he faced her. "I'm going to massage your feet."

"I'm not letting you do that!"

"Why not? You ticklish?"

Phoebe didn't look at him. "No."

"I think you're lying to me. Did you bring the lotion?"

She shifted to her right and put her hand in her housecoat pocket. She pulled out a bottle and handed it to him. Without even opening the bottle he recognized the scent he thought of as hers. He reached down, his hand wrapping her calf and lifting it to rest on his thigh.

"I'm getting you wet." She tried to pull her foot away.

He held it in place. "If it isn't bothering me, then don't let it bother you. Lean back and relax. Close your eyes."

He squirted a liberal amount of lotion into his palm and began rubbing Phoebe's foot. At the first touch she flinched and her eyes popped open. Their gazes met as he began to massage her skin. Seconds later, her eyes closed and she relaxed. As he worked the tissue on the bottom of her foot she let out a soft moan.

"Where did you learn this?" she asked almost with a sigh.

"In the army. The men in the hospital always seemed to respond and became calmer if they had a massage of some kind."

"I can understand that."

His hands moved to her ankle and then along her calf, kneading the muscles.

"I'm sorry if I put you in a difficult position when I asked to be your midwife." He squeezed more lotion into his hand and started at her toes again and pushed upward.

"It was sweet of you to ask."

He wasn't sure that Phoebe thinking of him as sweet was to his liking.

"Well, something that was said seemed to upset you." He gently pulled on one of her toes.

"It wasn't what you said as much as something I remembered."

"I guess it wasn't a good one." His fingers continued to work her toes.

"No. When Joshua was home the last time, we talked about separating."

"That's tough." He moved up to her knee and started down again.

"We had grown apart. I had my life and he had his. We just didn't make sense anymore." A tone of pain surrounded every word.

"I'm sorry to hear that. It must really have been difficult to deal with when you realized you were pregnant."

"That would be an understatement. How about an ocean of guilt?"

Ryan could more than understand that feeling. He placed her foot back into the pan and picked up the other one. He gave the second one the same attention as he had the first.

Phoebe leaned back and neither one of them spoke for the next few minutes. Ryan was content to watch the expression of pleasure on her face.

"You sure know the way to a woman's heart."

His hands faltered on her calf. He didn't want her heart. Having someone's heart meant they expected some emotion in return. He didn't get that involved with anyone.

Her eyes opened and met his look. There was a realization in them of what she'd said. Regardless of what his mind told him, his body recognized and reacted to the longing in her eyes. His hands moved to massage her knee and above, just as he had done before, but this time the movements requested more. Unable to resist, his fingers brushed the tender tissue of her inner thigh.

Phoebe was no longer thinking about her feet. This gorgeous, intelligent hunk of man in front of her wanted her. She couldn't remember the last time she'd felt desired. If it had ever felt this compelling.

Ryan's gaze captured hers. His eyes were storm-cloud gray. He held her leg with one hand and slowly trailed a finger upward past her knee to tease her thigh again before bring it down. It was no longer a massaging motion but a caress. With what looked like regret in his eyes, he lowered her foot into the water.

With his gaze still fixed on her, he offered both of his hands.

She took them. He gently pulled her closer and closer until she was in an upright position. Leaning forward, his mouth drew near. "I may be making a huge mistake but I can't help myself."

Ryan's lips were firm, full and sure as they rested on hers. He pressed deeper.

Phoebe wanted more but wasn't sure what that was or if she should want it. This was the first kiss she'd had since Joshua's parting one. She pulled away, their lips losing contact. Her eyes lifted and her look met Ryan's. He didn't hold it. Without a word, he scooped her up into his arms. She wrapped her hands around his neck.

"What?"

"Just be quiet." The words were a low growl. He carried her down the hall to her bedroom and stood her on her feet next to her bed. "Get in."

His tone was gruff. She didn't question, instead doing as he asked. He tucked the extra pillow under her middle and pulled the covers over her shoulders before he turned off the light and left the room. "Good night, Phoebe."

Had he been as affected by the kiss as she had? She still trembled inside. Ryan's lips meeting hers had been wonderful and shocking at the same time. He had surprised her. Everything had remained on a friendly level until his hand had moved up her leg. She'd wanted his kiss but hadn't been sure what to do when she'd got it.

Those days of schoolgirl insecurity had returned. She was soon going to be a mother. Did he feel sorry for her because of the baby? Joshua? Or just because he thought she needed the attention at the moment? The doubts had made her pull away. Now she regretted doing so. Her body longed for him. But it couldn't be. She wouldn't have Ryan feel obligated to her because of her situation. She'd put him on the spot when she'd shown up at his house and she had no intention of doing that to him again. It was best for them just to remain friends.

A few minutes later the front door was opened and closed. Ryan had gone. She didn't have to wonder if the pan and chair had been put away or the front door secured. Ryan would have taken care of that just like she knew she could rely on him to be there for her.

Ryan couldn't sleep and any time he couldn't do that he went to his workshop. What had he been thinking when he'd kissed Phoebe? That was the problem. He hadn't been thinking but feeling. Something he couldn't remember doing in a long time. The need to do more than touch her had pulled at him to the point he'd been unable to stand it any longer. When she'd raised those large questioning eyes...

How could he have done it? He had kissed his dead best friend's wife. Someone who had trusted him. Could there be a greater betrayal? He'd stepped over the line. Way over. Both personally and professionally. It wouldn't happen again. He could put his personal feelings aside and concentrate on the professional. That was enough of those thoughts.

He had the chest of drawers to finish and sand, and there was also the rocking chair to repair. Phoebe would be here in two days ready to work on them. Soon that baby's room would be complete and the baby here. Then he could back out of Phoebe's life. He would have done then what he could do to honor JT. Phoebe would no longer need him.

Had he seen a cradle at Phoebe's? She would need a cradle for the first few months to keep the newborn close. He'd been given some pink silkwood by an associate who was moving out of town. It had been stored away for a special project. This was it.

Would he have time to get it done before the baby came? If he worked on it every chance he had, he might make it. He'd finish the chest and then start on the cradle. If he worked on the rocker while Phoebe was busy painting, he could keep the cradle a surprise.

He had plenty to do so there wouldn't be time to think about Phoebe. The feel of her lips. The desire in her eyes. The need that was growing in him. With his mind and hands busy he wouldn't be tempted to kiss her again. He had to get control of his emotions. In Iraq he'd been the king of control. He needed to summon some of that now. Compartmentalize when he was around Phoebe. Keep that door she was pushing open firmly closed.

On Saturday morning Ryan came home as the sun was coming up. He'd been gone all night, delivering a baby. Phoebe would be there in a few hours. He wanted to get some sleep before she arrived. Taking a quick bath, he crawled into bed.

He woke with a start. Something wasn't right. The room was too bright. He groaned. He'd slept longer than he'd planned. But something else was off.

Music. His workshop. He had a radio there. Had he left it on?

Wearing only his boxer shorts, he headed for the kitchen. The music grew louder. The basement door stood wide open and a humming mixed with the song playing drifted up the stairs. He moved slowly down the steps, being careful not to make a noise. Halfway down, he bent over to see who was there.

Phoebe. She sat on a stool with her back to him, painting a side of the chest. She'd been smart enough to open the outside door to let out any fumes. Ryan trod on the next step hard enough that she would hear it. He didn't want to scare her by calling her name.

She twisted around. "Hey."

There was a tentative sound to her voice. Was she thinking about what had happened the last time they had seen each other? Was she worried he might try to kiss her again? He needed to put her at ease. "Hey, yourself. You're not afraid of being hurt when you come into someone's house while they're sleeping?"

"I knocked and knocked. I tried the front door and it was open. I came in and saw you were sleeping. I figured you'd had a late night and had left it open for me."

He nodded. Some of that was true, except he had planned to be up when she arrived. "I had a delivery early this morning."

"How's the mother and baby?"

He moved down the stairs going to stand beside her. "Great. Beautiful girl named Margaret."

"Nice. What do you think?" She indicated the work she'd been doing.

Phoebe had left the wood a natural color and was painting a vine with flowers down the side. "Looks great. What're your plans for the rest of it?"

"I'm going to paint the drawers different colors and paint the other side like this one."

"Sounds nice. Well, I'm going up and see if I can find some breakfast. Then I'll be back down."

He was headed up the stairs when Phoebe said in a bright voice, "Hey, Ryan. I like those boxers. Very sexy."

There was the straightforward Phoebe he'd come to appreciate. Ryan glanced down and shook his head. He'd forgotten all about what he was wearing. "Thanks. I do try."

Phoebe laughed. Ryan did have a good sense of humor. She liked that about him. In fact, she liked too much. He was sexy man and a good kisser, as well. He hadn't mention the kiss or even acted as if he would try again. She couldn't let that happen. Her life was already too complicated. She wouldn't add another emotional turn to it. If he didn't say something, she would have to.

A harsh word filled the air.

She heaved herself off the stool and walked to the door. Another harsh word and pounding on the floor filled the air. She climbed the stairs.

Ryan stood at the sink with the water running.

She moved to his side. "What happened?"

"I burned my finger."

Phoebe smirked at his whiny tone. She went to the refrigerator and opened the freezer compartment. Taking out an ice cube, she handed it to him. "Here, hold this over it."

With a chagrined twist to his mouth he took it. Phoebe looked around the kitchen, found a napkin from a fast-food restaurant and handed that to him, as well. He placed the ice in it and put it on his finger.

"Nothing like the big strong medic needing a medic."

"Hey, taking care of someone hurt is different than being hurt yourself."

She grinned. "Or cooking. Looks like you were having eggs and bacon."

Phoebe pulled the pan that looked as if it had been hastily pushed to the back burner forward and turned on the stove. The bacon was half-cooked.

"I didn't mean for you to come up and cook for me. I'm interrupting your painting."

"It can wait."

She picked up the two eggs sitting on the counter. Cracking them, she let them drop into the pan. There was a *ding*. The toast popped up.

Ryan pulled the slices out and placed them on a plate. "See, I can make toast without hurting myself."

"You get a gold star for that."

"Is that what you give your students when they're good?"

"Fifth years are too old for that sort of thing. Mostly they are happy to get to be first in line to lunch."

He stood nearer than she was comfortable with, but there was nowhere for her to go and still see what she was cooking. It made her body hum just to have him close. This was not what she'd told herself should happen.

"JT was very proud of the fact you're a teacher."

"Really? I always felt like he resented me having to go to work when he was home." Phoebe lifted the bacon, then the two fried eggs out of the pan, placing them beside the toast. She put the frying pan on the back burner and turned off the stove.

Ryan took the plate and sat down at the table. "Maybe that was because he wanted to spend as much normal time with you as possible. Nothing was normal where we were. People thought differently, ate differently, dressed differently. Everything was different. When I had leave I just wanted as much normalcy as I could get."

She slid into the chair across from him. "Then why did he always look forward to going back?"

"I don't know if I can really answer that question. Because it was his job. Because you feel like you're doing something bigger than yourself, something important. You're helping people who can't help themselves. Then there's the excitement. The adrenaline rush can be addictive.

"What I do know is that JT was good at his job. He was good to his men, protected them at any cost, even to himself."

She nodded. Some of the ache over their last words left her. "Thanks for telling me. Now I better understand why he always seemed so eager to return. Sometimes I worried it was more to get away from me. If you think you can finish up your breakfast without injuring yourself, I'll go and work on the chest."

Half an hour later Ryan went down the stairs. "I'm just going to work over here, out of your way."

"You're not going to be in my way."

Over the next hour they said little to each other as they both concentrated on their own projects. Every once in a while she glanced at Ryan. It appeared as if he was drawing off a pattern onto a plank of wood once when she looked. Another time he looked like he was studying a pattern he had spread across the workbench. There was something easy and comfortable about the two of them doing their own things together. It was the companionship she had been missing in her marriage.

Phoebe rubbed her hand over the baby as she looked at the painting she'd just completed. The world would be a good place for him or her. She felt more confident about that now. Glancing at Ryan, she found him with his butt leaning against the bench looking at her.

"Is something wrong?"

"No, I was just enjoying watching you."

Warmth flooded her. She had to stop this now or their new-found friendship might be damaged. She needed it too much to let that happen. "Uh, Ryan, about the other night…"

Ryan tensed slightly, as if he was unsure what she was going to say next.

"Why did you kiss me?"

"Because I wanted to." His eyes never wavered. Ryan was being just as direct.

She shifted on the stool. "That's nice but it can't happen again."

"Why not? We're both adults. I'm attracted to you. I believe you like me. So why not?"

"Because I don't think I can handle any more emotional baggage right now. I've lost a husband who died thinking I no longer loved him. Finding out I was expecting his baby was a shock of a lifetime. Realizing I'm going to have to raise a baby on my own is all I can handle right now. I can't take on more upheaval. I just think it would be easier if we remain friends and friends only."

He nodded. "I understand." Then he turned back to his work at the bench.

Phoebe believed he did. But she hadn't missed that he'd made no promises. She pressed her lips together. Did she really want him to?

Ryan opened the door to the examination room at the clinic the next Wednesday afternoon. To his shock, Phoebe was his next patient. He hadn't seen her since Saturday around noon when he'd had to leave her to deliver a baby. He'd told her she could stay as long as she wished and just to close up before she left as he doubted he'd be home before she was ready to leave.

Hours later he'd arrived home to a neat and tidy house. His bed had been made and his kitchen spotless. Even his pile of dirty clothes had gone. They were neatly folded on his bed. He'd had to admit it was nice to be cared for. It would be easy to get used to.

He'd been astonished at how much he'd missed Phoebe in the next few days and how much he was looking forward to seeing her again. After her statement about nothing more happening between them he didn't want to push her further away. Still, the thought of kissing her kept running through his mind. He'd be tempted when he saw her, but instead he would put on his professional hat and control himself.

"Hi, Phoebe," he said, as he stepped into the room and to the end of the table she was sitting on so he could face her. "This is a surprise."

She smiled. "Hey."

"Thanks for cleaning my house. You shouldn't have but I'm glad you did."

"It was nothing. It gave me something to do while I waited for the paint to dry. I saw the rocker. It looks great. You have a real talent."

"Thanks. Did you ask to see me for some reason?"

"I did. I'd like you to deliver my baby."

She had his complete attention.

"That is, if you still want to."

Ryan did. He owed it to JT. For not only his life when they had been pinned down, but because he had made a new start because of him. He had left the army, become a midwife and moved to Australia. Death was no longer a daily event. Ryan had been afraid that if he'd continued to be a medic that he would have never seen another side of life. Would have gone deeper into depression. He'd needed a change and JT had helped him see that.

That was what it had been about when he'd first asked but now, if he was truthful with himself, he wanted to be there for Phoebe and baby. They had started to matter more than he would have ever believed. "I'd be honored."

"I can't think of anyone I'd rather have."

"Thanks. So for your first official visit with me I'm going to listen to the baby's heartbeat, check your blood pressure, measure the size of the baby and check the position by feeling your belly."

"I understand." She said this more to the floor than him.

"Hey, Phoebe." She met his gaze. "Are you sure you're good with me taking over?"

"I do want you to do the delivery, it's just that this exam stuff the first time is a little…awkward."

"For both of us. So what do you say that we get it over with and go have some dinner? Why don't you lie down on the table and tell me what else you have planned for the baby's room?"

Ryan enjoyed her nervous chatter. He didn't blame her. More than once he reminded his hands not to tremble as he placed his hand on her skin and felt for the baby's position. "Well, you and the baby are doing great. You get dressed and we'll get that dinner."

"Do you invite all your patients out to eat?" she asked in a saucy tone.

"No, I do not. I save that for very special ones."

Less than half an hour later they were ordering their dinner at a café a few blocks from the hospital.

"I would have been glad to cook."

"You've done enough of that for me."

"As compared to all you have done for me?" Phoebe glared at him.

"Okay, let's not fight over who has done more." Ryan grinned back at her. "So how have you been?"

"I'm feeling fine. Just ready for this baby to get here and tired of people treating me like I can't do anything for myself. I was moving a box across the floor in my classroom the other day. It wasn't heavy but the janitor rushed to help me. On the tram on the way in a woman offered to hold my schoolbag. She said, 'Honey, isn't that too heavy for you?' I know she was just being nice but I'd like to go somewhere and enjoy being me instead of a pregnant woman."

"People are just naturally helpful when someone is carrying a baby."

The waiter brought their dinner.

"I know. But besides the baby, there's also Phoebe Taylor in here." She pointed to her chest.

He knew that too well. The sweet taste of her kiss still lingered in his memory like the fragrance of fresh-cut wood. Still, he shouldn't have stepped over that line. He owed her an apology but he couldn't bring himself to utter the words. Nothing in him regretted kissing her, not even for a second. Maybe he could show her he'd honor her decision in another way. He would show her he could be a gentleman. That she had nothing to fear on that level from him.

"Sophia really wants me at her wedding Friday evening. Would you like to go with me? We could dance the night away. I'll promise not to treat you like a pregnant woman." That was a promise he already knew he would break. He was far too attracted to her. The pregnancy hadn't even entered his mind when he'd kissed her. Still he would work not to go beyond that barrier Phoebe had erected.

At her skeptical look, he said, "No touching outside of dancing. Just friends."

"I don't know."

"Come on, Phoebe, you know you want to. Dinner and dancing. You don't want me to show up dateless, now, do you?"

She smiled at that. "I don't think you would have any trouble getting a date if you wanted one."

"It seems I'm having to work pretty hard right now to get one."

Phoebe smirked. "Okay, but only because you sound so pitiful. My dancing may be more like swaying."

"I don't mind. We'll just go and enjoy ourselves."

"All right. It may be a long time before I get to do something like that again."

"Well, every man wants to hear that kind of enthusiasm when he asks someone out."

"I didn't mean for it to sound like that. Thanks for inviting me."

The waiter stopped by the table and refilled their glasses.

"That was much better. Why don't I bring the chest of drawers and the rocker out when I come to pick you up? That's if you don't mind me dressing at your place."

"That sounds fine. I can hardly wait to see what they look like in the baby's room."

The wedding suddenly didn't seem like the drudgery that Ryan had thought it would be.

They finishing their meal talking about movies they'd enjoyed and places they would one day like to visit.

On Friday, Phoebe wasn't sure which she was looking forward to more, seeing the furniture installed in the baby's room or the evening of dancing with Ryan. Thankfully it was a school holiday so she didn't have to lose any of her leave time by being off that day.

Ryan had said she was special. She liked being special to someone and especially to him. But it wasn't something she was going to let go any further.

Ryan had taken over her care. As odd as it was, it seemed right to let him be there when the baby was born. In the last couple of weeks he had more than proved himself the compassionate and understanding person Joshua had promised he would be. She couldn't have asked for better help. And it had been cheerfully given. She liked Ryan too much. Appreciated his support. She could use all those attributes when she delivered.

He was as good as his word. Which she had learned Ryan always was. He pulled up in front of her house at three o'clock.

She stepped out onto the veranda when she saw a sports car followed by a red truck she recognized pull to the curb. Ryan stepped out of the car and waved. She strolled down the path toward him. A man almost as tall as Ryan climbed out of the truck.

"Phoebe, this is Mike. He came along to help me move the chest in."

"Hi, Mike, thanks for going out of your way to do this."

"Nice to meet you. No worries. Ryan has given me a hand a few times."

She looked at Ryan but he gave no explanation. Knowing him, he'd gone out of his way more than once to help people, yet he had no one special in his life. It was as if he was all about deeds but not about becoming emotionally involved. Did he feel the same way about her?

"Let's get these in. Phoebe and I have a wedding to attend," he said to Mike.

The two men undid the straps securing the chest and rocker in the truck bed. They carried the chest into the house.

"Show us where you want it," Ryan said to her. She followed them down the hall and into the baby's room.

She had them place it against the wall opposite the bed. "Perfect."

Ryan grinned. "I'll get the rocker."

"Thank you for your help," Phoebe told Ryan's friend as he followed Ryan out the door.

He waved an arm. "No problem, mate."

She waited there for Ryan to return.

Doing a back-and-forth maneuver, he brought the rocker through the doorway. "Where do you want it?"

"Next to the bed, I think."

He placed it where she'd suggested.

She gave the top of the chair a nudge and watched it rock.

"Aren't you going to try it?"

"Yes, I am." She promptly took a seat, placing her hands on the ends of the arms. Moving back and forth a couple of times, she looked up at him and said in a reverent tone, "It's wonderful. Just wonderful."

"I'm glad you like it."

"I do." She continued to rock and rub the arms with her hands.

"I hate to mention this but we need to get a move on or we'll be late to Sophia's wedding."

"I know. All I need to do is slip on my dress. It shouldn't take long." She pushed out of the chair with obvious reluctance.

"My suit is in the car. Mind if I change in the other bedroom?"

"Make yourself at home," Phoebe said, as she walked out of the room. She stopped and faced him. "Ryan, it's really nice to have you around. You have been a good friend the last few weeks. I really needed one."

* * *

A lump came to Ryan's throat he couldn't clear. His heart thumped in his chest. All he could do was look at her. Before he could speak she was gone. With those few words from her he received the same high he did when he delivered a baby. That the world could be a good and kind place. Her happiness was starting to matter too much.

What had he gotten himself into? As hard as he'd worked to keep their relationship centered on helping her get ready for the baby, he'd still grown to care for the fascinating and fabulous woman that was the mother. If he wasn't careful he could become far too involved with Phoebe. Start to care too much. Did he have that in him?

He'd dressed and was waiting in the living room for Phoebe when she entered, carrying her shoes. She wore a modest sleeveless pale blue dress that had pleats in front. Her hair was down but she had pulled one side of it away from her face. It was held in place with a sparkling clasp. She was beautiful in her simplicity.

"I hate to ask this but could you help me buckle my shoes? I've been working for five minutes to figure out how to do it around this baby and it's just not working."

Ryan smiled. "Have a seat and I'll give it a try."

She sat on the sofa and Ryan went down on one knee.

"You look like Prince Charming, dressed in your suit."

"More like a shoe salesman."

They both laughed.

She handed him a shoe and he lifted her foot and put it on.

Working with the small buckle, he said, "No wonder you were having such a hard time. This would be difficult for an aerospace engineer."

"Yes, but they look good."

Ryan rolled his eyes.

"Let's get the other one on. Man went to the moon with less effort than I'm putting into this."

She gave his shoulder a playful slap. "Remind me not to ask you for help again."

He gave her a pointed look. "And your plan for getting these off is?"

She smiled. "You are now acting like a shoe salesman and not Prince Charming."

He finished the task and stood. "Just so you'll recognize it, this is the part where I am Prince Charming." He reached out both hands.

Phoebe put hers in his and he pulled her up until she stood. Ryan continued to hold her hands as he stepped back and studied her. "You look beautiful."

She blinked and a dreamy smile spread across her face. "Thank you. That was very Prince Charming-ish. You look very dashing yourself."

He chuckled. A ripple of pride went through him at her praise. "I do try."

She removed her hands from his and went across the room to where a shawl and purse lay in the chair nearest the front door. "We should go."

"Yes, we should. It's an hour's drive and I've not been there before."

"I know how to get there. I've been by Overnewton Castle many times. I've always wanted to go there for afternoon tea but never have been in."

"Well, princess, this is your chance." Ryan opened the door.

As she went out onto the veranda she said, "Yeah, like I look like a princess. More like a duck."

Not to me.

CHAPTER SEVEN

PHOEBE HAD HEARD that Overnewton Castle was gorgeous but she'd never imagined it was anything like this magnificent. As Ryan drove up the tree-lined drive, the Victorian Tudor-style house came into view. It resembled a castle with its textured masonry, steep roofs and turrets. The multiple stories of corners and angles covered in ivy made it look even more impressive. The expanse of rolling hills and river below created a view that was breathtaking. It was a fairy-tale spot to hold a wedding or a princess for the evening.

"Wow, what a place," Ryan said, as he pulled into the car park that was secluded by trees. "After getting engaged in a hot-air balloon, I shouldn't be surprised that Sophia and Aiden would pick a place like this to marry."

"You don't like it?"

"Sure. It's just a little over the top for me."

"I love it." She did rather feel like a princess, being out with Ryan with the beautiful house as a backdrop.

He came around and helped her out. "I'm more like a beside-the-creek kind of guy but I have to admit this is a nice place."

"Getting married beside a creek, with the water washing over the rock, does sound nice." She pulled the shawl closer around her. When she had trouble adjusting it Ryan removed it, untwisted it and placed it across her shoulders once more. His hands lingered warm and heavy on her shoulders for a second. She missed his touch the instant it was gone.

"I think it's more about making a commitment and less about having a wedding."

Worry entered her voice. "You don't think Sophia and Aiden will last?"

"I'm not saying that. I think they'll do fine. It's just that I was in the service with too many guys whose wives had to have these big weddings and the marriages didn't last two years." He took her arm and placed it through his, putting his other hand over hers. She felt protected. Something that had been missing in her life for too long. They walked in the direction of the house.

"I had no idea you were such a cynic."

Ryan shrugged. "Maybe I am, but I just know what I've seen."

Her foot faltered on the stone path and he steadied her by pulling her against him. They continued down the path until it opened into a grassy area where white chairs had been arranged for the ceremony. Surrounding the area were trees, green foliage and brightly blooming flowers. It was a cozy place for a garden wedding.

"This must be the place." Ryan led her through the hedge opening.

Men and women stood in small groups between the house and the ceremony area. Phoebe recognized a few staff members from the hospital. An unsure feeling washed over her. Should she be here?

"Something wrong?" Ryan asked, as they made their way across the garden.

He always seemed to know when she was disturbed. She pulled away from him. "Are you sure you should have brought me? These are the people you work with and I'm not one of them."

"Look at me, Phoebe." She did. His gaze was intense. "I wanted you here with me." He took her hand. "I want to introduce you to some people I work with."

With Ryan beside her she was capable of facing anything. Phoebe had no doubt that he would remain beside her. She could rely on him. What it all came back to was that she could trust him. He would be there for her. This was the kind of relationship she'd been looking for, dreamed of. A man who would stand beside her. She glanced at his profile, and smiled.

Phoebe recognized a number of the guests from their pictures on the wall of the clinic but there was no reason that they would know her. She had only been a patient of Sophia, and now Ryan. Still, were they surprised to see him show up with a pregnant date?

She pulled on Ryan's hand, bringing him to a stop. "In that case, we both need to look our best. Let me straighten your tie."

"What's wrong with my tie?"

"It just needs an adjustment." Phoebe stepped so close that the baby brushed against him as she reached up to move his tie a centimeter to the left. "Now it's perfect."

Their gazes met.

"No, *you're* perfect." She blinked. His low raspy voice sent a ripple of awareness through her.

"Thank you," she said softly, "and thanks for this evening. It's already been wonderful." She meant that with all her heart.

His brow arched. "We haven't done anything yet."

"I know, but it was nice just to be invited out." *And to be treated as someone special.*

The group opened up as they approached to include

them. Ryan went around the circle, introducing everyone. His hand came to rest on the curve of her back. "And this is my friend, Phoebe Taylor."

She noticed that Ryan had presented her as a friend when he'd only introduced the people he worked with as his colleagues. It seemed as if he didn't have many people he considered friends. Yet he and she had formed what she would call a friendship. Why didn't he have more of them?

Ryan was acting nothing like he had the day she had met him. Was he hiding from the world for some reason? What had happened?

She smiled and listened to the conversation and banter between the members of the group. Ryan wasn't left out. He was obviously liked so why didn't he consider any of them his friends?

A few minutes later the notes from a harp sounded to announce it was time for the ceremony to begin. People started taking their seats.

"Sophia has pulled out all the stops for this wedding. I don't believe I've ever been to one with someone playing the harp," Ryan whispered. His breath brushed her neck as they stood in line, waiting for the usher to seat them.

Shivers ran down her spine. Thankfully her reaction went unnoticed because a tuxedo-wearing groomsman approached. He offered his arm and escorted her down the aisle, with Ryan following.

As they took their seats Ryan spoke to a couple of women sitting behind them. One he introduced as Isla, the head midwife in the maternity unit, and her husband, Dr. Alessandro Manos, who was one of the doctors there. Phoebe recognized Isla from visits to the clinic. A number of times Phoebe had seen her in the hallway. She was also very familiar with the prominent Delamere name. It appeared often in the society pages. She and Isla had something in common. Isla was pregnant as well but not as far along as she was. The other woman was Dr. Darcie Green. Phoebe was told she was a visiting obstetrician from London but she didn't catch her date's name.

After they were settled in their chairs she glanced at Ryan. He wore a stoic look. She leaned toward him. "This really isn't your favorite thing to do, is it?"

His shoulder touched hers. They must have looked like two lovers whispering. What would it be like to be loved by Ryan? Amazing would be her guess. She'd sworn to herself she wouldn't cross the line, had made Ryan pledge the same, but she wasn't sure she wanted it that way any longer.

"Do you know a man that enjoys this?"

She paused. "No, I guess not. We don't have to stay."

"I promised dinner and dancing and I don't plan to disappoint you." Ryan moved closer, putting his mouth to her ear. The intimacy made her grow warm. "*Men* do like food and holding women."

Was he looking forward to dancing with her as much as she was look forward to spending time in his arms? Thankfully, a woman stood in front and began to sing a hymn, leaving Phoebe no more time to contemplate the anticipation of having Ryan hold her. She wasn't sure she could have commented if she'd had a chance. Minutes later the parents of the bride and groom were seated. The harpist played again. The groom and groomsmen stepped to the altar, which was defined by a white metal arch.

Phoebe straightened her back as far as she could to see over the heads of those sitting in front of them. The men wore black tuxedos, making them look not only dashing but sophisticated. She glanced at Ryan and imagined what he would look like in a tux. Very handsome, no doubt. She could only see the top of the best man's head. He was in a wheelchair.

Ryan put his arm across the back of her chair and whispered, "That's Aiden's brother, Nathan, in the chair."

Phoebe nodded.

The harpist continued to play as the bridesmaids came down the aisle. They were dressed in bright yellow knee-length dresses of various styles. Each carried a bouquet of white daisies. As they joined the men, they made a striking combination against the backdrop of trees and plants.

A breeze picked up and Phoebe pulled her wrap closer. She felt Ryan adjusting the wrap to cover her right arm completely. His hand rested on her shoulder. There was something reassuring about the possessive way he touched her.

She looked at him and smiled.

It was time for Sophia to come down the aisle. At the first note of the traditional wedding march everyone stood. Phoebe went up on her toes to catch a glimpse of the bride going by.

"Move so I can see." She nudged Ryan back a step so she could peer around him.

He gave her an indulgent smile and complied.

What little she could observe of Sophia looked beautiful. When she reached Aiden all the guests sat.

Ryan's hand came to rest on her shoulder again. He nudged her close. "You really do like this stuff."

"Shush," Phoebe hissed.

He chuckled softly.

It wasn't long until Sophia and Aiden were coming back down the aisle as man and wife.

Ryan took Phoebe's hand as they filed out of their row. He continued to hold it while they walked across the garden toward the house where the reception would be held.

They entered the main hall through glass doors. Cocktails and hors d'oeuvres were being served there. Phoebe gasped at the beauty of the majestic circular staircase before them. It and the dark wood paneling were all the decoration required.

"Come over here," Ryan said, placing his hand on her waist. "If you plan to dance the night away, I think you need to get off your feet and rest while you can."

For once she accepted his concern and consideration. She'd gone so many years doing everything for herself that having someone think of her was fabulous. This evening she was going to enjoy being pampered. Having it done by Ryan would be even nicer.

There were high-backed chairs sitting along the wall and she took one of them. Ryan stood beside her. When the waiter carrying drinks came by they both requested something nonalcoholic, she because she was pregnant and he because he said he would be driving. She liked it that he was acting responsibly. Now that she was having a baby it seemed she thought about that more.

A number of people stopped and spoke to Ryan. While he talked to them, his fingers lightly rested against the top of her shoulder. It would be clear to everyone that she was with him. He never failed to introduce her. A few people gave her belly a searching look and then grinned at them. They must have thought they were a couple.

"Why, hello, Ryan. I never took you for a wedding kind of guy. I've never even seen you at a Christmas party." The words were delivered in a teasing tone by a woman who joined them.

Phoebe looked up at Ryan and he seemed to take the comment in stride.

"Hello, Vera. It's nice to see you, too. Sophia twisted my arm on this one. Couldn't get out of it. I'd like you to meet Phoebe Taylor." He directed the next statement to Phoebe. "Vera is the hospital's chief anesthetist."

"Hi." Phoebe smiled at Vera.

"Nice to meet you." Vera's attention went back to Ryan. "I had no idea you were expecting a baby."

"It's not mine."

"Oh." She made the word carry a mountain of suggestions and questions.

"Phoebe was a wife of a friend of mine in the service. He was killed eight months ago."

Vera looked down at Phoebe. "I'm sorry."

"Thank you." Somehow the pain of Joshua not being there had eased over the last few weeks.

"So when's the baby due?"

"In just a few weeks," Phoebe said.

"You're being followed at Victoria antenatal?" Vera showed true interest.

"You mean prenatal," Ryan quipped.

She glared at him. "I wished you'd get away from calling it that. I have to think twice when you do."

"And I have to think when you called it antenatal. Old habits die hard."

"I guess they do. Well, I'd better mingle. Nice to meet you, Phoebe."

"Bye." Once again Ryan had proved that he was well liked and respected. So why didn't he socialize with his colleagues?

A few minutes later the guests were called to dinner. On a table outside the room was a place card with Ryan's name on it and a table number. He picked it up and led the way.

The room was stunning. Round tables with white tablecloths covering them to the floor filled it. Chairs were also covered in white with matching bows on the back. At the front of the room, facing the guests, was one long table for the bridal party.

By the time they arrived at their table, Isla and Darcie, the two women who had sat behind them during the ceremony, were already there. Ryan took the chair next to Darcie, and Phoebe sat on his other side. Another couple who knew Isla joined them and took the last seats. Everyone introduced themselves. Most of Phoebe's time was spent talking to the woman beside her. Occasionally, someone across the table would ask a question but hearing was difficult with the amount of chatter in the room.

The bridal party was introduced and Sophia and Aiden took their places before the meal was served. The noise dropped as people ate.

"So, Phoebe," Isla asked from directly across the table, "when's your baby due?"

That was the most popular question of the evening. "In a couple of weeks."

"Are you being seen in the MMU?"

"I am. Sophia was my midwife but she thought falling in love was more important." Phoebe smiled.

"That does happen. Who's following you now?"

"That would be me," Ryan announced. There was a note of pride in his voice.

A hush came over the table. Phoebe didn't miss the looks of shock on the two women's faces. Was something wrong? She glanced at Ryan. It wasn't a secret. Why should it be?

"Phoebe needed someone and I volunteered," Ryan offered, as he picked up his water glass and took a sip.

Both women looked from him, then back to her and back again. Ryan didn't seem fazed by their reaction.

Finally Isla said, "Ryan's one of the best. You'll be happy with his care."

After they had eaten their meal, Ryan watched Phoebe make her way to the restroom. His attention was drawn away from her when Isla sat down in Phoebe's place.

Isla leaned close and hissed, "Just what do you think you're doing?"

He sat back, surprised by her aggression. "Doing?"

Darcie moved in from the other side, sandwiching him in. "You're dating a patient!"

"I am not."

"What do you call it when you bring the woman you're going to deliver for to a wedding as your date?" Isla asked.

"I call it dating," Darcie quipped.

"Look, Phoebe is the widow of a service buddy of mine. All I'm trying to do is be her friend. She doesn't have anyone else."

"That wasn't a friendly arm around her at the ceremony. Or a friendly look just a second ago when she walked away," Isla stated, as if she were giving a lecture to a first-year student.

"Or when you were looking at her as she fixed your tie," Darcie added.

"You saw that?" Ryan was amazed. They had seen what he'd believed he'd been covering well—his attraction to Phoebe.

"Yes, we…" Darcie indicated her date "…went past you and you didn't even see us, you were so engrossed."

"I was not."

"You can deny it all you want but I'm telling you what I saw. The point here is that you shouldn't be dating a patient. It's bad form and if someone wanted to make a big deal of it you might lose your job." Isla looked around as if she was checking to see if anyone was listening.

Ryan chuckled. "You're overreacting to two friends spending an evening together."

"I still say you better be careful. You're stepping over the line with this one," Isla said.

Darcie nodded her agreement.

He leaned back and looked at one then the other. "Well, are either one of you going to report me?"

The two women looked at each other. Both shook their heads.

"Thank you. I asked Phoebe to come with me because she's had a rough year, finding out her husband was killed and then that she was pregnant. This was her big night out before the baby comes. In any case, all of that about me delivering the baby will be a moot point in a few weeks. So, ladies, I appreciate your concern but I'm going to show Phoebe a pleasant evening and if that looks bad to you I'm sorry."

They grinned at each other.

"You were right, Isla. He does care about her." Darcie smirked.

Isla patted him on the shoulder. "Good luck."

Ryan wasn't sure what that meant but it was better than being reprimanded for something he didn't believe was a problem.

Phoebe returned, and Isla moved back to her chair and kissed her husband on the cheek as she sat down. She smiled at Phoebe.

After Phoebe sat she leaned over and whispered, "Is everything all right?"

He took her hand beneath the table, gave it a squeeze and held it. "Everything is great."

Dessert had been served by the time the bride and groom started around the room, greeting their guests. When they reached Phoebe and Ryan's table Sophia hugged each person in turn until she worked her way to Ryan.

"Well, I'm glad to see you. I wasn't sure you'd be here."

Ryan hugged Sophia in return. "O ye of little faith."

She laughed and turned to Phoebe. For a second there was a look of astonishment on Sophia's face when she saw her but it soon disappeared. "Phoebe, I'm so glad to see you. I'd like you to meet my husband, Aiden."

While Phoebe spoke to Aiden, Ryan didn't miss the look that passed between Sophia, Isla and Darcie.

Did his feelings for Phoebe really show that much? They must if they were that obvious to the three women. How had he let it happen? He glanced at Phoebe. The devil of it was, he hadn't. All it took was just being around Phoebe to make him care. And that he did far too much.

She giggled at something Sophia said. He wanted her too much. There was little that was professional about his feelings. How would she take it when he told her that he could no longer be her midwife?

The strains of an orchestra tuning up came from somewhere in the house.

Sophia's father asked everyone to join them for dancing and a toast to the bride and groom in the solarium. Ryan took her hand as they made their way there. It was as if he didn't want to break the contact with her. She didn't want to, either.

Phoebe had been sure that what she'd already seen of the castle couldn't be surpassed, but she'd been wrong. Two-thirds of the solarium consisted of glass walls and glass ceiling. It had turned dark and small lights above created a magical place.

Ryan directed her to one of the café-size tables stationed around the room. They sat and watched the bride and groom dance their first dance. The staff saw to it that everyone had a glass of champagne to toast the couple. Ryan smiled as he tapped her glass. Phoebe took the smallest sip and set the glass down. His joined hers on the table. The orchestra began to play again.

Ryan stood and offered his hand. "It's time I made good on my promise. Would you care to dance?"

"Why, sir, I think I would." Phoebe smiled at him and placed her hand in his.

"I'll have to tell you that I'm not a very good dancer," Ryan said, as he led her out on to the floor.

She laughed. "Have you looked at me lately? I'm not very graceful so I don't think it'll matter if you're a good dancer or not."

"Then I guess we're the perfect match."

Were they really?

Ryan took her into his arms, holding her close as they moved around the floor. He'd touched her before but had never put his arms completely around her. It was lovely to have him so close. He smelled like a warm forest after a spring rain. She leaned in and inhaled. Wonderful.

The overhead lights were turned low and the tiny ones became more brilliant. They slowly swayed to the music. Did fairy tales really come true? Phoebe had no idea if they were with the beat or not. It didn't matter. The next song was a faster one and they separated. She felt the loss of Ryan's warmth immediately and her body waited impatiently to have it returned. Not allowing her to completely lose contact, he continued to hold one of her hands. As soon as the faster dance was over, he brought her back into his embrace. Her fingers rested on his shoulders and his found her waist. As they moved slowly, they looked into each other's eyes. Something was occurring here that she'd never planned, never thought would happen. She was falling in love.

"Does dancing with me make you think of that game you might have played in gym class where you had to keep a ball between you and your partner without using your hands?"

He stopped moving. "How's that?"

"Dancing with the baby between us."

Ryan laughed. "I had skill at that game. Always won." He pulled her closer. "You're the best partner I've ever had."

Her hand cupped his face. "You're a nice guy."

Ryan's eyes grew intense and he cleared his throat. "It's warm in here. Why don't we go outside for a few minutes?"

She nodded. He led her through a half-hidden glass door that looked like part of the wall, onto a brick patio.

"It feels good out here." Phoebe breathed in the cold evening air. The music from inside drifted around them. It was painfully romantic. Was Ryan feeling the same need?

"It does." Ryan stood a couple of steps away, just out of touching distance.

She wanted his touch. Wanted to feel desired. It had been too long. Even with Joshua the last time she hadn't felt desire. Sex had become more of an obligation, expectation than anything else. There should be more than that in a relationship. There was with Ryan. Would he think she was too forward if she reached for him?

A wide set of steps led to a pond below. Surrounding it was an extensive grassy area. The lights of the solarium reflected off the water, making the view even more dreamlike. Phoebe started down the steps.

"Where're you going?" Ryan asked.

"I thought I'd stand in the garden and admire the solarium." She was already watching the others dance when Ryan joined her.

"It reminds me of a carousel music box I once had as a child. As it played, horses with people riding them went by in shadow. It was like watching something magical. I could look at it for hours. I loved it," she whispered, as much to herself as to him.

"You are a romantic." He now stood close enough that his arm brushed hers as their fingers intertwined.

"Because I think there can be fairy tales?"

He didn't say anything for a while. "I haven't believed in fairy tales for a long time, but somehow when I'm around you they do seem possible."

"I know you've lived through some horrible things you can't seem to leave behind, but you need to know there's good in life, too. Happy times that can replace the bad. Like this baby. Joshua is gone, yet in a way he's bringing new life into the world. Something good for me."

"Good can be hard to find."

His fingers tightened. Phoebe glanced at him. He stood rigid, as if the discussion was painful for him. His gaze met hers and she said, "It can be. And it can come from unexpected places, too."

"Like you?"

"I like to think so but I wasn't talking about me so much as from friends and family. Finding people that matter to you. Letting them know they are important to you."

"I can't do that."

She stepped closer, her body touching his. "I think you can. In fact, I know you can. You've been a friend to me these last few weeks."

They continued to stand there, not saying a word. It wasn't until the doors were opened wide by the Overnewton staff members that the spell was broken and they broke apart. The crowd poured out of the solarium and began lining up along the steps.

"I guess it's time for Sophia and Aiden to leave," Phoebe murmured.

"We should join everyone." Ryan didn't sound like he

really wanted to. Had their conversation put a dampener on the evening? She would hate that to happen. Had she ever enjoyed a wedding more?

As they stood at the bottom of the steps, a gust of wind caught her shawl. She shivered and pulled it closer.

"You're cold." Ryan removed his jacket and placed it over her shoulders. It still held his body heat. His scent. She pulled it tighter around her.

Someone near passed them each a small container of bird seed. As Sophia and Aiden descended the steps they were showered with the seed for good luck. When they reached Phoebe and Ryan, Aiden whisked Sophia into his arms and carried her to a waiting car.

Phoebe looked down at her expanded middle. "I'd like to see someone whisk me up like that."

Suddenly her feet were in the air and she was being held against a hard chest. "Oh."

Her arms went around Ryan's neck. He swung her around a few times. She giggled.

Ryan put her on her feet again. "I didn't see it as a problem."

As he smiled down at her, a tingle grew low within her from the warmth she saw in his eyes. She glanced around. Some of the crowd was watching them. She didn't care. What she wanted was to help make Ryan see that fairy tales could come true. He had the biggest heart of any-one she knew, loyal, caring and generous. With a wicked sense of humor that only made her love him more. That's what she felt. Love for him. She'd fallen under his spell. He wasn't going to leave her. More than once he'd proved he'd be there when she needed him. She could depend on him.

Phoebe's hands remained about his neck. She looked up into his eyes and smiled. "That was fun."

"I think it's time for us to go." He looked down at her, his voice coming out soft and raspy.

Ryan walked Phoebe to her door. She'd been quiet on their drive home. Had she been thinking about those moments when they had looked into each other's eyes? He'd known then there was no going back. He wanted her and she wanted him. It had been there in her crystal clear look of assurance.

As he'd pulled out onto the main road, he'd taken her hand and rested it on his thigh. She hadn't resisted. For once she hadn't fallen asleep during the drive. Had she been as keyed up as he'd been? He wanted her but he couldn't lead her on. Have her believe there was more than just a physical attraction between them.

Her hand had remained in his the entire way back to Box Hill. She had asked for his help with her shoes when they'd arrived at his car. He had obliged. When they'd arrived at her house she'd stepped out of the car carrying them by two fingers.

They walked to her front porch. "It was a perfect evening, Ryan. Thank you so much for inviting me."

"I'm glad you had a good time. Mine wouldn't have been near as nice if you'd not gone with me."

She fumbled with her purse.

"Hand those to me." Ryan indicated the shoes. She found her keys and unlocked the door, pushing it open. Ryan followed her in.

"Would you like some coffee?" Phoebe dropped her shoes beside the door.

"I thought you didn't drink coffee."

She turned to look at him. "I don't. I bought it for you."

"Then, yes, I would." It had been a long time since someone had bought anything especially for him. It meant she thought about him even when he wasn't around. That idea he liked far too much.

He followed her to the kitchen. He leaned against the door frame and watched as Phoebe put a kettle of water on a burner. He was fascinated by the combination of her in a beautiful dress with bare feet, preparing coffee. There was something so domestic about the picture that it made him want to run as far away from there as he could get while at the same time it pulled him in, making him wish for more, had him longing for someone special in his life.

Phoebe stood on her toes to reach the bag of coffee. Her dress rose enough that he had a view of the backs of her knees and thighs. An impulse to run a hand along all that skin and under her dress made his pants tighten. Heaven help him, he wanted her so badly. Right here, right now. The entire evening had been leading up to this moment. From the time he'd was on his knee, helping her put her shoes on, until now he'd known he had to have her.

He should walk away. Go out the door without a word said. The gentleman in him, the professional, screamed for him to leave. But he wouldn't. The temptation to kiss her was too great. Unable to resist, he closed the small distance between them. Pushing her hair away, he kissed her neck. He pressed his front to her back, letting his desire be known. "I know what I agreed to, but I can't stop myself. I want you."

Before he could say more, she pushed back against him, gaining enough room to face him. She wrapped her hands around his waist and lifted her face. Her eyes were clear and confident. The quiver of her lips gave him a hint of what this boldness was costing her. Still, she was offering.

Slowly his mouth met hers.

A flood of disappointment went through him when she

pulled away seconds later but quickly turned into a storm of longing as Phoebe's lips met his again. They were soft and mobile. Small cushions of bliss. This was better than he remembered. He wanted more.

Ryan reached around her and turned off the burner, then pulled her closer. He brought his lips more fully against hers.

Phoebe's hands moved to grip his biceps. She shifted, pressing her breasts to his chest.

The arousal he felt at the first touch of her lips grew, lengthened. Hardened. His mouth released hers and moved across her cheek. He left a trail of butterfly kisses on his way to the sweet spot behind her ear. Phoebe moaned, then tilted her head so that he could better reach her neck. She snuggled against him.

The desire to have her made his muscles draw tight. He wanted her here. Now. His hands caressed her back and settled low on her hips. He gathered her dress in his hands and pulled her against his throbbing need.

"Phoebe, you'll have to stop us because I can't," he murmured as his mouth pressed down on hers, begging her for entrance.

Her hands went to the nape of his neck in an eager movement, pulling his lips more firmly to hers. She opened her mouth, and his tongue didn't hesitate to gain entrance. Hers met his to tease and tantalize. It was a duel of pleasure that he didn't want to win.

His body hummed with a need that only Phoebe could ease.

She pulled her mouth away.

"Aw. What's wrong?"

"The baby kicked."

Damn. He'd forgotten all about the baby. How could he? Because he was so focused on his hunger for Phoebe.

He stepped back far enough that he was no longer touching her.

"I'm sorry. I didn't mean to hurt you."

"Silly, you weren't hurting me." She took a predatory step toward him. "Babies kick."

"I shouldn't, we shouldn't…"

"Come on, Ryan. We're adults. I'm certainly aware of the facts of life, and I'm sure you are, too. So we both know that what we were doing wouldn't hurt the baby. I want this. I want you. From what I could tell, you wanted me."

That would be an understatement.

"I'm going to my bedroom. I hope you join me. If not, please lock up on your way out."

She went up on the tips of her toes, kissed him and left the kitchen. Ryan stood there with his manhood aching and the choice of a lifetime to make.

How like Phoebe to be so direct. If he joined her, could he remain emotionally detached? He already cared more than he should and certainly more than he was comfortable with. But if he didn't, he would never know the heaven of being with Phoebe. There was no decision. A beautiful, desirable woman that he wanted was offering him the world. There was no question of whether or not to accept.

CHAPTER EIGHT

PHOEBE SAT ON the edge of the bed in her room. A lone lamp burned on her bedside table. She'd never been so brazen in her life. But how else was she going to get through to Ryan? She wanted him desperately. Needed his calm caring, his reliability and assurance in her life. It was so quiet in the house that she feared he'd slipped out and gone home. Seconds later her heart thumped against her ribs at the sound of footfalls in the hallway.

He'd stayed.

Ryan hesitated at the door. Their gazes met, held. He removed his tie and jacket and dropped them over the chair, then he stalked across the floor and pulled her to her feet and into his arms.

This was where she belonged.

His mouth met hers. She opened for him. Their tongues mated in a frenzied battle of touch and retreat. Heat flowed through her, strong and sure, pooling low in her. Ryan's lips left hers and he buried his face in her neck. He nipped at her skin. The desire that flickered in her blazed.

He gathered her dress along one leg, sliding a hand under the fabric. She hissed as his fingers touched her skin. His hand glided around her leg until it found the inside of her thigh and squeezed lightly. She shivered.

Ryan removed his hand. He met her gaze. Placing his hands on her shoulders, he turned her around.

"What…?"

"Shush," he all but growled. He gathered her hair, running his fingers through it. "Beautiful," he murmured, before placing it over a shoulder.

There was a tug at the top of her dress. He opened the zipper. The tug ended and his lips found the skin between her shoulder blades. A shudder traveled down her spine. His mouth skimmed over each vertebra to her waist. There he spent some time kissing and touching with the tip of his tongue the curve of her back.

She began to move but he said, "Not yet."

Ryan's fingertip followed the same path upward, then his palms until he brushed her dress off her shoulders. She crossed her arms, preventing the dress from falling away from her breasts.

He kissed the length of the ridge between her neck and arm. "So silky."

Phoebe sighed. This was too wonderful. "Let me turn off the lamp."

He guided her to face him. "Phoebe, look at me."

Her eyes rose to meet his gaze.

"You're beautiful." He placed his hands on either side of the baby. "That's a new life you're carrying. There's nothing more amazing or natural than that. Please don't hide it from me."

If she could have melted she would have. "You're sure?"

"Honey, I'm more than sure." Ryan moved closer to bring his taught length against her belly, leaving her in no doubt of his desire.

It was an empowering thought to know that was all for her.

Stepping back, he took both her hands and opened

her arms. The dress fell away, leaving her breasts visible, cupped in a lacy pink bra. Her dress gathered on her belly. Ryan gave it a gentle tug at the seams and the dress pooled around her feet on the floor.

His gaze fixed on her breasts. He sucked in a breath and she crossed her arms again.

"Please, don't. You're amazing. I want to admire you."

"They're so large." She couldn't look at him.

Ryan lifted her chin with a finger until her gaze met his. "I don't know a man in the world who doesn't love large breasts. Especially if they are his to admire."

The heat building in her grew. Ryan knew how to make her feel beautiful.

He removed her arms. Using a finger, he followed the cleft of her cleavage. Her nipples pushed against her bra as they swelled. A tingle zipped through her breasts. His finger traced the line of her bra first over one mound and then the other. She swayed and Ryan slipped an arm around her.

With a deft movement of his fingers he unclipped her bra. He slipped it off one arm. His tongue followed the same path as his finger. On the return trip, he veered off. At the same time his free hand lifted her right breast, his mouth captured her nipple.

Her womb contracted. "Ryan…" she muttered. She wasn't sure if she was begging for him to stop or to continue.

Ryan supported her as she leaned back, offering herself completely to him. Her hands went to his shoulders in the hope she could steady her body and her emotions. His mouth slid to the other nipple. Her fingertips bit into his shoulders.

Ryan's hand traced the line of her undies until he reached her center. It brushed her mound and retreated. Her center throbbed with the need for him to return. Using the arm around her waist, he pulled her toward him until she was no longer leaning back. His hand swept the other strap of her bra off and down her arm, letting the undergarment drop to the floor.

She looked at him. Ryan's gaze was fixed on her breasts. His hand reached up and stopped millimeters from her nipple. It had the slightest tremor to it. She would have missed it if she hadn't been watching. They both understood the facts of life well and still these moments of passion were overwhelming. He touched the tip of her nipple with the end of his finger.

Something similar to lightning shot through her.

"So responsive," Ryan murmured in a note of satisfaction as he ran a finger gently over her skin. It was as if a breeze had come through. He did the same to the other breast.

Phoebe quaked all over. There was something erotic about watching Ryan touch her. Her nerve endings tingled. She had to touch him. See his reaction.

He moved back and lifted both her breasts, kissing each one in turn. Taking a nipple in his mouth, he traced it with his tongue and tugged. She bucked against him.

"Clothes." The word came out as a strangled sound. "I want to see you."

A noise came low in his throat. Leaving a kiss on the curve of her breast, he stepped back. Undoing his tie, he jerked it from his collar and began unbuttoning his shirt.

While he did that she released his belt. She ran the back of her hand down the bulge of his manhood. His body's reaction to hers was stimulating. It gave her a boldness she'd never had before. She backed away until her legs found the side of the bed and she sat. Looking up at Ryan, she caught his gaze. "Come here. It's my turn."

His shirt fluttered to the floor. He stepped close enough

for her to touch him. Finding his zipper, she slowly lowered it. Her hand moved to touch him but he stopped her by capturing her hand and bringing it to his lips. "Don't." The word sounded harsh with tension. "I don't think I can control myself if you do."

Phoebe pulled her hand from his. Sliding her hands between the waist of his pants and his hips, she pushed. His trousers fell to the floor. He wore red plaid boxers that didn't disguise his size. Ryan was no small man anywhere.

He kicked off his shoes, then finished removing his slacks. Leaning over, he jerked off his socks.

Phoebe reached out and ran her hand through his hair. Her fingers itched to gather the mass and pull him to her. Had she ever been this turned on? She wanted Ryan beside her, on her and in her like she'd never wanted before. Her hands slowly slipped from his hair and Ryan looked at her. He nudged her back on the bed and came down beside her.

"I want to touch you like you did me." Phoebe rolled to her side.

He faced her.

Her heart leaped at his unspoken agreement. The lovemaking between Joshua and her had always been fast and desperate, never slow and passionate, as she was experiencing now.

Ryan wasn't sure he could stand much more of Phoebe's administering. As it was, he gritted his teeth to control his need to dive into her.

Her index finger traced the line of his lips. He captured the end and drew it into his mouth and sucked. Her eyes darkened. She slowly removed her finger. His manhood flinched. Did she have any idea how erotic she was?

Phoebe's small hand ran down the side of his neck in a gentle motion. It glided over his shoulder. She placed a kiss there. Her hair hid her face as it flowed over his skin like silk. He couldn't resist touching it, watching it move through his fingers. Pushing it away from her face, he cupped her cheek and brought her lips to his. She eagerly accepted. Her hands fluttered across his chest, moving up to the nape of his neck.

When he leaned over to take the kiss deeper, Phoebe pushed against his shoulders, breaking the connection. One hand at his neck dropped lower to run across his chest. She took an infinite amount of time tracing each of his ribs. As if she was trying to commit each curve, dip and rise of him to memory. His muscles quivered from the attention.

Her hand went lower, a finger dipping into his belly button. At his sharp inhalation she giggled. He loved the sound. Her hand moved to his side and rubbed up and down it to return to his stomach. She smoothed her fingers over his hip. The tips slipped under the elastic band of his boxers and retreated just as quickly.

Phoebe rose enough to accommodate the baby and kissed the center of his chest. At the same time her fingers went deeper under his boxers than before, touching the tip of his manhood.

Only with a force of control he hadn't known he possessed did he manage not to lose it.

Pulling her back, he gathered her to him and kissed her with a depth of need he was afraid to examine. She clung to him as if she never wanted to let him go.

"Phoebe, I need you now."

"I'm here."

Ryan scooted off the bed and removed his boxers. Phoebe's intake of breath made his manhood rise. He held out his hand and she took it, standing. His hands found the waistband of her undies and slipped them down her legs. She stepped out of them. He flipped the covers back to the end of the bed. Phoebe climbed in and seconds later he had her in his arms again.

"I don't want to hurt you. Or the baby."

She met his direct look with one of her own. "You would never do that."

The confidence she had in him shook him to the core. This wouldn't just be a physical joining but an emotional one, as well. He'd never intended to care but he did.

Ryan shifted to the center of the bed, then brought her over him until she straddled his waist. On her knees above him, her beautiful full breasts hung down like juicy melons, tempting him to feast. He wasted no time in doing so. As he savored all that was offered, Phoebe shifted so that her entrance teased his length. It ached in anticipation of finding home.

Phoebe kissed him as he lifted her hips and positioned her on him. He slid into her and they became one. He held his breath. It wasn't he but she who moved first. He joined her. Using his hands, he helped control their movements. At her frustrated sound he eased his grip and she settled farther down on him.

His hands remained lightly on her as he guided her up and down again and again. She was a beauty with her golden hair hanging down, her eyes closed and her head thrown back. With a shudder and a hiss of pleasure, she looked at him and gave him a dreamy smile.

Yes, he was the king of the world.

He kissed her deeply and flexed his hips against hers. After two powerful thrusts he found his own bliss.

Phoebe rolled off Ryan. Her head came to rest on his arm, a hand on his chest, her baby between them. She wished it would always be this way. She loved Ryan. He cared for her. She had no doubt of that. His lovemaking proved it.

But would he ever admit it to himself or her that he might want something lasting? It didn't matter, it wouldn't change how she felt.

She yawned. "I'm tired."

Ryan grinned. "Me, too. For a pregnant lady you sure can be rough on a man."

"So what you're saying is that you're not man enough for me."

Ryan pulled her to him for a kiss that curled her toes. His already growing manhood pushed against her leg.

"You need me to prove I'm man enough?"

"No, I think you did that just fine a few minutes ago. Right now, I need to rest. Too much dining, dancing and man." Her eyes closed to the feel of Ryan's hand rubbing her back.

Phoebe woke to the sun streaming through the bedroom window. She was alone. Panic filled her. Had Ryan left?

A clang came from the direction of the kitchen. She'd woken once during the night. Her back had been against his solid chest and his hand had cupped her right breast. It had been a perfect night. She wanted more of them.

He'd said nothing about how he felt. He had been an attentive and caring lover. She had never felt more desired. Still, she might be reading more into his actions than there was.

"Hey, I was hoping you were still asleep." Ryan walked into the room with a smile on his face and carrying a tray.

Phoebe pulled the sheet up to cover her chest. "Good morning to you, too. What do you have there?"

"It's supposed to be your breakfast in bed."

She'd never had anyone feed her in bed. Sitting up, she peered at the tray. "Really? That sounds nice."

He didn't seem to feel any morning-after awkwardness. She would be happy to follow his lead. Her biggest fear the night before had been that she would be a disappointment because of her size. The second fear had been that there would be unease between them this morning. Ryan had made it clear he wasn't turned off by her body. By his actions so far this morning, he was the same Ryan he had been last night.

He sat the tray at the end of the bed. She recognized it as one off the table in her living room. On it was sliced apples, two bowls of cereal and two glasses of orange juice.

"Lean forward."

Phoebe did as he asked. Ryan stuffed pillows behind her and she settled back. He joined her on the bed.

"No bacon and eggs?" She added a mock pout. "Afraid you'd burn yourself?

"You're so funny. I did what I was capable of doing. We can have something more substantial later."

"This looks wonderful to me."

She kissed him on the cheek.

"That wasn't much of a thank-you kiss. I think you can do better." His lips found hers. Seconds later Phoebe wanted to forget about their breakfast and concentrate on nothing but Ryan. Her arms went around his neck and she pulled him closer.

Ryan broke the kiss. "We need to be careful or we'll have juice and cereal everywhere. As much as I'd like to go on kissing you, I know you need nutrition."

"That sounded very midwife-ish."

He lowered his chin and gave her a serious look. "Well, that's what I am."

"And you are mine."

He was hers. Ryan liked the sound of that but he could never be what she needed. He couldn't commit to being hers, like she deserved. He wasn't who she thought he was. She should have someone who could love her whole-heartedly, holding nothing back. He had to see to it that their relationship remained light and easy. But after what had happened between them last night, that might be impossible.

"As your medical professional, I say eat."

"Can I put something on first?"

"I don't mind you the way you are." He grinned.

"That's sweet of you to say but I think I'd be less self-conscious with my gown on. After all, you have your underwear on."

Ryan stood. "Okay, if it'll get you to eat something, tell me where your gowns are."

She pointed to a chest. "Second drawer."

He didn't make a habit of going through a woman's personal things and found it almost too much like they were in a lifelong relationship to do so in Phoebe's. As quickly as he could, he pulled out a light blue gown. Returning to her, he helped her slip it over her head. Sitting on the edge of the bed, he asked, "Satisfied now?"

"Yes, I'm not used to breakfast in bed and I'm sure not used to sharing it with someone when I have no clothes on."

"I like you naked."

"Even with this beach ball of a belly?" She touched her middle.

He kissed her. "Women are at their prettiest when they are expecting. You glow."

She gathered her hair and pulled it over one shoulder. Her chin went up and she batted her eyelashes. "I glow? I like that."

"Yes, you glow but you would be brighter if you'd eat

something." Ryan pulled the tray closer and handed her a glass of juice.

They spent the next few minutes discussing the wedding, the weather and what other plans she had for the baby's room.

When they had finished eating Ryan stood, took the tray and was on his way out the door when Phoebe's squeak stopped him. He wheeled to look at her. Concern washed over him. Was something wrong? Should he take her to the hospital? "Are you okay?"

"Yes, just the baby making its presence known." She grinned. "I did have a little more activity last night than I normally do."

Relief flooded him. He needed to calm down, not overreact. Being a midwife, he should know better, but this was Phoebe. He cared for his patients but on no level did that came close to what he felt for Phoebe. How was he going to remain professional when he delivered the baby? Maybe it would be better if someone else did. "I'm sorry."

"I should hope not! Because I'm sure not."

"Thanks. My ego would have been damaged otherwise."

"I wouldn't want that to happen." She winced and shifted in the bed. "This baby is getting his morning exercise."

Ryan grinned. "I have an idea to help with those aches and pains. You stay there while I take this to the kitchen. I'll be right back. Don't move."

The anticipation of being in Ryan's arms again was enough to have Phoebe's blood humming. He soon returned with the bottle of lotion in his hand he had used the other night during her foot massage.

"Oh, I'm going to get another foot massage." She couldn't keep the eagerness out of her voice and started moving toward the edge of the bed.

"No. Stay where you are. Just move forward some." He put the lotion on the bedside table.

Her brow wrinkled but she did as he asked. What did he have planned this time?

Ryan climbed in bed behind her, putting a leg on each side of her hips so that she now sat between his.

"What're you doing?"

There was all kind of movement behind her until Ryan's arms came around her and pulled her back against his chest. "I was having a hard time getting the pillows to stay in place. Pull your gown up."

"What is this? Some special pregnant woman's sex position?"

He chuckled behind her. "Is that all you think about? Sex?"

"When you're around, yes."

He kissed her neck. "Thank you for the nice compliment but right now I have something else in mind. Now pull your gown up."

She did as he said until it was gathered under her breasts then adjusted the sheet over her thighs, giving her some modesty.

Ryan reached around her neck.

"Hey, is this a fancy way of choking me?"

"You sure are making it hard for me to be nice to you."

Cold hit her bare middle, making her jerk. "Ooh."

"That'll teach you not to have such a smart mouth," Ryan said in a teasing tone. His hands began to glide over her middle. "You're all tense. Lie back and enjoy."

She did, settling against his chest and closing her eyes. Ryan's hands made slow circles over her middle.

"This is wonderful. Did you learn to do this in the service, too?"

"No. But I did deliver my first baby there."

"Will you tell me about it?"

Ryan's body tensed behind her. He was quiet so long she wasn't sure he would say anything more.

"One weekend we were invited to a local celebration. I'm still not sure what it was for, but anyway some of the unit went along. We ate the food. Played with the kids.

"You know, kids are the same wherever you go. All they want is their parents there for them and to play and be happy. Every child deserves that." Ryan's hands drifted to the sides of her belly. His palms pressed lightly against her. "Especially this one."

Phoebe placed her hand over one of his. "He or she will have that. I promise."

It would be wonderful if Ryan would be a part of helping her make that come true. But he said nothing that indicated he wanted that kind of involvement in their lives.

"After the celebration we were going back to the base but had to stop because there was mechanical trouble with one of the trucks. There happened to be three or four huts that locals lived in nearby. There was a loud scream from that direction. A couple of the men went to investigate. It turned out that there was a woman having a baby. She was in trouble. They returned for me.

"I don't think I've even been in a house that had less. It was made of mud bricks, with a grass roof and dirt floor. Water was drawn from a barely running creek half a mile away. The kitchen consisted of a pot over a fire. In this horrible war-torn country, in this nothing shelter was a woman trying to give birth. The only people around were a couple of children about the ages of six and eight."

His hands stopped moving but continued to rest on her.

"I had the interpreter ask her if she would like me to help. Her culture dictated that she shouldn't agree but she was in so much pain she wouldn't tell me no. I had seen a baby delivered once. I'm not sure who was more scared, me or her. I sent everyone out but the interpreter. It took some explaining on the interpreter's part to get her to understand I needed to examine her. Finally she relented. The baby's shoulder was hung. I was thankful it wasn't breech, which was what I'd expected. It was work but I managed to help bring the baby into the world. It was exhilarating. The baby had a healthy cry and the mother a smile on her face when I left. Imagine living like that and still smiling. I knew then that it was far better than patching up men who had been shot or torn apart by landmines. As soon as I returned to camp I put in my papers to get out of the army."

"Did you ever see the baby again?"

"No. I never wanted to. I was afraid of what I might find. Children have a hard life in Iraq. You know, this conversation has suddenly taken a negative turn. Not what I intended. How about you tell me what you have planned for this week."

His fingers started moving over her skin again.

"I think I forgot to tell you that some of the teachers at school are giving me a shower on Monday after classes. I hope now I'll have some baby clothes to fill the drawers of the chest. I also hope to buy a few pictures for the walls. If I do, would you hang them for me?"

"As long as someone doesn't go into labor, I don't see why not."

She twisted to look at him. "Could you come out to dinner one night?"

Ryan's fingertips fluttered over her middle. "Sounds great to me. Sit up. I want to massage your lower back."

She did so and he pushed her gown up to her shoulders. He put more lotion in his hands and began to rub her lower back firmly.

"For a little bit you could get a permanent job doing that."

Ryan's hands faltered a second, then started moving again. Had she said the wrong thing?

"Well, I've done all I can to make you comfortable."

"It was wonderful. Feel free to stop by and do that any-time. If I got a foot massage and body rub on the same day, I might melt away."

"I wouldn't want you to do that. I like knowing you're around." Ryan moved out from behind her. "As much as I would enjoy staying in bed with you all day, I promised to cover for Sophia this afternoon and tomorrow until the new midwife takes over on Monday."

She hated to see this time with Ryan end.

"Mind if I get a quick shower?" he asked.

"Of course not," she said, pulling her gown back into place.

"Why don't you stay in bed, take it easy today?" Ryan suggested, as he picked up his clothes off the floor.

"Are you afraid you were too rough on me last night?"

His grin was devilish. "Are you kidding? It was more like you being rough on me. I had no idea a pregnant woman could be so aggressive."

She threw a pillow at him. "I'll show you aggressive."

Ryan's deep laughter filled the room even after he'd closed the bathroom door behind him.

Phoebe was in the kitchen when he came in to say good-bye. His shirtsleeves were rolled halfway up his forearms. He had his jacket over his arm and his tie in his hand. A couple of damp locks of hair fell over his forehead. She had never seen anyone look more desirable.

She resisted the urge to grab his hand and beg him not to

leave. When he went out the door she was afraid that fragile fairy-tale bubble they had been living in since yesterday afternoon would burst. Could she ever get it back again?

Phoebe stood with her back to the counter. "I'll be in town on Thursday for my next checkup."

"I'll see you then if not before. I have to go."

"I know. There are babies to deliver."

He grinned. "And they don't wait."

"I sure hope not. I'm ready now for this one to come." She looked at a picture on the wall instead of him, scared he might see her sadness. There had never been this type of emotion when Joshua had left and she'd known she wouldn't see him for months. She had it bad for Ryan.

Phoebe walked with him out to the veranda. At the steps he wrapped her in his arms and pulled her tightly against him, giving her a kiss. Letting her go, he hurried down the steps.

"A little overdressed for a Saturday morning, aren't you, dear?"

Phoebe smiled as Ryan threw up a hand and continued down the path. "Good morning, Mrs. Rosenheim. Beautiful day, isn't it?"

Phoebe waved as he pulled away.

"I see you found a young man who'll be around for you." Mrs. Rosenheim's voice carried across the gardens.

Phoebe waved and called, "I hope I have."

Ryan pulled up in front of his house, turned off the engine and banged his head against the steering wheel a couple of times.

What had he done? He knew the answer and didn't like it one bit. He'd spent the night with his best friend's wife. Crossed the professional line and, worse, he'd started to think of Phoebe as more than a friend. She was his lover. How low could he go?

He'd even spent most of the morning playing house with her. He had nothing emotionally to offer Phoebe. She needed someone to rely on, to love her and the baby. He wasn't that guy. He didn't commit to anybody. There wasn't even a cat or a dog in his life.

He had no intention of pledging himself to a woman with a child. Or to any woman, for that matter. He wouldn't be any good at it. Worse, didn't even want to try. He wouldn't take the chance on heartache. Fun while it lasted was all he'd ever wanted. He'd had all the pain he was willing to live with. He'd see to the practical things, like getting the baby's room ready and even delivering the baby, but then he was backing out.

Some other man would take his place. Phoebe was an attractive woman. No, that wasn't strong enough. She was beautiful and smart, funny, with a quick wit, and someone far better than him would come along. He was afraid he would hurt her, but over time she would get over it. Someone would enter her life and give her what she deserved. Maybe in time she'd forgive him.

He sat up and stared out the window. His hands tightened on the wheel. Someone else would share her bed. The thought made him sick. But it was the way things should be. For her sake and the baby's.

Ryan opened the door of the car and climbed out. There was a light mist, just as there had been the evening he'd found Phoebe on his doorstep. Would he always think of her when it rained? No, he couldn't let things go any further, but he worried they had already gone too far. He'd enjoyed her body too much, liked having someone to laugh with, eat with, to look forward to seeing. He'd never had trouble keeping himself shut off but now he couldn't seem to get past his feelings for Phoebe.

He needed to get into his shop, work. Push her out of his mind. He groaned. The project he was working on was the cradle. He wasn't even safe from her in his only sanctuary. How had she invaded his life so completely in such a short time? Why had he let her? Because he'd fallen for her. Cared about her more than he had anyone since JT. How ironic was that?

Disgusted with himself, he climbed out of his car and slammed the door before heading for his front door.

Maybe when he finished the cradle and Phoebe delivered, he would be able to get her out of his mind. A nagging voice kept telling him that wasn't going to happen.

CHAPTER NINE

PHOEBE WALKED THROUGH the archway entrance of the hospital on Thursday afternoon on her way to her appointment. Her soft-soled shoes made squeaking sounds as she crossed the tiles on the floor of the lobby. At the lift, she pushed the button for the sixth floor. She could hardly contain her excitement over seeing Ryan.

Despite their plans, she'd not seen him since he'd left her house on Saturday morning. She'd only heard from him once. That had been a quick phone call to say that he couldn't make it to dinner. It was a full moon and he'd been busy. He needed to remain near the hospital.

She understood. When it was her turn to deliver she would want to know he was close. He had asked how she was doing but otherwise the call had been short and to the point. Still, she had to remember that he worked odd hours and had no control over when those would be.

The doors to the lift whooshed open and she entered. Would he kiss her? Probably not. That would be very unprofessional during an antenatal visit. Maybe he would take her out to eat or, better yet, home. She had missed his touch but more than that she missed talking and laughing with him.

She was acting like a silly schoolgirl with her first crush. Here she was almost a mother and giddy over a man.

The lift doors opened again and Phoebe stepped out and walked toward the clinic. Inside, she signed in at the window. She took a chair and looked at the pictures of the medical staff lining the wall. They included Ryan. He looked handsome but far too serious in his picture. Nothing like the man with the good sense of humor that she knew. Besides him there were a number of people she'd met or recognized from the wedding.

"Phoebe."

It was Ryan's voice. She would have known it anywhere. Every night she heard it in her dreams. Her head jerked up and their gazes met. There was a flicker of delight in his before it turned guarded. Wasn't he glad to see her?

Phoebe smiled. "Hi."

He cleared his throat and said, "Hello. Are you ready to come back?"

She moved to stand. It took her a second more than she would have liked but Ryan hadn't moved from his position at the door. A few days ago he would have hurried to offer her help. "Yes, I'm ready."

"Come this way."

What was going on? Maybe he didn't want anyone to see him touch her or overhear them. Still, this was a little much. She'd always spoken in a friendly manner to Sophia. That was part of the appeal of having a midwife— it was more like having a friend there to help deliver her.

"Follow me," he said, and led her down the hallway to an exam room. Once she'd entered he closed the door.

She sat on the exam table.

"So how have you been?" Ryan asked, as if speaking to someone he'd just met.

Phoebe gave him a questioning look. Ryan couldn't see it because his focus was on the computer. Other than those few seconds when their eyes had met after he'd called her name he hadn't looked at her again.

"Any pains?"

Just in her heart all of a sudden. "No."

"Well, it won't be long now."

Why was he talking to her like that? As if he didn't really know her? Was he afraid someone might walk in on them? "No, it won't. Next week is my due date."

He finally looked up but his focus was over her right shoulder. "You know that the chance of a baby coming on a due date is slim. A first baby is almost always late."

"I know." This all business attitude was getting old. "How are you, Ryan? I've missed you this week."

He went back to studying the computer screen. "I've been busy. Sophia being out makes things a little complicated."

Apparently their relationship was included in that.

"Any chance we could get something to eat this evening?"

"I have a mother in labor on her way in. I'm going to the unit as soon as I'm finished here."

Phoebe had never received the brush-off before but she recognized it when she heard it. *I won't cry, I won't cry.* She clenched her teeth.

Ryan was acting as if they'd never been intimate. But they were at the clinic and he should act professionally. But he was overdoing it.

He left without giving her another look.

What had happened between now and Saturday morning that had made him so distant? He was acting like the guy she'd met that first night. When he returned she was going to find out what was going on.

She was prepared and waiting on the table when he returned. He wasn't by himself. A woman in her midtwenties followed him into the room.

"Phoebe, this is Stacy. She's the new midwife who has joined our group. Would you be willing to let her do the exam?"

She looked at him in disbelief. He wouldn't meet her gaze. Now he didn't even want to touch her.

"All right." Phoebe drew the words out.

Stacy stepped to the table. "Phoebe, may I check the position of the baby? I promise I have gentle hands."

Phoebe said nothing. She knew gentle hands and those belonged to Ryan.

As Stacy's hand moved over her expanded middle, she rattled off some numbers while Ryan typed on the computer.

"Well, you're doing fine. Everything is as it should be. I don't see why you won't have an uneventful delivery," Stacy gushed. "I look forward to being there."

"What?" Phoebe looked at Ryan. Nothing was as it should be.

He looked over her head as he spoke. "Stacy is going to step in for me. My, uh, caseload is heavy and she's taking some of my patients."

Stacy was all smiles when she said, "I'll see you here next week for your appointment or at the delivery, whichever comes first. Do you have any questions for us?"

Yes, she had a pile of questions but none that she could ask in front of Stacy.

"No" came out sounding weak.

"Okay, then. I'll see you next week," Stacy said, without seeming to notice the tension between her and Ryan.

He opened the door and left without even looking at her. Stacy followed.

Phoebe sat in silence. Stunned. Never had she felt so

used. She'd shared her body with Ryan. Opened her heart. Believed that she meant something to him. Now he was treating her like she was nothing. What a jerk. He didn't even have the backbone to tell her that he no longer wanted to help deliver the baby.

She climbed off the table and dressed. Had she ever felt more humiliated? Discarded?

Ryan was there four hours later when a new life entered the world. This time he missed the amazement he usually felt. All he could think about was Phoebe's large sad eyes when he'd left the exam room. What must she think of him? Probably the same as he was thinking of himself.

He had called to check on her a few days earlier, using all his self-control to wait as long as he had before he'd picked up the phone. Justifying the call, he'd told himself he was after all her midwife. But that hadn't been the real reason he'd done it. He'd been desperate to hear her voice. He'd done some difficult things in his life but acting as if he didn't care about Phoebe in front of her had been the hardest. It had been even more challenging not to touch her. She'd looked so dejected when he'd walked out of the room. The devil of it all was that he cared about Phoebe more than anyone else in the world.

The irony was that he had treated her the way he had because he couldn't deal with the depth of his feelings for her and his inability to handle the mountain of guilt for how he had treated someone who had been important to JT. He was so messed up he had no business being involved with anyone. Until Phoebe, he had managed to keep everyone at bay, but she had slipped past his defenses.

The dark of the night mirrored his emotions as he drove home hours later. For once in his life he wished someone was there to come home to. He let himself into his house and dropped his clothes on the floor. That was a habit that he and Phoebe shared. They both dropped things as soon as they came in the door. He his clothes and she her shoes.

Going to his bedroom, he flipped on the light. When he looked at his bed all he could see was the way Phoebe had lovingly admired his work. He'd never shared his workshop with anyone before. Even the few times female company had stayed over he'd never taken them down there. It had taken one sunny day of driving Phoebe around to garage sales to open it to her.

How quickly she had found a way into his home, his shop and his heart. But none of that mattered. He would never be able to be there for her as she needed. She deserved someone who could open his heart completely. Hold nothing back. Be there for her for the long haul. He wouldn't invest in people that way after he had he'd lost so many of them. He couldn't take the chance of going there again. It was better to let her go now.

Ryan turned off the light, removed his clothes but didn't bother to pull the covers back before he lay on the bed. He squeezed his eyes shut and put his arm over his eyes. All he could see was the confusion, then disappointment and pain in Phoebe's eyes.

Had he ever been happier than he had been in the last few weeks? When had he last thought about even being happy? It certainly hadn't been for a long time. He could remember that emotion. A few times when he'd been a kid. But he'd recognized happiness when Phoebe had kissed him on the cheek. Or when they had watched the little penguins waddle out of the water to take care of their chicks, or the look on Phoebe's face when she'd looked down at him as they'd become one. Because of her he'd known true happiness.

He hadn't realized how he'd shut out the world until she

had shown up on his doorstep, leaving him no choice but to rejoin it again. He'd carried the pain of war, the agony of trying to help men and women whose lives would never be the same, bottled up until Phoebe had started asking questions. He'd talked more about his time in the war in the last few weeks than he'd done in the last ten years. The more he'd told her the easier it had become to talk about those times. Now it felt like a weight had been lifted off his chest. After he'd returned from a difficult mission, he'd been required to talk to the shrink. He'd never thought it useful. Thanks to Phoebe, he was starting to see a value in not holding those memories in.

All this didn't matter anyway. He'd hurt Phoebe so badly today that even if he tried to have a relationship with her she would close the door in his face. No, it was better this way.

Phoebe leaned her head against the glass window of the tram. The clack of the cars made a rhythm that would have lulled her to sleep if her emotions hadn't been jumping like balls in a pinball machine. She fluctuated between disbelief and anger.

How had she let Ryan matter so much? Worse, how had she been misled by him?

He had made her believe he cared. It hadn't only been his lovemaking but the way he'd thought of little things to help her. Painting the baby's room, going with her to garage sales, massaging her feet. Her back. In just a few weeks he had done more for her and with her than Joshua had done during their entire marriage.

So what had happened to make Ryan do such an about-face?

Had she pushed too hard? Assumed things she shouldn't?

Had making plans for them to eat together, see each other scared him off?

When she heard her stop called she prepared to get off. She still had a few blocks to walk before she made it home. She was tired. Didn't even plan to eat anything before going to bed. If Ryan knew he would scold her. Maybe not, after what she'd experienced today.

Slipping her key into the lock a few minutes later, she opened the door. She entered and turned on the light. How different this homecoming had been from the one she had imagined. She'd hoped that Ryan would bring her home and stay the night. That bubble had been completely popped.

Phoebe kicked her shoes off. She chuckled dryly. The action made her think of Ryan dropping his clothes inside his door. Making her way to her bedroom, she turned on her bedside lamp, then undressed. She slid between the sheets and leaned over to turn the light off. The picture of her and Joshua caught her attention.

Had the fact that she was carrying Joshua's baby been the reason Ryan had suddenly slammed the door between them? Was the baby too much of a reminder that she would always be tied to Joshua? Or was it that they represented the painful loss of Joshua? Or the other men that Ryan had seen die. In some way they must be part of the past he worked so hard to shut out or forget.

Sliding the drawer out of the bedside table, Phoebe pulled out the crumpled letter Joshua had sent her. Opening it, she smoothed it out on the bed before reading it. Had Joshua known he wasn't coming home when he had written it? Had he known he was leaving on a dangerous patrol like Ryan had described? Even after they had discussed separating, had he wanted her to be happy, to find someone else? Had he thought Ryan might be that person?

Whatever it was, she'd done as Joshua had said and gone to Ryan. Joshua had been right. There she'd found the piece of her life that had been missing all these years. Moisture filled her eyes. But Ryan didn't want her. Once again she was on her own. Would she ever find a real partner in life?

Turning off the light, she curled around her baby. At least this little one would be someone to love who would return it.

Sunday afternoon there was a knock at the door.

Her heart leaped. Was it Ryan?

Phoebe answered it to find Mrs. Rosenheim waiting on the veranda. Phoebe's spirits dropped like a person falling off a bridge. Had she really expected it to be Ryan?

"Hello, dear. I was just checking on you. I've not seen you all weekend. Didn't want you to have that baby and me not know about it."

"I'm right here. No baby yet." She didn't want any company. How could she get rid of her neighbor gracefully?

"From the sound and look of you, something else is going on." Mrs. Rosenheim brushed past Phoebe into the living room.

Phoebe really didn't feel up to dealing with the older woman. She wanted to wallow in her misery alone.

"I haven't seen that nice young man around."

That was all it took for Phoebe to burst into tears.

"My goodness, it's all that bad?" Mrs. Rosenheim patted her on the arm. "Why don't you fix us some tea and tell me all about it?"

Phoebe swiped at her cheek, then nodded. Maybe it would be good to tell someone about what had happened.

As she put the kettle on and prepared the cups, Phoebe told Mrs. Rosenheim about how she'd met Ryan.

"Well, at least that absent husband of yours did one thing to show he cared," Mrs. Rosenheim murmured.

"Joshua cared—"

Mrs. Rosenheim waved her hand. "Let's not argue about that. So, what put you in this tizzy about Ryan?"

Phoebe placed a teacup in front of Mrs. Rosenheim and one in front of the chair across from her. She wouldn't sit in Ryan's chair. How quickly he had become a central part of her life.

Phoebe told her about how Ryan had acted during her clinic visit. During the entire explanation Mrs. Rosenheim sipped her tea and nodded.

"Sounds scared to me. So what do you plan to do?"

"Do? What can I do?"

"Yes, do. You're getting ready to have a baby. Do you want to bring a baby into the world feeling that kind of discord? Go and make Ryan explain himself. Tell him how you feel."

Phoebe sighed. "You're right. I need to talk him. Get the air cleared. I was so shocked and hurt by his actions that I've not been able to think."

"Then I suggest that you make yourself presentable and give that man a piece of your mind."

Ryan already had her heart, he might as well get part of her mind. If things stayed the way they were, she would lose him. To move on she needed answers, and those could only come from Ryan.

Phoebe bowed her head against the wind that was picking up as she walked along Ryan's street. Like the first time she had visited him, she had practiced what she was going to say on the tram ride there. She was going to demand answers. More than that, she was going to get answers.

Would Ryan be home? She'd thought of calling first but had been afraid that he would make some excuse as to why she couldn't see him. She would have none of that.

She had accepted Joshua's decisions. Knowing what he did was important hadn't disguised the fact he'd been more interested in fighting wars than being with her. She wouldn't let Ryan put her to the side. She'd stay at his place until she knew what was going on.

Phoebe walked past Ryan's car. He was home. She climbed the steps to his door and groaned. Her back was killing her. The baby had grown so large.

She hesitated. Would Ryan answer if he realized it was her? It didn't matter. She was staying until she found out what his problem was, even if she had to sleep on his veranda all night. That wouldn't happen. No matter how hard Ryan was trying to push her out of his life, he was too kind and tenderhearted to leave her out in the elements.

To come all this way and not knock was ridiculous. She was no longer the woman she'd been when she'd shown up on his doorstep last month. With or without him, she would have this baby and the two of them would make it. It would be wonderful to have Ryan in their lives, but if not, she and the baby would still survive. That much she did know.

Lifting her hand, she boldly knocked on the door. Seconds went by with no answer. There was no sound from inside. Again she knocked. Nothing. Maybe Ryan was in the basement and couldn't hear her. She turned to descend the steps and search for a way around back when the door opened.

Ryan looked as if he hadn't slept in days. There were dark circles under his eyes. His hair stood on end. He was still wearing his hospital uniform and it was rumpled, as if he'd been too distracted to change. Her heart went out to him for a second and then she reminded herself of why she was there. Life hadn't been kind to her since last Thursday, either.

CHAPTER TEN

PHOEBE.

Ryan's heart skidded to a halt then picked up the pace double-time. What was she doing here?

How like her to show up unannounced on his doorstep. Was that how they had started out?

She looked wonderful, irritated and determined all at the same time. He had missed her. There had never been another time in his life when he'd longed for someone like he had for Phoebe.

"What're are you doing here?"

"We need to talk." She stepped forward, leaving him no choice but to move and let her in.

"Talk?"

She whirled to face him with surprising agility. "You mean after your performance the other day you don't think we need to talk?"

Ryan closed the door. He really didn't want to do this. "Performance?"

"Really, Ryan? You don't think you owe me an explanation for your behavior at the clinic?"

"I did my job."

"Job? Was it your job to take pity on the poor widow woman and go to bed with her?"

Ryan flinched. That hurt. Yes, she was hitting below the belt but he deserved it.

"What I don't understand is why I let you get away with acting like there was nothing between us. Or why I've given you so many days to explain yourself. I didn't expect a public display at the clinic but I did expect you to act as if I had some importance."

"Stacy was there—"

"That's your excuse for going AWOL on me and not hearing from you? You know, I would never have taken you for a coward."

Ryan winced. That's what he had been. If he ran, then he wouldn't have to face what he'd done and how he felt about Phoebe. He sat in his chair. Phoebe's glare bore down on him. "Look, you don't understand."

"Oh, I understand. This is all about you hiding from the world, the things you saw in Iraq and your feelings. If you don't let someone in, then you don't have to worry about them dying, like your friends did. Like Joshua.

"You live mechanically. You just go through the days. Look at this place." She swung her arm around, indicating the room. "You just exist here. No pictures, no rugs, a sofa and a chair. Your bedroom is a step better only because of your woodwork. It shows some warmth. The one place where you actually look like you're living is ironically in your shop, and it's underground. You come up and do what you have to do and then disappear again like a mole that's afraid of the light, but in your case you're afraid of feeling anything for someone. You care more about that furniture downstairs than you do people. In fact, those inanimate objects in your bedroom have received more love than you show the rest of the people in your life."

She was right. There was nothing he could say to defend himself.

"You're afraid that if you care too much you'll lose part of yourself. But you'll never be happy that way. You have to let people in. Let them see the person I see. The warm and caring person. The fun and humorous one. The person who gives despite any pain to himself."

Ryan raised a hand with his index finger up. "Hey, don't be putting me on a pedestal. I'm not one of your fairy-tale knights on a white horse, riding in to save the day."

Phoebe looked at him. Was he right? Had she tried to make more of their relationship than there was? Had she been so desperate that she had clung to Ryan? Needed anyone to rely on? To fill the void of loneliness?

"I haven't." Her remark sounded weak even to her own ears.

"Haven't what? Become self-contained, built your own perfect little world where Joshua came home as the hero, loved you and left to return again? Where you were willing to accept a small piece of his life just so you could have someone to share that perfect life? Except it wasn't all that perfect, was it? You wanted more. A family, but you couldn't or wouldn't tell him that it was time to think of you."

She cringed. Was that what she had been doing? "You're wrong."

"Really? Did you ever once ask JT to take an assignment that would bring him home for longer than three months? Did you ever ask him to choose you over the army?"

She hadn't.

"I can see you didn't. What were you afraid of? That he would leave you all together? As strong as you act on the outside, you're a marshmallow of self-doubt on the inside. You don't understand why you weren't good enough to make JT want to stay at home. You feel sorry for yourself but cover it with acting as if you can handle everything on your own. No matter how hard I might try, I could never fix those for you. That's something you have to recognize and do for yourself."

All Ryan's accusations hit home. A number of them she didn't want to face.

"Phoebe, I can't be someone that I'm not. Seeing what humans can do to each other makes you stop and think before you get involved. I cared then and what did it get me? All I wanted was out." He spoke to the floor, then looked at her.

"That's understandable. But look at you now." She lowered her voice. "You help bring life into the world. You sure picked a funny occupation to not care about anyone."

"That was part of the appeal of being a midwife. I'm only involved in a patient's life for a short time. After the baby comes I'm done."

"How sad. You know you brought warmth and joy into my world. I came to your doorstep lonely, sad and afraid. For heaven's sake, I was weeks away from having a baby and I didn't even have a room ready. I was going through the motions, just like you, until we met. It was far past time for us both to start living our lives again."

"I have lived like that. I've had friends. Joshua was a friend and look what happened to him. You say that I'm afraid but you are afraid of something, too, and that is being alone. You've lost your parents, you brother is nowhere around, Joshua is gone, his parents are jerks and now you're clinging to me. People leave and die, it's a part of life."

Phoebe stepped forward. "I'm well aware of that. The question is, are you? People die. Do you think I don't understand that? He was my husband. My parents are gone. Even my brother is halfway across the world from me."

Ryan jumped up. Phoebe stepped backward. He move forward and glared at her. With his hands balled at his sides, he barked, "And I'm the man who slept with his best friend's wife."

Phoebe blinked and stumbled backwards. She quickly righted herself. That was what all of this was about? Some male idea of solidarity to his best friend. Ryan thought he'd betrayed Joshua.

He made a sound of disgust and turned away. His shoulders were tense. She wanted to reach out and touch him. Reassure him that he'd done nothing wrong. If she did, she feared he'd reject her forever. She had to reason with him, get through to him. Reaching into her pocket, she pulled out Joshua's letter. Maybe with Joshua's help she could.

"Ryan, Joshua is dead."

He jerked slightly.

"We're alive." She kept her voice low. "He doesn't stand between us. He's gone. You did nothing wrong. In fact, it was very right. Here, I think you should read this." She stepped around him and handed him the letter. "I'm going to leave you to read it."

Walking to the bedroom, she went into the bathroom. Her back was aching. Maybe the baby was just pressing against something it shouldn't. Would Joshua's letter help Ryan let go or would it only make things worse? She hoped with all her heart it made him see the truth.

Ryan opened the crumpled pages. Why had Phoebe given him something to read? He scanned the page and saw JT's name at the end. Guilt churned in his stomach. With his heart bumping against his chest wall and his hands shaking, he let his focus move to the top of the page.

Phoebe—

I know I've not always written like I should. For that I'm sorry. Especially when you have been so good about it. I know now that when we married you didn't bargain on us spending so much time apart. For that I'm sorry also. When we parted a few weeks ago I knew things had changed between us. We have spent too much time living separate lives to the point where our relationship has slipped into one of friendship instead of one that we both wish it could be. I have done you an injustice. You have such a large capacity to love that it was never fair of me to deny you that.

I wish for you a happy life. If you ever need anything and don't know where to turn I want you to find my friend, Ryan Matthews. He will help you. We are buddies from his army days. I trust him with my life and you can with yours. He lives in Melbourne. He will take care of you. Believe in him, he won't let you down. I think you will like him. I hope you do.

Take care, Phoebe. Have a good life.

Joshua

JT had sent Phoebe to him. As if he'd known they would needed each other. Had it been JT's way of giving his blessing to their relationship? He looked at the letter. How long had Phoebe had this? Why hadn't she said something sooner?

Ryan went into his room. Phoebe must have purposely taken her time in the bathroom because she was coming toward him. She stopped and stared at the cradle sitting in a corner. She must have missed it on her way to the bathroom because the closet door stood open, obscuring it.

It was his finest piece of work to date. He didn't know

if he would ever do better. It was as if his heart and soul had been emptied into it. It sat low to the floor with a high front and sides that wrapped around slightly. It looked like one that would be handed down in a wealthy family. It was as much like one he'd seen in a history museum back home as he could make it.

Going over to the cradle, Phoebe ran her hand along the smooth lip of one side. She pushed it and watched the slow movement back and forth.

"It's for the baby." The emotion in his voice made it come out as a croak.

She glanced at him. "It's the most beautiful thing I've ever seen."

He raised his hand with Joshua's letter in it. "This is why you came here that first night."

She nodded.

"Why didn't you tell me?"

"At first because you acted all cold and unwelcoming and I wasn't sure Joshua had been right about you."

His lips formed a tight line. "I wasn't at my best. I'm sorry. So why not later?"

She shrugged. "I started to trust you. You agreed to deliver the baby. I wanted you to and the letter didn't matter anymore. I had started to care about you. I had hoped you cared about me. Thought you did until I saw you on Thursday."

"I'm sorry I hurt you. I hated doing so but I didn't know how else to handle it. The night we made love was the most wonderful of my life but on my way home I thought of Joshua, of how I was not the best man for you. I knew we couldn't continue." He looked at the letter. "But after reading his letter, I wonder..."

"If it was Joshua's way of telling us both to move on? That we would need each other? I don't know if he thought this…" she pointed to him and then herself "…would happen, but I think he knew we could help each other. We were the two people he knew best in the world. I don't think what's between us is wrong. I think we honor him by caring about each other and living well. I love you, Ryan, and want you in my and this baby's life. By the way, you could have talked to me on Thursday, just like you are doing now."

His chest tightened. He'd rather die than not be the person Phoebe needed him to be. "I don't know if I can give what you and the baby should have."

Her look met his. "I don't think either one of us knows that for sure. Yes, there're risks but that's what love is all about. Think with your heart, not your head. I know you care." She touched her chest. "I feel it here. That was part of the reason I came." She grinned. "And because I was so mad. But everything you do proves you care. For example…" she touched the cradle "…you messed up with this. It shows your true feelings. You care. There's no doubt that you do, you're just scared of doing so.

"I've been waiting most of my life to have someone love me, really love me, want to be with me. I thought it was Joshua but I soon learned we didn't want the same things. I wanted the rocker on the veranda and watching the sunset and he wanted to always be going off somewhere. Don't get me wrong, what he was doing was important but that didn't bring me any closer to my dreams.

"I love you, Ryan. I don't want you doing anything for me out of obligation to Joshua any more. I want you to care about me for me."

Could he be a part of that? He wasn't sure. But he had been for the last six weeks. He'd never been happier. Had he found the place he belonged? The place where all the ugliness in life disappeared? When had the last time been he'd thought of the war? He'd already realized that talking to Phoebe had eased the past. Now, could he grasp what she was offering and hang on to it?

There was a silence between them. The air between them was heavy with tension.

"I guess I should be going."

She sounded defeated.

"I've said what I came to say. Found out what I needed to know." She moved past him and headed for the door.

Fear flooded him that surpassed any he'd ever felt before. Even when bullets had been flying over his head. If he let her go out the door he might lose her forever. He couldn't let that happen. His fingers wrapped around her forearm, stopping her.

Her gaze came up to meet his. There was a question there, along with hope.

"I don't want you to leave."

Her hand came up to cup his cheek. "I don't want to go."

The band around his chest popped, letting all the love he'd held back flow. He gathered her to him and brought his mouth to hers. Phoebe melted against him. Deep kisses, small sweet ones, filled his world until they broke apart.

"Can you stay the night?" Ryan looked down at her.

"Yes. My maternity leave starts tomorrow. No due babies?"

"Only this one." Ryan placed his hand on her belly. "And I intend to keep a close eye on him or her. Not let the mother out of my sight or out of my arms."

Phoebe smiled, one that reached her eyes. "That sounds perfect to me. I promise to be willing to accept life isn't about fairy tales if you're willing to believe they are a possibility."

"Agreed." Ryan kissed her again.

She broke away. "Augh." She reached behind her and rubbed her lower back.

"What's wrong?"

"My back aches."

He gave her an intense look. "When did it start?"

"On my way here."

He grinned. "You may be in labor."

"Really?" Her hands went to her belly and a dreamy look covered her face.

"We'll see what happens in the next few hours. It still might be Braxton-Hicks contractions or, in other words, false labor pains. Come with me. I have something we can do to keep your mind off them." He took her hand and led her toward the bath.

"Can we do that if I'm in labor?"

Ryan chuckled. "No, but there are plenty of other things that we can do that are almost as satisfying."

"Like a foot massage?"

"That could be arranged. But I have some new ideas in mind. Like starting with a nice warm shower."

Inside the bathroom, he reached in the tub area. Turning the water on, seconds later the shower sprayed water. Ryan turned back to her and began removing her clothes.

"I can do that."

"But I want to." He carefully worked each button out of its hole. Soon she was naked. He didn't touch her but he took his time looking.

"You're embarrassing me."

"Because I enjoy admiring you? I think you're the most amazing woman I know." With a look of regret he pulled the curtain back and offered her his hand. "Be careful. We don't need you slipping."

Phoebe took it and stepped under the steaming water. A few minutes later the curtain was pulled back and Ryan joined her. His manhood stood tall between them. He was dazzling. "Oh, I wasn't expecting you."

"I need a bath, too. Saves water to share. Turn around and let me massage your back."

Phoebe did as he instructed. He made slow circles with the pads of his thumbs pressing but not too hard.

"That feels great."

Ryan continued to ease the ache for a few more minutes before his hands moved around to make wide circular motions over her belly. He pulled her back against him. His length pressed against her butt. He didn't move but said close to her ear, "Hand me the soap."

She took it out of the holder and placed it in his hand. He stepped back and began to run the soap across her shoulders, then down her back. "Turn around."

Phoebe did. His hands traveled to her breasts. She watched the tension grow in his face. A muscle jumped in his jaw. He continued his ministrations. Her nipples grew and tingled. His hand moved on to her belly and down to do her legs. As he stood he kissed the baby.

Her breath caught and her lips quivered. She put her hands on both sides of Ryan's face and brought his mouth to hers. He returned her kiss, then set her away.

"You need to get out before the water turns cold."

"What about you?"

"I think I'll stay for a while."

Phoebe stepped out of the shower with a smile on her face. It was nice, being desired. She dried off. "Ryan, I don't have any more clothes. Do you have a large shirt I can wear?"

"You don't need any clothes. Just climb into bed. Is your back still hurting?"

"A little. It comes and goes."

A few minutes later Ryan came out of the bathroom in

all his naked glory. He was all man. Leaving the room, he returned with a fat candle and a pack of matches. He set the candle on the bedside table and lit it before he turned off the overhead light.

"Move over." He climbed in next to her. "Face me, Phoebe."

She rolled to her side and he did also. Ryan's hand started rubbing her belly and moving around to her back and forward again. He looked into her eyes.

A few minutes later he cleared his throat. "I loved the aggressive way you pushed your way in here tonight and made me see reason. JT and I could have used you on patrol with us a couple of times."

She snickered. "I actually learned that maneuver from Mrs. Rosenheim. She's been using it on me for a few years now. In fact, she did so this afternoon. She's the one who encouraged me to come and see you."

"Well, remind me to give her a kiss when I see her again."

Phoebe placed her hand on his chest. "You might not want to do that because she could expect it every time you see her."

"I think it'll be worth taking the chance." He captured her hand and held it against him.

"Ryan, I want you to know that I'm not going to push you for more than you can give or do. Ooh…" Phoebe tensed.

He looked at her closely. "Stronger?"

"A little."

"Why don't you try to get some sleep? You may need it later. I'll be right here." Ryan rolled to his back and pulled her closer. His length lay firm against her hip. Regardless of his obvious need, he made no move to do anything but care for her. She drifted off to sleep knowing she and the baby were in good hands. A sharp pain radiating around her waist woke her. The candle had burned low.

"How're you doing?"

"That pain was stronger."

Ryan set up in bed. "Then we need to start timing them. Let me know when you feel the next one."

She lifted one corner of her mouth and gave him a look. "I don't think you'll have to be told. I'm a wimp when it comes to pain. You'll hear me."

He chuckled. "I'll keep that in mind as this goes on. Do I need to call in someone else so they can lose their hearing?"

"You've already done that with Stacy."

Ryan had the good grace to look repentant. "I'm sorry about that. I'll try to make up for that by doing what I can to help make you comfortable. Do you need anything? Need more support on your back?"

"I'm fine right now but I do love to have my back rubbed."

"Then a back rub is what you'll get." He climbed out of bed.

"Where're you going?"

"I'm just going around to the other side."

"But I liked you here." She watched him walk by the end of the bed. Even in labor he turned her on.

"I appreciate the compliment but I can do a better job over here. Less distractions." His hands moved across her back.

"Like what?"

"Your beautiful face. When your pains get to twenty minutes apart we'll need to call Stacy and go to the hospital."

"Do we have to? I want you to deliver," she said in a melancholy tone.

"No, I guess we don't have to. Do you want to deliver at your house? If you do, we need to get moving."

"I'd like to have the baby here. In this beautiful bed. Just you and me."

Did he realize that if he agreed it would be a sign of commitment? He was giving her and the baby permission to enter his personal space. To share his home and bed for a significant event.

Ryan's hands stopped moving for a second then started again. "I would like that."

She smiled, then winced.

"I take it that was another pain. Try to breathe through them. It'll make it easier. Remember your lessons."

"Is this the moment that you morph into a midwife?"

"It's time. I'm going to get my bag and put on some pants. You stay put."

"You're going to put on clothes when I'm not wearing any?"

"It's a long shot that something might go wrong. If I have to call for help I don't want to get caught with my pants down, so to speak."

Phoebe laughed.

He gave her a reprimanding look. "You go on and make fun but it would be hard for me to live that one down."

She enjoyed the sight of Ryan's backside as he search a drawer. He pulled out some boxers and stepped into them. Going to the wardrobe, he came out wearing a pair of athletic shorts. He then left the room and returned with a backpack. Ryan flipped the bedside lamp on and blew out the candle.

"I liked it better the other way." Phoebe rolled toward him.

"I did, too, but I need to see." Ryan unzipped the back-pack and removed a stethoscope. He placed it on her belly, then listened to her chest and back. Finished, he put the stethoscope on the table. "Sounds good."

"I'm scared" slipped out before she knew it.

Ryan pushed her hair away from her forehead and kissed her. "There's nothing to be afraid of. I'll be right here with you all the way. This is a natural process."

"That's coming from a man who never had a baby."

"That's true, but I've been there when a lot of them have been born. I'll give you an example of how natural it is. My great-great-grandmother had twelve babies. They all lived. While she was in labor she would fix breakfast for the family and get everyone off to the fields. They were farmers in north Alabama. She would lie on the floor and have the baby, then tie the cord off with a thread from a flour sack because it was thin enough to cut the cord. She would clean herself and the baby up, then get into bed. At the end of the day when everyone came in from the field there would be a new baby to greet."

"Are you expecting me to do that?" Her voice rose.

Ryan took her hand and squeezed it. "No, I'm not. What I'm trying to say is that if my grandmother can do it by herself twelve times, then the two of us can certainly do it together once without any problem."

"I think I can do anything as long as I have you to help me."

Ryan leaned over and gave her a leisurely kiss. "I feel the same way, honey."

Another pain gripped her. She clutched Ryan's hand.

When it had passed he said, "Why don't you walk around some? It would help with the pain and get the labor moving along."

"I'm not going to walk around your place with no clothes on, in labor or not."

"Okay, let me see if I can find something comfortable

for you to wear." Ryan went to his wardrobe. The sound of hangers being pushed across a rod came out of the space. "This should do it."

He returned to the bed with a button-up shirt in his hand. "Swing your feet over the side and I'll help you get this on."

She did and he held the shirt while she slipped her arms into it. The sleeves fell well past her hands. Ryan buttoned it for her, then rolled the sleeves up to the middle of her forearms.

He reached out and wiggled his fingers. "Let me help you stand."

Phoebe took them and let him pull her to her feet.

Ryan stepped back and looked at her. "Cute. I do believe I like you wearing my shirt."

Phoebe pushed at her hair, trying to bring it to some kind of order. "Thanks. I just hope I don't mess it up."

"Not a problem. It'll be for a good cause.

"Okay, let's do some walking. There isn't as much space here as there is at the hospital but we'll just make do."

Ryan stayed by her side as they made a pass round the living room through the kitchen and back to the bedroom. "Let's do it again," he encouraged as she looked wistfully at the bed. With each contraction Ryan checked his watch, which he had slipped on his wrist before they'd started out of his bedroom.

"They're getting closer."

After one particularly lengthy pain he said, "Tell me about your shower at school."

It was his sly way of keeping her mind off what was going on with her body. She was grateful for his efforts. "It was wonderful. I received all kinds of cute baby things."

He touched her arm to encourage her to keep walking. "Did you get some baby clothes, like you were hoping?"

"I did. I filled a drawer and have some hanging in the wardrobe."

"You must have had a lot of people there."

They continued the slow pace around the house.

"I was surprised. Most of the teachers came. Those who didn't sent presents by others. Everyone was very generous."

"Why were you surprised? Haven't you been working there for some time?"

"I have but they have all seemed to be a little standoffish since Joshua was killed. It became worse when I told them I was pregnant. It was as if they didn't know what to say or do so they did nothing."

"I'm sorry you were so alone for so long. You should have come to me sooner."

She stopped and looked at him.

He put up a hand. "I know, I know. I wasn't very approachable at first. For that I'm sorry."

She smiled. "But you came around very nicely, so I'm happy." But he hadn't said anything about loving her. Even when she had confessed her love for him. She could wait. Ryan showed he cared in so many other ways. He was someone she could count on. Even if she couldn't, she had learned she could depend on herself. "Oh."

"Breathe. Don't hold your breath." Ryan showed her how.

They made small swooshing sounds together.

"I think it's time to get you settled in. I also need to check and see where that baby is."

Ryan led her toward the bedroom.

"How much longer?" As she went by the footboard, she let her fingers trail over the surface of the wood.

"Let me examine you, then I'll have an idea."

She sat on the edge of the bed while he prepared it.

"You're not going to make me lie on the floor like your great-great-grandmother did?"

"I hadn't planned to, but I can." He shook out a blanket as if getting ready to place it on the floor.

"I was kidding."

He smiled. "I'm glad to hear that. I was worried about my back hurting when I bent over to help deliver."

"What kind of midwife are you? Being more worried about your comfort than mine?"

Ryan put a hand down on the mattress on each side of her. His face was inches away from hers. "Honey, I care too much about you to let you be uncomfortable." Ryan kissed her deeply and moved away. He helped her settle into the center of the bed and then he did the exam.

"You're well on your way. Dilated five centimeters. When you get to ten you'll be ready to have a baby."

Another pain cramped her back and radiated around to her sides. She grabbed Ryan's hand. He rode it out with her, all the time whispering sweet encouragement.

Ryan had seen countless husbands in the delivery suite when their wives had been giving birth. Some handled the process with aplomb while others were just a step above worthless. Ryan knew what was going to happen and still waves the size of a tsunami rolled through his stomach because this time it was Phoebe having the baby and he was that significant other helping. He felt more like that guy who was useless.

She had taken over his life, captured his heart and made him a ball of nerves in a situation where he usually had all the confidence. Even with all his reassurances, he worried that something might not go right during the birth. If she died or the baby did, he didn't know what he would do.

He'd survived other deaths but he didn't think he could live without Phoebe.

"You look worried all of a sudden. Is something wrong?" Phoebe asked.

"No, everything is fine. You're doing wonderfully. Keep up the good work."

"I need to go to the bathroom?"

"Sure." Ryan stood and helped her up. "I'll leave the door open. If you need me I'll be right out here."

While Phoebe was in the bathroom Ryan pulled out his cellphone and called the hospital to let them know that he was in the process of delivering Phoebe's baby. He wanted them aware so that if there was a problem someone could be here to help in minutes.

"Ryan!"

"Yes?" He hurried toward the bathroom.

"My waters just broke."

"Well, this baby is getting ready to make a showing. Stay put and I'll help you get cleaned up. I'll find you something dry to wear."

He left to search for another shirt. This time he went to the chest of drawers and found a T-shirt. It might not fit over all of her middle but at least it would cover her lovely breasts so that he could concentrate on delivering the baby. He went back to Phoebe.

"You're going to run out of clothes." She pushed a button through a hole.

"If I do, I won't mind. I like you better naked anyway."

Moisture filled her eyes and she gave him a wry smile. "Thanks. You really are being wonderful."

"Not a problem." A delivery had always been a matter-of-fact event for him. A job with a happy ending most of the time. But with Phoebe it was much more. This was an event to cherish.

He helped her pull the T-shirt over her head.

"This doesn't cover much," she complained.

"I need to see your belly and you can pull the sheet up to cover yourself if you must. I don't know why you're being so modest. I've seen all of you and there isn't anything or anyone more stunning. Now, come on and get into bed. We have a baby to welcome into the world."

Another pain shot through her.

"Let's get you settled and I'm going to have another look." He help her move to the center of the bed.

"I'm feeling pressure."

"Good, then you're almost ready. Bend your legs."

Ryan placed her feet in the correct spot so he could see. He put on plastic gloves and checked her. "You're almost there."

"Here comes another one." Phoebe gritted her teeth.

"Look at me," Ryan demanded.

She did.

"Now, let's breathe together."

Phoebe followed his lead.

With the contraction over, Ryan lightly trailed his fingers over her middle until the tension left her and she lay back.

"I need to get a few things out of the bathroom and find something soft to swaddle the baby in. You should have let me know you were planning this tonight and I could have been better prepared."

"You're a funny man, Ryan Matthews."

"I thought you could use some humor right about now." He found the things he needed and placed them at the foot of the bed within arm's length.

Another pain took Phoebe and she met his look. They went through it together. This was one time he didn't mind looking into the pain in someone's eyes.

"I feel pressure. I need to push."

"Hold on just a second."

"This baby isn't waiting for you," she growled.

Ryan examined her. "The head has crowned." He moved to the end of the bed and leaned over the footboard. "Phoebe—" his voice was low "—I want you to look at me. On the next contraction I want you to push."

Her gaze met his between her knees. They didn't have to wait long. "Push."

Ryan reached for the baby's head and supported it. His look went to Phoebe again. "You're doing beautifully."

Another contraction hit. His gaze held hers. He wished he could hold her hand and comfort her but he couldn't be at two places at once. "Push, honey."

Ryan glanced down. The baby's shoulders slid out and the rest of the tiny human followed. He saw birth all the time but none had been more amazing.

Exhausted, Phoebe fall back on the bed.

"It's a boy," Ryan announced. He tied off the umbilical cord before cutting it and laid the baby on Phoebe's stomach.

She reached a hand up to touch the tiny head.

At the baby's squeaking sound, Ryan came around to the bedside table and reached for the suction bubble. He cleaned the air passages and mouth. Grabbing a clean towel, he wiped the newborn.

The sight before him was more beautiful than any he'd ever witnessed. His heart swelled. For once he could understand the feeling new parents had when their child was born.

"He's perfect, Phoebe." Ryan couldn't keep the reverence out of his voice.

She looked at him with a tired smile. "He is, isn't he?"

Ryan leaned down and kissed her on the forehead. "No

more perfect than you. I'm going to lay him beside you and go get a washcloth and finish washing him up. You and I still have some work to do." He took a towel from the end of the bed. Wrapping the baby in it, he placed him beside her.

Phoebe secured him with her arm.

"Don't move." Quickly he went to the bathroom and prepared a warm washcloth. Returning to Phoebe, he cleaned the baby boy, swaddled him in a sheet and placed him in the cradle.

Going to the end of the bed, Ryan said, "Okay, Phoebe, I need a couple of big pushes and we'll be done here. Then you can rest."

Half an hour later Ryan had Phoebe settled with the baby at her breast. He stood at the end of the bed and watched them. He was so full of emotion all he could do was stare. It had been an honor to be a part of such a special event. Phoebe's eyelids lifted.

They were full of love that extended to him.

"What's your middle name?"

"James."

Phoebe looked down at the baby. "Joshua James Taylor." She looked back at Ryan. "We'll call him JJ."

Ryan's eyes watered.

"Why don't you join us and get to know your namesake?"

Ryan didn't hesitate to join them on the bed. Phoebe lifted her head and he slipped an arm under her neck. JJ mewed as if he wished the two adults would stop interrupting his sleep. He soon quieted. Ryan ran his palm over JJ's silky head. Despite having delivered hundreds of babies, Ryan had never spent any time enjoying the touch and feel of a newborn. He picked up the tiny hand and JJ wrapped it around Ryan's finger. His heart was captured.

Ryan had spent so much of his life alone and now he wanted more. He would never go back to living closed off from people. His world was right here in his arms and he was going to hold on to it tight.

He looked at Phoebe. Her eyes were clear and confident. "We are yours. All you have to do is accept us."

"I love you, Phoebe. And I love JJ. I want to be a part of your lives if you will let me."

"And we love you. We are family now."

Ryan kissed her tenderly on the lips. When he lifted his mouth from hers Phoebe's eyelids had already closed. He shut his, releasing a sigh of contentment. He'd gone from being a man alone and caring nothing about the future to a man who had everything he could hope for, including a bright future. Life was worth living.

* * * * *

BEST FRIEND TO PERFECT BRIDE

JENNIFER TAYLOR

For Charlotte, who told me about the boat Gallina, and for James, who owns her.

Many thanks for providing me with the perfect home for my hero.

CHAPTER ONE

SHE HADN'T CHANGED. Tall and slender, her red-gold hair coiled into an elegant knot at the nape of her neck, Bella English looked as beautiful today as she had done the last time he had seen her. On her wedding day.

'Mac! I heard you were back. Good to see you, mate. How are you?'

'Great, thanks, Lou.'

James MacIntyre—Mac to all who knew him— turned and grinned at the elderly porter. Out of the corner of his eye he saw Bella move away from the desk but he kept his attention firmly focused on the other man. After what his old friend Tim had told him, he wasn't all that eager to speak to her.

'You're looking well, I must say, Lou. Obviously, moving to the new paediatric A&E unit has done you the power of good. You look a good ten years younger than the last time I saw you!'

'I wish!' Lou's grizzled face broke into a wry smile. 'It'd take major surgery to turn me into Dalverston's very own version of George Clooney.' He glanced over Mac's shoulder and grimaced. 'Anyway, I'd better get going. Catch you later.'

'Yep.'

Mac didn't need to check to see what had caused Lou to beat a hasty retreat. He could smell her perfume, that subtle fragrance of freesias that Bella always wore. She had told him once that it was made especially for her and that had fitted perfectly with everything he knew about her. Bella was the sort of woman who would have her very own perfume. Nothing about her was ordinary or commonplace.

Mac turned slowly around, taking stock of all the details he had missed before. Although Bella had always been slender, she was verging on thin now, he realised. And even though her complexion was as creamy as ever, there were dark circles under her green eyes that hinted at far too many sleepless nights. Was it guilt that had kept her awake? he wondered a shade bitterly. A noisy conscience clamouring to be heard, even if it was too late in the day? After all, even Bella must feel some degree of remorse about ending her marriage to Tim.

'Hello, Mac. I heard you were back. How are you?'

The greeting was almost identical to Lou's, but Mac had to admit that it made him want to respond very differently. He experienced an uncharacteristic urge to take her by the shoulders and shake her, demand to know why she had done such a cruel thing.

She had ruined Tim's life—didn't she care? Didn't she care either that she had broken all those promises she had made three years ago to love, honour and cherish the man she had married? He had sat through the ceremony, listened to her cool clear voice swearing a lifetime's devotion, and had believed every word. If he was honest, he felt almost as let down as poor Tim must do.

The thought shocked him so that it was a moment before he answered. He and Bella had never been anything more than friends—he had made sure of that. So why should he feel so disillusioned? He blanked out the thought, knowing it was foolish to dwell on it. If he and Bella were to work together for the next few months, he couldn't allow recent events to stand in the way.

'Fine, thanks. Looking forward to working in the new unit.' He glanced around and nodded. 'It looks great, I must say. Obviously, no expense has been spared.'

'No. Everything is state of the art. We've been open for almost a month now and I still have to pinch myself when I come into work. I can't believe that we have such marvellous facilities to hand.'

She gave a husky laugh and Mac tensed when he felt the tiny hairs all over his body spring to attention. He had forgotten about her laugh, forgotten how soft it was, how *sexy*. It had been her laugh that he had noticed first, in fact. He had been standing in the lunch queue in the university's refectory when he had heard a woman laugh and he had turned to see who it was...

He ditched that thought as well, not needing any more distractions. He knew where his loyalties lay, knew that if he had to take sides then he would be firmly allied to Tim. Tim had poured out the whole sorry tale, told him what had happened from start to finish, and whilst Mac was realistic enough to know that it was rarely all one person's fault when a marriage ended, it was obvious that Bella was more at fault than Tim. No, Tim's biggest mistake had been to love Bella too much and be too soft with her. The thought firmed his resolve and he smiled thinly at her.

'Is that what brought you to Dalverston, the chance to work in a wonderful new facility like this? I must confess that I was surprised to learn you had moved out of London.'

'It was one of the reasons, yes.'

Bella's expression sobered and Mac's heart twisted when he saw the pain in her eyes. Maybe Tim *was* hurting but Bella was hurting too, it seemed. The idea affected him far more than it should have done, far more than he wanted it to do. It was an effort not to let her see how he felt when she continued.

'I needed to get away and moving up here seemed like the right thing to do. It's a fresh start for me and, hopefully, it will be a fresh start for Tim as well.'

Bella could feel the animosity coming off Mac in huge waves and it hurt to know that he had judged

her and obviously found her wanting. She knew that
Tim would have told Mac his version of the story
but she had hoped that Mac would wait until he had
spoken to her before he started apportioning blame.
However, it appeared that he had accepted what Tim
had said without question. *She* was the one at fault,
the bad guy who had called time on her marriage,
while Tim was the innocent victim.

She swung round, refusing to stand there and try
to justify herself. She had made up her mind that she
wouldn't retaliate after she had found out that Tim
had been spreading all those lies about her. She had
seen that happen with other couples, had watched
as the situation had deteriorated into an unseemly
sparring match, and she had sworn that she wouldn't
go down that route. People would believe what they
wanted to believe anyway. If she tried to contest Tim's
claims that she had been unreasonable, that she had
ruined his career, that she had ended their relationship rather than have a baby with him, few would
believe her.

She had always been the reticent one in the relationship, the one who took longer to make friends,
whereas Tim had always been very outgoing. Tim
drew people to him and made instant friends of them,
and if he tended to drop them just as quickly later,
then nobody seemed to mind. No, if there were sides
to be taken then most folk would take Tim's. Including Mac, it seemed.

Pain stabbed her heart as she led the way to Reception. Even though she knew it was silly, she hated to think that she had sunk so low in Mac's estimation. Dredging up a smile, she turned to Janet Davies, their receptionist, determined that she wasn't going to let him know how she felt.

'This is Dr MacIntyre, Janet. He'll be covering the senior registrar's post until Dr Timpson is fit to return to work following her accident.'

'Oh, I know Mac. Who doesn't?' Janet got up and hurried around the desk to give Mac a hug. She grinned up at him. 'So where was it this time? Africa? India? Outer Mongolia?'

'The Philippines.'

Mac hugged Janet back, his face breaking into a smile that immediately warmed Bella's heart. He had always had the most wonderful smile, she thought, then pulled herself up short. Maybe Mac had smiled at Janet with genuine warmth but he certainly hadn't smiled at her that way.

'Oh, grim.' Janet grimaced. 'Was it as bad as it looked on TV?'

'Worse.'

Mac shook his head, his dark brown hair flopping untidily across his forehead. It needed trimming, Bella decided, even though it suited him, emphasising his craggy good looks and that air of toughness he projected. Mac looked exactly like the kind of man he was: tough, unflappable, someone you could depend on, someone who would never let you down.

Her heart ached even harder at the thought. She could have done with Mac's support this past difficult year.

'The typhoon destroyed whole cities and left people with nothing except the clothes they stood up in. We had a devil of a job getting hold of even the most basic supplies in the beginning,' he continued.

'How awful!' Janet shuddered as she went back to her seat. 'Makes you grateful that you live here, doesn't it.'

'It does indeed.' Mac grinned. 'Even if it does rain a lot in this part of the world!'

Janet laughed as she reached for the telephone when it started ringing. Bella moved to the whiteboard and checked the list of names written on it, determined to start as she meant to go on. Maybe there were certain issues that she and Mac needed to address, but they were colleagues, first and foremost, and she intended to keep that at the forefront of her mind. There were just three children in cubicles and each of them had been seen and were currently awaiting the results of various tests. She pointed to the last name on the list when Mac joined her.

'I'd like you to take a look at this one, if you wouldn't mind. Chloe Adams, aged eight, admitted at four a.m. this morning complaining of a severe headache. She'd also been vomiting.' She sighed. 'Apparently, she's been suffering from violent headaches for several weeks. Mum took her to their GP, who thought it was probably a sinus infection, but I'm not convinced.'

'So what are you thinking?' Mac queried. 'That it's something more sinister?'

'Yes. I noticed a definite lack of coordination when I was examining her. It made me wonder if it's a tumour. I asked Mum if she'd noticed anything— clumsy gait, frequent falls, that kind of thing—but she said she hadn't.' Bella shrugged. 'Chloe is one of five children and I get the impression that her mother is finding it hard to cope since their father upped and left them at the beginning of the year.'

'I see. It must be difficult for her when she's been abandoned like that,' Mac said blandly, so blandly in fact that Bella knew he was thinking about her situation.

Colour touched her cheeks as she led the way to the cubicles. She hadn't abandoned Tim! She had left because Tim had made it impossible for her to stay. She had tried to help him, tried everything she could think of, but nothing had worked. He had been too dependent on the painkillers by then to give them up. Oh, he had promised that he would, swore that he had umpteen times, but he had lied. The drugs had changed him from the man she had married, turned him into someone who lied and deceived at the drop of a hat. It had reached the point where she simply couldn't take any more and she had left and, amazingly, it had been the best thing she could have done for him.

Tim had sought help after that. He had admitted himself to rehab and finally kicked his habit. Maybe she should have gone back to him then—she had thought about it. But then she had found out about his affair and there hadn't seemed any point. She would only have gone back out of a sense of duty and that hadn't seemed right or fair to either of them.

It made her wonder all of a sudden if she had ever really loved him—loved him with the depth and intensity that people were supposed to feel when they married—if she hadn't been prepared to fight for him. The problem was that she had never been truly in touch with her feelings. As the only child of career-minded parents, she had learned at an early age to keep her emotions in check. Even after she had grown up, she had always held back, had always been wary about letting herself feel. Tim had seemed like a safe bet—the type of man she was used to, someone from her own social circle, someone she felt comfortable with. Unlike Mac. Mac had been very different. Even though they'd only been friends, his self-assurance and experience of life had unsettled her. Everything about him had seemed alien. Dangerous. A threat to her peace of mind. He still was.

Bella's breath caught. If Mac had seemed danger-ous all those years ago, he was even more of a threat now that she was so vulnerable.

* * *

'Mrs Adams? I'm Dr MacIntyre. Dr English has asked me to take a look at your daughter.'

Mac smiled at the harassed-looking woman sitting beside the bed. He knew that Bella was standing right behind him and forced himself to focus on the other woman. He had sworn that he would behave with the utmost propriety and wouldn't take Bella to task about what she had done. Maybe he *did* believe that she had behaved deplorably by ending her marriage, but it wasn't his place to say so.

'She's feeling a lot better now, aren't you, Chloe?' Donna Adams turned to the little girl, urging her to agree, and Mac sighed. No matter how long this took or how inconvenient it was for the mother, they needed to get to the bottom of Chloe's problem.

'That's good to hear but I still think it would be best if we carried out a couple more tests.' He smiled at the little girl. 'We don't want you having any more of those horrible headaches if we can avoid it, do we, Chloe?'

'No.' She smiled shyly back at him, clutching tight hold of a battered old teddy bear.

Mac grinned at her as he sat down on the edge of the bed. 'What's your teddy's name? I have a bear just like him and he's called Bruno.'

'William.' Chloe gave the bear a hug. 'He's my best friend and I take him everywhere.'

'I expect he enjoys it.' Mac took hold of the bear's

paw and solemnly shook it. 'It's nice to meet you, William. My name's Dr Mac.'

Chloe giggled at this piece of nonsense, but Mac knew that it was important to gain her trust. He smiled at her again. 'So, now the introductions are over, I need to ask you some questions, Chloe. There are no right or wrong answers, mind you. And if you want William to help you then that's also fine. OK?'

'OK,' Chloe agreed happily.

'So, Chloe, have you noticed that sometimes you don't seem quite as steady on your feet as normal and fall over?'

'Sometimes,' Chloe murmured. She glanced at her mother then hurried on. 'It happened in school the other day. I got up to fetch a piece of paper to do some painting and fell over. Teacher thought I was messing about and told me off.'

'I see.' Mac glanced at Bella and saw her nod. Poor balance could point towards a disturbance to the function of the cerebellum and was often an indication of a tumour. Although he hoped with all his heart it wasn't that, it was looking increasingly likely.

'And have you found it difficult to walk sometimes, as though your feet don't want to do what you tell them to?' he continued gently.

'Yes. Sometimes they keep going the wrong way,' Chloe told him guilelessly.

'I'm sorry, Doctor, but what has this got to do with Chloe's headaches?' Donna Adams demanded.

'It all helps to build up a picture of what might be wrong with Chloe,' Mac explained, not wanting to go into detail just yet. If their suspicions were correct then there would be time enough for the poor woman to face the fact that her child was seriously ill. He stood up and smiled at Chloe. 'I'm going to send you for a special scan, Chloe, so we can see what's happening inside your head. I just need to make a phone call first and then the porter will take you and your mum downstairs to have it done.'

'Will it take long?' Donna Adams asked anxiously. 'Only I've got to get the others ready for school. They're with my neighbour at the moment but I can't expect her to see to them. She's in her eighties and it's far too much for her.'

'The scan itself won't take very long,' Bella said gently. 'However, Chloe will need to stay here until we get the results back. Is there anyone else you can contact who could see to the children?'

'No.' Donna's tone was bitter. 'There's nobody since their dad upped and left.' She glanced at her daughter and sighed. 'They'll just have to miss school today, I suppose.'

Mac didn't say anything as he followed Bella from the cubicle, but it didn't mean that he wasn't thinking it. Breaking promises was a definite no-no in his view. He only had to recall his own father's despair after his mother had walked out on them to know that it was something he would never do. If he ever made a commitment then he would stick to it, no matter what.

He glanced at Bella and could tell from her expression that she knew what he was thinking, but it was hard luck. Letting Tim down the way she had was beyond the pale, in his opinion. She had promised to love and cherish Tim for the rest of her days but she hadn't meant it. She couldn't have done if at the first sign of trouble she had turned her back on him. He felt guilty enough about not being there when Tim had needed his support, even though he'd had no idea what his friend had been going through. However, Bella *had* been there and, as Tim's wife, she should have been the one person he could rely on. It was little wonder that his friend was so devastated.

Mac's mouth thinned as he followed her into the office. Maybe it was unfair of him to be so judgemental but he had always considered Bella to be the ideal woman. Not only was she beautiful, but she was highly intelligent too. Although he had been deeply attracted to her when they had met at Cambridge, he had been ever so slightly in awe of her as well. The fact that she had kept herself aloof from the rest of their class had only added to her allure, in fact.

He had never been the reticent type. His upbringing, on a council estate on the outskirts of Manchester, hadn't allowed for such luxury. He had learned early on that he needed to be tough to survive, focused and determined if he hoped to achieve his goal of becoming a doctor. Bella had been very different from the girls he had known at home, different too from the rest of the women in their year at university. Although many of them had come from privileged backgrounds too, Bella had stood out: her perfection had made her special. To discover that she wasn't perfect after all had hit him hard. For all these years he had put her on a pedestal but the truth was that Bella was just a woman like any other, a woman who could make and break promises. She wasn't special. And she wasn't out of his league, as he had always believed.

Mac frowned. It was the first time that thought had crossed his mind and he didn't like it. Not one little bit. Or the one that followed it. There was nothing to stop him making a play for Bella now.

Sadly, the results of Chloe's scan only confirmed their suspicions. Bella sighed as she studied the monitor. 'There's no doubt about it, is there? That's definitely a tumour.'

'It is.'

Mac leant forward to get a better look and she tensed when his shoulder brushed against hers. She moved aside, not enjoying the fact that her heart seemed to be beating far faster than it normally did. She cleared her throat. The last thing she needed was Mac thinking that he had any kind of effect on her.

'It's probably a medulloblastoma, wouldn't you

say? That's one of the most common types of brain tumour that occur in children.'

'Oh, yes. The fact that it's arisen in the cerebellum makes it almost a certainty,' he concurred.

'Chloe's going to need immediate treatment,' Bella said, focusing on their patient in the hope that it would stop her thoughts wandering again. Maybe she did seem to be unusually aware of Mac, but that was only to be expected. Ever since she'd heard he was back in England, she had been on edge. After all, Mac was Tim's best friend and it must be hard for him to accept what had happened. It was bound to lead to a certain degree of…well, *tension* between them. The thought was reassuring and she hurried on.

'From what I've read, medulloblastomas can grow very rapidly and spread to other parts of the brain as well as to the spinal cord.'

'That's right. Chloe needs to be seen by an oncologist ASAP so we shall have to set that up. She'll probably need radiotherapy as well as chemotherapy if she's to have any chance of surviving this.' He shook his head and Bella saw the sorrow in his eyes. 'I feel sorry for her mother. It's going to be a huge shock for her.'

'It will be a lot for her to deal with, especially with having the other children to look after,' Bella agreed quietly. 'Just travelling back and forth to hospital while Chloe receives treatment will be a major task with her not having any backup.'

'It will.'

Mac's tone was flat. Although there was no hint of censure in his voice, Bella knew that he was thinking about the way she had seemingly deserted Tim in his hour of need. The urge to tell him the truth—the *real* truth, not the version that Tim was determined to tell everyone—was very strong but she refused to go down that path. It wouldn't improve Mac's opinion of her if she tried to apportion blame; it could have the opposite effect, in fact.

It was hard to accept that there was very little she could do, but Bella knew there was no point agonising about it. Switching off the monitor, she turned to leave the office. 'I'll go and have a word with Mrs Adams,' she said over her shoulder. 'The sooner she knows what's going on, the better.'

'Fine. Do you want me to phone Oncology and start the ball rolling?' Mac offered, following her out to the corridor.

'If you wouldn't mind… Oh, they've got a new phone number. They're starting the refurbishments today so they've moved temporarily into the old building. I'll get it for you.' Bella went to go back into the office and staggered when she cannoned into Mac.

'Sorry.' He grinned as he set her safely back on her feet. 'I didn't expect you to turn round so suddenly, or that's my excuse, anyway. It's got nothing whatsoever to do with me being born clumsy!'

'No harm done,' she assured him, although she could feel heat flowing from the point where his hands were gripping her shoulders. She stepped back, setting some much-needed space between them, or much-needed by her, at least. Mac appeared unmoved by the contact. 'Janet should have Oncology's new number, now that I think about it,' she said, hastily squashing that thought. 'Let me know what they say, won't you?'

'Will do.'

He sketched her a wave as he headed to Reception. Bella watched until he disappeared from sight then made her way to the cubicles. She wasn't looking forward to the next few minutes. Breaking bad news to a parent was always difficult and one of the few things she disliked about her job...

Her breath caught as she felt the heat finally consume her entire body. It felt as though she was on fire, burning up, inside and out, and all because Mac had touched her. She couldn't recall ever feeling this way before, couldn't remember when the touch of a man's hands had set her alight, not even when Tim had made love to her. What did it mean? Or didn't it mean anything really? Was it simply the lack of intimacy that had made her so susceptible all of a sudden?

Once Tim had become hooked on the painkillers, they had stopped making love. He hadn't been interested in anything apart from where his next fix was coming from and she hadn't been able to stand the thought of them being intimate when it wouldn't have meant anything. It was almost two years since they had slept together and there had been nobody else since, or at least not for her. Was that why she felt so aware of her body all of a sudden, so emotionally charged? It wasn't Mac's touch per se that had aroused her but the fact that she had been denied an outlet for her feelings for such a long time?

Bella told herself that it was the real explanation; however, as she entered the cubicle, she knew in her heart that it was only partly true. Maybe the lack of intimacy was a contributing factor but she doubted if she would have reacted this way if another man had touched her the way Mac had done. The truth was that she had always been aware of him even though they had never been anything more than friends. There was something about him that she responded to, even though she had refused to acknowledge it. It made her see just how careful she needed to be. The last thing she wanted was to start craving Mac's touch when it was obvious how he felt about her.

CHAPTER TWO

IT WAS A busy day but Mac enjoyed every second. Although he had worked in emergency medicine for some time, paediatric emergency care on this scale was a whole new ball game. The newly opened paediatric A&E unit accepted patients from a wide area and not just from Dalverston itself. Built on a separate site to the main hospital, it boasted the most up-to-date facilities available. Everything was geared up for children, from the bright and airy waiting room, which sported comfortable couches rather than the usual hard plastic chairs, to the on-site Radiography unit. X-rays, CT and MRI scans were all carried out in rooms that had been made as child-friendly as possible. Colourful murals adorned the walls and the staff wore brightly coloured polo shirts instead of their usual uniforms. Even the gowns the children were given to wear were printed with cartoon characters and had easy-to-fasten Velcro tabs instead of fiddly ties.

Whilst Mac knew that all these things were incidentals, they helped to put the children at their ease and that, in turn, helped him and the rest of the team do their job. By the time his shift ended, he knew that he was going to enjoy working there. Not only would it allow him to develop his skills in paediatric medicine, but it promised to be a fun place to work too. Several of the nurses were leaving at the same time as him so he held the door open for them, bowing low as they all trooped past.

'After you, ladies,' he said, grinning up at them.

'Thank you, my man,' one of them replied, sticking her nose into the air as she sallied forth.

They all laughed, Mac included, and it was a pleasant change to enjoy a bit of light-hearted banter. He hadn't been overstating how bad things had been on his most recent aid mission. It had been extremely grim at times and it was a relief to feel that he could legitimately enjoy himself, even though he didn't regret going and would do the same thing again if it were necessary. He often thought that he had the best of both worlds: he got to help people who were in dire need of his skills and he also had a job he loved to come back to. There was nothing else he could wish for…except, maybe, someone to share his life.

'Thank you.'

The cool tones brought him up short. Mac straightened abruptly when he recognised Bella's voice, feeling decidedly awkward at being caught on the hop. Although he and Bella had spoken several times during the day, their conversations had been confined to work. He had made sure of it, in fact. Although he had promised himself that he wouldn't say anything to her about Tim, he had realised how hard it was going to be to bite his tongue. Bella had let Tim down. Badly. And it was painful to know that she was capable of such behaviour when he had expected so much more from her.

'You're welcome.' He forced himself to smile even though his insides were churning with all the conflicting emotions. On the one hand he knew it was none of his business, yet on the other it still hurt to know that she had fallen so far short of the picture he had held of her. 'It's been a busy day, hasn't it?' he said, struggling to get his feelings in check. It wouldn't serve any purpose whatsoever to tell her how disappointed he felt, how let down. After all, why should she care how *he* felt when she obviously didn't care about Tim?

'It has. We're seeing more and more children now that word has spread that we're open. Obviously, the other hospitals know we're up and running, but it's the parents bringing in their children that has made the difference.'

She gave a little shrug, immediately drawing his eyes to the slender lines of her body, elegantly encased in an emerald-green coat that he knew without needing to be told was from some exclusive designer's collection. Bella had money—a great deal of money that she had been left by her grandparents—and it showed in the way she dressed, even though she had never flaunted her wealth. It was a tiny point in her favour and Mac found himself clinging to it. Maybe it was silly but he wanted to find something good about her, something to redress the balance a little. His smile was less forced this time.

'It must take the pressure off the other A&E departments if more kids are being treated here. That can only be a good thing.'

'Yes, although so many A&E units have closed that the ones which are left are still under a great deal of pressure.'

Bella headed towards the car park, making it clear that she didn't expect Mac to accompany her. He hesitated, wondering why he felt so ambivalent all of a sudden. He had been planning an evening doing nothing more taxing than watching television. It was what he needed, some downtime after the hectic couple of months he'd had and yet, surprisingly, he was loath to spend the evening slumped in front of the box. He came to a swift decision even though his brain was telling him that he was making a mistake.

'Do you fancy grabbing a bite to eat?' he said as he caught up with her. He saw the surprise on her face when she glanced round but he ignored it. For some reason he didn't intend to examine too closely, he wanted to spend the evening with her. 'Nothing fancy, just a curry or something.'

'I don't know if it's a good idea.' She stopped and looked him straight in the eyes and he could see the challenge in her gaze. 'It's obvious how you feel, Mac. You blame me for what's happened, don't you?'

'So why don't you set the record straight and tell me your side of the story?'

He shrugged, wishing he felt as indifferent as he was trying to make out. Maybe he was wrong to blame her, but he couldn't help it when he felt so let down. For all these years he had considered her to be the model of perfection and he didn't want to have to change his view of her, especially when he sensed that it could have repercussions. Now that Bella had fallen from her pedestal, she was just a woman like any other. A woman he had always been deeply attracted to.

The thought made his insides churn and he hurried on. 'It seems only fair to me.'

'Sorry, but it isn't going to happen. I have no intention of trying to justify myself to you or to anyone else.'

She carried on walking, ignoring him as she got into her car. Mac stared after her, wondering why she was being so stubborn. Leaving aside his reasons for wanting to get at the truth, surely it would make sense for her to explain why she had called time on her marriage? Nobody liked being blamed for something they hadn't done and Bella must be no different…

Unless the truth was that she was too embarrassed to admit that she *had* been at fault.

Mac's mouth thinned as he watched her drive away. Bella knew that she had been wrong to abandon Tim when he had needed her so desperately and that was why she couldn't face the thought of talking about it. Although his opinion of her had already dropped way down the scale, it slid even further. Bella was a long way from being perfect, it seemed.

Bella spent a miserable evening. Not even the latest bestseller could take her mind off what had happened. Should she have done as Mac had suggested and told him her version—the *real* version—about what had gone on?

She kept mulling it over, wishing that she had and then just as quickly dismissing the idea. Once she set off down that route there would be no turning back; she would have to wait and see if Mac believed her. The thought that he might think she was lying was more than she could bear. It would be better not to say anything rather than have to endure his contempt.

She was due in to work at lunchtime the following day. By the time she arrived, there was quite a long queue of patients waiting to be seen. Janet waved as she crossed Reception and Bella waved back although she didn't stop. There was a child screaming and it seemed propitious to go and check what was happening before the other children started to get upset. The noise was coming from the treatment room so she went straight there, frowning when she opened the door and was assailed by the shrill screams of an angry toddler.

'What's going on?' she asked, dropping her coat onto a chair.

'Alfie fell off his scooter and cut his knee,' Laura Watson, one of their most experienced nurses, told her. She rolled her eyes. 'Unfortunately, he won't let me look at it 'cos it's sore.'

'I see.' Bella crouched down in front of the little boy. He was clinging to an older woman who she guessed was his grandmother. 'That's an awful lot of noise, Alfie. You're going to scare Robbie if you scream like that.'

The little boy stopped screaming and peeped at her through his fingers, distracted by the mention of the unknown Robbie. Bella smiled at him. 'That's better. Have you met Robbie yet? He's rather shy and only comes out of his cupboard when he thinks nobody is looking. I'll go and see if I can find him.'

Standing up, she crossed the room and opened one of the cupboards that held their supplies. Robbie, the toy rabbit, was sitting on a shelf so she lifted him down and carried him back to the little boy.

'Here he is. He must like you, Alfie, because he came straight out of his cupboard and didn't try to hide.' She handed the toy to the child then glanced at the older woman. 'If you could pop him on the bed then I can take a look at his knee,' she said sotto voce.

The woman quickly complied, sighing with relief when Alfie carried on playing with the toy. 'Thank heavens for that! I thought he would never stop screaming.' She smiled at Bella. 'You must have children, my dear. It's obvious that you know just how to distract them.'

'Sadly, no, I don't.'

Bella smiled, trying to ignore the pang of regret that pierced her heart. Having a family had always been her dearest wish, something she had assumed would happen once she had got married, but Tim had never been keen on the idea. Whenever she had broached the subject, he had brushed it aside, claiming that he had no intention of being tied down by a baby at that stage in his life. It was only after she had told him that she wanted a divorce that he had tried to persuade her to stay with promises of them starting a family, but she had refused. The last thing she'd wanted was to have a child to hold their marriage together, a sticking-plaster baby.

'Then you should.' Alfie's grandmother laughed ruefully as she ruffled her grandson's hair. 'Oh, they're hard work, but having children is one of life's blessings. And there's no doubt that you'd make a wonderful mother!'

Mac paused outside the treatment room. The door was ajar and he had heard every word. He frowned as he recalled the regret in Bella's voice when she had explained that she didn't have any children. Quite frankly, he couldn't understand it. According to Tim, Bella had refused his pleas to start a family, claiming that her career came first and that having children was way down her list of priorities, but it hadn't sounded like that, had it? It made him wonder all of a sudden if Tim had been telling him the truth.

It was the first time that Mac had considered the idea that his friend might not have been totally honest and it troubled him. He had accepted what Tim had said without question but had he been right to do so? What if Tim had tried to cast himself in a more favourable light by laying the blame on Bella? What if it hadn't been all her fault that the marriage had failed? What if Tim had been more than partly to blame?

After all, it couldn't have been easy for her to cope with Tim's dependence on those painkillers. Mac had worked in a rehab unit and he knew from experience how unreasonable people could be when they were in the throes of an addiction. Bella must have been through the mill—struggling to help Tim conquer his addiction, struggling to support him even when his behaviour probably hadn't been as good as it should have been. As he made his way to the cubicles, Mac realised that he needed to get to the bottom of what had gone on. Although Tim was his oldest friend, he owed it to Bella to ascertain the true facts. The thought that he might have misjudged her didn't sit easily with him, quite frankly.

Mac didn't get a chance to speak to Bella until it

was almost time for him to go off duty. He was on his way to the office when he saw her coming along the corridor. She gave him a cool smile as she went to walk past, but there was no way that he was prepared to leave matters the way they were. It was too important that they got this sorted out, even though he wasn't sure why it seemed so urgent.

'Have you got a second?' he asked, putting out his hand. His fingers brushed against her arm and he felt a flash of something akin to an electric current shoot through him. It was all he could do to maintain an outward show of composure when it felt as though his pulse was fizzing from the charge. 'There's something I need to ask you.'

'I'm just on my way to phone the lab about some results I need,' she said quietly. However, he heard the tremor in her voice and realised that she had felt it too, felt that surge of electricity that had passed between them.

'Oh, right. Well, I won't hold you up. Maybe we can meet later? You're due a break soon, aren't you? How about coffee in the canteen?' he suggested, struggling to get a grip. What on earth was going on? This was Bella, Tim's wife—OK, technically, she was Tim's *ex-wife*—but it still didn't seem right that he should be acting this way, yet he couldn't seem to stop it.

'Why? I don't mean to be rude, Mac, but why do you want us to have coffee?'

She stared back at him, her green eyes searching his face in a way that made him feel more than a little uncomfortable. If he came straight out and admitted that he wanted to check if she was solely to blame for the demise of her marriage then it would hardly endear him to her, would it? He came to a swift decision.

'Because we need to clear the air.' He shrugged, opting for a half-truth rather than the full monty. 'I get the impression that working with me is a strain for you, Bella, and it's not what I want. It's not what you want either, I expect.'

'You're imagining it. I don't have a problem about working with you.' She gave him a chilly smile. 'Now, if you'll excuse me...'

She walked away, leaving him wishing that he hadn't said anything. After all, he hadn't achieved anything, probably made things even more awkward, in fact.

Mac sighed as he made his way to the office. That would teach him to poke his nose into matters that didn't concern him. What had gone on between Tim and Bella was their business and he would be well advised to leave alone.

Bella worked straight through without even stopping for a break. Although they were busy, she could have taken a few minutes off if she'd wanted to, but she didn't. Mac's request to talk to her had unsettled her and she preferred to keep her mind on her patients rather than worry about it. She dealt with her final patient, a ten-year-old boy who had fallen off his bike and broken his arm. Once the X-rays had confirmed her diagnosis, she sent him to the plaster room and cleared up. Helen Robertson, one of the new F1s on the unit, grinned when Bella made her way to the nurses' station to sign out.

'Off home to put your feet up, are you? Or are you planning a wild night out?'

'No chance. It's straight home, supper and bed for me,' Bella replied with a laugh. 'My days of tripping the light fantastic are well and truly over!'

'Oh, listen to her. You'd think she was in her dotage, wouldn't you?' Helen looked past Bella and raised her brows. 'Maybe you can convince her that she can forgo the carpet slippers for a while longer!'

Bella glanced round to see who Helen was talking to and felt her heart lurch when she saw Mac standing behind her. She knew that he was supposed to have gone off duty several hours before and couldn't understand what he was doing there... Unless he had stayed behind to talk to her? The thought filled her with dread. She didn't want to talk to him about anything, neither her marriage nor what Tim had and hadn't done. If she told Mac then she would have to face the possibility that he might not believe her and she couldn't bear that, couldn't stand to know that he thought she was lying.

She hurriedly signed her name in the register, adding the time of her departure. Mac was still talking to Helen, laughing at something the young doctor had said, so Bella headed for the door. It hummed open and she was outside, walking as fast as she could towards the car park. She could hear footsteps behind her and knew that Mac was following her but she didn't slow down. He had no business harassing her this way! She had made it perfectly clear that she didn't intend to discuss her marriage with him and he should accept that. All of a sudden anger got the better of her and she swung round.

'Please stop! I don't want to talk to you, so leave me alone.'

'Why? What are you so scared about?' He shrugged. 'If I were in your shoes, I'd want to tell my side of the story, unless I had something to hide. Do you, Bella?'

'No.' She gave a bitter little laugh, unable to hide how hurt she felt at the suggestion. 'I have nothing to hide but Tim's told you what happened, and you obviously believe him, so what more is there to say? Why should I try to justify myself to you?'

'Because I thought we were friends.' He held out his hands, palms up, in a gesture of supplication that she found incredibly moving for some reason. 'I can tell that you're hurting and if there's anything I can do to make it easier for you then that's all I want.'

He paused. Bella had a feeling that he wasn't sure if he should say what was on his mind and she bit her lip because she wasn't sure if she wanted to hear it either. She steeled herself when he continued.

'I guess what I'm trying to say is that I care about you, Bella. It's as simple as that.'

CHAPTER THREE

MAC HELD HIS BREATH, hoping against hope that Bella would believe him. It was the truth, after all—he *did* care. He cared that she was hurting, cared that she had behaved so out of character. The Bella he knew would *never* have broken her marriage vows unless there had been a very good reason to do so.

'Maybe you mean what you say, Mac, but it makes no difference.' Bella's icy tones sliced through the thoughts whizzing around his head and he flinched.

'I do mean it,' he said shortly, annoyed with himself. What possible reason could there be to excuse the way she had treated Tim? Tim had needed her, desperately, and she had failed him. There was no excuse whatsoever for that kind of behaviour, surely? And yet the niggling little doubt refused to go away.

'Fine.'

She inclined her head but Mac could tell that she didn't believe him and it stung to know that she doubted his word. Couldn't she see that he was telling her the truth? Didn't she know that he wouldn't

lie about something so important? It was on the tip
of his tongue to remonstrate with her when it struck
him that he was doing the very same thing. He was
doubting *her*, blaming *her* for the demise of her marriage. What right did he have to take her to task when
he was equally guilty?

The thought kept him silent and she obviously took
it as a sign that he had given up. She went to her car,
zapping the locks and getting in. Mac stayed where
he was until the sound of the engine roused him. He
had no idea what he was going to do but he had to do
something. Maybe Bella was at fault, but he couldn't
just ignore the pain he had seen in her eyes. Fling-
ing open the passenger door, he climbed into her car,
holding up his hand when she rounded on him.

'I know what you're going to say, Bella. You don't
want to talk about your marriage. I also know that I'm
probably poking my nose in where it's not wanted…'

'You are,' she snapped, glaring at him.

'OK. Fair enough. And I'm sorry. But, leaving all
that aside, I meant what I said. I really do care that
you're upset.' He reached over and squeezed her hand,
hurriedly releasing it when he felt the now familiar
surge of electricity scorch along his nerves. He didn't
want to scare her, certainly didn't want her to think
that he was trying to take advantage of her vulnerability by making a play for her!

Heat rose under his skin, a hot tide of embar-
rassment that was so unfamiliar that it would have

brought him to his knees if he hadn't been sitting down. Making a play for Bella had never been on the cards. From the moment they had met, Mac had known that she was beyond his reach and he had been perfectly happy with that state of affairs too. Although he had earned himself a bit of a reputation at university by dating a lot of women, he'd had no intention of settling down. He had been determined not to get involved with anyone, although he had been genuinely pleased when Bella and Tim had started seeing one another. They had been so well suited, their backgrounds so perfectly in tune that he couldn't have found a better match for either of them.

It had been the same when they had announced their engagement some months later; he had been truly thrilled for them both and absolutely delighted when Tim had asked him to be his best man. It was only at the wedding that he had started to feel a little bit odd. Listening to Bella swearing to love, honour and care for Tim for the rest of her days had, surprisingly, made Mac feel as though he was about to lose something unutterably precious...

He drove the thought from his head. It was too late for it now; far too late to wish that he had said something, done something, stopped the wedding. How could he have jumped up in the middle of the ceremony and declared that he didn't want Bella to marry Tim because he wanted her for *himself*? No, he had done the right thing—sat there and played his part to the best of his ability. And if there'd been an ache in his heart, well, he had accepted that he would have to learn to live with it.

That was why he had decided to sign on with Worlds Together, a leading overseas aid agency, after the wedding. He had been on over half a dozen missions to date and although he knew that he had helped a lot of people during that time, he had gained a lot too. He'd had three years to rationalise his feelings, three years to make sure they were safely under wraps. Why, if anyone had asked him a couple of weeks ago how he felt then he would have confidently told them that he was back on track. But not now. Not now that Bella was no longer Tim's wife. Not now that she was available.

Mac swallowed his groan. Maybe he did want to help Bella but it could turn out that he was creating a lot of problems for himself by doing so.

Bella had no idea what was going on but the tension in the car was making her feel sick. She licked her parched lips, trying to think of something to say, but what exactly? If she ordered Mac to get out of the car, would he do so? Or would he ignore her and stay where he was? It was the not knowing that was the scariest thing of all because it denoted a massive shift in his attitude.

Mac's behaviour towards her had always been impeccable in the past. He had treated her with an old-fashioned courtesy that she had found strangely endearing. Few men in the circles she had frequented had been so polite. The old 'Hooray Henry' syndrome had been very much alive, so that Mac's thoughtfulness and maturity had set him apart. That was why she had enjoyed spending time with him, she realised in surprise. He hadn't needed to shout or tell risqué stories to make himself stand out. Whenever Mac was around, people always knew he was there.

The thought stunned her. She had never realised before just how much Mac had impressed her. He had been an unknown quantity in so many ways, his background so different from hers that she had been afraid of saying something stupid that would betray her ignorance. Now, after working in the NHS for the past ten years, she had a much better idea of the world. She had treated many people from backgrounds similar to Mac's and understood the hardships they faced. That Mac must have had to overcome all sorts of obstacles to qualify as a doctor merely highlighted his strength of character, his determination, his commitment. Few men could have taken on such a challenge and won.

Bella's head whirled as thoughts that she had never entertained before rushed through it. Added to the strain she'd been under since the breakdown of her marriage, it made her feel very shaky. Leaning forward, she rested her throbbing forehead on the steering wheel.

'Are you all right? Bella, what's wrong? Answer me!'

The concern in Mac's voice brought a rush of tears

to her eyes. Although her parents had expressed polite sympathy when she had told them about the divorce, they hadn't really cared about the effect it had had on her. They were too wrapped up in their own lives to put her first. As Mac had just done.

'It's just all too much,' she whispered, unable to lie.

'No wonder!' Anger laced his deep voice as he got out of the car. He strode round to her side and flung open the door. 'When I think what you must have been through recently—' He broke off as he lifted her out of the car. Bella got the impression that he didn't trust himself to say anything more as he carried her round to the passenger's side. He gently deposited her on the seat and snapped the seat belt into place then looked at her. 'Right, where to? You can go straight home or you can come back to my place. You decide.'

Bella bit her lip as she weighed up her choices, even though by rights she knew that she should tell him to take her home. She didn't want to talk to him, especially not tonight when she felt so raw, so emotional, so very vulnerable.

'Come on, Bella. Just choose where you want to go and I'll take you there.' His tone was so gentle, so persuasive, and Bella wanted to be persuaded so much…

'Yours.'

Mac nodded as he closed the door. Walking round to the driver's side, he got in and backed out of the parking space. He didn't say a word as he drove out of the hospital gates. Bella had no idea where he lived and quite frankly didn't care. Wherever it was, it had to be better than the soulless apartment she was renting. They drove for about fifteen minutes, the roads becoming increasingly narrow as they headed away from the town centre. Bella had done very little exploring since she had moved to Dalverston and had no idea where they were going until she saw the pale glint of water in the distance and realised they were heading towards the river. Mac slowed and turned down a narrow lane, drawing up on the grass verge.

'We have to walk from here,' he told her. 'It's not far, just five minutes or so, but we can't take the car any further.'

Bella nodded as she unfastened her seat belt. She slid to the ground, breathing in the musky scent of damp vegetation. She could hear the river now, the softly sibilant whisper of the water providing a backdrop to the sound of the birds performing their evening chorus. It was so peaceful that she sighed.

'It's wonderful not to hear any traffic.'

'One of the big advantages of living out in the sticks,' Mac replied with a smile that made her breath catch.

He turned and led the way along the path, leaving her to follow, which she did once she had got her breath back. It was the way he had smiled at her that had done the damage—smiled at her the way Mac had used to do. Did it mean that he had forgiven her for her apparent misdemeanours? She doubted it, yet all of a sudden she felt better than she had done in ages. The world didn't seem quite so grim now that Mac had smiled at her. How crazy was that?

Mac paused when they reached the riverbank. It was almost nine p.m. and the light was fading fast. In another month, there would still be enough daylight to light their way along the towpath but he was afraid that Bella would trip up in the dark. Holding out his hand, he smiled at her, determined to keep a rein on his emotions this time. He was offering to hold her hand for safety's sake and not for his own nefarious reasons!

'You'd better hold on to me. The path's a bit slippery after all the rain we've had recently. I don't want you ending up taking a dip.'

There was a moment when he sensed her hesitate before she slipped her hand into his. Mac sucked in his breath when he felt his libido immediately stir to life. OK, so, admittedly, he hadn't made love to a woman in a very long time, but that had been his choice, hadn't it? He had grown tired of dating for dating's sake, had become weary of sex that hadn't really meant anything. It had seemed better to step out of the game rather than continue the way he had been doing. However, it was completely out of order for him to start lusting after Bella. She'd been through enough without him making her life even more complicated.

Mac gave himself a stern talking-to as he led her along the towpath and, thankfully, it seemed to work. There were several boats tied up along the riverbank and he guided her around their mooring lines. They came to the last boat in the row and he stopped, suddenly feeling on edge as he wondered what she would make of his home. Although he loved the old boat—loved everything about it, from the tranquillity of its mooring to the fact that it was the first home he had owned—Bella had been brought up to expect so much more. He couldn't help feeling a little bit...well, *nervous* about what she would make of it.

'This is it,' he announced, wincing when he heard the false note of bonhomie in his voice. It wasn't like him to put up a front and he hated the fact that he'd felt it necessary. If Bella didn't like his home—so what? It wouldn't make a scrap of difference to him... Would it?

'You live on a boat!'

The surprise in her voice made his teeth snap together as he forced down the urge to start apologising.

'Yep. I bought it when I moved here. I couldn't afford a house so I opted for this instead. It's the perfect base when I'm in the UK. Come on. I'll show you round.'

He helped her on board and unlocked the cabin door, turning on the oil lamp so that she could see where she was going. 'The steps are quite steep,' he warned her. 'So take your time.'

Bella nodded as she cautiously stepped down into the cabin. Mac followed her, turning on more lamps as he went so that the cabin was suddenly bathed in light. Bella stopped and looked around, her face looking even more beautiful in the lamplight. And Mac's libido wriggled that little bit further out of its box.

'It's beautiful. So warm and welcoming... Oh, I do envy you living here, Mac. It must be marvellous!'

There was no doubt that she was telling him the truth and Mac's nerves evaporated in a rush of pleasure. He had no idea why it meant so much to hear her praise his home but it did. He laughed out loud.

'I was worried in case you hated it,' he confessed as his confidence came surging back. 'After all, it is *rather* different from what you're accustomed to.'

'And that's why I love it so much,' she said simply. 'You can keep all your architectural gems as far as I'm concerned. I much prefer somewhere like this— a real home.'

She sat down on the old couch that he had spent so many hours reupholstering and smiled up at him. Mac felt himself melt as relief washed over him. Bella liked his home—she *genuinely* liked it! He wanted to leap up and punch the air in triumph even though he knew how stupid it was.

'Thank you, although you'd better not be too lavish with the compliments or I'll get a swelled head,' he said, trying to joke his way through such a truly amazing moment. 'Not a good idea in a place as small as this!'

'Not small—compact. Or maybe that should be bijou if you prefer estate agent speak.'

Her smile was gentle, making him wonder if she had guessed how nervous he'd felt, but how could she? Bella had no idea that he had always felt at a disadvantage around her in the past, thanks to his background. He had gone to great lengths to hide his feelings and had thought that he had succeeded too. Thankfully, he no longer felt that way. The passage of time had given him the confidence to accept himself for who he was, which was why it was all the more surprising that he had been worried about her reaction.

'Hmm, I'm not sure if most estate agents would class it as that,' he replied lightly, not wanting her to guess how disturbed he felt. He hadn't realised that she understood him so well, hadn't thought that she even *cared* enough to try. And that thought was the last one he needed when he and his libido were having such a hard time sorting themselves out.

'Right. I'll make us some coffee.'

He hurriedly set about filling the kettle. Opening a cupboard, he took out a couple of mugs and placed them on the worktop. There was fresh milk in the tiny fridge and sugar in the jar so he fetched them as well. By the time he had done all that, he was feeling far more in control. Maybe it had come as a surprise to discover that Bella knew him rather better than he had thought she did, but he wasn't going to allow it to throw him off course. Maybe he *did* want to hold her, kiss her, do all sorts of things to her he had never even contemplated before, but he wasn't going to forfeit their friendship for a night of rampant sex. Bella was too important to him; he cared too much about her. And not even what Tim had told him could change that.

It was a moment of revelation, a light-bulb moment that suddenly made everything so much clearer. He may have accepted what Tim had told him. He may even have been hurt and angry about what Bella had done, but he still cared about her. And he always would.

'Thank you.' Bella accepted the cup of coffee. It was too hot to drink and she set it down on the table in front of the couch.

Everything was scaled down to fit, yet, surprisingly, it didn't feel cramped. She found herself comparing it to the vast amount of space in her rented apartment and realised that she much preferred it here. In fact, she had never felt so at ease in any of her previous homes, not even the house she and Tim had started their married life in.

Tim's parents had insisted on buying the elegant Georgian town house for them as a wedding present and her parents, not to be outdone, had insisted on furnishing it. However, the designer-styled rooms with their expensive furniture and luxurious fabrics couldn't hold a candle to this place, she decided. The house had been more an expression of wealth than a real home and it was a relief not to have to live there any longer.

The thought immediately made her feel guilty. It reminded her of how relieved she'd been when she had finally plucked up the courage to leave. It had taken her months of soul-searching before she had reached her decision and it still hurt to know that she had broken her marriage vows, even though she'd had no choice. Tim's behaviour had become increasingly erratic by that point; he had become a danger to his patients as well as to himself. Leaving him had been the only thing she could think of to shock him into seeking help and it had worked too. But did Mac understand that? Did he understand just how hard it had been for her to break her vows? All of a sudden Bella knew that she needed to find out.

'It wasn't an easy decision to leave Tim,' she said quietly. Out of the corner of her eye, she saw Mac stiffen and experienced a momentary qualm. She had sworn that she wouldn't try to justify her actions, but she needed to make Mac understand how impossible the situation had been. 'I agonised over it for months but in the end I realised that I didn't have a choice. It was the only thing I could think of that might bring him to his senses.'

'Wouldn't it have been better if you'd stayed and encouraged him to get help?' Mac suggested and she flinched when she heard the cynicism in his voice.

'I tried that, but Tim refused to listen to anything I said. He insisted that he didn't have a problem and that I was making a fuss about nothing.' She shrugged, recalling the vicious arguments they'd had. The drugs had changed Tim from the man she had married into someone she had barely recognised. 'He couldn't see that he was addicted to the painkillers and needed help.'

'So you upped and left him?'

Mac regarded her from beneath lowered lids. It was hard to tell what he was thinking, although she could guess. Mac believed that she should have stayed with Tim no matter what, but he hadn't been there, had he? He hadn't witnessed the rows, the lies, the empty, meaningless promises to stop taking the drugs.

'Yes. I hoped that it would shock him into admitting that he had a problem and it worked too. He went into rehab a couple of weeks later.'

'I see. So why didn't you go back once he was clean?' Mac's brows rose. 'Tim told me that he begged you to go back to him but you refused. If you loved him then surely that would have been the right thing to do?'

'It wasn't that simple,' Bella said quietly. She stared down at her hands, wondering if she should tell him about Tim's affair. Would she have gone back if she hadn't found out about it or had it been the excuse she had needed? Her feelings for Tim had reached rock-bottom by then; the thought of trying to make their marriage work had filled her with dread. The truth of the matter was that she had no longer loved him, always assuming that she had loved him in the first place, which she now doubted.

'No? It seems pretty straightforward to me.' Mac's tone was harsh. 'What about all those promises you made when you got married? Were they just so many empty words at the end of the day?'

'Of course not!' Bella said angrily, hating the fact he seemed determined to blame her for everything. 'I meant every word I said, but it needs two people to uphold a promise, although Tim obviously didn't see it that way.'

'What do you mean?' Mac shot back. 'It was you who left him.'

'Forget it. It doesn't matter.'

Bella picked up her coffee mug, feeling infinitely weary. No matter what she said, Mac would continue to blame her. Even if she told him about Tim's affair, there was no way of knowing if he would believe her. The thought that he might think she was lying about that to save face was more than she could bear. It would be better to say nothing than take that risk.

They finished their coffee in silence. Bella put her mug on the table and rose to her feet. It was gone ten p.m. and time she went home, even though the prospect of going back to the apartment wasn't appealing. 'I'd better go. Thank you for the coffee and everything.'

'Do you know how to get back?' Mac asked gruffly.

'I'll use the satnav.' She bent and picked up her bag, swaying a little as exhaustion suddenly caught up with her. It had been a long day and add to that the ongoing guilt she felt about the divorce and it was little wonder that she felt so drained.

'Sit down.' Mac eased her back down onto the couch. Taking the bag off her, he placed it on the table then crouched down in front of her. 'There's no way that you can drive yourself home in this state. You'll have to stay here tonight.'

'Oh, but I couldn't possibly,' Bella began but he ignored her. Standing up, he crossed the cabin and opened a door at the far end to reveal a tiny bedroom complete with double bed.

'You can sleep in here,' he informed her brusquely. Picking up one of the oil lamps, he placed it on the shelf next to the bed, turning down the wick so that the room was bathed in a soft golden glow. 'The sheets are clean and you should be comfortable enough. Bathroom's through there,' he continued, pointing to a door leading off from the bedroom. 'It's only basic but there's everything you'll need.'

'But where are you going to sleep?' Bella protested, more tempted than she cared to admit. Maybe it was foolish but the thought of staying on the boat was the most wonderful thing she could think of. She felt safe here—safe, secure, protected: all the things she hadn't felt in ages.

'The couch pulls out into a bed so don't worry about me,' Mac told her. Opening a cupboard, he took out a T-shirt and tossed it onto the bed. 'You can use this to sleep in. I haven't anything else, I'm afraid.'

'It's fine. Thank you,' Bella said softly.

She sank down onto the bed after Mac left, feeling the last vestige of strength drain from her limbs. Picking up the T-shirt, she held it to her cheek, savouring the softness of the cotton against her skin. Tears filled her eyes again and she blinked them away but more kept on coming, pouring down her face in a scalding-hot tide. She hadn't cried before, not even when Tim had said all those awful things to her after she had told him that she wanted a divorce. Now Mac's kindness had unleashed all the feelings she had held in check and they came spilling out, all the hurt and the pain, the guilt and the relief, every single thing, including how she felt about Mac himself.

Bella took a deep breath. She didn't want to think about Mac and how confused he made her feel. It had always been the same and yet she couldn't understand why he made her feel so mixed up. Normally she had no difficulty making up her mind. Every decision she had ever made had been carefully considered, rationalised, even when she had agreed to marry Tim.

Marrying Tim had seemed like the right thing to do. He had come from a similar background to hers, had held the same values as well as the same expectations. To her mind, their marriage was bound to be a success; however, with the benefit of hindsight, she could see that it hadn't been enough. It had needed more than the fact that they had been compatible on paper—her feelings for Tim had needed to be much stronger, especially after he had become addicted to those drugs. She had failed Tim because she hadn't cared enough, because she wasn't sure if she was *capable* of feeling that deeply about anyone.

Lying down on the bed, Bella clutched the T-shirt to her as sorrow overwhelmed her. She had spent so many years ignoring her emotions that she had lost touch with them. No wonder she couldn't understand how she felt about Mac.

CHAPTER FOUR

THE GENTLE MOTION of the boat woke Mac from a restless sleep. It had been the early hours of the morning before he had finally dozed off, his mind too busy to allow him to rest. Last night had been unsettling for so many reasons, the main one being that Bella had slept right here on the boat. Several times he had heard her crying and he'd had a devil of a job to stop himself going to her. However, the thought of what might happen if he did had helped him control the urge. It would have been far too easy to allow the need to comfort her to turn into something more.

His body responded with predictable enthusiasm to that thought and he groaned. He had to stop this! Maybe it was time he thought about breaking his self-imposed vow of celibacy. So what if sex had become merely a physical release, like an itch that needed scratching? Surely it would be better to deal with the itch than allow it to turn into a major problem.

Rolling out of bed, he filled the kettle and set it to boil then opened the hatch to let some fresh air into the cabin. It had been raining through the night and he grimaced as raindrops splashed onto his head and shoulders. Picking up a tea towel, he dried his face then looked round when he heard the bedroom door open, his heart lurching when he saw Bella standing in the doorway. She was wearing the T-shirt he had lent her and although it came midway down her thighs there was still an awful lot of her shapely legs on view. His gaze ran over her, greedily drinking in every detail. Although his T-shirt was huge on her, somehow the washed thin cotton managed to cling to her body, outlining the curve of her hips, the hand-span narrowness of her waist, the swell of her breasts…

Mac sucked in a great lungful of air when he saw her nipples suddenly pucker beneath the cotton. Rationally, he knew that it was no more than a physical response to the chilly air flowing through the cabin, but after the night he'd had, thinking rationally wasn't easy. His wayward thoughts flew off at a tangent as he found himself imagining how it would feel to watch her nipples harden as he caressed her…

He groaned out loud, hurriedly turning it into a cough when he saw her look at him in alarm. 'Hmm, a bit of a frog in the throat this morning,' he muttered, reaching for the coffee.

'It is a bit chilly in here,' she replied, hugging her arms around herself, and Mac saw the exact second when she realised what was happening. Colour rushed up her face as she hurried back into the bedroom. Picking up her sweater from the end of the bed, she dragged it over her head. 'That's better,' she said brightly as she turned round.

Mac wanted to disagree. He wanted to do it so badly that the words got all clumped up in his throat and almost choked him. He had to content himself with nodding, which was probably the safest response anyway.

'Anything I can do? Make the coffee? Or how about some toast—I could make that, if you like?'

Bella hovered uncertainly in the doorway and Mac's feelings underwent yet another rapid change. Tenderness swamped him as he pointed to the bread bin. Bella's composure was legendary. Even when they'd been students, she had always appeared to be totally in control. He couldn't remember her looking so out of her depth before, so that all he wanted to do was to put her at ease.

'Seeing as you've volunteered, you can be on toast duty. There's no toaster, I'm afraid. You have to do it the old-fashioned way under the grill.' He lit the grill for her. 'Butter's in the fridge and there's marmalade in that cupboard over there.' He pointed everything out then headed to the bedroom. 'I'll have a shower while you're doing that if it's OK with you?'

'Of course.'

Bella nodded as she took a loaf out of the bread bin. Picking up the bread knife, she started to cut it into slices, the tip of her pink tongue poking out between her lips. Mac turned away, not proof against any more temptations so early in the day. He didn't want to think about her tongue and how it would feel stroking his…

There was plenty of hot water for a shower but he turned the dial to cold instead. Stepping under the icy spray, he shivered violently. If there was one thing he loathed more than anything else it was a cold shower but he didn't deserve a hot one, not after the way he'd been behaving.

Lusting after Bella simply wasn't on! Quite apart from the fact that it would ruin whatever friendship they had, he couldn't do it to Tim. Tim may have kicked his drug habit but, like any addict, he was very vulnerable. Mac couldn't bear to imagine the harm it could cause if he and Bella had an affair, not that it was on the cards, of course. However, the fact that he was even *thinking* about Bella in such terms was a warning in itself. Now that she had forfeited her married status, it didn't mean that he was free to make a play for her. No, to all intents and purposes nothing had changed. It was still Bella and Tim.

Bella had their breakfast ready by the time Mac reappeared. He was wearing a pair of navy chinos with a blue-and-white striped shirt, and it was a relief to see him safely covered up. Maybe he had been decent enough before but the T-shirt and shorts he had worn to sleep in hadn't left very much to the imagination. To her mind, there'd been a rather disturbing amount of leanly muscular body on show.

Heat flowed under her skin as she hurriedly placed the toast on the table. She added the coffee pot along with the milk jug and sugar bowl, determined not to allow her mind to get hijacked by any more such foolish ideas. She had seen men wearing a lot less than Mac had worn that morning in the course of her work so it was stupid to start acting like some sort of...*inexperienced virgin*!

'I could grow used to this.' Mac grinned as he sat down and reached for the coffee pot. He filled both of the mugs, adding milk and several spoons of sugar to his. 'It's a real treat to have my breakfast made for me.'

'It's the least I can do,' Bella murmured, sitting down opposite him. Her knees bumped against his and she hastily drew her legs back out of the way, steadfastly ignoring the odd tingling sensation that seemed to be spreading from the point where their knees had touched.

She was bound to feel *aware* of him, she reasoned, adding a dash of milk to her coffee. After all, it wasn't as though she had made a habit of spending the night with a man, was it? She had never had an affair, had never even indulged in any one-night stands like so many of her contemporaries at university had done. She had only ever slept with Tim, in fact, so spending the night with Mac was a whole new experience for her.

The thought unsettled her even more. It seemed to imply that she'd had an ulterior motive for spending the night on the boat. It wasn't true, of course; it had been necessity that had forced her to stay, the need to rest and recoup her strength. The past year had been extremely hard. Between the stress of the divorce and the move to Dalverston, it was little wonder that it had felt as though she had reached rock-bottom last night. However, she felt much better this morning, less anxious and more like her old self. Spending the night here with Mac had worked wonders and it was just a shame that she couldn't do it again.

Bella bit into her toast, more surprised by that thought than she could say. Bearing in mind how confused Mac made her feel, she should be trying to avoid him, surely? And yet there was no denying that if he had offered to let her stay again tonight *and* the night after that, she would have accepted with alacrity. Being with Mac might be unsettling but in a good way.

They finished their breakfast, making desultory conversation as they ate. Mac sighed as he drained the last dregs of coffee from his mug. 'I'd better get a move on or I'll be late. Are you working today?'

'No.' Bella picked up her mug and plate. She carried them to the tiny sink and pumped water into the bowl. 'I'm working over the weekend so I've got today and tomorrow off.'

'Lucky you.' Mac picked up his dishes and brought them over to the sink. He checked his watch and grimaced. 'I really will have to fly. Fingers crossed that they haven't changed the times of the buses, otherwise I am going to be seriously late.'

'Bus? Why do you need to take the bus?' Bella queried, rinsing their mugs and setting them to drain.

'I left my motorbike at the hospital last night.'

Bella sighed. 'Because you drove me back here? Of course. Sorry.'

'It doesn't matter.' He reached for his jacket, patting the pockets to check that he had everything. 'Look, I'm sorry but I'm going to have to cut and run...'

'Here. Take my car.' Bella picked up her car keys. She shook her head when he started to protest. 'I insist. It's my fault that you left your motorbike at the hospital so it's the least I can do.'

'But what about you?' he demanded, his dark brows drawing together. 'How are you going to get home?'

'Don't worry about me. I'll call a taxi.' Bella pressed the keys into his hand. 'Go on, off you go or you'll be late.'

'Yes, ma'am.' Mac grinned at her. 'Has anyone told you how bossy you are?'

'Not lately,' Bella retorted. She followed him up

to the deck, pausing when he stopped. His blue eyes were very dark as they met hers.

'Sure you'll be OK? I feel as though I'm abandoning you.'

'Don't be silly,' she said briskly, although she was deeply touched by the sentiment. It had been a long time since anyone had worried about her this way. 'I'll be perfectly fine. I'll tidy up then phone for a cab… Oh, wait, what's the address? I've no idea where we are.'

'Too-Good Lane.' Mac dug into his pockets and pulled out a crumpled supermarket receipt. He jotted down a number on the back and handed it to her. 'Phone Dennis and ask him to come for you. He's a nice chap and very reliable. You'll be safe with him.'

'Oh, right. Thank you.' Bella went to slip the paper into her pocket before she remembered that she didn't have any pockets. She took a hasty step back when she spotted a jogger running along the towpath, suddenly conscious of her state of undress. She could just imagine what people would think if they saw her standing here wearing one of Mac's T-shirts. They would assume that she and Mac had spent the night together and, although they had, they hadn't *slept* together! Heat flowed under her skin as the thought triggered a whole raft of images: Mac's eyes, so deep and dark as he stared down at her; the feel of his hands as he stroked her body from throat to thigh…

A shudder passed through her and she turned

away, terrified that she would give herself away. She heard Mac call a cheery goodbye as he leapt off the boat, even managed to respond, but everything seemed to be happening at one step removed. All she could think about were Mac's hands stroking and caressing her.

Bella hurried back inside the cabin and stood there with her arms hugged tightly around herself. She had never felt this way before, never experienced this overwhelming surge of desire. Although she had enjoyed making love with Tim in the beginning, she had never yearned for his touch. However, with a sudden rush of insight she realised that if Mac made love to her it would be very different. She wouldn't be able to remain detached then—she wouldn't want to. If Mac made love to her, she would be unable to hold anything back, not even a tiny scrap of herself. Mac would unleash her passion, awaken her desire and, once that happened, it would be impossible to go back.

She shuddered. She would be changed for ever, a completely different person, a woman who not only felt but *needed* to feel too. She wasn't sure if she could cope with that.

Mac was thrown in at the deep end as soon as he arrived at work. There'd been an accident on the by-pass involving a lorry and a coach ferrying children to the local high school. Thirty-three casualties were brought through their doors and each one needed to be assessed and treated. Fortunately, Trish Baxter, one of their most experienced staff nurses, was on duty and she performed triage. The less seriously injured children—those with only minor cuts and bruises—were told to wait while the rest were farmed out between cubicles, treatment rooms and Resus. Fortunately, there were just two children badly injured enough to require the facilities of resuscitation and Mac dealt with them. Twelve-year-old twins, Emily and Ethan Harris, had been sitting together at the exact spot where the truck had hit the coach.

'Hi, I'm Mac and I'm a doctor,' Mac explained as the paramedics rolled the youngsters in on their respective trolleys. He listened attentively while the crew outlined the children's status. Emily had injuries to her right arm and was in a great deal of pain, while her brother was having difficulty breathing. Ethan had been thrown into the aisle by the force of the impact and trapped under the seat, which had come away from its housing. It was more than likely that he had fractured ribs which could be compromising his breathing if they had pierced the pleura—the two layers of membrane that covered the lungs and the chest wall. If blood had entered the pleura cavity it would compress the lungs and cause a partial collapse. Mac knew that the boy required urgent treatment and turned to Helen Robertson, the F1 student, who was working with him.

'You take the girl. She'll need X-rays first and then we can tell exactly what we're dealing with. If her shoulder has popped out its socket it will need putting back before the nerves are damaged. You also need to check if the humerus is fractured. OK?'

Helen nodded, looking a little daunted at being put in charge of a patient. Mac watched as she hurried to the phone to request the services of the duty radiographer. She would manage fine, although he would keep a close eye on her. However, if she was to develop her skills then she needed to step up to the plate, as every young doctor had to do. He turned his attention to Ethan, checking his pulse and oxygen levels. Bailey Thomas, the Australian specialist resus nurse, was assisting him and Mac nodded when he asked if Mac intended to aspirate.

'Yep. I reckon there's blood in the pleural cavity, don't you? Let's see if we can drain it off and help him breathe a bit easier.'

Bailey fetched what they needed and Mac set to work, easing the needle through the tough intercostal muscles between the boy's ribs. He was unsurprised when he immediately drew off bloody fluid. 'Definitely a haemothorax,' he said, glancing at Bailey. Out of the corner of his eye, he saw that the radiographer was putting Emily's X-rays up on the monitor. Even from where he was standing, Mac could see that the girl's humerus was fractured although he didn't say anything. He wanted Helen to find her feet and spotting the fracture herself would help her do that.

'Let's see if we can get any more out of there,' he said, turning back to Ethan. He aspirated some more blood before he was satisfied that he had alleviated the problem. Ethan's sats were back to what they should have been and he was breathing steadily so it was time to assess what other injuries he had sustained. Mac called over the radiographer and asked her to do a whole-body X-ray. While she was doing that he went to check on Helen.

'So, how's it going?' he asked, leaving her to explain her findings.

'It's as you suspected—the humerus is fractured at the upper end.' Helen pointed out the fracture and Mac nodded.

'So it is. Well spotted. Her shoulder's also dislocated so that needs sorting as well.'

'What should I do?' Helen asked uncertainly. 'Should I try to reduce the dislocation and pop the humerus back into its socket or what? I've not dealt with a case where the humerus is fractured as well.'

'It would be far too painful for Emily if we did it here. Plus there's the problem of the fracture, which complicates matters,' he explained. He always enjoyed helping the younger doctors and, unlike a lot of his peers, never considered it to be a waste of his time. The more everyone knew, the easier it was for the rest of the team, he reasoned.

'Phone Theatre and book her in ASAP. They'll take care of the lot and that way Emily won't know a thing about it. You just need to get her parents' permission for the operation to go ahead, so see if they've arrived yet and if not get the police to contact them. Tell them it's urgent.' He grinned at her. 'We don't want to waste any time so lay it on thick. It's the one time you're allowed to lie to the police!'

'Will do!' Helen was laughing as she hurried out of Resus to set the wheels turning.

Mac smiled as he went back to his patient. From what he had seen so far, Helen had the makings of a really good doctor. She would learn a lot from working here too. It made him suddenly glad that he had agreed to cover the paediatric A&E unit until their own registrar returned to work. Oh, he'd had his doubts when he had found out that Bella was working here. After everything that Tim had told him, it was only natural, although now he could see that he had been a little too hasty. OK, so maybe there had been a few teething problems but he and Bella seemed to be getting on remarkably well, all things considered.

The radiographer interrupted his thoughts just then to tell him the films were ready and he turned towards the monitor. There would be time enough to think about his relationship with Bella later.

Mac's heart skipped a beat. When had it turned into a relationship? It definitely hadn't been that before last night, had it? At the very most, he would have classed it as friendship—he and Bella were friends and that was it. However, deep down he knew it wasn't that any longer. At least not *only* that. Friendship had been hiked up to another level, to the point of becoming a relationship. He wasn't sure if that was a good thing or not, but he was powerless to do anything about it.

He took a deep breath as he stared at the screen. He and Bella had a relationship. Pick the bones out of that!

Bella squared her shoulders as she watched the taxi drive away from the hospital. She would collect her keys from Mac and head straight home. The sooner she was back in her apartment, the sooner she would be able to rid herself of the ridiculous notion of asking him if she could spend another night on the boat. Maybe it had helped to stay there last night, but she had to stand on her own two feet. She couldn't expect Mac to *mollycoddle* her.

She went straight to Reception, only to come to a halt when she saw all the children milling around in the waiting area. It didn't take a genius to work out that something major must have happened so she made her way to the nursing station. Trish Baxter was adding more names to the whiteboard, squeezing them in around the edges. She grimaced when she saw Bella.

'We're fast running out of space. I'll have to resort to taping up a bit of paper soon!'

'What's happened?' Bella demanded, glancing at the list. From what she could see, there were fifteen children waiting to be seen, plus another six receiving treatment: three in cubicles, one in the treatment room, plus two more in Resus.

'A lorry ran into the bus taking the kids to the high school,' Trish explained. She put the cap back on the pen and placed it in the tray. 'To say it's been a tad chaotic in here this morning is an understatement.'

'I can imagine,' Bella agreed, shrugging off her jacket. 'Right, who's next on the list? Freya Watson from the look of it,' she continued, answering her own question.

'I thought you were supposed to be off today,' Trish pointed out as they went back to Reception.

'I am. But I can't just take off and leave you to it when something like this has happened.' Bella picked up the girl's notes and looked around the waiting room. 'Freya Watson?' She smiled reassuringly when a tall red-haired girl hesitantly stood up. 'Come with me, Freya, and we'll get you sorted out.'

Bella led the girl to a cubicle. According to her notes, Freya was sixteen years old and in her last year at the high school. She looked extremely nervous as she sat down on the bed and Bella smiled encouragingly at her. 'This must have been a big shock for you. You're bound to feel rather shaken up and even a little bit tearful, but that's perfectly normal. I'm just going to check you over and make sure you're all right and then, as soon as your parents get here, you can go home.'

Freya didn't say anything as she stared down at the floor and Bella frowned. Although her notes stated that Freya appeared to have suffered only minor bruising, she couldn't rid herself of the feeling that there was something else wrong with her. She didn't say anything, however, as she set about examining her. If there was something wrong then it would soon become apparent. There was quite heavy bruising to the girl's thighs and it was obviously painful because she winced.

'How did this happen, do you know?' Bella asked, gently examining the area.

'A bag fell off the luggage rack and landed on me,' Freya muttered.

'I see. That must have hurt,' Bella said sympathetically. 'Can I just check your tummy? I need to see if it's caused any bruising there as well.'

She went to unbutton the oversized cardigan that Freya was wearing but the girl pushed her hands away. There was real fear in her eyes when she looked at Bella.

'I'm all right!' she said sharply, attempting to stand up. The words were barely out of her mouth, however, when she doubled up in pain.

Bella caught her as she fell and eased her back

down onto the bed. 'Obviously you're not all right, Freya, so I need to examine you. Come on, don't be silly. I only want to check that you're not badly injured.'

Tears started to stream down the girl's face as Bella unfastened her cardigan. As soon as she had done so, she realised what was wrong. Freya was pregnant and, from the look of her, at full term too. She chose her words with care, knowing how important it was that she gained the girl's trust.

'Do you know when your baby is due, Freya?'

'No. Not really. I just kept hoping it wasn't actually happening.' She looked up and Bella's heart ached when she saw the fear in her eyes. 'My mum and dad are going to kill me when they find out! They're always banging on about me not getting myself into any trouble.'

'I'm sure they will be fine once they get over the shock,' Bella said soothingly, mentally crossing her fingers.

She quickly examined the girl, her heart sinking when she realised that the baby's head was engaged. As she'd suspected, Freya was at full term and, when she let out a groan, Bella realised that there was no time to waste; the baby was about to be born. Hurrying to the phone, she rang Maternity and asked them to send over a midwife as soon as possible. In the meantime, she would have to manage as best she could, although it was a long time since she had delivered a baby. Poking her head out of the cubicle, she beckoned to Trish, who had just finished seeing her patient. She lowered her voice, not wanting anyone to overhear. Although there was little hope of keeping the baby's arrival a secret for very long, at least Freya should be able to tell her parents before her classmates found out.

'We've a bit of a situation in here. It turns out that Freya is pregnant and the baby is on its way. I've asked for a midwife to attend but I don't know how long it will be before she gets here, so we're going to have to manage as best we can. Can we move her into Resus to give her some privacy? Apparently her parents have no idea that she's pregnant.'

'Blooming heck!' Trish exclaimed. 'I know her parents and, believe me, they're going to have a fit when they find out. They're very strait-laced, from what I know of them. Pity help the poor kid is all I can say.'

'Great!' Bella sighed. 'I'll get onto Social Services as soon as I can, but my main concern right now is keeping a lid on this so that the rest of the school doesn't find out. Has Mac finished in Resus, do you know?'

'I'll go and check. Won't be a sec.'

Trish hurried away as Bella went back into the cubicle. Freya was moaning softly and clutching her stomach, obviously in the throes of labour. Bella checked her over once again, grimacing when she discovered that Freya's cervix was fully dilated. From the look of her, it wouldn't be long before the baby arrived.

'It shouldn't be long before your baby is born,' she told her gently. 'I know it hurts, sweetheart, but once the midwife gets here she'll sort out some pain relief for you. Do you understand what happens when a baby is born?'

Freya nodded. 'We did it in biology, how the cervix has to dilate and soften so that the baby can make its way out of the birth canal.'

'Good. At least you have some idea of what's happening and that will help.'

Bella looked round when she heard the curtain open, feeling her heart leap when she saw Mac coming into the cubicle. Although it was barely an hour since they had parted, it was as though she was seeing him through fresh eyes. Her gaze ran over him, taking stock of the dark brown hair falling over his forehead, the midnight blue of his eyes, the strongly masculine set to his features. There was no doubt at all that Mac was an extremely attractive man and she couldn't understand why she had never realised it before…

Her breath caught as she was suddenly forced to confront the truth. Deep down, she had always been aware of his appeal, only she had been too afraid to admit it.

CHAPTER FIVE

FREYA'S BABY ARRIVED just twenty minutes later. It was a little girl and she was absolutely perfect in every way, despite the fact that her mother had received no antenatal care. Mac gently placed the little mite in her mother's arms, wondering what was going to happen now. Bella had explained the situation to him and although he understood what a shock it was going to be for Freya's parents, surely they would support their daughter during this difficult time?

He sighed, realising that it could be wishful thinking. He only had to recall what had happened to his own mother to know that the happily-ever-after scenario wasn't guaranteed. His maternal grandparents had refused to have anything to do with his mother after he had been born. As his father had been brought up in care and hadn't had any contact with his family, it had meant that his parents had had to struggle along on their own. Although his dad had done his best, his lack of qualifications had meant that he'd had to take a series of low-paid jobs, so money had been tight. Coming from a comfortable middle-class background, his mother had found it very difficult to adapt to the change in lifestyle, so it wasn't surprising that she had left.

'The midwife should be here shortly.' Bella came back from phoning the maternity unit. 'Apparently they're short-staffed and that's why it's taken them so long to send anyone over here. However, they've promised to get a midwife to us as soon as they can.'

'Not much they can do now,' Mac replied laconically, trying not to think about how much he had missed his mother after she had left. It was all water under the bridge and had no bearing on his life these days.

'No, I suppose not. I'm only glad that you were here. It's been ages since I delivered a baby and I'm rather rusty, I'm afraid.'

'I've delivered my share over the past few years,' he said wryly, returning his thoughts to the matter at hand. After all, he'd had his father, hadn't he? So he'd been far luckier than a lot of kids. 'You have to turn your hand to most things when you're working overseas.'

'Well, all the practice definitely stood you in good stead today.' She smiled but there was a wariness about the look she gave him that made Mac wonder if something had upset her. However, before he could attempt to find out, Trish popped her head round the door.

'Mr and Mrs Watson are here. How do you want to play this, Bella? Shall I show them straight in here or do you want a word with them first?'

'I'd better have a word with them first,' Bella replied with a sigh. She turned to Mac after Trish left. 'I'll send Jenny in to sit with Freya. You must have loads to do.'

'I need to check how many kids are still waiting to be seen,' Mac agreed, following her to the door. He looked back and frowned as he watched Freya cradling her baby. 'It's going to be a massive shock for her parents so let's hope they can rise to the occasion. That girl is going to need a lot of support in the coming months.'

'She is,' Bella agreed soberly. 'Having a baby at her age is a lot to cope with.'

'It is. My parents were only a year or so older than Freya when they had me.' He opened the door but he could sense Bella's curiosity as she stepped out into the corridor and suddenly wished that he hadn't said anything. Maybe it was the birth of the baby or thinking about his parents, but he was very aware that his emotions were rather too near the surface for comfort.

'I didn't know that your parents were so young when you were born,' she said quietly as they made their way to Reception.

'There's no reason why you should have known,' he countered. 'It's not something that came up in conversation, I imagine.'

'No. Probably not.' She hesitated. 'It must have been difficult for them, though. Did your grandparents help?'

'Nope. Dad was brought up in care and he'd lost touch with his family. As for my mother, well, her parents took the view that she'd made her decision and it was up to her to live with the consequences. They wanted her to have a termination, apparently, but she wouldn't hear of it,' he added when Bella looked at him questioningly. 'They refused to have anything more to do with her after that.'

'Really? Oh, how awful for her!' She touched his arm and he could see the sympathy in her eyes. 'And awful for you, too.'

'I survived.' Mac dredged up a smile, afraid that he would do something really stupid. Maybe it did hurt to know that his grandparents had turned their backs on him but he was far too old to start crying about it at this stage! He swung round, determined that he wasn't going to make a fool of himself. Maybe Bella *had* touched a chord but there was no way that he intended to let her know that. 'Right, I'll go and check how we're doing. Catch you later.'

'I expect so.'

There was a faintly wistful note in her voice but Mac refused to speculate on the reason for it. He went to the desk and checked how many children were still waiting to be seen. There were just half a dozen left so he took the next one to the cubicles and got him sorted out. While his mind was busily engaged it couldn't start wandering, could it? he reasoned.

He sighed, uncomfortably aware that he had never experienced this problem before. He wasn't someone who wore his heart on his sleeve and yet the minute Bella had expressed her sympathy, he had turned to mush. What was happening to him? First there had been all those crazy thoughts he'd had last night— the ones that had involved him, Bella, and a bed— and now this. He had to get a grip. Maybe Bella *did* make him feel things he had never felt before but he had to remember that, to all intents and purposes, she still belonged to Tim. No way was he going to be responsible for Tim suffering a relapse! No, Bella was off limits. She always had been and she always would be too.

It was almost lunchtime before Bella felt that she could leave. The last of the children had been seen and sent home and the department was more or less back to normal. Granted, there was a lot of paperwork that still needed doing, but she felt that she could justifiably leave that to Mac. After all, it was supposed to be her day off and there was no reason to feel guilty about going home. It was only when she was halfway across the car park that she remembered that she had forgotten to ask Mac for her keys.

She sighed as she turned round and headed back. She could have done without having to speak to him again, if she was honest. What he had told her earlier in the day about his family had affected her far more than she would have expected. She couldn't help thinking how hard it must have been for him to grow up knowing that he had been rejected by his grandparents.

Bella gave herself a mental shake as she reached the main doors leading into the hospital. She had to stop thinking about Mac all the time. Maybe she did feel incredibly aware of him, but she couldn't afford to let it take over her life the way it was doing. The sooner she got it into her head that he was just a colleague, the simpler it would be.

She was just about to enter the hospital when Mac himself appeared. He smiled ruefully as he held up her car keys.

'You need these, don't you? Sorry! I should have handed them back before.'

'Don't worry about it.'

Bella dredged up a smile as she took the keys off him but it was hard to behave naturally. Why had she never noticed before what a gorgeous shade of blue his eyes were, like the sky on a summer evening? And how come she had never realised just how tall he was, not to mention how lean and fit his body looked? Her thoughts skittered this way and that so that it was a moment before she realised that he had asked her a question.

'Sorry,' she said hurriedly. 'What did you say?'

'I was just wondering how it went with Freya's parents.'

Bella felt a shiver ripple through her at the sound of his deep voice. She had to make a conscious effort not to show the effect it was having on her. If she hadn't noticed his eyes or his physique before then she certainly hadn't noticed how seductive his voice sounded!

'Not too good, I'm afraid. They wouldn't believe me at first, insisted that it couldn't be their daughter and that there must have been a mix-up with the names. Then when I took them in to see Freya, they lost it completely and started shouting at her.' She sighed, deliberately reining in her wayward thoughts. 'It was so bad, in fact, that I had to ask them to leave in the end.'

'Sounds grim. How did Freya take it?'

'Pretty much as you'd expect. It took me ages to calm her down but it's a lot to deal with at her age.'

'It is. What's going to happen when she leaves hospital? Are her parents going to take her home and support her?'

'I doubt it, from what I heard.' Bella shrugged. 'I've spoken to Social Services and they've promised to visit her. They said that they will arrange accommodation for her and the baby when she's discharged. In the unlikely event that Mr and Mrs Watson change their minds, they will cancel the arrangements.'

'I'm not sure which is worse,' Mac said grimly.

'Being dumped in some grotty flat or going home and being faced with constant recriminations. That won't do her or the child any good, will it?'

'It won't. But there's not much we can do except pray for a miracle,' Bella said sadly.

'Pray that Freya's parents will have a change of heart, you mean?' He shook his head. 'In my experience, it rarely happens so I wouldn't hold out too many hopes on that score.'

'Your grandparents never changed their minds?' Bella said quietly, hearing the echo of pain in his voice.

'No. Oh, Mum tried to persuade them to see sense, but they were adamant that they wanted nothing to do with her or me. I never met them, in fact.'

'How sad. Not just for you and your mother, but for them too. They could have had the pleasure of watching you grow up if they hadn't taken such a rigid stance.'

'Obviously, they didn't see it that way. The shame of their unmarried daughter having a baby outweighed everything else.'

'I can't understand why people feel like that,' Bella admitted. 'Oh, I know my parents were more interested in their careers than in me, but I'd like to think they would have supported me if I'd found myself in that position.'

'There wasn't much chance of that happening, though, was there?' Mac observed drily.

Bella's brows rose. 'What do you mean?'

'Nothing. Forget it. Right, I'd better get back. Thanks again for the loan of your car.'

He started to go back inside but Bella knew that she couldn't let him leave without explaining that cryptic comment. She caught hold of his arm, feeling a flutter of awareness run through her as she felt the warmth of his skin seep through her fingertips. It was all she could do not to release him immediately, but she needed to know what he had meant.

'I want to know what you meant,' she said firmly, determined that she was going to put a lid on all these crazy feelings. All she was doing was touching his arm, for heaven's sake, not making mad, passionate love with him! The thought wasn't the best she could have come up with, but she stood her ground. For some reason it seemed vitally important that she found out what he was talking about. 'Well?'

'Tim told me that you'd refused to have a baby.' His eyes met hers and she felt chilled to the core when she saw the condemnation they held. 'It was obvious how upset he was and I don't blame him. Having a child could have been exactly what he needed to keep him on track.'

'Is that what Tim told you? Or is that your expert opinion?' Bella laughed harshly, more hurt than she could say. Once again Mac was blaming her for what had happened and it was even more hurtful after last night. She'd thought that he was starting to accept that she wasn't solely at fault for the demise of her marriage but she'd been wrong. All of a sudden the need to set him straight overcame everything else.

'Don't bother answering that—it really doesn't matter. The only thing that matters is why I refused to have a baby. I don't suppose Tim explained that, did he?' She didn't give him a chance to answer. 'I refused because there was no way that I was bringing a child into the world who wasn't really wanted. Oh, maybe Tim claimed that he wanted a baby but he only wanted one *after* I told him I was leaving him. He'd always refused to start a family before that, told me that he had no intention of having children when they would only tie him down. However, once I asked him for a divorce, he changed his mind.'

She stared back at him, wondering if he would believe her. Maybe he would and maybe he wouldn't, but she intended to tell him the truth. What he made of it was up to him. 'I refused point-blank and I don't give a damn if you think I was wrong to do so. There was no way that I was prepared to have a baby just to try and save our marriage. That was well and truly over, believe me!'

She swung round, ignoring Mac's demands for her to stop. Walking over to her car, she got in and drove out of the car park without a backward glance. She wasn't sure how she felt, if she was honest, whether she was more angry than hurt by his continued refusal to believe that she wasn't solely to blame. However, what she did know was that she wouldn't make the mistake of thinking that he was on her side ever again. Maybe it had appeared that way last night but it wasn't true. Mac's loyalties didn't lie with her but with Tim. It just proved how little he really cared about her, despite his claims to the contrary.

Mac felt absolutely dreadful for the rest of the day. He couldn't rid himself of the memory of how hurt Bella had looked as she had driven away. By the time his shift ended, he knew that he couldn't leave things the way they were. He had to see her and clear the air. If he could.

He collected his motorbike and headed into the town centre. He had got Bella's address from the staff files and knew that she lived in one of the new apartments that had been built on the site of the old brewery. He'd heard that the cost of renting an apartment there was extremely steep, not that it would worry Bella, of course. She was in the fortunate position of having a private income and it was yet another reminder of why he needed to quash any fanciful thoughts he might be harbouring. Although he earned a decent salary, he wasn't in Bella's league!

Mac parked the motorbike and walked to the entrance. There was an intercom system so he pressed the bell, steeling himself when he heard her voice coming through the speaker. He wouldn't blame her if she refused to see him, but he really and truly needed to sort this out.

'Bella, it's me—Mac. I need a word with you.'

'I'm afraid now isn't a good time,' she began, but he didn't let her finish. He had a nasty feeling that if he didn't resolve this issue tonight, he might never be able to do so. If Tim had lied to him then he needed to know.

'I understand that you're angry but we need to sort this out, Bella, once and for all.'

'Why?' She gave a harsh little laugh and his insides twisted when he heard the pain in her voice. 'What difference will it make to you if Tim was spinning you a line? You're still going to take his side, aren't you, still going to blame me for ending our marriage? As far as you're concerned, Mac, I should have stuck with him come hell or high water, so what's the point of talking about it?'

'The point is that I need to know the truth.' Mac took a deep breath, aware that he was stepping into dangerous territory, yet how could he avoid it? Bella deserved to be given a fair hearing and that was what he intended to do. If she would agree. 'I know it's asking a lot but, please, Bella, let me in so we can talk this all through.'

He held his breath, hoping against hope that he had managed to persuade her. When he heard the door lock being released, he almost shouted out loud in relief. He hurried inside and made straight for the lift, half afraid that she would change her mind. Her apartment was on the fifth floor and he tapped his foot in impatience as the lift carried him upwards. He wasn't sure how he was going to set about this; maybe it would be simpler just to wait and see how it panned out? If he started asking questions, there was always a chance that he would say something to alienate her. He sighed as the lift came to a halt. Normally, he wouldn't have given it a second thought; he would have simply asked Bella what had gone on and that would have been it. But this wasn't a normal situation, was it? Someone was lying and he needed to find out who it was.

Bella must have heard the lift stop because she opened the door. She didn't say a word, however, as she led the way inside the apartment. Mac placed his motorbike helmet on the console table in the foyer then followed her into the living room, stopping abruptly when he was greeted by the most spectacular sight. One whole wall was made of glass and the view of the mountains that surrounded the town was stupendous.

'What a fabulous view!' He went over to the window and stood there for a moment, drinking it in. It was only when he became aware of the silence that he remembered why he had come. He turned slowly around, his heart aching when he saw how distant Bella looked. She had always had a tendency to withdraw into herself if something had upset her and it was obvious that was happening now.

'Thank you for letting me in,' Mac said quietly, trying to rein in the guilt he felt. It didn't make him feel good to know that he had upset her, even though it hadn't been intentional. He sighed, aware that he could make the situation worse if he continued probing, but what choice did he have? He needed to get at the truth.

'What you told me before about Tim not wanting a child until you asked him for a divorce—was it true?' he said before his courage deserted him.

'Yes. Not that I expect you to believe me.'

Mac heard the challenge in her voice but it didn't disguise the pain it held as well and his heart ached all the more. That she was loath to discuss what had gone on was obvious and in other circumstances he wouldn't have pushed her. However, making sure that he could trust her was even more important than finding out if Tim had lied to him.

The thought stunned him because it aroused feelings that he'd believed he had conquered many years before. After his mother had left, he had found it impossible to trust anyone. He had been only seven when Laura MacIntyre had walked out of their home but he could still remember how terrified he had been in case his father had left him as well.

Was that why he had avoided commitment? he wondered suddenly. Was it the reason why he always called time on a relationship before it became too serious? He was afraid of letting himself fall in love in case he was let down. His breath caught as one thought led to another: was it also the reason why it was so important that he made sure he could trust Bella?

Mac felt panic assail him when he realised just how complicated the situation actually was. His feelings for Bella weren't nearly as clear-cut as he had believed. They seemed to be changing on a daily basis, in fact. He had started out feeling disillusioned, angry even about the way she had behaved, yet he couldn't put his hand on his heart and swear that was how he felt now.

A trickle of sweat ran down his back as he looked at her and remembered how he had felt the night before, how he had ached to touch her, kiss her, feel her body, warm and responsive under his. It certainly hadn't been anger or disillusionment he had felt then!

Bella wasn't sure what Mac was thinking but there was something about the way he was looking at her that made her heart start to race. She bit her lip, determined that she was going to keep a lid on her emotions. If they were to sort this out then she had to remain detached. She had told Mac her version of what had happened, the *true* version, and now it was up to him to decide if he believed her. The one thing she mustn't do was get emotionally involved. Something warned her that would be a mistake of gigantic proportions.

Turning, she went over to the drinks trolley and poured a little brandy into a couple of crystal glasses. Although she rarely drank spirits, she felt in need of some Dutch courage to see her through the next few minutes. Walking over to one of the huge black leather sofas, she sat down, placing the drinks on the glass-and-steel coffee table. She had rented the apartment fully furnished and hadn't made any changes to it. It was merely a place to eat and sleep when she got back from work, yet all of a sudden she found herself wondering what Mac would make of it. Having experienced the welcoming warmth of his boat, she couldn't imagine that it would appeal to him on any level.

For some reason she found the idea upsetting but she refused to dwell on it. It wasn't her taste in furnishings that Mac was interested in but her honesty! Anger rippled through her as she picked up a glass and took a sip of the brandy. She had done nothing wrong and the sooner he accepted that the better.

'So, seeing as you've seen fit to come here to talk to me, I suggest you get on with it.' Bella stared at him over the rim of the glass, wanting to make it clear that she didn't intend to allow this to drag on. She had been genuinely upset when she had got home but she'd had time to calm down now and she had no intention of getting upset again, no matter what he thought. *She* knew she was telling the truth and that was what mattered, wasn't it?

She clamped down on the tiny flicker of doubt, knowing how quickly it could turn into something much bigger. Mac came and sat down opposite her, although he didn't make any attempt to pick up his glass. He stared down at the floor for a moment and her heart surged when she saw how grim he looked when he finally raised his head.

'Why would Tim lie to me, though? That's what I don't understand.' He pinned her with a look of such intensity that she was hard-pressed not to look away, but somehow she managed to hold his gaze.

'You'll have to ask him that.'

'But doesn't it make you angry that he's blaming you for everything that happened?' he retorted.

'Yes, it does.' Bella managed to suppress a shiver when she heard the anger in his voice. Was he angry because Tim had lied to him or because he didn't believe her? She had no idea but she couldn't afford to let it worry her, certainly couldn't allow it to unleash all the emotions that were churning around inside her.

'Then how can you sit there so calmly? Surely, you want to do something to address the situation, Bella.'

'What do you suggest? That I contact everyone I know and tell them that Tim is lying?' She gave a bitter little laugh. 'Maybe some people will believe me, but not very many, I'm afraid. Most will take Tim's side simply because he's always been far more outgoing than me. I have a tendency to keep myself to myself, and that doesn't help if you're trying to get people on your side. I mean, even you aren't sure who to believe, are you, Mac? And you know me better than anyone else does.'

CHAPTER SIX

Mac felt his blood pressure rocket skywards. Bella thought that he knew her better than anyone else? Coming on top of everything that had happened recently, it was almost too much to take in and yet he couldn't pretend that he didn't experience a rush of pleasure at the idea. Knowing Bella, inside and out, was his dearest wish.

'Which is why I want to get to the bottom of this.' He cleared his throat when he realised how uptight he sounded. Until he was sure who was telling the truth, he needed to remain impartial. The thought of how easily he could be swayed by all the emotions rampaging around inside him was sobering. Mac deliberately cleared his head of everything else while he focused on the reason why he had come to see her.

'So you're just going to leave things the way they are and not try to defend yourself?'

'Basically, yes.' She sighed. 'I can't see any point in making a fuss, if I'm honest. Tim obviously has his reasons for blaming me and, quite frankly, I don't intend to end up having a public slanging match with him to clear my name. *I* know what really happened and that's what matters most of all.'

'So what you're saying is that you don't care what anyone else thinks,' Mac said slowly. He shook his head. 'That doesn't seem fair to me. I mean, why should everyone believe you're to blame when it wasn't your fault?'

'It's just the way things are.' Bella shrugged, trying not to get too hung up on the thought that Mac must care if he was so keen to straighten things out. She'd been down that route last night and she wasn't about to make the same mistake again. Maybe Mac did care but out of a sense of justice: it wasn't personal.

'Maybe Tim finds it easier to deal with what's happened by blaming me,' she said flatly, not wanting to dwell on the thought when it evoked so many mixed feelings. She and Mac had never been more than friends and it would be stupid to think that their relationship had changed. 'After all, he's been through a very difficult time. Dealing with his addiction can't have been easy for him. You know as well as I do how hard it is for an addict to get clean and stay off the drugs.'

'Yes, I do.' His tone was flat. 'I grew up in an area where drugs were part of everyday life, so I understand the damage they cause. That Tim managed to overcome his addiction is to his credit but it still doesn't excuse what he's doing, going around telling everyone a pack of lies. He needs to accept responsibility for his actions. Then maybe there's a chance that you two can get back together.'

'That isn't going to happen,' Bella said quietly. 'Our marriage is over and there's no chance of us trying again.'

'But you must still have feelings for him. Oh, I know it's been tough, Bella. Probably tougher for you than it was for Tim, in fact, because he was more concerned about where his next fix was coming from.' He leant forward and she could see the urgency in his eyes. 'But you loved him once, otherwise you wouldn't have married him, would you? So why not give it another shot?'

'As I said, it isn't going to happen.'

She stood up, wanting to make it clear that she didn't intend to discuss the matter any further. She and Tim were never getting back together for one simple reason: she didn't love him and she never had loved him either.

The thought was incredibly painful as it seemed to highlight how out of touch she was with her own emotions. As she led the way to the door, Bella felt a wave of despair wash over her. How could she ever trust her own judgement again? How could she be sure if she did fall in love that it was the real thing this time? The thought of living out her life in a state of lonely uncertainty was more than she could bear, especially with Mac there—Mac, who always seemed so sure of himself, so confident about what he wanted. She couldn't imagine Mac experiencing all these crippling doubts!

Bella opened the door, her heart aching as she fixed a smile to her lips. 'Thank you for coming. I'll see you in work, I expect.'

'So that's it, is it? I've said my piece and you've said yours and that's the end of the matter?' His dark brows drew together as he glowered down at her.

'I can't think of anything else that we need to say.' She gave a little shrug, aiming for a nonchalance she wished she felt. Maybe it was silly, but she had always dreamt of finding the right man and falling in love. However, it seemed unlikely that it would happen now. 'I've told you my side of the story and now it's up to you to decide who you believe.'

'In other words, you don't give a damn if I think you're lying.' He laughed harshly, so harshly that she flinched. 'I have to hand it to you, Bella. Your self-confidence is amazing!'

'You're wrong. I don't feel confident at all,' she shot back. 'I have no idea if you believe me, Mac, but what can I do about it? Should I try to convince you by telling you about all the horrible things Tim said to me or all the lies he told? Should I tell you about his affair to try and gain your sympathy?' She shook her head. 'Sorry, but it isn't going to happen. Either you believe me or you don't—it's as simple as that.'

'Affair? What do you mean? What affair?'

The shock in his voice cut through her anger. Bella bit her lip, wishing she hadn't told him that. It hadn't been intentional, but the words had somehow slipped out.

'It doesn't matter...' she began.

'Of course it matters!' He gripped hold of her by the shoulders as he bent to look into her eyes, and maybe it was the fact that she was feeling so wrung out, but all of a sudden she couldn't contain her feelings any longer. Tears began to pour down her face and she heard him groan.

'Oh, Bella, I'm sorry! I didn't mean to upset you.' He drew her to him, cradling her against the solid strength of his body, and she cried all the harder. It had been such a long time since anyone had held her like this, since anyone had cared.

'Shh. It's OK, sweetheart. Don't cry. Everything's going to be fine, I promise you.'

He drew her closer, running his hand down her back in a gesture that was meant simply to comfort, and she sighed. She could feel his fingers gliding down her spine, warm and wonderfully soothing as they traced the delicate column of bones. His hand reached the curve of her buttocks and stopped. Bella could feel the heat of his fingers burning through her clothing and shuddered. All of a sudden the air seemed thick with tension, filled with a sense of anticipation that immediately dried her tears. She realised that she was holding her breath as she waited to see what would happen...

His hand slid back up, following the route it had already travelled. When it reached the nape of her neck it stopped again, resting lightly beneath the heavy knot of her hair. Bella bit her lip, suddenly unsure about what she should do. Should she break the contact, step away from him and make it clear that she didn't welcome this kind of intimacy? But surely that would be a lie? Having Mac hold her, caress her, make her feel all these things *was* what she wanted.

Desperately.

Helplessly, her eyes rose to his and she felt her heart lurch when she saw the awareness on his face. She knew in that moment that Mac understood how confused she felt because he felt the same. Maybe it was that thought, that single mind-blowing thought, that unlocked all her reservations, but she didn't pause to consider what she was doing as she reached up and drew his head down. Their mouths met, clung, and it was like nothing she had experienced before. There was desire, yes, but there was so much more to the kiss than passion. The feel of Mac's mouth on hers made her feel safe, secure, protected. It was as though she had found her way back home after a long and exhausting journey.

Bella wasn't sure how long the kiss lasted. It could have been seconds or a lifetime for all she knew. She was trembling when they finally broke apart, but so was Mac. He ran the pad of his thumb over her swollen lips and his eyes were alight with a tenderness that filled her with warmth. It was obvious that she wasn't the only one to have been so deeply moved by what had happened.

'I didn't plan this, Bella, but I'm not sorry it happened and I hope you aren't either?'

His voice was low, deep, and she shivered when she heard the desire it held. She had done this to him, she thought in amazement. She had aroused his passion and it was a revelation to realise that she was capable of making him want her this much.

'I'm not. I'm not sorry at all,' she said in a husky little voice that made his eyes darken. When he reached out and pulled her back into his arms, she knew what was going to happen. Maybe they hadn't planned it, but there was no point pretending. They had both thought about it—thought about how it would feel to lie in each other's arms and make love. And tonight it was going to happen.

When he swung her up into his arms and carried her into the bedroom, she didn't protest. Why would she when it was what she wanted so much? He laid her down on the huge bed and sat down beside her, his hand trembling just a little as he cupped her cheek.

'Are you sure, Bella? Absolutely certain this is what you want?'

'Yes.' She captured his hand, gently biting the pad of flesh at the base of his thumb, and didn't even feel shocked by her own temerity. This was Mac and whatever happened between them tonight felt right. 'I'm sure, Mac. Completely and utterly sure.'

He made a sound deep in his throat as he stood up and started to strip off his clothes. His body was lean and fit, the muscles in his chest flexing as he dragged his T-shirt over his head and tossed it onto the floor. Bella's eyes ran over him, greedily drinking in the sight of his body, so beautiful in its masculinity. She bit her lip as her gaze came to rest on his erection because there was little doubt about how much he wanted her. Her eyes rose to his and she realised that she must be blushing when he laughed softly and tenderly.

'It's hard for a man to hide how he feels. When he wants a woman as much as I want you, Bella, then it's pretty obvious, I'm afraid.'

'Don't apologise,' she said with a bravado that would have shocked her once upon a time but felt completely natural now. She laughed up at him. 'It's good to know that it isn't all one-sided.'

'Oh, it most definitely isn't!' He lay down on the bed and gathered her into his arms while he kissed her with a passion that made her tingle both inside and out. Propping himself up on his elbow, he smiled into her eyes. 'You're a great kisser, Bella English. I have no complaints on that score.'

'Thank you,' she retorted. 'I hope you don't have any complaints on any other score, either.'

'Maybe just one.' He kissed the tip of her nose and grinned at her. 'You're decidedly overdressed for what I have in mind. Still, it shouldn't take long to resolve the problem.'

His hands went to the buttons on her shirt and Bella sighed. Her lack of experience hadn't prepared her for his relaxed approach to lovemaking. Passion was tempered by humour and, amazingly, that only seemed to heighten her desire for him. By the time he reached the final button, she was trembling with need but it was obvious that he didn't intend to rush things.

He parted the edges of her shirt with exquisite slowness and stared down at her breasts, barely concealed by the lacy white bra she was wearing. His eyes were filled with so many emotions when he looked up that her heart overflowed. Was this how it should be? she wondered giddily. Was this what she had missed, having a man look at her as though she was the most wonderful sight he had ever seen? She had no idea what the answer was but she knew that she would remember this moment for the rest of her life—the moment when she discovered how it really felt to be a woman.

'You're so beautiful, Bella. So very, very beautiful…'

The rest of the words were swallowed up as he bent and drew her nipple into his mouth. Bella cried out at the explosion of sensations that erupted inside her. The moist heat of his tongue, the erotic stimulation of the damp lace against her flesh, the sensual whisper of his breath as he raised his head and blew gently on the hard nub made her tremble with longing. When he turned his attention to her other breast, lavishing it with the same attention, she wasn't sure if she could bear it. She could feel her passion mounting, feel her desire growing more and more urgent with every delicate stroke of his tongue. Lacing her fingers through his hair, she raised his head, uncaring if he could tell how much she needed him.

'Mac, I don't know if I can take much more of this,' she whispered hoarsely.

'Sweetheart!' He kissed her hard and hungrily, then stripped off the rest of her clothes until she was naked to his gaze. His eyes grazed over her and she shivered when she saw the desire they held as he raised his head. 'Tonight is going to be special, Bella. I promise you that. Just give me a second.'

He slid off the bed and, picking up his trousers, took out his wallet and removed a condom from it. Bella closed her eyes as he lay down beside her again and took her in his arms, shuddering as he entered her. There wasn't a doubt in her mind that he was right. Tonight *was* going to be special. For both of them.

Mac lay on his back, one arm resting across his eyes. It was almost midnight and the daylight had disappeared a long time ago, but they hadn't switched on the lamps. Maybe they had both felt a need to preserve the status quo. Casting light onto the scene might spoil things; it might make them question the wisdom of what they had done. He didn't want to do that and he sensed that Bella didn't want to do it either.

He sighed softly. He was still finding it difficult to accept how quickly his feelings had changed. The anger he had felt about the way Bella had treated Tim seemed to have melted away. Finding out that his friend had had an affair had been a shock but it wasn't only that which had made him see that he had been unfair to her. Holding her in his arms, being close to her had done more than merely satisfy his desire for her. It had made him remember exactly who she was, and that certainly wasn't the sort of woman who would turn her back on someone in need. No, Bella had been forced into ending her marriage by Tim's appalling behaviour and it made him feel incredibly guilty to know how badly he had misjudged her. Now he could only pray that he hadn't made her life even more difficult by what they had done.

'Penny for them, Dr MacIntyre.'

Her voice was low but Mac heard the uncertainty it held and lowered his arm. Rolling onto his side, he pulled her to him and kissed her softly on the lips. Maybe he did have doubts, but he intended to keep them to himself. He didn't want her worrying unnecessarily.

'I'm not sure they're worth as much as a penny,' he countered, clamping down on the rush of desire that flooded through him. They had made love not once but twice and he really shouldn't be feeling this need again, he told himself sternly, but to very little effect. 'I was just letting my mind drift rather than thinking actual thoughts.'

'So you weren't regretting what we've done?' She looked steadily into his eyes and he sighed, unable to lie to her.

'No. I don't regret it, but I do wonder if it was right. I...well, I don't want it to affect our friendship, Bella, and make life even more complicated for you.'

'Neither do I.'

She smiled but there was something about her expression that made him wonder if he had phrased that badly. Getting into a discussion about the problems it could cause if they had an affair didn't seem right, but maybe he should have made his feelings clearer? However, before he could try to make amends, she tossed back the quilt and stood up. Mac gulped as he was treated to a tantalising glimpse of her beautiful body before she pulled on a robe.

'I'll have a shower then make us some coffee. There's a second bathroom along the corridor if you want to use that,' she told him briskly.

'Thanks.'

Mac stayed where he was until she had disappeared into the en-suite bathroom. Getting out of bed, he gathered up his clothes and made his way to the bathroom. There was a heavy feeling in his heart, a suspicion that he had upset her, and he hated to think that his clumsiness had caused her any pain, but what should he do? Sit her down and explain how awkward he felt about encroaching on Tim's territory?

Although Bella had claimed that there was no chance of her and Tim getting back together, she could change her mind. He had seen it happen to other couples, watched as time had softened the bad memories and brought the good ones into focus. He wouldn't want to stand in the way of that happening. Neither would he want to be left with a broken heart if it did. If Bella did rediscover her love for Tim then how would it affect him?

Once again the fear of finding himself rejected reared its ugly head. As Mac got dressed, he tried his best to rationalise it away. He was a grown man, after all, not a scared seven-year-old child, and if anything happened he would deal with it. However, no matter how he tried to reason the fear away, it wouldn't budge. In all those dark places he didn't visit very often, he knew that losing Bella would be far worse than anything that had happened to him before. Once he had allowed himself to fall in love with her, his heart would no longer be his. It would belong exclusively to her.

Bella had the coffee ready by the time Mac appeared. She loaded everything on to a tray and carried it through to the sitting room. He was standing by the window, ostensibly enjoying the view, but she sensed that his thoughts were far removed from the charms of the moonlit scene. Was he afraid that he had allowed his judgement to be swayed by passion? Was he worried in case she had used sex as a means to convince him of her innocence? That thought stung more than any other could have done. The only reason she had slept with him was because she had wanted to!

She plonked the tray on the table with a thud that made him swing round and she felt her heart scrunch up in her chest when she saw the strain on his face. Whatever thoughts he was harbouring obviously weren't pleasant ones. Picking up the pot, she poured coffee into the mugs, wishing that some passing genie would spirit her away. She wasn't up to this! She couldn't face the thought of explaining why she had slept with him when it was obvious that her reasons were a world removed from his. Oh, so maybe he had wanted her; she'd seen definite proof of that! However, it meant nothing if he now regretted what they had done.

Bella's hand shook as she put the pot back on the tray. She couldn't believe how painful it was to know that Mac wished tonight had never happened. It felt like another rejection, just like the way Tim had rejected her when he'd had that affair. What was wrong with her? Was it her inability to show her emotions that drove men away?

That was what Tim had said during one of those terrible rows they'd had. He had accused her of being so cold that she had driven him into the arms of another woman. He had even blamed her coldness for his drug addiction and, although Bella knew that he had been trying to excuse his behaviour by blaming her, the words had stuck in her mind. Now they rose to the surface again to taunt her.

She was incapable of showing her true emotions because there was something missing from her make-up, some vital element she was lacking. No wonder Mac was having second thoughts about what had happened tonight. After all, what man would want to get involved with someone like her? Someone who wasn't a *real* woman.

Mac drank his coffee as quickly as he could. It was scalding hot but, he gulped it down anyway, uncaring if it burnt his tongue. He needed to get away and the sooner the better, preferably. He had never gone in for the *wham, bam, thank you, ma'am* routine; he'd had far too much respect for the women he had slept with to treat them that way. However, he would have given his right arm to simply cut and run without offering up any explanations. If he started to explain to Bella why he wanted to leave so desperately, who knew what he'd end up admitting? The thought of laying his soul bare gave him hot and cold chills and he stood up abruptly. He had to leave. Right now, this very second. No matter what Bella thought of him!

'I have to go.'

He headed for the door, hating himself for leaving her like this, yet unable to do anything about it. He knew that he was within a hair's breadth of falling in love with her and the thought scared him witless. It was all very well telling himself that he could cope with anything that happened, but could he if it involved losing Bella? Could he honestly see himself carrying on if he loved and subsequently lost her? Just the thought made his head spin, round and round, faster and faster, until it felt as though his thoughts were swirling on a merry-go-round. Losing Bella would be the one thing he couldn't handle, the thing that would bring him down, and he couldn't take that risk.

He stopped when he reached the front door, forcing himself to smile as he turned to her. His heart stuttered to a halt when he saw the pain in her eyes but he had to be strong, had to do what was right for her as well as right for him. It wasn't just himself he had to think about, after all. How Bella was going to feel was even more important. He couldn't bear to think that she would be consumed by guilt about what they had done if she did decide to go back to Tim.

'I know we crossed a lot of boundaries tonight, Bella,' he said gruffly, trying to batten down the thought of how he would feel if that happened. 'But there's no need to feel…well, *awkward* about what's happened. We've always been friends and I hope that we can still be friends from now on too.'

'If that's what you want.'

Her voice echoed with scepticism and Mac grimaced, understanding completely why she had difficulty believing him. Friends didn't usually make mad passionate love, did they? They definitely didn't cross that boundary! The thought of how hard it was going to be to think of her as a friend after tonight was too much to handle and he shrugged, opting for the easier route, a half-truth.

'It is. I value our friendship, Bella. I always have.' Bending, he dropped what he hoped was a friendly kiss on her cheek, drawing back when he felt his body immediately respond. So much for friendship, he thought wryly as he opened the door. All it took was one chaste little kiss and he was up and running again!

He made his way to the lift, pausing briefly to wave before he stepped inside. He heard the apartment door close as the lift set off and sighed. If only that was the end of the matter, but there was no point kidding himself: tonight was going to have far-reaching consequences for both of them. He and Bella had slept together and even if they ignored what had happened, it wouldn't go away. It would be like the proverbial elephant in the room whenever they were together, always there but never acknowledged.

He groaned. What in heaven's name had he done?

CHAPTER SEVEN

THE DAYS FLEW PAST. With the schools breaking up for the long summer holiday, there were a lot of visitors in the area and that meant they were busier than ever in the paediatric A&E unit. Bella started early and finished late but she didn't complain. It was easier when she was working. It was when she was on her own that it became a problem. With nothing to distract her, her mind kept returning to what had happened that night in her apartment. She and Mac had made love and whilst she knew that a lot of women would have taken it in their stride, she couldn't do that. That night had been a turning point for her. She had not only discovered how it felt to be a real woman but she had also realised how inadequately suited she was to the role. It was much easier not to have to think about it.

It was a Saturday evening, three weeks after that fateful night, when Bella found herself working with Mac. Up till then their paths had crossed only fleetingly; if she'd been working days, he had been working nights. However, that night they were both rostered to work and she knew that she would have to deal with it. He was already there when she arrived, standing by the desk, laughing at something Laura Watson was saying to him. Bella felt her heart jolt as the memories came flooding back. Mac had looked like that when they had made love. His expression had been softened then by pleasure. If she lived to be a hundred, she would never forget that night, no matter how hard she tried.

He suddenly glanced round and she took a steadying breath as his gaze landed on her. Although neither of them had said anything, they were both aware of the rules. If they were to continue behaving as friends then there must be no harking back to what had happened. They must focus on the here and now, not on what they had done that night.

'It sounds as though you two are having fun,' she said lightly, going over to the desk to sign in.

'Laura was just telling me about one of the children she saw this morning,' Mac explained. He stepped back, ostensibly to give Bella some room, although she suspected that in reality he was trying to avoid touching her. A spurt of anger suddenly shot through her. He had been more than eager to touch her that night, hadn't he?

'Oh, yes?' She smiled up at him, her green eyes holding a hint of challenge. Maybe they had agreed to behave as though nothing had happened, but it wasn't true. They had made love and not once either, but twice. Whether he liked the idea or not, he couldn't just ignore what they had done. 'So what happened?'

'Oh, nothing much. The kid just got a bit confused, that's all.' He glanced round when the phone rang. 'I'll get that.'

He headed to the phone, leaving Bella seething even though she wasn't sure why exactly. After all, it made far more sense to pretend that nothing had happened, especially when there was no chance of there being a repeat. She snorted in disgust as the thought slid into her head. There definitely wasn't going to be a repeat. One night in Mac's arms had caused enough upheaval in her life!

Bella worked her way through the list. There was nothing really serious, just a lot of cuts and bruises, as could be expected when so many children were on holiday. She patched up several cut knees and sent a couple of youngsters for X-rays, and that was it. By the time she was due to take her break, there was just one child waiting to be seen. Mac had finished with his patient and arrived at the desk at the same time as her. He shrugged as he reached over and picked up the last file.

'I'll take this if you want to go for your break, Bella. We may as well make the most of it while it's quiet.'

'Fine.'

Bella headed for the lift. Although she wasn't hungry, a cup of tea would be very welcome. Mac had taken his patient to the cubicles and the waiting room was empty. She was about to step into the lift when the main doors opened and a couple of police officers came in. The female officer was carrying a baby in her arms and Bella paused, wondering what was going on. When Janet, their receptionist, beckoned to her, she hurried over to them.

'What's happened?'

'We received a report to say that a baby had been left at home on its own,' the male officer explained. 'When we got to the flat, we found the front door open. The child was inside, screaming its head off. It doesn't appear to be injured, from what we can tell, but we need you to check it over, just to make sure.'

'Of course.' Bella led the way to the treatment room. 'If you can put the baby on the bed, I'll examine it.'

She undid the poppers down the front of the child's sleepsuit and slipped it off then removed its vest and nappy. It was a little girl and she appeared to be both clean and well-nourished. Bella carefully checked her over and shook her head.

'No, there's nothing wrong with her. She's a little bit dehydrated but that can soon be sorted out once we give her a drink. Do you know where the mother is?'

'No idea. The neighbour who phoned in the report wasn't able to tell us very much.' The officer sighed. 'Apparently, she's little more than a kid herself, from what we can gather. We've been on to Social Services and we're hoping they might be able to help us.'

'Do you know her name?' Bella asked slowly, although she had a feeling that she already knew the name of the baby's mother.

'Yes. The neighbour was able to tell us that much at least.' The officer consulted his notebook. 'Freya Watson. We're trying to find out if she's local. If we can trace her family then they might know where she's gone.'

'I can give you their address.' Bella brought up Freya's file on the computer. She gave the policeman the Watsons' address then quickly explained the situation. 'I'd like to think that Freya's parents know where she is, but they were furious when they found out about the baby and refused to have anything more to do with her,' she concluded. 'If Freya has been living in the flat on her own with the baby then it doesn't look as though they've had a change of heart, does it?'

'No. It doesn't.' The policeman sighed as he wrote everything down in his notebook. 'Right, then. It might turn out to be a waste of time but I'll get on to the station and ask them to send someone round to speak to the girl's parents. The sooner we find out what's happened to her, the better.'

Both officers went outside to make the call, leaving Bella alone with the baby. She sighed as she picked her up and cradled her in her arms. It was no wonder that Freya had found it difficult to cope. Caring for a child on your own was a lot for any woman to deal with. Why, even she would find it hard and she was a lot older than Freya and had far more resources at her disposal. Quite frankly, she couldn't imagine how she would cope if she found herself in the position of being a single parent, not that it was likely to happen. Mac had taken great care to ensure she didn't get pregnant that night they had made love.

A tiny ache awoke in her heart, even though she knew how stupid it was. However, his determination to make sure that there were no consequences from their night of passion simply proved how he really felt about her. Maybe he'd been keen enough to sleep with her but he certainly wasn't looking for anything more.

Mac was surprised to see the police there when he got back from attending to his patient. He went over to the reception desk and asked Janet what was going on.

'They brought in a baby that had been left home alone.' She lowered her voice. 'From what I overheard just now, they seem to think it's Freya Watson's baby.'

'Really?' Mac exclaimed.

He glanced round when he heard footsteps, feeling a whole raft of emotions hit him when he saw Bella walking towards him, carrying the baby in her arms. He had never really thought about having children. Although he liked kids, the fact that he had always avoided commitment meant that it had never been

an issue before. Now, however, as he looked at Bella
holding the baby, he realised all of a sudden what he
was missing.

He could picture it now, imagine how wonderful it would be to have a child of his own, a son or a
daughter to love and cherish. His vision blurred as the
image inside his head grew stronger. He could see a
chubby little baby laughing up at him from its mother's arms now. It was only when the mother's face
started to become clearer that Mac realised what was
happening and groaned. Picturing Bella as the mother
of his children was something he mustn't do! It was a
mistake of gigantic proportions to allow himself that
much licence. Maybe Bella would have children one
day, but one thing was certain: their father would be
someone very different from him, a man who came
from a background similar to her own.

Bella was relieved when her shift finally ended. It
had been a stressful night for so many reasons. The
police were still searching for Freya Watson and it
was obvious that they were becoming increasingly
concerned as time passed and they failed to find any
trace of her. The baby had been placed with a foster
carer so at least she had the comfort of knowing that
the infant was being looked after. However, as she
left the hospital, she couldn't shake off the feeling of
gloom that weighed her down.

Tim had only wanted to have a child with her to

stop her divorcing him—he'd certainly not wanted one before then. And Mac had been at pains to ensure that nothing untoward happened in that department either. Even though she couldn't blame him for behaving responsibly, she couldn't rid herself of the thought that her inability to get in touch with her emotions had a huge bearing on the way both men had acted. The future had never seemed bleaker than it did right then and she realised that there was no point going home as she would never be able to sleep with all these thoughts whizzing around her head.

She left the hospital and headed to a supermarket on the outskirts of town that should open shortly. She hadn't done any food shopping for several weeks and the cupboards were bare. She filled a trolley then paid for her shopping and loaded everything in to her car. At least it had helped to distract her but, as she set off home, she found the same thought churning round and round inside her head: unless she got in touch with her emotions she would never be truly happy.

Maybe it was the stress, but somehow she must have taken a wrong turning because she found herself on a road she had never driven along before. She drove on for a few more miles, searching for any clues as to where she was. The car's satellite navigation system wasn't any help; it just showed an unmarked road and nothing else. When the road suddenly petered out into a track, Bella decided to turn round rather than risk going any further and getting completely lost. She carefully manoeuvred the car, shunting it backwards and forwards across the narrow track. She had almost completed the turn when there was an almighty bang from the rear of the vehicle.

She got out, her heart sinking when she discovered that one of the back wheels had hit a boulder and had buckled under the impact. There was no way that she could change the wheel herself, but maybe there was a farm up ahead and people who would help her?

Lifting her bag out of the car, she started walking. Although it was almost the middle of the morning, heavy black clouds hung overhead, obscuring the tops of the surrounding mountains, and she shivered. Although she was wearing a jacket, it wouldn't be much use if it started to rain.

She must have walked a couple of miles before she decided to give up. There had been no sign of a farmhouse and it seemed pointless carrying on. She turned back, grimacing when she felt the first drops of rain start to fall. Within seconds, it was pouring down, sheets of water falling from the sky and soaking through her clothing. Bella walked as fast as she could but the increasingly slippery ground hampered her progress and it took her twice as long to get back to the car.

She climbed in, shivering violently as she started the engine and switched on the heater. Digging in to her bag, she found her mobile phone, intending to call the local garage and ask them to come out and fetch her. It was only when she saw the phone's blank screen that she realised the battery was flat. Tipping back her head, she groaned. What a perfect end to a miserable night!

Mac couldn't shake off the feeling that there was something wrong with Bella. Oh, he understood that it must have been a strain for her to work with him—heaven knew he hadn't found it easy, either. Nevertheless, he couldn't rid himself of the nagging thought that there was something else troubling her. As he left the hospital, he knew that he wouldn't rest until he found out what was the matter, even though he doubted Bella would appreciate his concern. If last night was anything to go by, she would much prefer it if he steered well clear of her!

He drove into town, drawing up in front of the apartment block where she lived. There was no sign of her car in the courtyard and he frowned. He had assumed that she would go straight home after working all night but maybe she had stopped off along the way. He decided to wait but when she still hadn't appeared an hour later, he realised that he might as well give up. There was no point in him hanging around if she had gone off somewhere. He would just have to try again later.

Mac headed home and went straight to bed but, even though he was tired after the busy night, he couldn't sleep. His mind kept churning over all the reasons why Bella might be upset. The fact that Freya had gone missing was bound to have upset her, but was it really that which was troubling her or something of a more personal nature? Try as he might, he couldn't come up with an answer and it was frustrating, to say the least, not to be able to find an explanation.

In the end he gave up any attempt to sleep and got up. He made himself a cup of coffee and stood on the deck while he drank it. It had started to rain but he barely noticed. Was it something he had said? Or was he deluding himself by thinking that anything *he* did could affect her?

He sighed. The truth was that he had no idea how Bella really felt about him. Maybe he should be glad that she seemed to have put what had happened that night behind her, but in his heart he knew it wasn't relief he felt. It was something far more disturbing, an emotion he shouldn't allow himself to feel. To wish that Bella would never forget that night, as he would never forget it, was selfish in the extreme.

Bella trudged on. Although the rain had eased off, it hadn't stopped and cold little flurries of raindrops stung her face as she made her way back along the track. She had decided to walk back to the main road and try to flag down a car in the hope that she could beg a lift into town. However, she hadn't realised just how far she must have driven. At this rate it would be midnight before she reached the road!

Spurred on by the thought, she quickened her pace then had to slow down again when she came to a section where the hillside had caved in. Mud and boulders had been washed down by the rain and covered the track. Bella carefully made her way around the obstruction, pausing when she heard a cry coming from somewhere to her left. She looked around, trying to determine where it had come from, and gasped when she spotted a woman huddled against some bushes. She hurried towards her, her feet slipping this way and that on the muddy ground. It was only as she got closer that she realised it was Freya Watson.

'Freya! What are you doing out here?' she demanded, crouching down beside her.

'I've hurt my ankle,' the girl told her. She ran a grimy hand over her face and Bella's heart went out to her when she realised that she was crying.

'It's OK,' she said, putting her arm around the girl's shoulders. 'We'll get it sorted out so don't worry. Here, let me take a look.'

She eased up the leg of Freya's jeans, hiding her grimace when she saw her ankle. It was very badly bruised and swollen, the flesh black and purple in places. 'Can you wiggle your toes?' she asked, trying to assess if it was broken or badly sprained, not that it made much difference. It must be extremely painful whichever it was.

'No. I can't move them. Is it broken, do you think?' Freya asked miserably.

'It looks like it.' Bella unwound her scarf from around her neck. 'I'm going to use this as a temporary support. I'll be as gentle as I can but it might hurt a bit.'

Leaving the girl's shoe and sock on, she carefully wound the scarf in a figure of eight fashion around Freya's foot and ankle. 'That should help,' she said after she had finished. 'How did it happen, though? And what were you doing out here in the first place?'

'I was hiding from a man who gave me a lift,' Freya told her. She bit her lip, looking for all the world like a child who knew she had done something wrong.

Bella sighed. 'I think you'd better start from the beginning. But, before you do, have you a mobile phone I can use to call the mountain rescue services? My battery's flat.'

'No. My dad used to pay for my phone but he stopped it after I had Ava and I can't afford to pay for it myself.'

'Don't worry. We'll work something out,' Bella told her, wondering what sort of parents could treat their child the way the Watsons were doing. She would never do that to *her* child, she thought angrily, then sighed when it struck her that it was highly unlikely that she would ever be in the position of having a child of her own.

'So what happened, sweetheart?' she asked, trying not to think about how bleak the future seemed. 'I know you walked out of your flat because the police brought Ava into the hospital to be checked over. She's fine,' she said hastily when she saw the fear in Freya's eyes. 'She's with a foster carer at the moment so she's being well looked after. But what made you leave her in the first place?'

'She wouldn't stop crying,' Freya explained. Tears began to stream down her face once more. 'I tried everything I could think of, too. I fed her and changed her, rocked her and sang to her, but she wouldn't stop. I know I shouldn't have left her on her own but I just couldn't stand it any longer.'

'It must be hard when you don't have anyone to help you,' Bella said gently. 'I take it from what you just told me that your parents haven't had a change of heart?'

'No. They won't even speak to me when I try phoning them.' Freya dried her eyes with the back of her hand. 'I know I was stupid, but it's not as though I've *murdered* someone or anything like that!'

Bella wholeheartedly agreed although she didn't say so. To her mind, the Watsons had behaved deplorably. 'So what happened after you left your flat?'

'I got on a bus. I've no idea where it was going 'cos it really didn't matter. I just needed to get away, you see. The trouble was that when I tried to catch a bus back home, it was after midnight and they'd stopped running.' Freya sighed. 'I started walking when this car drew up and the driver offered me a lift.'

'And you accepted?' Bella asked, her heart sinking at the thought of Freya getting into a stranger's car.

'Yes. He said he'd drive me home but he brought me here instead.' Freya's eyes welled with tears again. 'I was so scared! I managed to jump out of the car when he stopped and hid until he had left. It was pitch-dark and I had no idea where I was so I just stayed here until the morning. I was making my way back to the road when I slipped and hurt my ankle. If you hadn't come along then, I don't know what I'd have done,' she added tearfully.

'Well, I did come so let's not think about that,' Bella said rousingly. She stood up. 'Now, we need to get you back to the main road. Do you think you can hop if I support you? It's either that or leave you here while I go for help.'

'Oh, don't leave me!' Freya exclaimed, obviously terrified by the thought of being left on her own once again.

Bella looped the girl's arm across her shoulders as she helped her to stand up. It wasn't going to be easy to get Freya back to the road, but what choice did she have? Nobody knew they were here and nobody would come looking for them either. Just for a second the thought that Mac might notice her absence crossed her mind before she dismissed it. Mac wouldn't miss her, as he had made it abundantly clear.

CHAPTER EIGHT

MAC WAS GROWING increasingly concerned. He had tried phoning Bella several times but she hadn't responded. He would have put it down to the fact that she didn't want to speak to him, only it appeared that her mobile phone had been switched off. It seemed odd to him, bearing in mind how conscientious she was. How would work contact her in case of an emergency if her phone was switched off?

In the end he went back to her apartment. Although there was still no sign of her car, he rang the bell anyway. There was always a chance that her car had broken down and she had made her way home by some other means. However, after half a dozen rings on the bell, he gave up. She obviously wasn't here, so where was she?

He stood there, trying to think where she might have gone. He knew for a fact that she had made very few friends since she had moved to Dalverston. Although she was well regarded by their colleagues, the fact that she kept herself to herself didn't encourage close friendships—he definitely couldn't picture her dropping in to someone's house for coffee and a chat! No, what friends she did have were all in London, so was it possible that she had driven down there?

It seemed unlikely but it was the only lead he had. He phoned half a dozen mutual friends but drew a blank. Nobody had seen or heard from Bella in months, it seemed. That left him with just one other option, the least appealing one too. He dialled Tim's number, filled with such a mixture of emotions that it was difficult to speak when Tim answered. He had come to Dalverston, sure in his own mind that Bella had been responsible for the demise of her marriage. However, he no longer believed that and it was hard to behave with equanimity as he asked Tim if he had heard from her. He had been wrong to blame her— so very, very wrong. If he lived to be a hundred he would always regret it.

Once again Mac drew a blank. Tim hadn't heard from Bella either, apparently. Mac cut him off, knowing that he would lose it completely if he had to listen to Tim blackening her name again. Although she hadn't gone into any detail about Tim's affair— she'd not had time!—he believed her. And the thought filled him with all sorts of uncharitable feelings towards his former friend. Tim had deliberately lied to him and he wasn't sure if he would ever be able to forgive him for that.

He went back to his motorbike, his face set as he

revved up the engine. He was going to find Bella even if it took him all day!

Progress was excruciatingly slow. They had to stop every few minutes while Freya rested. Bella glanced at her watch, sighing as she realised how much time had passed. They'd barely travelled half a mile and it was already gone midday. She helped Freya sit down in the lee of a large rock and sat down beside her while she tried to decide what to do. It had started to rain again, which would only exacerbate the problem. With the ground becoming increasingly slippery there was a very real danger that Freya might fall again. Bella came to a swift decision, prompted by necessity.

'Look, Freya, this isn't working. I know you don't like the idea of being left on your own but I need to fetch help.' She patted Freya's hand when she started to cry, feeling terrible about abandoning her. However, she would be much faster on her own. 'I'm going to leave you here while I go back to the main road. There's bound to be a car coming along it and I'll flag it down and get them to phone the mountain rescue people. Once they receive the call, it won't be long before we're out of here.'

'You will come back for me?' Freya asked anxiously. She looked round and shuddered. 'What if you can't remember where I am? I mean, it all looks the same to me!'

'I'll use my blouse as a marker.' Bella hurriedly undid her jacket and stripped off her blouse. Rooting around on the ground, she found a sturdy branch and knotted the blouse's sleeves around it. 'Look, I'll push the end of the branch into this crevice in the rock—it will act as a marker so that we'll be able to find you.'

'I suppose so,' Freya agreed reluctantly, obviously unsure about what she was proposing.

'It will be fine, Freya. I promise you.'

Bella gave her a hug then hurried away before *she* started doubting the feasibility of her plan. She had to leave Freya here, otherwise they could be stuck out in the open all day long. The thought spurred her on and she made rapid progress, although it still took her over an hour to reach the main road. She stood at the side of the carriageway, praying that a car would come along soon. She was cold and wet and unutterably weary and all she wanted was to go home and have a long hot bath then climb into bed. Just for a second the image of Mac lying beside her popped into her head before she drove it away. Mac wouldn't be sharing her bed today or in the foreseeable future!

Mac drove all around the town but he still couldn't find any sign of Bella. He tried to imagine where she might have gone but his mind was blank. He sighed as he pulled up outside a coffee shop. Maybe a shot of caffeine would help restore some life to his flagging brain cells. He went in and ordered a triple espresso to go. He added a couple of sachets of sugar to the brew to give it an extra kick then left, stopping when he came face to face with Helen Robertson, their F1 student. She grimaced as she studied the concoction he was nursing.

'You're obviously in need of some serious stimulation if you're thinking of drinking that. It looks lethal to me.'

'Hmm, it probably is. But needs must, and my brain definitely needs a major pick-me-up,' Mac replied with a grimace as he gulped down the coffee.

'It must have been a rough night,' Helen observed, laughing. 'I saw Bella at the supermarket earlier and she looked really washed out.'

'You saw her!' Mac exclaimed. He grabbed hold of Helen's arm. 'When was this?'

'First thing this morning,' Helen told him, looking startled. She glanced over at a young man who was obviously waiting for her and shrugged. 'David and I had been out at a club all night and we popped into the supermarket for some breakfast on our way home. We saw Bella at the checkout, although I don't think she saw us.'

'Thank you so much!' Mac impulsively hugged her. He let her go and grinned. 'I've been worried sick because she wasn't at her apartment or answering her phone. At least I have some idea where she went now.'

'Probably needed to stock up, from the amount of shopping she had,' Helen said lightly.

'Probably,' he agreed.

He said his goodbyes and hurried over to his motorbike. Climbing astride it, he headed out of town to the supermarket, mentally crossing his fingers that he would find Bella there. He sighed. And if he didn't find her, then what? He could hardly report her missing and call out a search party on such flimsy evidence, could he? After all, there was no proof that anything had happened to her—nothing, apart from this gut feeling he had.

He snorted in disgust. Try explaining that to the authorities. They would think he was deranged!

It must have been half an hour before a car finally appeared. Bella stepped into the middle of the road and flagged it down. There was an elderly couple inside and she could see how nervous they looked as she approached the driver's window. Bending down, she smiled reassuringly at them.

'Thank you for stopping. Do you have a mobile phone I can use to call the mountain rescue service? There's been an accident, you see—a young girl has been injured and she needs help.'

The man quickly gave her his phone. Bella made the call, checking with the driver as to their location. Fortunately, he was a local man and he was able to explain exactly where they were. Bella thanked him as she handed back the phone. When the couple asked her if she would like to sit in the car while they waited for the mountain rescue team to arrive, she gratefully accepted. It would be wonderful to get out of the rain even for a short time.

The first of the rescue vehicles arrived just fifteen minutes later and was quickly followed by several others. In a very short time, Bella was leading the team back to where she had left Freya. Thankfully, her makeshift marker had survived the wind and the rain and proved a big help in locating her. Once Freya was loaded onto the stretcher, they headed back. Bella was exhausted by then and finding it difficult to keep up. Relief overwhelmed her when she saw the road up ahead. Just a few more minutes and that would be it, she thought. It was only when she spotted the motorbike parked behind the other vehicles and the man standing beside it that her heart began to pound.

What on earth was Mac doing here?

It had been pure chance that Mac had happened upon the scene. After failing to find Bella at the supermarket, he had driven around, trying to decide what to do next. Although reporting her missing might have seemed premature, that gut feeling he had that something was wrong was growing stronger by the minute. When he came across the mountain rescue vehicles parked beside the road, he could hardly contain his fear. He just *knew* that Bella was involved!

He climbed off the bike, his legs trembling as he went over to speak to one of the team. He was just about to ask the man if he knew the name of the casualty when a shout went up and he turned to see the rest of the group walking towards them. His heart started to pound when he saw the figure lying on the stretcher. Was it Bella? Was she badly injured? All of a sudden the strength came flooding back to his limbs and he raced towards them. It was only as he drew closer that he realised it wasn't Bella on the stretcher but Freya Watson and he didn't know whether to feel relieved or terrified. Where on earth was she?

'Mac? What are you doing here?'

The sound of her voice had him spinning round. Mac just had a second to take in the fact that she was right there in front of him before instinct took over. Dragging her into his arms, he held her to him, held her as though he would never let her go again. Maybe he wouldn't, he thought giddily. Maybe he would follow his heart and not allow his fear of being rejected, of being left, to ruin things. If he could find the courage to believe in her, to believe in *them*, he could have everything he wanted: Bella in his arms and in his life for ever more.

The next hour passed in a blur. Although Bella did everything that was expected of her, her mind was far removed from what was happening. She kept thinking about the expression on Mac's face, about the way he had held her so tightly, so desperately, and it didn't make any sense. He had behaved as though he truly cared about her but that couldn't be true…

Could it?

The question nagged away at her as she and Freya were ferried to hospital in one of the rescue vehicles. They were taken straight to A&E, where they were met by the senior registrar. Bella quickly explained what had happened, nodding when he immediately decided to send Freya down to X-ray. Once they knew for certain if Freya's ankle was fractured, he could decide on the appropriate course of treatment.

After Freya left, Bella reluctantly agreed to be checked over as well. Although she was sure she was fine, there were procedures to follow and it would be wrong to create a fuss. As expected, she was given a clean bill of health and told that she could leave whenever she wanted. And that was when the tricky bit started. As she exited the cubicle and saw Mac sitting in the waiting room, she had no idea what to do. Had she correctly interpreted his reaction as rather more than relief for the safe deliverance of a friend?

Bella's heart began to race as that thought unlocked the door to several others. Did she want him to feel more than friendship for her, maybe even love? But if he did then how could *she* be sure that she wouldn't ruin things and that her inability to show her true feelings wouldn't destroy whatever he felt? Pain shot through her. Quite frankly, she didn't think she could bear knowing that yet again she had failed as a woman.

* * *

Mac could feel the tension building inside him as he waited for Bella to return. He knew that his behaviour must have aroused her suspicions and he was honest enough to admit that the thought scared him too. However, if he intended to win her then he couldn't back down. He had to fight for her. Tooth and claw!

'They said I could go home whenever I liked.'

He started when he realised that she was standing in front of him. He shot to his feet, almost overturning the chair in his haste. 'No damage done, then?' he said and winced at the sheer inanity of the comment.

'No, I'm fine.'

She gave him a quick smile and headed for the door. Mac followed her, pausing when he realised that it was still raining outside. Bearing in mind the soaking she'd had already that day, it seemed decidedly off to drive her home on the back of his motorbike.

'I'll phone for a cab,' he said, hunting his mobile phone out of his jacket pocket.

'What's wrong with your bike?' she asked, one brow arching in a way that made all sorts of complicated things start to happen inside him.

'Oh, ahem, nothing,' he murmured, trying to wrestle his libido back into its box. 'I just thought you'd prefer not to get drenched again.'

'I don't think it matters. I'm soaked as it is, so a drop more rain isn't going to make much difference.'

She gave a little shrug, her breasts rising and fall-

ing beneath the clinging folds of her wet jacket, and
Mac's libido won the battle, hands down.

'Oh, well, if you're sure, then.'

Mac didn't give her chance to reply as he led
the way to where he had left his motorbike. Quite
frankly, he couldn't believe how crassly he was behaving. Usually, it took more than the lift of a brow
or the wiggle of a woman's breast to arouse him. He
groaned as he took the spare helmet out of the box
beneath the seat. Who was he kidding? Bella only
had to look at him and he was putty in her hands!

He helped her on with the helmet then swung his
leg over the bike, tensing when she settled herself behind him on the seat. He could feel her body pressing against the length of his back and sent up a silent
prayer that he would manage to hold out. There must
be no stopping along the way, he told himself sternly.
And absolutely no thoughts of pulling into a secluded
lay-by. He wasn't a teenager but a mature adult who
had given up such behaviour years ago. No, he would
drive Bella home, make sure she was safely inside
her apartment and leave…

'Can we go back to the boat?'

Mac jumped when she leant forward and spoke
directly into his ear. He could feel the warmth of her
breath on his skin and shuddered. It took every scrap
of willpower he could muster not to respond as he
yearned to do. 'You don't want to go home to your
apartment?' he said hoarsely.

'No. I...well, I would prefer to go to the boat, if you don't mind.'

There was something in her voice that made his skin prickle. Mac nodded, not trusting himself to speak. He drove out of the car park, trying to get a grip, but it was impossible. How could he behave calmly when every instinct was telling him that the reason Bella wanted to go back to the boat was because she wanted to be with *him*?

As he followed the familiar route, he could feel his tension mounting, could feel all sorts of things happening which he had steadfastly avoided in the past. He had refused to allow himself to fall in love before—completely and totally rejected the idea, in fact. He had witnessed his father's devastation when his mother had walked out on them and he had sworn that love wasn't for him; but not any more. Not now that Bella was in his life.

His breath caught as he was forced to confront the truth. How could he *not* fall in love with her when he wanted her so desperately?

Bella took a deep breath as she stepped down from the motorbike. Had she been mad to ask Mac to bring her here? Oh, she knew what was going to happen— there was no use pretending that she didn't. She and Mac would make love again because it was what they both wanted. But surely that would only complicate matters even more?

'Come on. Let's get you inside before you're completely waterlogged.'

Mac placed his hand at the small of her back to urge her onto the boat and she shivered. Just the feel of his fingers pressing against her flesh made her senses reel. She stepped on board, waiting while he unlocked the cabin door. He turned to her and she could see the uncertainty in his eyes even though he smiled. Did he have doubts about the wisdom of what they were doing too? she wondered. And knew it was true. He was no surer about this than she was.

'Take care on the steps,' he advised her. 'They can be a bit slippery when it rains.'

Bella nodded as she made her way inside the cabin, feeling her nervousness crank itself up another notch or ten. The fact that Mac had doubts only seemed to heighten her own misgivings so that all of a sudden she found herself wishing that she had never suggested coming back here. She should have gone straight home to her apartment, chosen the sensible option rather than placed herself in this position. If they made love again it would be that much harder to do the right thing. No matter how she felt about Mac, she wouldn't *coerce* him into having a relationship with her. It wouldn't be fair. Mac needed a woman who didn't have all these hang-ups. A woman who understood her own feelings and was able to show them too. What he didn't need was someone like her.

The thought was more than she could bear. Bella

knew that she had to leave before anything happened. She spun round so fast that she cannoned right into Mac as he stepped down from the last tread. There was a moment when they both froze, when it felt as though time itself had stood still, and then the next second he was hauling her into his arms.

'I was so scared when I couldn't find you!'

His voice grated with fear and a host of other emotions, and she shuddered. It was hard to believe that she had made him feel all those things. Her eyes rose to his and she knew that he could see how she felt—how shocked, how amazed, how overjoyed.

'I didn't think anyone would notice I was missing,' she said truthfully.

'Well, I did!' He rested his forehead against hers and she felt the tremor that passed through him and was shocked all over again.

She had never believed that she was capable of arousing such strong emotions in another person. She had always been so diffident in her approach to life that she had honestly thought it was beyond her, but maybe she had been mistaken. Maybe her experiences with Tim weren't the yardstick by which she should measure any future relationship? The thought made her head reel even more because it opened up so many possibilities that she had thought were denied to her. If she could make Mac feel this way then perhaps there was a future for them after all?

When he bent and kissed her, Bella didn't hesitate.

She simply kissed him back, wanting him to know just how much she needed him. When he murmured something deep in his throat, her heart overflowed with joy. That he wanted her too was blatantly obvious. Swinging her up into his arms, he carried her into the tiny bedroom and laid her down on the bed and she shuddered when she saw the desire burning in his eyes.

'I want to make love to you, Bella, but only if it's what you want as well.'

'It is.' She held out her hand. 'It's what I want, Mac. More than anything.'

He didn't say a word as he took hold of her hand and raised it to his lips, but he didn't need to. The expression on his face said everything that she wanted to hear. Bella could feel herself trembling as he lay down beside her and drew her into his arms. No one had ever looked at her like this before. Looked at her as though she held the key to their future. In that second she knew that, no matter what happened, she would make sure that he didn't get hurt. She loved him so much—far too much to risk his happiness. Maybe she always had loved him too, she thought as she closed her eyes and let their passion sweep her away. She had just been too afraid to admit it before.

They made love with a voracious hunger that had them both trembling. Every kiss, each caress only seemed to fuel their desire for one another. Mac's whole being was consumed by the need to be inside her, but somehow he managed to hold back. He wanted this to be as amazing for Bella as it was for him.

'Mac, *please*!'

The desperation in her voice tipped him over the edge and he entered her with one powerful thrust. He couldn't have held back then even if he'd tried but he didn't need to. Bella was with him every step of the way, her body arching under his as he drove them both to the heights of passion and beyond. They were both shaking when they came back down to earth, both stunned by the sheer intensity of what had happened. Mac knew that he had visited a place he had never been before and that he would never visit again without Bella. It was only with Bella that he could experience such rapture, such a feeling of completeness. Only Bella whom he loved.

The need to tell her how he felt was very strong but something stopped him, a tiny vestige of that fear of rejection that had blighted his life for so long. Although he hated himself for being such a coward, he knew that he needed to come to terms with how he felt before he could take the next step.

Rolling onto his side, he smiled into her eyes, loving the way her face lit up when she smiled back at him. If that weren't proof that she felt something for him, he thought, then what was?

'Now that I've had my wicked way with you, Dr

English, I suppose I'd better feed you,' he said, battening down that delicious thought. Maybe she *did* care about him but he had to be sure—one hundred per cent *sure*—before he went any further. 'How about bacon and eggs—would that hit the spot?'

'Mmm, lovely.' She batted her eyelashes at him. 'I don't suppose you offer your guests breakfast in bed, do you? I'm feeling far too relaxed and comfortable to get up.'

'I suppose I could stretch a point just this once.' He huffed out a sigh, playing up the role of martyr to the full. 'I must warn you, though, that I don't plan to provide such luxuries on a regular basis.'

'Oh, so there are going to be other occasions like this, are there?'

She grinned up at him, her green eyes filled with laughter, and Mac couldn't resist. Bending, he dropped a kiss on her lips, feeling his body immediately stir. Catching hold of her around the waist, he lifted her on top of him.

'I think so. In fact, I'd go so far as to say that I *know* there will.'

He ran his hand down her back, feeling her tremble as her hips were brought into intimate contact with his. That she could feel how much he wanted her wasn't in any doubt. He kissed her long and hungrily, not even surprised by the depth of his desire. Even if he made love to her a dozen times a day, he would still want her, he thought.

Their lovemaking was just as fulfilling the second time round. Mac had to drag himself out of bed afterwards. He knew that Bella must be hungry and he wanted to feed her and take care of her every need. The thought filled him with tenderness as he dragged on his clothes and went to start preparing their meal. Bella had decided to take a shower and he smiled when he heard the water running. He could get used to sharing his life here on the boat with her. Very easily too.

It was the first time he had ever considered such an arrangement and it shocked him. Although he'd had many girlfriends over the years, he had never lived with any of them. It had seemed like a step too far and yet he knew without even having to think about it that living with Bella was what he wanted more than anything. He wanted the intimacy that came from living together, wanted to get to know all the little things that made her tick, like her favourite food and which programmes she enjoyed watching on television. His head began to spin because if he went down that route then it was just a small step to the next, but was he ready for that, ready for the ultimate commitment—marriage?

He wished he knew, wished with all his heart that he could simply close his eyes and *know* it was what he wanted but he couldn't. Not yet. That last pesky remnant of fear was still niggling away at the back of his mind and, until he had rid himself of it, he couldn't make the final decision. He sighed heavily. Please heaven, he prayed he wouldn't leave it too late and end up losing her.

CHAPTER NINE

'I AM ABSOLUTELY STUFFED!'

Bella groaned as she laid down her knife and fork. She had eaten far too much but it had been hard to resist when Mac had placed the meal in front of her. Now she smiled at him, loving the way his eyes lit up as he smiled back—another indication of how he felt about her, perhaps?

'Are you trying to make me fat, Dr MacIntyre?' she said, trying not to get too hung up on the idea. Maybe they *had* made love and maybe it *had* been marvellous but she mustn't take anything for granted. 'Because you're definitely going to succeed if you keep cooking me meals like that!'

'From what I can recall, there's no danger of you getting fat.'

He smiled into her eyes and Bella felt a wave of heat flow through her when she realised that he was remembering how she had looked when they had made love. She bit her lip as she was suddenly assailed by the memory of his powerful body. The strange thing was that she had never been aroused by a man's physical appearance in the past. Even as a teenager she hadn't done what most teenage girls did and stuck posters on her wall of the latest male heart-throb. Looks hadn't aroused her and yet the memory of Mac's body, so lean and yet so powerful, made her tremble. Picking up her cup, she buried her face in it, praying that he wouldn't guess what she was think-ing. Lusting after him definitely wasn't something a woman of her age should be doing!

'Bella?' His voice was so bone-meltingly gentle that she reacted as though he had actually touched her. Her hand was trembling as she placed the cup on the table and she saw him look at her in con-cern. Leaning forward, he covered her hand with his. 'You're not upset about what we did, are you, sweet-heart?'

'No.' She shook her head to emphasise that she meant what she said. She didn't regret making love with him again, although she couldn't help wonder-ing what was going to happen from here on. Would Mac expect them to be friends who occasionally slept together from now on? She hoped not, even though she wasn't sure exactly what she did want them to be.

'Then what's wrong?' He squeezed her fingers. 'Tell me. I want to know if there's something wor-rying you.'

'There isn't. I'm fine.'

She smiled brightly back at him, not wanting to

admit her fears when she felt so ambivalent. Did she want Mac in her life for ever and ever or simply for the foreseeable future? Oh, she loved him—she was sure about that. But *for ever* was a long time and she had no idea if it was expecting too much to aim for that.

All of a sudden the situation seemed way too complicated. Bella pushed back her chair and started gathering up their plates. She needed time to think, time to work out what she really wanted... Her breath caught as she turned to carry the plates to the sink and saw Mac watching her. She wanted Mac. But did she have the right to want him when she wasn't sure if she could fulfil his needs?

'I think I'll have a shower.' Mac stood up. Picking up their cups, he brought them over to the sink. He put them down on the counter then bent and dropped a kiss on the nape of her neck. Bella shuddered when she felt his lips brush against her skin. It was hard to be sensible and act responsibly when she felt this way!

'Bella.'

Her name on his lips was like a caress. When he turned her into his arms, she didn't hesitate. Maybe she didn't know what was going to happen in the future but she did know what she wanted to happen right now. Lifting her face to his, she kissed him back, her mouth clinging to his as she sought reassurance. Surely this desire they felt for one another could be seen as a good omen?

* * *

They made love once again and once again it was unlike anything Mac had experienced before. The feel
of Bella's satin-smooth skin gliding beneath his fingertips aroused him as nothing had ever done in the
past. He could only marvel at how different it was to
make love to her. How special. How totally fulfilling.
It wasn't just his senses that were engaged when they
made love but his spirit too. It felt as though he had
found himself in her arms, discovered the real person beneath the public image. He hadn't realised to
what extent he put up a front between himself and the
world, but he did now. With Bella he could be himself. Completely and wholly himself. The thought was
so poignant that it washed away the last remnants of
fear. Framing her face between his hands, he looked
deep into her eyes.

'I love you, Bella.' He had to break off at that point
because words failed him; only to be expected when
it was the first time he had ever uttered them. Not
once had he told a woman that he loved her because
it wouldn't have been true, but it was true now. He
loved Bella with all his heart and with every atom
of his being too.

'I…' Bella started to speak and then stopped. Mac
could see the shock on her face and understood. It was
a momentous occasion for both of them. He laughed
softly as he dropped a kiss on the tip of her nose.

'I know. I feel as stunned as you do, my love. I

think we both need a few minutes to get our heads round the idea, don't you?'

He stood up, feeling tenderness engulf him when he saw the expression on her face, a mixture of shock mingled with a growing excitement. Obviously, his announcement hadn't come as an unwelcome surprise then, he thought a shade smugly. As he made his way into the bathroom, Mac could feel happiness bubbling up inside him. Telling Bella how he felt had been a huge gamble, but it appeared to have paid off. Clearly, she had feelings for him too, and now all he needed to do was to persuade her to admit that she loved him back and they could look towards the future.

He grinned as he poured shower gel into his palm and started to lather himself. Maybe he was guilty of putting the cart before the horse, but it looked very much as though he and Bella might be riding off into the sunset. Together!

Bella washed the dishes and put them away in the cupboard. Mac kept the boat immaculately tidy and she didn't want to leave everywhere in a mess. After all, she would hate to think that he considered her to be a nuisance…

She sat down abruptly on the couch as all the strength suddenly seeped from her limbs. From what Mac had said before, there seemed little danger of that! He had told her that he loved her, but could it be true?

A tremor ran through her as she recalled the expression on his face as he had made the admission. He was either a brilliant actor or he had been telling her the truth and all of a sudden she knew which she wanted it to be. She wanted Mac to be a permanent part of her future!

Her breath caught as her mind raced away with the idea. Being with Mac, day in and day out, would be like a dream come true. He would always be there for her, always support her, always put her first. His loyalty and steadfastness were qualities she had admired ever since they had first met. Even though she had been a little wary of him initially because of the differences in their backgrounds, she had always known that he would be there for her. That was why it had hurt so much when he had blamed her for the failure of her marriage. She had expected him to understand why she'd had to end it and the fact that he hadn't done so had knocked her for six. Did he now accept that she wasn't at fault? she wondered suddenly. She hoped so. If they were to have that glorious future she longed for then they had to trust one another completely.

It was a tiny doubt, like a black mark on an otherwise bright and shiny canvas. Bella knew that she needed to talk to him about it before they went any further. She made a fresh pot of coffee while she waited for him to finish showering, feeling her nervousness increasing by the second. If Mac didn't believe in her innocence then this could be the beginning and the end for them.

'Mmm, coffee.' Mac came into the cabin. He grinned as he came over and caught her around the waist. 'Not only beautiful and sexy, but you can read my mind as well. It's no wonder that I love you, Bella English.'

He kissed her lingeringly, his lips teasing hers until Bella's head reeled. She kissed him back, feeling the tiny niggling doubt disappear. Mac wouldn't feel this way unless he believed in her. And it was the most marvellous feeling in the world to know that his love for her was everything he professed it to be. When he raised his head, she knew that this was the moment she should tell him how she felt too. She loved him and now that all her doubts had been erased, she wanted to make that clear.

'Mac, I…' She got no further when at that precise moment his phone rang. Mac groaned as he glanced over at where it lay on the table.

'Typical! Why do the wretched things always ring at the most inconvenient times?' Reaching over, he picked it up and she saw his expression change as he glanced at the screen.

'Hello, Tim,' he said flatly. He paused while he listened to what the other man was saying. 'Yes, I found her and she's fine… Of course. She's right here.'

Bella's heart bumped painfully against her ribs as he handed her his phone. She wasn't sure why Mac looked so distant all of a sudden. Surely he didn't think that she was eager to speak to her ex after what had just happened between them?

She was curt almost to the point of rudeness as she told Tim that she had taken a wrong turning on her way back from the supermarket and that was why she had gone missing. She didn't add anything about Freya and what else had happened because she wanted to end the call as quickly as possible.

She glanced at Mac, who had gone to stand by the sink, and felt her heart start racing when she saw how grim he looked. Mac obviously believed that she was pleased to hear from Tim, but nothing could be further from the truth. That part of her life was over and there was no chance of her and Tim getting back together. She realised that she needed to make that clear to Tim, so when he asked if they could meet up, she agreed. She couldn't move forward until she had drawn a line under the past.

'Tim was just calling to check that I was all right,' she said quietly as she ended the call. Mac didn't say anything and she hurried on, wanting to make the situation clear to him as well. 'He wants to see me and I've agreed.'

'So I heard.' Mac's expression held a contempt that chilled her to the core. 'Maybe I should congratulate you. It appears that you two have resolved your differences at last. I hope you will be very happy together.'

'No! It isn't like that,' she began but he didn't let her finish.

'Don't bother explaining. It's obvious that Tim still loves you if he's so eager to talk things through with you. And you obviously still love him if you've agreed to meet him after everything that's happened.' He gave a dismissive shrug that made her heart curl up inside her. 'I'm only glad that I was able to help in some small way. It appears that sleeping with me has helped you realise exactly what you want from life, and it certainly isn't an affair with me.'

Bella couldn't believe what she was hearing. Oh, she understood the words all right—they were plain enough. However, the fact that Mac believed that she had slept with him to help her decide if she should go back to Tim was beyond her comprehension. If he loved her, as he claimed to do, then he would *know* that she was incapable of such behaviour.

All of a sudden she couldn't take any more, couldn't bear to stand there and listen to him accusing her of such terrible deeds. Snatching up her bag, she pushed past him and ran up the steps to the deck. She heard him shouting her name but she didn't stop. What was the point? He had said everything that needed to be said, made it abundantly clear how he felt. Oh, maybe he had thought that he loved her but it wasn't true. It couldn't be when he didn't know in his heart that she would *never* go back to Tim after what they had done. Once again the thought that it was all down to her rose to the surface to taunt her. If she had only shown Mac how she really felt, convinced him that it was *him* she wanted and no one else, told him she loved him too even just once then maybe things would have turned out very differently.

Tears streamed down her face as she ran along the towpath, tears of grief for what she'd had so fleetingly and lost so quickly. It hurt so much, far more than when her marriage had ended, but that was to be expected. This time she had given her heart and had it ripped to shreds and thrown back at her. It had to be the most painful rejection of all.

Mac sank down onto the couch after Bella left. He knew that he should go after her but he felt incapable of doing anything at that moment. Bella was planning to go back to Tim; could it be true? But if it wasn't true then why had she agreed to meet Tim?

His head reeled as question after question assailed him. He realised that he needed to find out the answers before he drove himself mad, and leapt to his feet. There was no sign of Bella when he reached the deck so he set off at a run, expecting to catch up with her in the lane, but there was no sign of her there either. His heart began to thump as he wondered where she had gone. It was only when he caught a glimpse of the bus disappearing around the bend that he had the answer to that question at least. As for all the others, well, he would need to speak to her. She was the only one who knew the truth.

Mac made his way to where he had parked his motorbike. He started the engine, feeling his stomach churning with dread as all his old fears of rejection surged to the forefront. Maybe he did need answers but he could only pray that he was strong enough to hear them.

'Four-year-old in cubicle three—Oscar Starling. Mum thinks he's swallowed some detergent. Who wants it? You or Mac?'

'I'll take it.'

Bella grabbed the child's notes, turning away when she saw Trish look at her in surprise. There was no way that she intended to explain why she was so eager to take the case. Mac had been trying to get her on her own all morning long, but she had no intention of talking to him. That was why she hadn't answered the door when he had turned up at her apartment yesterday after she'd got back from the boat. What was there to say, after all? That she had no intention of going back to Tim? Why should he believe her when she had such difficulty expressing her true feelings?

Bella pushed back the curtain, preferring to focus on her patient's needs rather than her own problems. There was a little boy sitting on the examination couch and he smiled when she went in.

'I've got a new tractor,' he told her importantly, holding up a bright green toy tractor for her to admire.

'You lucky boy. It's beautiful.' Bella took the toy off him and ran it across the couch, making appropriate tractor noises. She handed it back then turned to his mother and smiled. 'Hello, I'm Dr English. I believe Oscar may have swallowed some detergent—is that right?'

'Yes.' Louise Starling sighed. 'He was playing in the kitchen with his tractor. He never normally goes in the cupboard where I keep the detergent but he did today. I'd gone upstairs and when I came down, he had the box on the floor. I use those liquid capsules and one of them was broken open. The liquid in them is bright blue and I could see that Oscar's lips were stained blue as well.'

'I see.' Bella turned to the little boy. 'Did you swallow a lot of mummy's detergent, Oscar?'

He shook his head. 'No, 'cos it tasted funny.' He zoomed the tractor across the couch and grinned at her. 'I spat it out on the floor.'

'Good boy.'

Bella ruffled his hair, thinking how adorable he was. It must be wonderful to have such a bright and happy child. The thought naturally reminded her of her own situation and she swallowed her sigh. There was little chance of her ever having a child when she ended up driving away every man she met. She tried to put the thought out of her mind as she asked

Louise Starling if she had brought any of the capsules with her.

'I brought the box.' Louise handed Bella the box of detergent capsules. She grimaced. 'I saw something on TV about taking the container with you if your child swallows something he shouldn't. I remember thinking that it would never happen to Oscar as I'm so careful, but it just goes to show, doesn't it?'

'You mustn't blame yourself,' Bella said sympathetically. 'Even the most careful parents can't always predict what their children are going to do. Right, I'll go and phone the National Poisons Information Service and see what they advise. However, I don't think that you need to worry too much. From what Oscar has told us, he didn't ingest very much of the detergent.'

Bella went to the desk and called the NPIS helpline. They kept a list of household products on file and were able to advise her on the best course of treatment. Fortunately, these particular capsules weren't highly toxic and, because so little of the detergent had been ingested, they agreed that Oscar wasn't in any immediate danger. Bella went back and broke the good news to the little boy's mother then set about treating him, which involved getting him to drink a large tumbler of water. He was as good as gold and drank it all without a murmur, making her smile.

'You are a good boy, Oscar. I want you to drink an-

other glass of water when Mummy takes you home—
will you do that for me?'

Oscar nodded, more interested in his tractor than
in what was happening. Bella laughed as she lifted
him off the couch. 'Come with me and I'll see if I can
find you a sticker for being such a good boy.'

He happily held her hand as she led the way from
the cubicle. They kept a pile of stickers behind the
desk so Bella sorted through them until she found
one with a tractor on it. Crouching down, she stuck
it onto the child's T-shirt. 'There you go. It says, "I'm
a star patient!"—which you are.'

Bella smiled as Oscar excitedly showed the sticker
to his mother. She told Louise to bring him back if
she was at all worried then sat down to write up the
child's notes after they left. It was almost lunchtime
and, once she had finished her notes, she would go
to the canteen and make herself eat something. She
hadn't been able to force down anything except a cup
of coffee that morning and she couldn't keep going
on that alone. If she was to do her job properly then
she needed to look after herself. After all, if she was
never going to have that family she had longed for
then she would need to focus on her career.

It seemed like a poor substitute even though she
loved her job but Bella knew that she had to be realistic. Oh, maybe she did have dreams and maybe it
was hard to relinquish them, especially the dreams
she'd had about her and Mac and the golden future

they would enjoy together, but the longer she clung to her dreams, the more painful it would be. She and Mac had had their chance and it hadn't worked out. The sooner she accepted that, the better.

By the time lunchtime rolled around, Mac was finding it difficult to contain his frustration. Bella had evaded his every attempt to speak to her. Oh, he had tried—tried umpteen times, in fact—but she had managed to avoid him. It was fast reaching the point where the rest of the team were bound to notice that something was going on, but hard luck. It wasn't his doing; it was Bella's. And if people started gossiping about them then she only had herself to blame!

Mac grimaced, aware that he was being very unfair. He had started this by making those accusations. He had spent a sleepless night, thinking about what had happened, and by the time morning arrived he knew that he had been wrong to jump to such hasty conclusions. Bella would never have tried to use him that way—it simply wasn't in her nature. He had allowed his fear of getting hurt to skew his judgement and he owed her an apology, but the big question was: would she accept it? From the way she had behaved towards him that morning, he very much doubted it.

His spirits were at an all-time low as he saw his patient out and returned to the desk. He paused when he spotted Bella sitting at the computer. There was nobody else around so maybe this was the moment he'd been waiting for. The thought of losing her if she went back to Tim was bad enough, but it would be so much worse if they parted on such bad terms. He needed to make his apologies and at least try to salvage something from the situation even if it was all too little. He took a couple of hurried strides then stopped when the emergency telephone rang. It felt as though he was being torn in two. Part of him desperately wanted to ignore the phone and speak to Bella, while another part urged him to respond to the summons.

In the end duty won. Mac snatched up the receiver, listening intently while the operator relayed the details. There'd been an accident at a level crossing on the outskirts of town. A train had hit a car that had stalled on the track and a number of people had been seriously injured, including several children. Mac confirmed that they would send a team and hung up then pressed the call button to summon the rest of the staff. Once everyone had gathered around the desk, he explained what had happened and what they would do.

'Bella, Laura and I will attend the accident as we've all done the major incident training course. That leaves Helen, Trish and Bailey to cover here.' He turned to Janet. 'Can you phone Adam and ask him to come in?' he asked, referring to their consultant, Adam Danvers. 'He was at a finance meeting this morning but it should be over by now so it shouldn't be a problem.'

Once everything was organised, Mac led the way to the room where they kept all their equipment. After they had donned weatherproof suits, they each collected a backpack containing everything they might need, from basic dressings to surgical instruments. It was impossible to foretell what they would have to deal with and they needed to be prepared. A rapid response car was waiting when they exited the building. Bella didn't look at him as she climbed into the back and beckoned to Laura to sit beside her.

Mac's mouth compressed as he slid into the passenger seat. He had missed his chance to try and sort things out with her and, if she had anything to do with it, he wouldn't get another opportunity either. Maybe he should think about cutting short his contract and signing on for the next aid mission? He had planned on staying in England for a while, but it would be better than having to work with Bella if she and Tim got back together. To see her day in and day out, knowing that she didn't love him but someone else, would be unbearably painful. Quite frankly, he doubted if he could handle it.

He closed his eyes as they set off with lights flashing and siren blaring, trying to blot out the thought of the dark and lonely future that lay ahead of him. Without Bella in his life, it felt as though he had very little to look forward to.

CHAPTER TEN

IT WASN'T THE FIRST major incident that Bella had attended but it had to be the most serious. The train was a high-speed express and many of its carriages had been derailed. The fire and rescue crews were working their way along the track, searching for any injured passengers, and by the time they arrived there were over a hundred people gathered at the side of the railway line. It was more than a little daunting to be faced with so many people who needed help, but Mac took it in his stride.

'We need to find out where the children are. It may seem hard-hearted to ignore the adults but there are other teams of medics who can deal with them. Our brief is to concentrate on the kids first and foremost.'

Bella nodded, feeling her initial panic subside in the face of his calmness. 'So what do you want us to do?' she asked, her heart lifting when he smiled at her. She battened it down, knowing how easy it would be to allow herself to think that it meant something.

Mac had proved beyond any shadow of a doubt that he didn't really love her and she must never forget that.

'I'll have a word with the officer in charge. Incident control said that there were two children who'd been seriously injured, although there may be others. However, we'll start with them.'

'Fine. Laura and I will go and check on that group over there,' Bella replied dully, confining her thoughts to what was happening. There was no point thinking about how much she loved him when it wouldn't make any difference. Mac may have thought that he loved her; however, the way he'd reacted yesterday proved it wasn't true. If he had loved her, as he'd claimed, then he would have known that she would never go back to Tim!

Her heart felt like lead as she and Laura made their way over to a group of teenagers huddled beside the track. There were three boys and two girls in the party and they all looked deeply shocked. One of the boys had a large gash on his forehead so Bella cleaned it up and applied butterfly stitches to hold the edges together. He would need to go to hospital and have a scan to check that he hadn't suffered a head injury. The rest of the group had suffered only minor cuts and bruises so she told them to wait there until they were told they could go home. They all had mobile phones and they'd called their parents so she guessed it wouldn't be long before they were collected.

As for the aftermath of what they had witnessed,

that was something no one could predict. Some would put it behind them and get on with their lives, while others might be permanently affected. It all depended on the type of person they were. Take her, for instance. She had spent her life distancing herself from other people so it was doubly ironic that now she had finally got in touch with her emotions, it was to have them thrown back in her face. It was a sobering thought but thankfully she didn't have time to dwell on it as Mac came over just then and drew her aside.

'The injured children are still on the train. The crew who found them decided it was too risky to try and move them.'

'Sounds bad,' Bella said quietly, her heart sinking. 'Do you know which carriage they're in?'

'One of the crew's going to take us to them.' Mac looked at her. 'Are you OK about this, Bella? I know how upsetting this kind of situation can be, so say if it's too much for you.'

'I'm fine,' she snapped, determined that she wasn't going to let her newly discovered emotions get the better of her. Mac didn't love her. If she said it often enough then maybe she would believe it and not keep reading too much into everything he said.

'Fair enough.'

He shrugged but she saw the hurt in his eyes and had to bite her tongue to stop herself saying something. He didn't need her reassurances. He didn't need anything at all from her. The thought stayed with her as they followed one of the fire crew along the track. They came to the first two carriages, the ones directly behind the engine, and Bella grimaced. The carriages were lying on their side, in a mangled mess halfway down the embankment, and it was hard to believe that anyone sitting in either of them had survived.

'You're going to need to be extremely careful,' the fireman warned them. 'There's a lot of broken glass and metal in there. We've tried to stabilise the carriages as best we can to stop them sliding any further down the embankment but if we tell you to get out then no arguing—just do it. One of the kids is in the first carriage and the other is in the second, but you'll need to make your way inside through here. A couple of our guys are waiting with them.'

Bella nodded, saving her breath as she set about levering herself up into the carriage. It was a long way and there were very few footholds so it wasn't easy.

'Here. Put your foot in my hands and I'll give you a boost up.'

Mac made a cup with his hands and after a moment's hesitation Bella placed her foot in it. He boosted her up until she could grab hold of the fireman's hand. He hauled her the rest of the way, waiting until Mac joined them before he led them inside. It was strangely disorientating to walk along what was actually the side wall of the carriage, scrambling over seats and tables that had sheared away from their housings. Bella was glad when they reached the first casualty, a young girl, roughly ten years of age.

'You stay with her and I'll check out the other child,' Mac told her as they paused. His eyes darkened. 'Just mind what you're doing, Bella. It's only too easy to have an accident yourself in this kind of situation.'

Bella nodded, unable to speak when her throat felt as dry as a bone. She crouched down and began examining the girl, focusing all her attention on what she was doing. It would be a mistake to read anything into the way Mac had looked at her, she reminded herself sternly. Her heart began to thump because there was no way that she could stop herself. Despite what had happened, she wanted Mac to be concerned about her.

She took a deep breath but the truth had to be faced. She wanted him to feel all *sorts* of things when he looked at her, and especially love.

Mac did his best but the boy's injuries were just too severe. He died a short time later and now all that was left to do was to inform his parents. They had been injured as well and had already been ferried to hospital.

His heart was heavy as he made his way back through the train. Breaking bad news to relatives was always hard and even worse when it concerned a child. He couldn't imagine how people coped with such a tragedy; he knew he'd find it impossibly difficult. If he had a child then he would love it with every fibre of his being, and it was such a poignant thought in the circumstances. Bella was the only woman he had ever wanted to have a child with and it was never going to happen.

It was hard to hide how devastated the thought made him feel as he stopped beside her. She looked up and he had to bite back the words that were clamouring to get out. It wasn't fair to put her under any pressure, to make her feel guilty because she loved Tim and not him. People couldn't choose who they fell in love with, although even if he could have done he would have still chosen Bella. Right from the first moment they had met, he had known in his heart that she was the only woman for him.

It was hard to contain his emotions at that thought but somehow he managed to get them under control. 'Have you nearly finished here?'

'Yes. She's stable and ready to be moved. How about the other child?'

Mac shook his head, feeling tears welling behind his eyelids. He was at emotional overload and it would take very little to make him break down. 'He didn't make it.'

'Oh, I'm so sorry!' Reaching up, she touched his hand, just the lightest, briefest of contacts, but he felt the touch like a brand burning into his skin.

He turned away, terrified that he would do something crazy. He mustn't beg her to stay with him, mustn't try to *coerce* her. She had to want him as much as he wanted her, otherwise there was no point. She would only end up by leaving him and he couldn't bear the thought of that happening... Although could it be any worse than what was happening right now? Could he feel any more devastated than he did at this very moment, knowing that he had lost her?

The questions thundered inside his head as he made his way from the train. He had intended to find the officer in charge and update him about what had happened to the boy. However, he'd only gone a couple of yards when he heard shouting behind him and spun round. His heart seemed to seize up as he watched the wrecked carriages start to slide down the embankment. There was a sickening screech of metal being ripped apart, the sound of glass shattering, and then silence.

Mac stood where he was, unable to move as fear turned his limbs to stone. Bella was trapped somewhere inside that tangle of broken glass and metal!

Bella had been about to stand up when she heard someone shouting and the next second she felt the carriage begin to move. Grabbing hold of a table, she clung on as it gathered momentum, jolting and bouncing its way down the embankment. Bits of broken glass and metal were being flung around and she gasped when a shard of metal cut into her neck. She could feel the warm stickiness of blood pouring from the cut but she was too afraid to let go of her hand-hold to check it out. Fortunately, Katie, the young girl she'd been treating, was wedged between a couple of overturned seats and they provided some protection for her. However, Bella could see the fear in her eyes and reacted instinctively.

'It's OK, sweetheart. The carriage has just slipped a little but it will stop in a moment.'

Reaching out, she squeezed Katie's hand, praying that she wasn't being overly optimistic. The bank was very steep at this point, falling away to the river at the bottom, and she didn't want to imagine what would happen if it slid all the way down. When they suddenly came to a jarring halt, she was overwhelmed by relief. She gingerly straightened up, holding on to the table when she felt the carriage sway. She could see out of the window now and her heart sank when she realised that the carriages had come to rest against some scrubby-looking trees. It seemed unlikely that they could support their weight for very long.

'We need to get you out of here.' The fireman who had accompanied them onto the train appeared. His expression was grim as he glanced out of the window. 'Those trees won't be able to support this weight for much longer, so we're going to have to move you and the girl straight away.'

'I understand,' Bella said quietly, doing her best to hide her concern for Katie's sake. Crouching down, she concentrated on making sure that the supports she had placed around the girl's hips and legs were securely fastened. Katie had a fractured pelvis plus fractures to both femurs and it was essential that the breaks were stabilised before they attempted to move her. Once Bella was sure that she had done all she could, she stood up. 'Right, there's nothing more I can do. Let's get her out of here.'

The fire crew carefully eased the girl out from between the seats. They had a stretcher ready and they slid her onto it, passing it from hand to hand as they lifted her over all the debris. Bella followed them, biting her lip against the pain from the cut in her neck. It had stopped bleeding, thankfully, but it was definitely going to need stitching from what she could tell. They reached the door at last and the lead fireman turned to her.

'We'll get you out first. That way, you'll be on hand if she needs anything.' He lowered his voice. 'It won't be easy to get her out of here, so be prepared, Doc.'

Bella nodded, understanding how difficult it was going to be. Not only would the crew need to lift the stretcher up to reach the opening, they would have to raise it at an angle to get it through the gap. She could only pray that the pain relief she had given the girl would be sufficient. In other circumstances, she would have insisted on them waiting while she topped it up but that wasn't an option right now. At any moment, the carriages could start to move again and the consequences of that happening didn't bear thinking about. She allowed one of the crew to boost her up to reach the opening, gasping when she discovered that Mac was there waiting to help her down. He gripped tight hold of her hands and she could see the relief in his eyes.

'Are you all right?' he asked, his deep voice throbbing with an emotion that made her heart start to race.

'I…I think so.'

'Good.'

He squeezed her fingers then quickly lowered her down to the ground where another member of the crew was waiting to escort her to safety. Within seconds Bella found herself at the top of the embankment. She sat down abruptly on the grass as her head began to whirl. Maybe it was the stress of what had happened the previous day allied to the amount of blood she had lost, but all of a sudden she felt incredibly dizzy. Putting her head between her knees, she made herself breathe slowly and deeply but the feeling of faintness simply got worse. As she slid into unconsciousness, the last thing she heard was Mac's frantic voice calling her name.

CHAPTER ELEVEN

MAC WAS ALMOST beside himself with fear by the time he returned to Dalverston General. He would have happily sold his soul to the devil if it had meant he could have gone with Bella in the ambulance that had ferried her and Katie to the hospital, but there'd been no way that he could have left Laura on her own. He'd had to stay, even though it had been the hardest thing he had ever done. Bella was injured and he needed to be with her even if it wasn't what she wanted.

The thought weighed heavily on him as he made his way to A&E. Nick Rogers, one of the senior registrars, was on duty and he grinned when he saw Mac coming in. 'Bit of excitement today, eh? I drew the short straw and had to stay here. Story of my life—I never get the really interesting jobs!'

Mac knew that Nick was joking and that he was as committed to his job as they all were, but he took exception to the comment. 'You wouldn't say that if you'd seen the state of those poor souls who were on the train,' he snapped.

'Sorry.' Nick held up his hands in apology and Mac sighed, aware that he had overreacted.

'No. It's me. Take no notice. Anyway, you've got Bella in here. Can I see her?'

'Sure. She's in cubicle four... No, wait a sec; she's just gone down to radiography.'

'Radiography?' Mac repeated. His heart gave a little jolt as he looked at Nick in horror. 'She's having an X-ray?'

'Yep. That cut on her neck is deep and I wanted to check there was nothing lodged in it so I've sent her down for an X-ray.'

'I was hoping it would just need stitching,' Mac murmured, his stomach churning sickeningly. If there was something lodged in the cut—a piece of glass or a sliver of metal, perhaps—then Bella might need surgery and he couldn't bear the thought of her having to go through such an ordeal.

'Probably will,' Nick replied cheerfully. 'It's just best to err on the side of caution, as I said.'

'I...er... Yes, of course.'

Mac did his best to pull himself together as he thanked the other man. He knew he was overreacting but he couldn't help it. This was Bella and he simply couldn't take a balanced view where she was concerned. He hurried to the lift, tapping his foot with impatience as it carried him down to the radiography unit. There was nobody in the waiting room so he pressed the bell, his impatience mounting as

he waited for someone to answer. When the door to
one of the X-ray suites opened, he spun round, his
heart leaping when he saw Bella being wheeled out
by a porter.

'Mac, what are you doing here?' she exclaimed
when she saw him. 'I thought you'd still be at the
accident.'

'All the children have been either moved to hospital or sent home,' he explained as he went over to
her. 'Nick told me you were here, having an X-ray
done on your neck.'

'Yes. Thankfully, there's nothing in it. Once it's
stitched up I should be right as rain.'

She dredged up a smile but Mac could see the
wariness in her eyes and realised that she wasn't sure
what was going to happen. All of a sudden he couldn't
stand it any longer, couldn't bear to tiptoe around any
more. He loved her! He wanted her! And he wanted
her to know that too.

His heart was thumping as he turned to the porter and told him that he would take Dr English back
to A&E. Once the man had disappeared, he pushed
Bella to a quiet corner where they wouldn't be disturbed. Crouching down in front of the wheelchair,
he looked into her eyes, knowing that he was about
to take the biggest gamble of his life. Telling her that
he loved her had felt like a huge risk at the time, but
it wasn't nearly as massive as this. This was so enor-
mous that it scared him witless and yet it was what

he *had* to do if he was to have a chance of achieving what he wanted so desperately—Bella and that happy-ever-after he yearned for.

Capturing her hands, he raised them to his mouth, feeling his panic subside as soon as he felt the warmth of her flesh against his lips. He could do this. He really could! 'I love you, Bella. I know I already told you that but then I went and ruined things by overreacting when Tim phoned. There's no excuse for what I said. I was wrong and I bitterly regret it.'

'I would never have slept with you just to work out how I feel about Tim,' she said softly.

'I know that.' Mac had to force the words past the lump in his throat when he heard the pain in her voice. He knew that she was telling him the truth and the fact that he had caused her such anguish filled him with guilt. 'I am so sorry, my love. Can you ever forgive me?'

'Yes. If I'm sure that you believe me.' She looked steadily back at him. 'I couldn't cope if you kept on doubting me all the time. I have to know that you believe in me, Mac. Our relationship won't work if you're continually wondering if I'm telling you the truth.'

'I know that.' He sighed as he leant forward and kissed her gently on the mouth. He drew back when he felt his body immediately stir. It was too soon for that. They needed to sort this out before they went any further. *If* they went any further. The thought spurred him on.

'I hate myself for hurting you, Bella. However, the truth is that I've always had a problem about trusting people since I was a child and my mother left.' He dredged up a smile, uncomfortable about admitting to what he considered a weakness. 'I know I should have got over it years ago, but sometimes it comes back to haunt me.'

'We're all the product of our upbringing, Mac.' She lifted his hand to her lips and pressed a kiss to his palm and her voice was so gentle, so tender that it brought a lump to his throat.

'Think so?' he murmured huskily.

'Oh, yes.' She smiled into his eyes. 'Look at me. My parents aren't demonstrative people and they didn't encourage me to show my feelings either. That's why I've always had such difficulty relating to other people—I tend to hold everything inside me rather than show how I really feel.'

'Really?' His brows rose and he grinned at her. 'I would never have guessed from the way you responded when we made love.'

'That was different,' she protested, a rush of colour staining her cheeks.

'Was it? Why?' He brushed her lips with the lightest of kisses, drawing back when he felt her immediately respond. His heart filled with joy, although he shouldn't assume that her response meant that it was *him* she wanted…

All of a sudden Mac couldn't wait any longer. Cupping her face between his hands, he looked into her eyes, knowing that this was the most important moment of his life. Whatever happened in the next few seconds was going to determine his whole future.

'Do you love me, Bella? I know I shouldn't put you on the spot like this, but I need to know before I drive myself crazy!'

Bella could feel her heart thumping. It was beating so hard that she could barely think, let alone answer the question. And then slowly through all the confusion in her head one thought rose to the surface. Of course she loved him. There was no doubt about that.

'Of course I love you,' she said indignantly, glaring at him. 'I'd have thought that was obvious.'

'Not to me.'

His voice was filled with a mixture of pure amazement and utter joy. Bella felt her indignation melt away as fast as it had appeared. Placing her hand on his cheek, she smiled at him, stunned by the fact that he was so vulnerable. Mac had always been so together, so in charge of himself—or so she had thought. To suddenly discover this whole different side to him was a revelation. She realised in that moment that she would do everything in her power to make sure that he never regretted letting her see the

real man beneath the confident façade he presented
to the world at large.

She kissed him softly on the mouth, letting her
lips show him in no uncertain terms how she felt.
She loved him so much and she wanted nothing more
than to spend the rest of her days proving it to him...

If he would let her.

She drew back, feeling the first tiny doubt gnaw-
ing away at her happiness. Mac had asked her if she
loved him. He had told her that he needed to know.
However, he hadn't said why.

'I love you, Mac, but are you sure that you love
me? You were so quick to think that I'd used you to
clarify my feelings for Tim and you wouldn't have
done that if you'd really loved me. You would have
known that I would never have slept with you for
that reason.'

It was the hardest thing Bella had ever done. She
had never done anything like this before, never delved
into emotional issues, and it scared her to do it now
when it was so important. Whatever Mac told her
would affect the rest of her life and she wasn't sure
if she could handle the thought.

She stood up abruptly, suddenly too afraid to sit
there and listen to what he had to say. If Mac didn't
want her then there was nothing she could do about
it. She had to accept his decision and not make a
scene, certainly not make a fool of herself by begging him to reconsider! Tears stung her eyes as she

went to push past him but he was too quick for her. Reaching out, he drew her to a halt, his arms closing around her so that she couldn't move, couldn't escape him or the truth.

'Bella, stop! I know you're scared because I'm scared too, but you can't run away. I won't let you.' Bending, he pressed a kiss to her lips and she felt the shudder that passed through his body and into hers. Raising his head, he looked steadily at her. 'We both need to be brave if we're going to make this work. I love you and I want to spend my life with you. I think...*hope*...that you feel the same. Do you, my darling? Do you love me enough to live with me from now to eternity because I warn you that's what I want. Nothing less.'

Bella could feel her heart thumping. This was it. Whatever she said now would determine her future. Did she want to be with Mac for ever? Did she want to live with him and spend each and every day making him happy? Of course she did!

Reaching up, she drew his head down and kissed him, letting her lips answer his question. There was a moment when he held back, a tiny beat of time when he seemed to hesitate as though he wasn't sure that what was happening was real, and then he was kissing her back, kissing her with a hunger he didn't attempt to hide. They were both trembling when they broke apart, both shaken by the depth of their feelings for each other. Mac cupped her cheek and she could hear the love resonating in his voice.

'I didn't know it was possible to feel this way, Bella, to want someone *this* much.'

'Me neither.' Turning her head, she pressed a kiss against his palm and felt him shudder. It felt like the most natural thing in the world to tell him how she felt, to lay bare her emotions completely and totally. 'I want you so much that it hurts, Mac. I want to spend my life with you and spend every single second of every minute loving you. Even then it won't be enough. Nothing would be when I feel this way.'

'And you're sure? Sure that you want me and not Tim? After all, you agreed to meet him—'

'Yes, I did.' She laid her fingertips against his lips to silence him. 'And the reason I agreed was because of how I feel about you. I wanted to draw a line under past events and, if possible, make my peace with Tim. I want the future—our future, together—to be perfect and not tainted by anything that's happened in the past.'

'Oh, my love!'

He kissed her again, hunger replaced by a bone-melting tenderness that brought tears to her eyes. He smiled as he wiped them away with his fingertips. 'Don't cry, sweetheart. Although I have to confess that I feel very much like shedding a tear or two myself.'

'Just not right for your macho image,' she teased, smiling up at him through her tears.

'Definitely not. I should really be beating my chest right now, shouldn't I?' He grinned back at her. 'I mean, I've just won the woman I love and I should be celebrating before dragging you back to my cave.'

'Hmm. Let's not get too carried away by the macho theme.' She laughed up at him. 'I'm a modern woman, after all, and I value my independence.'

'And so you should. I don't want you to change, Bella. I want you to stay exactly the same as you've always been.'

'I don't think that's possible,' she said quietly. 'I've changed a lot in the past few weeks and changed for the better too. I now understand my feelings and I'm not so afraid to show them, thanks to you. And, hopefully, I shall get even better at it as time passes too.'

'I've always thought you were perfect from the moment we met.'

His voice grated and Bella's eyes filled with tears once more because it was obvious that he was telling her the truth. Mac loved her exactly how she was and it was marvellous to know that he didn't want her to change. Reaching up, she kissed him, showing him without the need for words how much she loved him and how much she needed him. He'd said she was perfect but to her mind he was perfect too!

EPILOGUE

One year later...

MAC CAREFULLY LAID the baby in her crib. It was two a.m. and the rest of the town was sleeping. With a bit of luck, three-week-old Isobel Grace MacIntyre would follow suit.

'Has she dropped off at last?'

'Not yet.'

He turned, thinking that Bella had never looked more beautiful as she sat there propped against the pillows in their bed. They had married as soon as they had discovered that she was expecting the baby. He knew that they would have got married anyway but he had discovered that he was surprisingly old-fashioned in many ways and had wanted their child to be born in wedlock. The simple ceremony in the hospital's chapel had been perfect too, the final seal on their happiness, not that they had needed to prove it. He loved Bella with every fibre of his being, just as she loved him, and anyone could see how they felt too!

'I think she's debating whether or not to give her poor mum and dad a break.'

He lay down on the bed and gathered Bella into his arms, inhaling the warm womanly smell of her. She had decided to feed Isobel herself and he loved watching her do so, loved how her face filled with adoration for their baby, loved how fulfilled she looked with the infant nursing at her breast. Love, as he had discovered, was infinite and expanded on a daily basis.

He kissed her gently on the lips, drawing back when he felt his body immediately stir. It was too soon for them to make love because Bella needed time to heal after the birth. Anyway, waiting only made his desire for her even stronger, not that it hadn't been pretty strong to begin with!

'Mmm. I think I can guess what's on your mind,' she said, pulling back so she could look into his eyes, and he chuckled.

'Is it that obvious?'

'Yes.' She snuggled against him and sighed. 'Not just on your mind either.'

'Never mind. Just another couple of weeks and we can resume relations, as they say,' he said comfortingly, pulling her back to him.

'I can't wait,' she murmured against his chest. She suddenly drew back again. 'Did I tell you that I spoke to Freya this morning? Apparently, the results of her mock A-levels were so good that she's been offered a place at Lancaster. She will make a brilliant nurse, don't you think?'

'I do. I'm so glad that her parents saw sense in the end. She needs their support if she's to make a success of uni,' he said, pulling her back into his arms. He kissed the tip of her nose and smiled. 'Another set of grandparents who've been won over.'

'Like my parents, you mean.' She burrowed against him. 'Dad phoned as well this afternoon to let me know they're coming up to visit us at the weekend.'

'Again?' Mac laughed softly. 'That's the third time in as many weeks. Why do I get the feeling that they're going to turn into doting grandparents?'

'Oh, I've no idea, but don't knock it. Dad mentioned something about him and Mum babysitting if we wanted to go out for dinner. Sounds good to me.'

'Me too. So long as Isobel is all right, of course,' he added, glancing over at the crib.

'She'll be fine.' Bella snuggled even closer. 'Now, why don't we take advantage of the fact that she seems to have dropped off at last?'

'Mmm, sounds interesting. What do you suggest?' he asked, leering comically at her.

'I'm not sure. I shall leave that up to you.'

Mac laughed as he pulled her to him and kissed her hungrily. Maybe they couldn't make love just yet but there were other ways to show how they felt about one another. They just needed to be creative…

* * * * *

LET'S TALK

Romance

For exclusive extracts, competitions
and special offers, find us online:

 facebook.com/millsandboon

@MillsandBoon

@MillsandBoonUK

Get in touch on 01413 063232

For all the latest titles coming soon, visit
millsandboon.co.uk/nextmonth

MILLS & BOON
MEDICAL
Pulse-Racing Passion

Set your pulse racing with dedicated, delectable doctors in the high-pressure world of medicine, where emotions run high and passion, comfort and love are the best medicine.